CURSE *of the* PAINTED LADY

BOOK 3

THE ANLON CULLY CHRONICLES

K. PATRICK DONOGHUE

Published by Leaping Leopard Enterprises, LLC

CURSE OF THE PAINTED LADY
Copyright © 2018 Kevin Patrick Donoghue
All rights reserved.
eISBN: 978-0-9973164-7-6
ISBN: 978-0-9973164-6-9 (paperback)
ISBN: 978-0-9973164-8-3 (hardcover)

Published by Leaping Leopard Enterprises, LLC
www.leapingleopard.com

First edition: March 2018, updated August 2020

Cover art and design by Asha Hossain Design LLC

Author photograph by Down Owens Photography

DEDICATION

To my sons,
Michael and Stephen.
Dream big, work hard, be kind
and always remember you are loved!

Contents

Acknowledgements

The creation of *Curse of the Painted Lady* was only possible due to the support, feedback and encouragement I received from a host of people, including my family, publishing team and readers of my stories. To each, I owe a round of thanks.

To my wife, Bryson, and sons, Michael and Stephen, thank you for creating and maintaining a supportive atmosphere for me to conceive and write my stories. Your continued encouragement, support and understanding are deeply appreciated!

To my editor, Katherine Pickett of POP Editorial Services, thank you for helping me continue to improve as a writer and storyteller. To design artist, Asha Hossain, thank you for conceiving compelling cover art that reinforces the vibe of the story. To design artist, Amber Colleran, thank you for enhancing the look and feel of the printed editions' interior layout. To proofreaders, Cheryl Hollenbeck and Lisa Weinberg, thank you for your eagle-eye scrutiny and valuable editorial suggestions. To photographer, Donna Owens, thank you for encouraging me to smile (one day I'll get there). To my website designers, James Lee and Kevin Maines of JML Design, thank you for continuing to evolve and improve my author website.

Last, but not least, I would like to thank my readers, fans and super-fans. I am grateful for your interest in my stories as well as your constructive feedback. I especially thank those of you who share your opinions of my stories with other readers (and me) via reviews, Facebook comments and personal messages. The thoughts you share are inspirational, even when delivered with a dose of tough love.

Preface

Greetings to one and all! Thank you in advance for choosing to read *Curse of the Painted Lady*, the third book in The Anlon Cully Chronicles series.

I hope you are excited to dive into the finale of the archaeological mystery explored in the first two books in the series, *Shadows of the Stone Benders* and *Race for the Flash Stone*! I think you'll find *Curse of the Painted Lady* contains plenty of action and plot twists — some of which will hopefully catch you by surprise and make for an entertaining read.

As was true in the previous installments of the series, the story told in *Curse of the Painted Lady* blends fiction with real-world archaeological mysteries and ancient mythologies (artifacts, monuments and legends) that appear to challenge conventional views of humankind's historical record and societal development.

For those of you who have not read the first two books in the series, I encourage you to tackle those first before reading *Curse of the Painted Lady*. Otherwise, I believe you may find it challenging to fully appreciate the plot lines, terminology and characters.

For those who read *Shadows of the Stone Benders* and/or *Race for the Flash Stone* some time ago, I would encourage you to at least revisit *Race for the Flash Stone* before reading *Curse of the Painted Lady*, as the plot lines in *"Painted Lady"* commence where the *"Flash Stone"* plot lines end. To assist in connecting these two stories, the Prologue of *Painted Lady* provides a synopsis of the ending points of the three main *Flash Stone* plot lines in the form of news articles (similar to the method I employed in *Flash Stone's* Prologue).

For all readers, I have once again included a glossary of important terms toward the rear of the book, as well as an illustration of the *Sinethal* etching, a key artifact featured in the story. A quick scan of both reference tools prior to starting *Painted Lady* may prove helpful. eBook readers can quickly access these sections by clicking on the links for each in the table of contents.

With those comments in mind, please enjoy the story! *Kaeto*!

Prologue

In the News
September 11-16

UNUSUAL STONE-AGE ARTIFACTS UNEARTHED IN NICARAGUA

*Discoverers claim artifacts are magnetic tools
forged by long-lost civilization*

MANAGUA, NICARAGUA – September 11 – An archaeological research team today announced the discovery of sophisticated magnetic tools that may date to 8000 B.C.E.

The announcement, made at a press conference held at the Nicaraguan Bureau of Cultural Affairs in Managua, challenges notions of Stone-Age humans as simple cave dwellers. At least, that's the view put forth by archaeologist and team spokesperson Dr. Cesar Perez.

"In the team's eyes, the find is significant in that it suggests the existence of an advanced society at a much earlier point in human history than most archaeologists deem possible," Perez said.

Perez told reporters the team believes the tools were crafted by a culture known as the Munuorians, an ancient race of mariners who possessed a sixth sense — an ability to sense and interact with the Earth's magnetic field. "They applied this sixth sense to create precision magnetic instruments out of stone and diamonds, and they used these tools to build, farm, hunt and heal injuries, among other purposes."

According to Eleanor McCarver, a member of the team who joined the press conference by video feed, the tools were found inside a sealed crypt in the Indio Maiz Biological Reserve in eastern Nicaragua.

"As far as we have been able to determine, the Indio Maiz crypt is the first-known discovery of a fully intact Munuorian archaeological site, and we believe the artifacts found inside are over 10,000 years old," McCarver said.

When pressed by members of the media for the team's proof of the artifacts' authenticity and age, McCarver indicated the team would invite a group of independent archaeologists and anthropologists to examine and validate the artifacts' heritage once the collection has been cataloged and the site fully excavated.

McCarver further indicated the team's leader, scientist and amateur archaeologist Dr. Anlon Cully, planned to establish a museum to display a sampling of the discovered artifacts in Greytown, a small coastal Nicaraguan town near the Indio Maiz crypt. Speaking in her capacity as the museum's newly appointed curator, McCarver said the exhibition would be named after the late Dr. Devlin Wilson, a prominent archaeologist and Cully's uncle.

In written remarks provided to reporters, Cully said, "Devlin Wilson was the team's true inspiration. He devoted a decade of his life to the search for evidence to prove the Munuorians' existence but died before realizing his dream. Fortunately for us, Devlin left behind enough clues in his research files to lead us to Indio Maiz and the evidence he sought for so long. We are proud to honor Devlin's legacy by dedicating our discovery, and the museum, to him."

McCarver concluded the news conference by announcing Cully also planned to form and endow the Alynioria

Foundation, an organization pledged to preserve Munuorian artifacts and share insights about their unique culture with the world.

BENNINGTON WOMAN'S DEATH
PUZZLES AUTHORITIES

Woman found dead in garden, police suspect foul play

BENNINGTON – September 15 – An unidentified Bennington woman was discovered dead in her flower garden yesterday afternoon by Bennington Police responding to a call from a concerned neighbor. The dead woman has yet to be identified, pending notification of family members.

According to officers responding to the call, a neighbor's dog wandered into the dead woman's yard around 1 p.m. yesterday and began wailing loudly.

The dog's owner, who requested her name be withheld from this report, indicated the animal's excited behavior was uncharacteristic. The neighbor entered the dead woman's yard to retrieve the dog and discovered the body. She immediately called rescue personnel and the police.

An unnamed police official with knowledge of the incident said the circumstances surrounding the woman's death indicated foul play. According to the official, the woman had been electrocuted.

As there was no source of electricity in the immediate vicinity, police suspect the woman was killed elsewhere and placed in the garden. The official also indicated robbery as a possible motive. Officers entering the home discovered evidence of a break-in. The official described the crime scene as "chaotic."

BIZARRE MURDER AT FINCA
6 MUSEUM REMAINS UNSOLVED

Police suspect murderer may have been
American fugitive wanted by FBI

PALMAR NORTE, COSTA RICA – September 16 – Costa Rican police officials remain baffled by the September 5 murder of a male tourist at the remote Finca 6 Museum and the subsequent abduction of the suspected murderer from museum grounds.

As previously reported, police were summoned to Finca 6 by the museum's security chief after three men dashed through the visitor's center carrying a bloodied, unidentified woman. According to witness statements, the men allegedly loaded the woman into an SUV in the parking lot outside the center and sped away.

When police arrived on scene to investigate the kidnapping, they discovered the body of a man whose throat had been slit. After examining video footage from security cameras mounted around the museum grounds, police determined the dead man had been attacked by the female kidnap victim prior to her abduction.

But in the days since the murder the police investigation has produced little new evidence. The dead man remains unidentified, the murder weapon has yet to be recovered and there has been no further news of the whereabouts of the kidnapped woman. Police are also stymied regarding the motives behind both crimes. Suggestions of a drug deal gone bad have been circulating in the media, but police have been quick to dispel the speculation as unfounded.

The only potential new clue surfaced yesterday, when police revealed fingerprints belonging to an American named Margaret Corchran were discovered in an abandoned rental car at Finca 6. According to U.S. embassy officials in San Jose, Corchran is wanted by the FBI in connection with the murder of a fellow American citizen, Devlin Wilson.

Yet, police acknowledge there is no evidence beyond the fingerprints linking Corchran to the crimes. No one matching Corchran's description was observed at Finca 6 by witnesses, nor was she spotted on security camera footage. Further, police have found no record of Corchran entering Costa Rica and the rental car was not registered in her name.

1

Needle in the Haystack

Bennington, Vermont
September 25

Detective Timothy Hall stood at the edge of the garden and pointed at a flattened patch of wildflowers and milkweed. "They found her right here."

Jennifer Stevens leaned forward to examine the crushed plants, then held up a photograph of the crime scene. In the picture, Anabel Simpson was splayed face up with a horrified expression frozen on her face. Mouth agape as if cut down in midscream, Anabel's lifeless eyes stared straight ahead. Her outstretched and twisted limbs were gruesome to behold, but they paled in comparison to the charred hole through her chest and her disfigured, bloodied hands. Jennifer handed the picture to Detective Dan Nickerson. "God, she put up one hell of a fight."

Nickerson examined the photograph, then asked Hall, "Any other defensive injuries, other than the hands?"

Scratching at his beard-covered chin, Hall said, "It's hard to say. There were other contusions, but the medical examiner said they could have been caused by the jolt she received. We won't know for sure until he's done with the autopsy."

"Where do you think she was killed?" Jennifer asked.

"We don't have a solid idea, yet. All we know for sure is she was placed in the garden after she was killed." Shaking his head, the ginger-haired Hall confessed, "It's the damnedest thing. There's so much evidence, it's overwhelming, but none of it points us in a direction any of us feels good about.

"Just about every room inside was turned upside down, but, on the surface, it looks more like a search than a struggle. No blood stains, signs of fire. So, it doesn't look like it happened in the house. Outside, we haven't found anything of significance either. No singed plants. No blood trail and no source of electricity nearby. Plus, we haven't found anyone who heard or saw any disturbance. Given the condition of the body, it seems impossible someone wouldn't have noticed if it happened in her yard."

Nickerson nodded in agreement and then pointed at the wilting garden. "When you say 'no blood trail,' I assume you combed the whole property?"

"Correct. When we didn't find any clues near the body or in the house, we expanded the search area a few hundred yards in every direction. Into the neighbors' yards, into the woods behind the garden. Nada," Hall said.

"And her car is missing, right?" Jennifer asked.

"Yes. Silver Honda CR-V, 2010 model year. We don't know for sure, but we're fairly certain it was stolen the same day Ms. Simpson was discovered." The Vermont State Police detective explained they'd interviewed the surrounding neighbors, including the woman who found Anabel, as well as the postal carrier who delivered mail on Anabel's street. The carrier and two of the neighbors said they were positive the car was in the driveway the day before Anabel's body was found. "Unfortunately, no one saw the car leave, so we don't know whether it was taken before or after she was killed. We've got warrants out to review video surveillance cameras around town. Hopefully we'll get lucky."

While Hall spoke, Jennifer scanned the garden. It was hard to believe how much the plot had changed in the six weeks since she had last visited Anabel. Then, it had been bustling with color and life. Hundreds of butterflies had floated in the air above the forest of flowers while others competed with bees for the nectars of the various blooms. Now, however, the garden looked pale and withered. All that remained were brittle, drooping stalks of yellow, brown and gray. She could understand why the Bennington police quickly reached the conclusion that Anabel had been killed elsewhere and moved here afterward. Given the intensity of the burns to her chest and hands, one would have expected the dead, dry stalks to ignite like tinder if Anabel had been standing near the garden when she was electrocuted.

But had she really been electrocuted? For that matter, had she really been murdered? Or, could she have been Muran? If so, had she instead transferred her mind to a new body, as Jacques Foucault claimed she had done many times before? And the abuse to Anabel's body — could that have been delivered after the fact to send a message to someone? Anlon, maybe? Thus far, Jennifer thought there were aspects of the crime scene that favored Foucault's theory, but other aspects argued against it.

As she walked around the perimeter, Jennifer noticed something she hadn't seen in August when the garden was full and lush. There were bowling-ball-sized holes in places throughout the garden. She bent down on hands and knees to examine the closest one she could see from the garden's edge. Peering through the thicket, she spied two others of similar size deeper in the garden.

Calling over her shoulder, she asked Hall, "What did your forensics guys make of these holes?"

Hall crouched down next to her. "Pretty weird, huh?"

"I'll say," Nickerson said as he leaned forward to get a better look.

"At first, we thought someone dug holes looking for something buried," Hall said. "But there's only crumbs of displaced dirt and no footprints or trampled plants around the holes. When the techs took a closer look, they said it looked like stone markers had been set in them, but that didn't make sense either."

"How so?" Jennifer asked.

"The holes go about three feet deep, so we're talking pretty large stones. There's no way someone could lift out rocks of that size without leaving some trace, but there were no shovel marks or other signs of digging. If someone used a crane or tractor to pull them out, there would be tracks all over the place, but there aren't any. And no one saw or heard any heavy machinery or anyone digging," Hall said.

"You're convinced they were stones?" Nickerson asked. "How about something ornamental? Faux rocks, maybe some kind of hollowed cast stone?"

"I'm not convinced of anything, but there were black flecks of rock inside the holes. The M.E. seemed to think they were metallic, so we did a sweep of the garden with a metal detector. The whole garden gives off magnetic readings, but they were strongest around each hole," Hall answered.

Jennifer raised up and brushed the grass and dirt from her hands. Pushing a strand of blond hair behind her ear, she asked, "You called them markers. What do you think they marked?"

Hall stood and shrugged. "Beats me. They were arranged in a hexagon pattern. Six holes, spaced evenly apart."

When they entered Anabel's kitchen, Jennifer barely recognized the place. The cabinets were all open and their contents scattered on the shelves. Some of the china plates and cups had fallen and smashed onto the counter, while pieces of others littered the floor. The drawers beneath the counters had been pulled free and emptied onto the floor, then tossed aside into a haphazard pile next to the refrigerator.

Jennifer knelt down and spied the severed head of a Holstein figurine that had once served as a napkin holder. She looked at the smiling cow's face and thought of sitting at the table with Anabel while sipping on *enjyia*.

Standing up, she turned and scanned the kitchen counter for Anabel's rack of ornamental eggs. Among the debris and clutter on the counter, she spotted the mangled, empty rack. Stepping gingerly over piles of flatware, utensils, dish towels and broken glass, she moved closer to the counter and searched for the marble, egg-shaped *Terusael* among the wreckage.

"Geez, does the rest of the house look like this?" Nickerson asked Hall.

"Pretty much," he said, shoving his hands in his pants pockets. "The kitchen, living room and her bedroom took the worst of it."

"Fingerprints?" Nickerson asked.

"Yep, all over the place. Multiple sets. Whoever did this didn't care about leaving fingerprints. Found a few hair fibers, too. Appears to be at least two people, possibly three," Hall said. "We'll know more after the fingerprint analysis is complete."

"Have you been able to verify if anything was taken?" Jennifer asked, examining a pile of odds and ends by the kitchen sink. Still no *Terusael*.

"No. That's another strange thing. Her purse was searched, but no cash or credit cards were taken. In the bedroom, she had jewelry in a box on her dresser. They went through it, but there are several expensive pieces still in the box. In the dining room, she had some signed Norman Rockwell prints. They're each worth a few thousand dollars from what I'm told. They were taken down from the walls, and the paper on the back of the frames was slit open, but the prints are undamaged," Hall explained. "There are other expensive items in the house, too. Antiques. Vintage clothing."

"So, you're thinking the perps were looking for a very specific item," Nickerson said.

Hall nodded. "Yep. Something small. Something concealed."

Jennifer overhead the comment and joined them. "Like what?"

"We don't know. We've been kicking it around. Our Major thinks it's a document. A couple of the other detectives think it's a key. Could be something else entirely. But, whatever it was, it was something small. Come with me, I'll show you."

They walked into the small dining room on their way to the living room. As they passed through, Hall pointed out the Norman Rockwells stacked facedown on the dining room table, their paper backings slashed open. Jennifer looked at the tattered paper and frowned. So far, the house definitely appeared as if it had been burgled, and that didn't gibe with the theory of "Anabel as Muran."

When they arrived in the living room, Hall stopped and lifted an empty picture frame from the floor. "This is another oddity. Every picture frame in the house was emptied. Most of the photographs that were in them were just tossed on the floor. We've been able to find most of the photographs, but not all."

"Hmmm...They took some of the photographs?" Jennifer asked. Another clue that could be read in two ways, she thought.

"Yeah. Too bad we don't know which ones were taken. Suggests there was something incriminating in the photos," Hall said.

"Maybe," Jennifer said, recalling the photos she inadvertently left with Anabel during her August visit. It was also possible that Muran had taken photographs as sentimental mementos of her time as Anabel, she thought.

Hall pointed to a small, empty writing desk in the far corner. "You can't tell now — we boxed all the evidence — but there was paper strewn everywhere on and around the desk. Under the papers, we found about a dozen keys lined up. Found some more keys laid out on her bedroom dresser."

Jennifer scanned the room and frowned again. Where was Anabel's *Terusael*? "Can we see her bedroom?"

"Yep. This way," Hall said.

They walked down a narrow hallway, past a sparsely furnished guest bedroom, a small bathroom, a linen closet and an open ceiling panel leading to the attic. The guest room and hallway closet had been ransacked to the same degree as the rest of the house. When they arrived at Anabel's bedroom, the first thing that caught Jennifer's attention was the clothing tossed about the room. Piles and piles of clothes were everywhere: atop the small bureau, hanging out of drawers, on the floor by the open closet and on the bed. The volume of clothing was surprising given the small size of the dresser and closet. Equally bizarre was the makeup of the scattered wardrobe. Most of the items on the bed and by the closet looked more like costumes than they did clothing. And none of it looked like anything Jennifer had seen Anabel wear.

"What's with all the costumes?" she asked.

"Heck if I know," Hall answered. "But the M.E. said they aren't costumes. They're 'vintage' dresses and such. Most of it is from the 1800s. There's some World War Two–period clothes, too."

Nickerson asked, "Where did it all come from? That closet doesn't look big enough to hold all this stuff."

"There are four empty steamer trunks in the attic," Hall said.

Different period clothes? Mark another clue for the body-switch theory, Jennifer thought.

As Nickerson milled about the room, Jennifer scanned the contents of the open jewelry box. Much like the odd mix of clothes, the jewelry was a mishmash of styles, too. The main compartment held everyday jewelry, mostly earrings and necklaces with pendants, including several featuring Holsteins. Below the main compartment were two small drawers. In the left drawer, there were several classical pieces including a strand of pearls, two sets of diamond earrings and a few gemstone rings. In the right-hand drawer, there were vintage broaches of rose gold, several cameo pendants and a round, gold locket. It was facedown and she could see there was an inscription on its casing, but it was too faded to read at a distance.

Curious to read the inscription, Jennifer was tempted to pick it up, but she knew it was a no-no to touch anything that might be evidence. Hall had been decent enough to allow her to join Nickerson's tour of the crime scene, something he didn't have to do given Jennifer was no longer a detective, so she didn't want to do anything to betray his trust.

She pulled out her cell phone and activated its flashlight. She leaned forward and pointed the flashlight at the casing. While she endeavored to read the inscription, she thought back to her last visit with Anabel. Had she worn any jewelry that day? She visualized Anabel sitting at the kitchen table, pouring from the pitcher of *enjyia*, but couldn't recall any earrings or other jewelry. The flashlight illuminated the italicized inscription. It was in English, but Jennifer had a difficult time making out the words given the extravagant flourishes of the lettering.

In the background, Hall and Nickerson discussed the vintage clothes. Peeking over her shoulder, Jennifer couldn't resist the temptation. With her back turned to block Hall's view, she used her fingertips to lift the locket from inside the jewelry box. Holding the flashlight as close as she could without touching the casing's surface, she was finally able to read the inscription: *Forever One.*

Aw, thought Jennifer. Devlin was so sweet for such a rakish bachelor. She shoved the phone back into her jacket pocket. After checking over her shoulder again, she flipped the locket over to look at its face. She whispered, "Whoa…"

Jennifer had expected to see Anabel's engraved initials or an embossed heart or some other sappy, sentimental ornamentation. Instead, the front of the gold locket looked like a mask or a shield. At its center was the face of a man or woman wearing an elaborate headdress. Jennifer smoothed her thumb across the face's raised surface. While some of its features looked more masculine than feminine, the ears were adorned with large earrings. To Jennifer, they appeared similar to modern-day gauges. But when the earrings were combined with the shaping of the eyes, they gave the face a distinctly feminine appearance.

The headdress depicted a bird, like an eagle or a hawk, with its beak protruding above the face's forehead. Surrounding the face was an intricate, circular design that reminded Jennifer of Mesoamerican art she'd seen the previous month during her research of Devlin's "fish man" statuette. She was not expert enough to tell whether it was Olmec, Mayan, Incan or Toltec, but it was definitely related to one of those cultures. Jennifer opened the locket. She blinked and mumbled, "What the…"

"Jen?" Nickerson asked.

She clasped her hand around the locket and turned toward Nickerson. "Yeah?"

"Find something interesting?" he asked.

"Oh. Um, not really," she said, slowly moving her hand behind her back. "Just surprised they left the diamond earrings."

Nickerson frowned. Jennifer could feel her face turning red. Change the subject quick! she thought. She asked Hall, "Did you find her cell phone?"

"Yep, we have it. She also had a tablet and a laptop. All three are with our forensics team," said Hall. He paused and then asked Jennifer, "Now that you've been through the whole crime scene, any suggestions as to what the perps were after?"

Jennifer crouched down to examine some of the clothes piled on the floor. As she scanned a collection of sweatshirts and sweaters, she slid the locket into her jacket pocket. She said, "Well, if it was a document, it could have been a map. The people who killed Anabel's lover were looking for a map. It was in Anabel's possession for a little while, but I know for a fact she passed it on to someone else back in May."

"What kind of map?" Hall asked, scribbling a note.

"It was hand-drawn. About the size of a folded newspaper. It marked some archaeological sites," Jennifer said, careful to avoid the words "Waterland Map."

"Was it common knowledge that she had the map?" Hall asked.

"At the time she had it? I would say no," Jennifer said, standing to join Hall and Nickerson. "But I know at least two people became aware of it after she gave it away."

"Names?" Hall asked, pen poised over his notepad.

Nickerson said, "The two guys I told you about on the phone: Thatcher Reynolds and Pacal Flores. Reynolds is missing. Flores is dead. He's the one who kidnapped Ms. Simpson last May."

"Ah, right," Hall said, jotting down more notes. "You also mentioned a brother and sister in our call. The brother's in prison. The sister's missing. Did they know about the map?"

"Margaret and Kyle Corchran," Nickerson said with a nod. "They knew the map existed. They were after it, too. But as far as we know, they didn't know Ms. Simpson had it."

"Don't forget about Klaus Navarro," Jennifer called out over her shoulder as she left the room.

"Klaus who?" Hall asked.

While Nickerson detailed Navarro's connection with the Corchrans and the Argentinian's pursuit of Devlin Wilson's artifacts, Jennifer snuck back into the living room. Looking behind her to ensure they hadn't followed, she opened the locket again and tried to make sense of the photo and a second inscription inside. She squeezed her eyes closed. Opening them again, she stared at the sepia photo and wondered if her mind was playing tricks. Before she could examine it more closely, she heard the two detectives approaching. She shut the casing and quickly returned it to her jacket pocket.

Her face flushed as she moved across the room to the writing desk. When the men arrived in the living room, Jennifer overheard Hall say to Nickerson, "So, it's possible someone came looking for the map, unaware that Ms. Simpson no longer had it."

"Or...maybe the person thought Anabel kept a copy," Nickerson replied.

With her back turned toward the others, Jennifer pretended to examine the desk while exhaling slowly through pursed lips to calm her heartbeat.

"Hell, maybe she did keep a copy," Nickerson said. "What do you think, Jen?"

Jennifer leaned forward to spy into each of the empty cubbyholes of the shelf attached to the desktop. She said, "It's possible. I caught Anabel in some lies when I met her here last month. One of them was about the map. She claimed to know nothing about it other than saying Devlin asked her to hold it for him, but I'm pretty sure she knew a lot more than she let on."

"Well, one way or another, it sure sounds like the map's a possible motive for at least the burglary," Hall said. "I know there was no map in the papers we collected, but maybe she kept a copy on her computer."

Jennifer didn't want to dissuade Hall from the notion, but the fact the computer was left by the thieves made it seem doubtful the forensics guys would find a file containing the map. Then again, she thought, if the thieves searched files on the laptop, the forensics team might find evidence of the search. As she scooped another loose strand of hair behind her ear, a different thought occurred to her. She mumbled, "Keys."

"Eh?" Hall asked.

"Oh, sorry," Jennifer said, turning to face Hall. She pointed to the desk surface. "You said earlier that there were keys lined up here."

"Yep, and there were others on her bedroom dresser," Hall said.

"What kind of keys? How many?" she asked.

"There were ten on the desk and six on the dresser. A mix of different sizes and types. Why?"

"Any of them look like locker keys? Safe-deposit box keys?"

"We thought of that, too," Hall said. "A couple of the keys look like contenders for a storage locker or padlock."

Nickerson joined the conversation. "I see where you're going. You think she might have hidden the map off-site?"

Jennifer scanned the room again. She thought of the missing *Terusael* and said to Nickerson, "Maybe. But I think we're getting a little too focused on the map. There are other possibilities that stand out to me. For instance, I know Anabel had a collection of rare artifacts, or at least she said so. Anlon told me they were worth several million dollars."

Hall's pen froze in midstroke. He looked up at Jennifer with a surprised expression. "Say what? We didn't find any artifacts."

"Yes, that's curious, isn't it? An archaeology professor with no artifacts," Jennifer said. She briefly considered telling Hall about the *Terusael* but decided against it. It would have meant opening up the whole can of worms about the Munuorians, the *Lifintyls* and Muran. Which, in turn, meant discussing the possibility of Anabel being a ten-thousand-year-old woman who could switch her mind from one body to another.

Jennifer looked through the open doorway leading to the dining room. In a soft tone, she said, "I should have noticed that when I was here in August, but come to think of it, we met in the kitchen and out by the garden. We never came in here."

"Do you know what these artifacts look like? How many there are?" Hall asked.

She darted a brief look at Nickerson and said, "No, I don't."

"Well, she didn't have an alarm system. Pretty bold if you're keeping Rockwells and expensive jewelry in the house, let alone stuff worth millions," Hall said.

"What about the steamer trunks?" Nickerson asked. "The ones in the attic. They have locks, right? Could they have been looking for keys to open them? Maybe Anabel kept her artifacts inside the trunks?"

Hall stopped taking notes for a moment and scratched at his beard, pen in hand. A swoosh of blue ink marked his cheek. "They definitely have locks. We found the keys on the dresser."

"So, maybe they found what they were looking for in the trunks," Nickerson said.

"Hmmm, I don't know, Dan," Jennifer said. "I'm more in favor of an off-site storage place."

"You're probably right," Nickerson said. "But, then again…"

"Then again, what?" Hall asked.

Nickerson pointed in the direction of Anabel's bedroom. "Presuming the retro clothes came from the trunks, why haul them all out, bring them down from the attic and go through them in the bedroom? Why not just go through them in the attic?"

"I'm not sure I follow you, Dan," Jennifer said.

"The mountain of clothes in the bedroom gives the impression the killers searched the clothes looking for something. The empty cases in the attic give the impression the clothes were the only things in the trunks. But what if the artifacts were hidden in one or more of the trunks, maybe wrapped up in the clothes or hidden underneath them?"

Nickerson's theory was plausible, Jennifer thought. Anabel might have wrapped the artifacts inside the clothes and stored them in the trunks. If only she knew more about the artifacts in question. To Jennifer's knowledge, Anlon had never seen them and the only one

she had seen herself was the *Terusael*. And she was pretty sure Anlon had said Anabel's artifacts were gifts from Devlin, and not necessarily Munuorian *Tyls*. The others might be pieces of jewelry, pottery or God knows what else. If the pieces were small enough, the
trunks might have indeed made for decent hiding places.

"Definitely seems possible," Hall said. "I'll have forensics come
back for the trunks and vintage clothes."

He lowered his head and jotted several more notes before closing
his notepad. "Anything else either of you noticed?"

Nickerson grumbled under his breath.

"What's that?" Hall asked.

"Oh, sorry. I was just thinking out loud," Nickerson said.

"About what?" Jennifer asked.

Waving his arm in a circle around the room, Nickerson said, "I
don't know. The whole crime scene in here bugs me. Everything
looks and sounds staged. Keys lined up on the desk. Papers scattered, pictures slashed. Open trunks in the attic. Fingerprints everywhere. I think most, if not all, of it is intended to throw us off,
confuse us. Same with the body in the garden and the missing car."

While Jennifer listened to Nickerson, she fidgeted with the
locket in her pocket. There certainly was a slew of conflicting
evidence, but in her mind the *Lifintyls* were at the root of the
crimes in one way or another. In fact, she could imagine three
viable scenarios centered around the *Tyls* that might explain the
confusing array of evidence.

Option one: Anabel had been Muran. Feeling pressure that her true
identity was about to be discovered, she switched into a new body and
discarded Anabel's. She took her *Tyls* with her and arranged the scene
to make it look like a burglary and murder.

Option two: Anabel had been Muran, and she fell for the trap Foucault supposedly set, the one he mentioned at Indio Maiz. Under this
scenario, Foucault killed Muran and took her *Tyls*, or he searched the
house looking for them, or for evidence of where they were kept. The
brutality of the murder had been driven by Foucault's sense of revenge
and justice. The ceremonial display of the body in the garden was his

way of laying her curse to rest. The evidence of a burglary in this scenario was legit.

Option three: Anabel was not Muran and was killed by someone who knew she had *Tyls* or someone who thought she had a copy of the Waterland Map. Someone familiar with the Munuorian Stones, or Anabel's connection with Devlin. Margaret Corchran? Klaus Navarro? Thatcher Reynolds? The murder in this scenario was to silence Anabel. The brutality a sign of torture? The burglary the true motive of the crime.

Jennifer would have loved to share all three scenarios with Nickerson and Hall, but she knew the first two would not go over well. Plus, she wanted some time to ponder the locket, for it didn't fit with any of the scenarios.

She tuned back into Nickerson and Hall's conversation as Nickerson said, "I don't envy you, Tim. This is a hard one."

"Tell me about it," Hall said, sliding his notebook and pen inside his coat pocket. "Unless there's something else you'd like to see, I'd like to wrap up and get back to Burlington. The team will be anxious to hear the new angles you've given me."

With that, the Vermont detective led Jennifer and Nickerson back outside. While Hall locked and sealed the house, Jennifer and Nickerson stood by his unmarked police car. A gust of wind whipped through the trees, causing a flurry of leaves to drift to the ground. Jennifer blew on her hands and whispered to Nickerson, "Sure would like to talk with the M.E., hear what he's found so far."

"Today?" Nickerson asked, while looking at his cell phone.

"Yeah. Can you swing that?" she asked.

"No can do, Jen. The captain will bust a vein if I'm not back at HQ by four."

"Do you think Hall will let me meet with the examiner without you there?"

"No harm asking," Nickerson said. "By the way, what's with your pocket?"

Jennifer froze as Nickerson pointed at her jacket. He said, "Looks like you left a flashlight on."

2

Vengeance Is Mine

Fort Ticonderoga, New York
September 25

When Aja arrived at the battlement's edge, a cavalcade of icy gusts swirled up from the lake. Tightening the collar of the worn barn coat around her neck, she turned her back to the wind and maneuvered between a cannon and a band of tourists admiring the view of Lake Champlain. Shivering, she headed for the comparative calm of the fort's Place D'Armes.

She passed through the courtyard's stone-arched entrance and spied a solitary stone stela directly ahead. Guarded on each side by a black cannon, the small, rectangular monument bore a black-faced memorial plate. When she reached the stela, she read the plate inscription.

> *From this fortress went Gen. Henry Knox in the winter of 1775–1776 to deliver to Gen. George Washington at Cambridge the train of artillery from Fort Ticonderoga used to force the British army to evacuate Boston.*

Above the inscription was a scene depicting an oxen-drawn sledge laden with a cannon. The oxen were shown trudging through a snowy forest under the watchful eye of a proud colonial general. Running down the left side of the memorial plate was a relief map tracing the path of the Knox Trail from Fort Ticonderoga to Cambridge.

Aja frowned and softly said, "Poor honor for a great deed."

Earlier, inside the fort's museum, she'd listened to a docent recount the tale. The docent declared it as a story of courage, perseverance and sheer will. A deed that tilted the Revolutionary War's early balance of power toward the upstart colonials. A bold and daring military triumph that stunned the British army encamped outside Boston so badly, they quit the city without a fight.

According to the docent's recital, twenty-five-year-old Henry Knox, then a lowly Massachusetts militiaman, was commissioned by General Washington to do the impossible. In the depth of winter, Knox was tasked with transporting fifty-nine artillery pieces from the conquered Fort Ticonderoga on the banks of Lake Champlain all the way to the outskirts of Boston. It was a journey of nearly three hundred miles through snow-covered forests and mountains and punctuated by detours across frozen lakes and rivers. The ten-week trek included several near catastrophes and ended with a volley of surprise cannon fire on the British encampment in Cambridge.

Looking down on the diminutive monument, Aja frowned again. It was a disgrace to memorialize such an amazing feat with so flat a tribute. But it came as no surprise to her. These days, monuments served only to mark territory and deliver facts. They no longer displayed the grandeur of the deeds they were erected to commemorate. Gone were the ages when great achievements were honored with monuments of profound artistry — artistry that inspired whole populations to build, fight and worship.

Her nostalgic thoughts were interrupted by a voice from behind. "I am *so* sorry I'm late. The ferry was running behind schedule."

She turned to face the voice and inspected the speaker with the intensity of an unhappy drill sergeant. Unable to escape her withering gaze, the man lowered his head. She stepped forward and lifted his chin with the fingers of her glove-covered hand. When their eyes met, she softly smiled and kissed him. "It's okay, my pet."

Her lips parted and they kissed again. Pressing her body against his, she slipped her tongue from inside his mouth and whispered in his ear, "I've missed you."

He squeezed her tightly and whispered back, "Me, too. More than you could possibly know."

"Patience, my love," she said, touching her forehead to his. "As soon as we have them, it will be like Guatemala all over again."

He kissed her forehead and they separated. With a sly smile, he said, "That may be sooner than we thought."

Aja gripped his wrist. "You found them?"

"I think so," he said. "But it won't—"

His words were drowned out by the booming voice of a docent entering the courtyard with a large tour group in tow. Pointing to where Aja and the man stood, the docent proclaimed, "And right here we have the famous starting point of Henry Knox's noble train of artillery."

Hearing the commotion approaching them from behind, Aja sighed and took her companion by the arm. "Ugh. It's always something. Let's get out of the way before we get trampled."

They serpentined through the throng of tourists and retreated to the museum café. Given the early hour, the restaurant was empty save for a party of four sitting by the windows looking out at Mount Defiance and chatting over coffee. Aja chose the farthest table from the small party and ordered tea for the two of them. Once the waitress was out of range, Aja said in a low voice, "You were saying?"

The man leaned over the table. "I rented a safe-deposit box, as you instructed. I saw the boxes. Side by side. Bottom row. They're big, the biggest boxes you can rent in the vault."

"I knew it! I knew the sneaky bitch was lying," Aja said with a snarl.

"It seems so," he said. "It won't be easy to get into them. You won't have much time to go through them once you're in."

"I will manage," she said, crossing her arms.

"There are cameras everywhere. Inside the vault, above every teller, the lobby, outside the building," he said.

"Yes, I know. You Americans. So fascinated with surveillance. Security guards?"

"None that I saw, but that doesn't mean they don't have one. I'd count on at least one."

"Show me the layout."

He retrieved a pen from his blazer pocket. After pulling a napkin from the table dispenser, he started to draw the outline of the bank.

As he finished the rough layout, the waitress arrived with their hot tea. He discreetly covered the napkin while she poured their cups. When she had finished, she placed the pot on the table and walked back to the kitchen. While Aja stirred in a half packet of sugar, her companion described the layout.

The bank was on Main Street in the heart of Middlebury, he told her. The building itself was old — stone with pillars adorning the entrance. Inside, directly opposite the entrance was a bank of teller stations, three in total. A long, narrow counter stood in front of the teller stations, presumably for customers to use when filling out checks and deposit slips. To the left of the teller stations were windows overlooking a small alley between the bank and the adjacent bookshop. To the right were three glassed-in cubicles for account representatives and loan officers. Down a narrow hallway beyond the cubicles was the bank manager's office and two other unmarked doors. At the end of the hall was a heavy-duty door with security keypad entry. Beyond the door was a small vestibule area with the gated vault dead ahead and two small "privacy" cubicles where customers could view, add to or remove items in their safe-deposit boxes.

"I was at the branch shortly after it opened for the day. There were two tellers and two reps working. The bank manager hadn't arrived yet. Two customers were in there as well. By the time I left, the bank manager still hadn't showed, and the bank lobby was empty. Who knows how many will be there when you go, but you'll have at least four people to deal with," he said.

"So long as they don't activate the alarm before I get into the boxes, it should be fine," she said.

"God, I wish I could be there to see you in action. It makes me hot just thinking about it," he said with a lecherous look.

Aja reached across the table and stroked his index finger with two fingers of her own. "You do your part and I'll tell you every little detail."

He lowered his head and pulled his hand away. He whispered, "You shouldn't tease me like that."

"I'll do more than tease you, but first…you know what you must do. Round up Kora and go get me the girl."

"Yes, my Queen."

After he departed, Aja returned to the battlements. There, she hoped the breeze would cleanse her mind of his fawning gaze and insipid voice. He was an unworthy consort, and she rued the prospect of allowing him into her bed again. But it was a necessary sacrifice, for there was a chance now to set things right, to restore majesty to her name. An opportunity to once again rise above the designs of weaker men…and women.

She closed her eyes and inhaled deeply. The dusty, earthy smell of the stone fort and the feel of the wind ruffling through her hair brought to mind images of standing atop her Naranjo temple on the eve of her first battle with the mighty city of Tikal. Though the memory was more than twelve hundred years old, she could still recall looking down on thousands of faithful warriors at the base of the fortress-like temple. They had reverently bowed for her blessing before marching off to conquer Tikal, chanting her name as they disappeared into the jungle.

It was a memory she revisited often. For she had been at the peak of her power in those days, unmatched by any living thing on Terra. If she had desired it, she could have swept her hand over any land and taken it for her own. But she hadn't. There had been no need. Once her adversaries witnessed her wielding the *Lifintyls*, they shrank from the battlefield and pledged any tribute she demanded. The men she had summoned to her bedchamber in that age were captains and warriors, men who earned the honor of pleasing her through their victorious deeds.

As Aja savored the memory, another group of tourists flowed out from the museum and spread along the battlement. One of them bumped into her while he backed up to snap a selfie against the backdrop of the lake. He mumbled a brief, hollow apology as he stepped to the side and fiddled with his smartphone camera. As she glared at the man, bitterness filled her heart. Such a misstep in older days would have cost the clumsy man his head, but now it was a daily occurrence.

No matter, she thought as she turned to leave. One day soon, her powers would be restored and she would inflict unrelenting vengeance for the centuries of her suffering — suffering that had commenced with the incompetence of Evelyn Warwick and had descended to its nadir through her treachery.

Amsterdam, The Netherlands

On good days, Julian Van der Berg always took the long way home. He would begin his victory lap by strolling past Christie's and the other premier auction houses. As he sauntered by, Van der Berg would bow and tip an imaginary cap to each of his competitors. After paying his respects, he would continue to the Stedelijk and Van Gogh museums and eventually curl in front of the Rijksmuseum on his way to the twists and turns of the Vondelpark. As he moved through the throng of tourists and bicycling commuters, he would smile at any eyes that met his as if he was one of the Dutch Masters accepting praise from admirers.

Tonight, he walked through the Vondelpark at a more leisurely pace than usual, his face aglow. Instead of dodging the thick two-way stream of cyclists on the trails, Van der Berg opted to cut his own path across the grassy parklands. Using his umbrella as a walking stick, he whistled a tune and strolled along with nary a care.

And he had good reason to feel upbeat. The day's auction had been a record-breaking event for his boutique firm. His client, an aging German industrialist with a mountain of debt and unpaid taxes, had been quite pleased with the outcome despite bemoaning the surrender of his precious Egyptian collection. There had been frothy bidding and a buzz of excitement as each lot was presented.

Before the auction ended, reporters in attendance were tweeting and posting the eye-popping prices for the world — and Van der Berg's competitors — to see. Yes, it had been a very good day, he thought. A day worthy of a long walk, a hearty meal, an extra tot of cognac and maybe a late-night visit to the red-light district.

With these pleasant thoughts in mind, he approached the park exit and watched the last of the sun dip below the horizon. Van der Berg was so immersed in reliving his triumph, he paid no attention to the two shadows scampering toward him from behind. Nor did he notice the van idling at the curb by the park exit, a blazing cigarette dangling from the driver's lips. No, when the blow struck against the back of his head, Van der Berg was instead fantasizing about the headlines he would read in the morning newspapers...

Nationaal Park Zuid-Kennemerland, The Netherlands

The van followed the looping N200 exit ramp until the driver eased to a full stop at the intersection with Zeeweg. Turning right, the van continued north along Zeeweg until the driver spotted the park access road, Parnassiaweg, to his left. Extinguishing the vehicle's headlights, he cautiously turned down the dark lane. Bordered on both sides by sand dunes, scrub bushes and marsh grass, Parnassiaweg led into the heart of Nationaal Park Zuid-Kennemerland, passing various campgrounds along its way. The driver struggled to adjust to the pitch-black terrain ahead, a condition made worse by the bright city lights of Zandvoort attacking his eyes through the rearview mirror. On a couple of occasions, the van scraped against the dunes and kicked up a thick plume of sandy debris in its wake.

In the backseat of the van, Julian Van der Berg belted out a fresh round of muffled protests through the gag wedged in his mouth. On his left and right sat two men. Though Van der Berg could not see them through the thick bag covering his head, he could feel their hulking figures pressed against his body. Each time he squirmed against the zip ties binding his hands and feet, one or the other captor would silence his movement with a stiff elbow to the ribs.

At first, Van der Berg had thought the men who snatched him were robbers who mistook him for an American tourist. As the van sped away from the Vondelpark exit, he had tried to tell them as much and pleaded for his release in Dutch, German and English. The men had ignored his entreaties as they roughly applied the zip ties. Van der Berg had screamed for help, hoping pedestrians on the narrow streets would take notice. The men hadn't said a word. Instead, they beat him until he stopped screaming. Dazed, Van der Berg had been unable to resist when the gag was shoved in his mouth and bag tugged over his head. Later, when his head began to clear, he had screamed again for help. This had caused the men to laugh and mock his muffled, high-pitched bleats.

For over an hour, the van had bumped along the roads leading from Amsterdam to the Atlantic coast. Once the initial shock of the abduction had begun to fade, Van der Berg had abandoned his smothered pleading. For the longer they traveled, the more he realized simple robbery was not the likely motive for the abduction. After all, if they had meant to rob him, they could have easily taken his wallet, watch and briefcase and kicked him out on the side of the road ten minutes outside Amsterdam. But they hadn't. In fact, they'd made no effort to search him and, as best as he could tell, they hadn't rummaged through his briefcase either.

The more likely target, Van der Berg now reasoned, was his gallery. More specifically, the vault in his gallery. Two of the pieces auctioned earlier in the day were still in the vault, awaiting delivery instructions from the winning overseas bidder. In addition, the safe held several other valuable artifacts awaiting auction, as well as a few pieces in Van der Berg's personal collection. He concluded his captors meant to interrogate him for the gallery security code and vault combination. It would be a foolhardy move, Van der Berg thought. Even if they coerced the information from him, there were security cameras at every entrance, in every room and inside the vault itself. To boot, a security guard was posted inside the gallery twenty-four hours a day, and the Amsterdam police routinely patrolled the city-center grouping of galleries, auction houses and museums.

Yet, if they were successful, even if they got away with just one piece, Van der Berg's reputation would be demolished on the very eve of his greatest triumph. Yes, insurance would cover any losses, he thought. But there was no policy that would help recover the trust of his hard-won clients, and the prospects of attracting new clients would take a devastating blow. Though his competitors would publicly express sympathy, he knew they would privately circulate doubts about his security measures for years to come. Van der Berg sighed as he imagined his reputation dragged through the mud. The possibility cut deeper than any financial loss he might incur in the theft.

Anger swelled inside him as the van came to a halt. The engine turned off and Van der Berg heard a door open. In the background, he detected the sound of crashing waves, and then he heard a man's voice through the open door. Van der Berg recognized the language as either Portuguese or Spanish, but he did not catch the man's words. Squeezing his blood-deprived, tingling hands, he took a deep breath and tried to corral his emotions. He would have to be level-headed to negotiate with the thieves.

There was a light rapping on the side of the van, followed immediately by the sound of another door opening. The men bracketing Van der Berg gripped his arms and hauled him through the open door. They dragged him up a small rise, jostling him with each step. The sound of waves grew louder as they descended the far side of the rise. Finally, they stopped and dropped him onto the sand. Van der Berg rolled onto his side and tried to speak.

A hand grasped the bag covering his head and yanked it off. Van der Berg's eyes fluttered open and he spied four dark figures hovering above him. One of them crouched by his side. "Hello, Julian."

The voice was familiar to Van der Berg, but he could not see the man's face. The distant lights of Zandvoort reduced the man's features to an inky silhouette. He turned his head away from the lights and squeezed his eyes shut. The crouching man spoke to the other figures, and several hands grasped Van der Berg by the shoulders and arms. They pulled him up and twisted him around before planting him back in the sand in a kneeling position. When the hands let go, Van der Berg briefly teetered but he managed to steady himself. He opened his eyes again and found he was still facing the crouching silhouette, but the beach town's lights no longer assaulted his vision. He first noticed the ponytail. Then, the pirate's smile. Wild-eyed, he bit down on the gag and spat the man's name.

"That's right, Julian. Surprised to see me?" asked Klaus Navarro.

Van der Berg writhed against his binds and raged with livid protests.

"Shhh," Navarro said, gently patting Van der Berg's shoulder. "You will get your chance to speak. Right now, be quiet and listen."

The patronizing tone of Navarro's voice only fueled Van der Berg's ire. His body shook as he cursed the Argentinian.

"Julian, please," Navarro said. He motioned to one of the other men. A swift kick to the abdomen crumpled Van der Berg into the fetal position. The Dutchman gasped through sandy nostrils.

"It will get *much* worse if you don't settle down," Navarro said. "All I want is some information. Lie still and listen."

As Van der Berg tried to calm his breathing, his mind fought to make sense of the situation. What was going on? Why was Navarro doing this? What information could he possibly want that would warrant such harsh treatment?

Navarro's shady reputation was well known to Van der Berg, but he had always been a good client. He never quibbled over fees and often paid far more than necessary to win auctions. On past occasions, he had sought inside information about pieces coming to auction, but that was not unusual among serious collectors in Van der Berg's experience. Some wined and dined him, hoping the libations would loosen his tongue. Others offered bribes, sometimes subtly, other times not. But, to the best of his memory, Navarro had never done more than suggest trades of information, which Van der Berg always politely rebuffed. But to kidnap and beat him? Looking up at Navarro, he wondered again what information was so important that Navarro would resort to bullying him?

"Are you ready to listen now?" Navarro asked.

Van der Berg nodded.

"Good." Navarro instructed his men to lift Van der Berg from the sand, and they once again propped him up on his knees. Once he was face to face with the auctioneer, Navarro said, "Someone tried to kill me, Julian. And you know who he is."

Navarro paused and leaned forward. Glaring at Van der Berg, he said, "I want to know his name."

Van der Berg stared back at him with a puzzled expression.

"The name, Julian. The anonymous collector with the stone I wanted," Navarro demanded, his voice cold and sharp.

A flash of recognition washed across Van der Berg's face. Now he remembered! Navarro had come to him in search of an Olmec stone known as the Serpent's Tooth. Navarro had asked for his assistance in canvassing museums, auction houses and private collectors for anyone who might possess the stone. He had offered Van der Berg a hefty commission for his assistance, a commission that had yet to be paid.

Navarro prodded again. "His name?"

The demand drew a muffled response from Van der Berg. Navarro motioned for one of the men to remove the gag. A hand cupped Van der Berg's head from behind while another hand gruffly pulled the cloth from between his teeth and let it droop around his neck. The Dutchman greedily drew air into his mouth while moving his jaw from side to side. He tried to speak, but his throat was too dry to make sound. He coughed several times and whispered hoarsely for water.

"Tell me the name and you can have all the water you want," Navarro said.

Van der Berg knew the name, of course, but he had no intention of telling Navarro under the present circumstances. He whispered, "Water first."

Navarro lowered his head and sighed. Standing up, he brushed sand from his black Armani slacks and rattled off a command in

Portuguese. All three men converged on Van der Berg and lifted him off the sand. Carrying him like a log, they walked toward the gurgling waves. He twisted his body and cried out with a croaky voice, "What are you doing? Put me down! Stop!"

The men ignored his pleas. When they reached the surf, they dropped him into the foamy, ice-cold water. While Van der Berg yelped in protest, one of the men bent down and jabbed a knee in his back. As a new wave approached, the henchman pulled Van der Berg's head up by his hair. While the other two men stood back, the one with his knee boring into Van der Berg's back leaned forward and said, "Drink up, amigo!"

The wave plowed into both of them. Navarro's man stumbled but managed to stay upright while Van der Berg took the wave's full fury in the face. As the wave began to recede, the man dragged the auctioneer deeper into the water and pressed his head down into the sludgy sand. Unable to breathe, Van der Berg flailed violently. Message delivered.

The man released his grip on Van der Berg's head and raised it above the water. Taking hold of the soaked gag hanging around his neck, the man dragged Van der Berg away from the surf and deposited his retching body at Navarro's feet.

Navarro crouched down again, shifting his dangling ponytail back over his shoulder. "No more delay, Julian. The name."

Coughing out a mixture of sand and saltwater, Van der Berg said, "Why are you doing this? Why are you treating me this way?"

From inside his blazer pocket, Navarro withdrew a thin, dark object. He held it up and the lights of Zandvoort glinted off the blade. "This, my friend, is the weapon your client gave to his assassin, the one who tried to kill me. You would find it most interesting. I've never seen another like it. It's old, inexplicably ancient, yet as deadly as the day it was forged."

He lowered the knife from the light and gripped it tightly in his hand. "I mean to return it to its owner. I need your help to find him."

"He didn't tell me his name," Van der Berg said.

With a sigh, Navarro shook his head. "Julian, Julian. I know you better than that. You would not have called me unless you knew he was a credible seller."

He thrust the blade into Van der Berg's thigh. Muted by the crashing waves, the Dutchman's grisly shriek did not travel beyond the dunes. Navarro slowly slid the knife from the wound and briefly hovered it above Van der Berg's chest before readying the dripping weapon to strike again.

"Stop!" Van der Berg begged. "Please, stop!"

Navarro rammed the blade into his shoulder. Another sickening scream echoed around the dunes.

"Foucault!" he cried. "Jacques Foucault."

In between sobbing groans, he pleaded again for Navarro to stop. The Argentinian withdrew the knife and wiped the bloody blade across Van der Berg's blazer. While the wounded man continued to whimper, Navarro stared out into the ocean. "Foucault...Foucault. I have heard the name before, but I do not know where."

Turning back to Van der Berg, he asked, "He is a client of yours?"

Van der Berg nodded.

"French or Belgian?"

"French," Van der Berg said between panting groans. "Please, I've told you what you want to know. I beg you, let me go. I'm bleeding badly."

Twirling the knife shaft in his hand, Navarro asked, "You have his address, of course?"

"Yes, yes," he said. "Please, Klaus! I swear to God, I thought he wanted to sell you his piece. That's all. You must believe me."

The crouching Navarro patted the man's knee and put away the knife. "I believe you, Julian."

Rising up, Navarro rattled off instructions to his men in Portuguese and then turned to walk away. As Van der Berg watched him sashay toward the dunes, the men lifted Van der Berg from the beach. At first, the weakened auctioneer closed his eyes and whimpered with relief. His nightmare was over. Within a few steps, however, Van der Berg realized the men were not following Navarro. Instead, they were carrying him back to the surf.

He protested and squirmed against their hold. The men laughed as they staggered through the tide, once again mocking Van der Berg's feeble protests.

Navarro stood by the van with cell phone in hand. As he scrolled through results of his search on the name Jacques Foucault, he listened to Van der Berg's urgent screams disappear beneath the crashing waves. He shook his head and said, "So sorry, Julian. You should have chosen your clients more carefully."

A few moments later, his men appeared over the dune. Navarro motioned them to hurry. When they reached the van, Navarro placed a hand on one man's shoulder. "Manuel, it is time to fetch the girl with the pretty new necklace. Then we will all go together to pay a visit to Monsieur Foucault and return his special blade."

3

A Weave in Time

New York, New York
September 26

Anlon Cully stood by the hotel window and peered down at competing waves of pedestrians moving along the sidewalks of Fifty-Ninth Street. With determined gaits, they dodged around one another, barely breaking stride, as they made their way toward Columbus Circle in one direction and Fifth Avenue in the other. On the street itself, drivers nudged their vehicles forward in fits and starts, generously applying their horns to urge movement. Raising his gaze, Anlon sipped coffee and looked out on Central Park and the eerie shadows that stretched across its green canopy from the east. He sighed and turned away from the window. As much as he preferred to linger, watching and listening as Manhattan awoke, it was time to call Foucault.

First, though, he walked to the sofa and used his phone to send off a quick text to Pebbles. "Hey, good morning! Getting ready to call JF, then meeting Cesar. I'll call you after I wrap up with Cesar."

To his surprise, he received a reply within seconds. "Good morning back atcha."

What is she doing up at this hour? he thought. It wasn't even four thirty yet in Tahoe. He typed, "Up awful early. Everything okay?"

"Awful is right," she replied. The message was punctuated by an angry-faced emoticon. A second text followed shortly after. "I'm ok. Just couldn't sleep after call with Jen."

"Ah. Sorry," Anlon wrote. "If any consolation, I had a rough night, too."

The three-way call had been disturbing, to say the least. Jennifer had arranged it to run through the highlights of her meeting with the police at Anabel's house. In the call, Jennifer had provided a vivid description of Anabel's death scene and detailed the confusing array of evidence inside the house and out — including her discovery of the gold locket. They had discussed Jennifer's theories of the possible scenarios and motives and debated whether to get involved in the investigation.

In the end, they had agreed there was no choice but to get involved. One way or another, Anabel's death was connected with the *Lifintyls*. As such, until an investigation produced a definitive answer as to who was responsible, there was a risk that the killer might come looking for more of the *Tyls*. The weight of the discussion and the decision had kept Anlon's mind buzzing all night long. He typed, "How are you feeling about it this morning?"

"Icky. Angry. A little scared."

"Scared?"

"Yeah. The whole Muran 'boogey-monster' thing."

"I understand what you mean, but that's only one possibility."

"Yeah, I know," Pebbles replied. A moment later she sent a follow-on message. "Other possibilities aren't exactly peachy, either. Navarro. Margaret Corchran. Yada yada."

"I hear you," Anlon answered.

"Even if JF tells you he did it, still got the heebie jeebies. What he did to her was sick. Twisted."

There was no way to argue with that point, Anlon thought. Looking at the time, he realized he was late for the call with the aforementioned Foucault. He texted Pebbles, "Hey, gotta run now. Check in with you after my meeting with Cesar?"

"K. Good luck. Tell Cesar I said hello! xo"

"Will do. Try and go back to sleep. xox"

When Foucault answered the call, his voice was light and friendly. "*Allô?* Dr. Cully?"

"Hello, Count Foucault. Yes, it's Anlon Cully. I'm sorry I'm a little late calling. Is this still a good time to talk?"

"*Oui, oui.* I have been on pins and needles since receiving your email last night," Foucault said.

"I'm glad it got through to you. I appreciate you responding so quickly."

"Of course. I trust you are well?"

"Yes, I'm fine. And you?"

"*Comme ci comme ça*," Foucault said.

"How is your man, Christian? Is he on the mend?" Anlon asked.

"*Oui.* He is progressing nicely, thank you. I will tell him you asked about his health," Foucault said. "I saw the announcement about Indio Maiz. Your project goes well?"

"So far, so good. Cesar has had some productive talks with the Nicaraguans, and Pebbles has really rolled up her sleeves to get the museum underway."

"*Bon!* I'm pleased to hear it," Foucault said. "Now, what is this matter you wished to speak about so urgently?"

Leaning forward on the sofa, Anlon bowed his head. "I have some sad news to share."

"Oh?"

"Anabel is dead."

There was a long pause before Foucault said, "I'm afraid you have me at a loss. Who is Anabel?"

"Anabel Simpson. She was a close friend of Devlin's. You knew her, right?"

"*Non.*"

Anlon noted the nonchalant lilt with which Foucault delivered his one-word answer. Was it a sincere reaction or was Foucault putting on an act? "I'm surprised to hear that. She was a retired archaeology professor. She often traveled with Devlin."

"I see. You said she is dead?"

"She was murdered."

"*Mon Dieu*," Foucault whispered. "Murdered?"

"Yes. Electrocuted."

"Oh, my. I'm very sorry. A friend of Devlin's, you say?"

"Yes, they shared a long romance."

"I see…"

"I'm not sure you do. Anabel's the one who gave me Devlin's map after he died," Anlon said.

There was no answer from Foucault. Anlon stood and tilted the phone closer to his mouth. "Foucault, are you there? Did you hear me?"

"*Oui*, Dr. Cully, I heard you," whispered Foucault.

After another uncomfortable silence, Anlon said, "You have nothing to say?"

"What should I say? What do you expect me to say?" Foucault asked.

Anlon began to pace in front of the sofa. "Look, forgive me for being so bold, Foucault, but I need to know. Did you have anything to do with it? Did you kill her?"

"*Non!* Absolutely not!" Foucault said with quick defiance. "What makes you think this?"

Clearing his throat, Anlon said, "Well, at the top of the list — right before you left us at Indio Maiz, you told us you had laid a trap for Muran."

"*Oui*. This is true. What of it?"

"Was Anabel the target of your trap?"

"*Non*." Foucault paused, then said, "Dr. Cully, you seem to be suggesting this woman was Muran."

"You tell me," Anlon said.

"I have never heard of this woman. Of that you may be certain. What makes you think she was *The Painted Lady*?"

"There are some things about Anabel, about her death, that suggest she could have been Muran, or at least had contact with her."

"You intrigue me. What things?"

"Well, for one, we think Anabel might have been the person who passed Malinyah's *Sinethal* to Devlin," Anlon said.

When Foucault replied, there was a noticeable difference in his tone. To Anlon, he seemed anxious. "What did this woman look like? Do you have a picture you can send me?"

Anlon frowned. "Uh, not with me. But I'm sure you can find one if you do a search online."

Anlon heard the sound of typing, and then Foucault mumbled something. Why did Foucault want to see a picture of Anabel? he wondered. The only answer he could come up with startled him. "Foucault, do you know what Muran looks like?"

"One moment, please," Foucault said. Anlon heard several more keystrokes before the Frenchman spoke again. "It is not her."

"You *do* know what she looks like, don't you? Why the hell didn't you tell us that before?"

Another silent stretch. Unbelievable! Anlon thought. He circled the suite's living room, waiting for Foucault to answer. As he walked, another question leapt to mind. If Anabel hadn't been Muran, and Foucault hadn't killed her, then who the hell did and why?

"Dr. Cully?"

"Yes?"

"I think we should meet. There are certain things you should know. And others I wish to know. But it is a conversation we should have face to face."

"That suits me. I'm in Manhattan for a few days. Can you come to New York?" Anlon asked.

"*Bon.* I will. When will you be free to meet?"

"You name it, I'll make it happen. I don't want to drag this out."

"Agreed. It will take me a day or two to set things in order. Will Friday work?"

"It's actually perfect. Pebbles and Jennifer will be here by then."

"Excellent. I will bring Christian…and Mereau," Foucault said.

"Mereau?"

"*Oui.* And Malinyah should be there as well. In fact, her presence is vital."

"Vital? What do you mean?" Anlon asked.

There was a long sigh on the other end of the line. When Foucault spoke, his voice was nearly a whisper, "She holds the key that can help us break the curse of *The Painted Lady.*"

Hall of South American Peoples
American Museum of Natural History
New York, New York

Anlon hustled up the stairwell until he reached the second floor. Turning right, he passed through two halls full of cultural exhibits and finally spied Cesar Perez at the far end of the second hall. As Anlon approached, Cesar looked up and waved. Anlon extended his hand. "Sorry, Cesar. Got hung up in the subway. Waited forever at Columbus Circle. Could have walked here in less time."

"No trouble at all. I occupied myself quite happily," Cesar said, shaking Anlon's hand. "How are you?"

"Okay, I guess. A little frazzled," Anlon said.

"Anabel?" Cesar asked.

"Yeah, Anabel. Guess who I talked to this morning. Our friend from Indio Maiz, Jacques Foucault."

"Ah. What did Count Foucault have to say?"

"I'll tell you later over lunch. Right now, I want to hear about this mystery relic of yours," Anlon said.

"Very well. Come this way."

They walked through an archway into the Hall of South American Peoples, and Cesar guided Anlon to a glass-encased exhibit featuring fabrics. As Cesar started to speak, a group of children descended upon them. Cesar paused and motioned for Anlon to step aside. Together, they gave way as the children filed past the display case. A few of the middle schoolers stopped to glance at the ancient textiles behind the glass, but most darted away in a boisterous hunt for mummies.

When the last of the gaggle zipped by, Cesar turned to Anlon and shook his head. "Mummies. It's always mummies and dinosaurs with the *niños.*"

Anlon laughed and patted him on the back. "Don't take it personally, Cesar. It's hard to beat mummies."

"Yes, yes. I know," Cesar said. Waving his arm around the hall of displays, he sighed. "Still, there is so much history surrounding us, and yet so few bother to look for more than a second."

"Well, you've got *my* full attention," Anlon said, resuming his place in front of the display. He pointed at two small cloth fragments. "You were about to say something about these ones."

Cesar withdrew reading glasses from his tweed blazer and stepped up next to Anlon. He slid on the eyewear and leaned forward for a closer look. "Notice the fine twining. The intricate pattern of the weaving."

Squinting through the high-polished glass, Anlon examined the four-line placard positioned beneath the two tattered fabrics. It read, "Site of discovery: Huaca Prieta, Peru. Culture: Unknown. Estimated date of origin: 1000–500 B.C.E. Discovered: 1946."

The cloth fragments were each about the size of a small washcloth. Unlike other textiles displayed in the same case, the two at the center of Cesar's focus lacked colorful threading and fanciful designs. Instead, they were a solid color, a drab, yellowish-brown hue. Yet, despite their plain appearance when viewed at a distance, there was extraordinary detail in each artifact's weaving. Anlon said, "It's hard to believe these were hand-sewn."

"Agreed. The craftmanship is so refined, it looks like it was machine-made," Cesar said.

"Is that what drew your attention to these?"

"Partially. There have been other textiles found at the same site which are more intriguing."

"Yeah? How so?" Anlon turned to Cesar and crossed his arms.

"As soon as Dr. Sinclair arrives, you will see for yourself," Cesar said with a smile.

Before Anlon could reply, another surge of schoolchildren raced through the hall. The two men retreated to a nearby bench to avoid falling victim to the Pamplona-like stampede while they awaited Dr. Elton Sinclair. Anlon said, "If you won't tell me about your 'intriguing' textiles, at least tell me a bit more about where they were found."

"Huaca Prieta? It's in northern Peru, very close to the Pacific coastline," Cesar said.

"Have you been there?" Anlon asked, crouching down to wipe away a child's dusty footprint from the top of one of his boots.

"Oh, yes, several times. The first extensive excavations were done well before my time, in the forties. Since then, there have been numerous digs in and around the first site," Cesar explained. "From a distance, Huaca Prieta looks like a big mound sitting close to the beach. It instantly catches the eye because the land around it is flat and unremarkable."

"Is there mythology associated with the site?" Anlon asked.

Cesar said, "Not outright. There are artifacts from multiple cultures from different time periods in different layers spread around the site, so it's a bit of a jumble. It doesn't appear to have been a strong cultural center for any one civilization."

"What led you to take an interest, then?"

"Believe it or not, it was your uncle who first urged me to go there."

"Devlin? Why?"

"It was about ten years ago. We were at an archaeology conference in London and we had just finished listening to a presentation about the discovery of textile imprints embedded in copper artifacts at Harappa and Mohenjo-daro in Pakistan," Cesar said.

Anlon feigned a yawn. "Sounds fascinating."

"Actually, it was!" Cesar laughed. "Anyway, Devlin leaned over and whispered something in my ear. I didn't hear what he said at first, I was distracted by the applause for the speaker. When I asked him to repeat it, he said, 'Huaca Prieta.' Without explanation, he got up and dashed over to speak with the presenter.

"Later, over dinner, he explained his excitement. He said he thought there was a strong similarity in the weave pattern of one of the Harappa imprints and one from Huaca Prieta. The bottom one there, the one with the patterned border," Cesar explained, pointing toward the display case.

"Was he right?" Anlon asked, leaning forward to spy the cloth fragment again.

Cesar shrugged. "I didn't think so for a long time. Harappa is nearly ten thousand miles from Huaca Prieta, separated by the Pacific Ocean. Though one finds examples of trading between cultures at many archaeological sites, they are mostly confined to cultures that resided on contiguous land masses, or later periods when sea travel was more common. And the Harappan artifact was much older, two thousand years older."

"But something changed your mind?" Anlon asked.

"Yes. Early last year, a few months before Devlin died, I heard of a new discovery by Dr. Sinclair at Huaca Prieta. The details piqued my interest, so I called him. He invited me out and showed me his discovery."

Cesar stopped speaking and stared off toward the entryway of the hall. Anlon edged forward on the bench and nudged Cesar's shoulder. "And? What did he say?"

A smile spread across Cesar's face and he rose off the bench. He took several steps forward and waved his hand. Anlon followed the direction of his wave and noticed two smiling people waving back. One was a squat man with a Santa Claus–worthy beard of snow white. He wore a battered fedora, leather jacket and blue jeans. Beside him was a much younger woman with olive skin and long, jet black hair. Anlon guessed her to be a graduate student. As they drew closer, Anlon noted she was dressed more formally than the man: tweed skirt, tan blouse and heels. Black-rimmed eyeglasses and a leather satchel clutched in her hand completed her appearance.

Cesar greeted the man heartily while the woman politely stood to the side. Anlon approached the woman. She smiled and extended a hand. "You must be Anlon Cully. Ow ya goin, I'm Diane Jones. Everybody calls me Jonesey."

Her Australian accent surprised Anlon. As did the strength of her grip. "You got it right, I'm Anlon. Nice to meet you, Jonesey."

In the middle of their handshake, the bearded man slapped Anlon on the shoulder. "So, you're the nephew of the great Devlin Wilson. God, I miss that man!"

"Me, too," Anlon said. "Elton Sinclair, I presume."

"The one and only," Sinclair said, removing his hat to reveal his shiny pate.

"It's good of you to meet with us," Anlon said.

"No trouble at all, young man. I'm always thrilled to talk about my work," Sinclair replied. "Cesar tells me you're interested in our mysterious shawl."

"Uh," Anlon said, darting a quick glare at Cesar, "why, yes."

Cesar grinned at Anlon and then said to Sinclair, "I have not told Anlon much, Elton. I wanted him to see it first."

Jonesey stepped forward and introduced herself to Cesar. Sinclair slapped his thigh and said, "Forgive me, Jonesey. How rude of me." He turned to Anlon and Cesar, "Dr. Jones is an expert in early Mesoamerican cultures. I told her you were coming to take a gander at the shawl and invited her to tag along."

With the introductions completed, Sinclair slapped Anlon once more on the shoulder. "Follow me. Let's see if you've got some of Devlin in you."

The quartet made their way to the nearest staircase and ascended two floors. As they walked toward the museum's research library, Sinclair pummeled Cesar with questions about the Indio Maiz discovery, while Anlon chatted amiably with Jonesey.

When they reached the library, Sinclair spoke to a clerk who led them behind a door with a small sign that read "Official Use

Only. Do Not Enter." They proceeded down a hallway with several closed doors. The clerk unlocked the first door to their right and ushered them in. To Anlon, it looked like a smaller version of Devlin's barn office. There was a central examining table with high-power lighting fixtures overhead. Clamped to each corner of the table were magnifying lamps. To one side of the table, there was a counter with an assortment of precision tools and brushes. The clerk marched to the counter and retrieved latex gloves for all members of the party, including himself. From a portable rack behind the door, he provided each with a laboratory coat and tugged on his own as he left the room.

The clerk returned shortly with an oblong carrying case layered atop his outstretched forearms. Anlon thought it looked like the kind of case one might expect to be used to transport a musician's keyboard. The clerk placed it on the table with care and slowly unhinged its buckle locks. Then, he reverently lifted out the inner case holding the ancient textile.

The full-length shawl was pressed between two panes of glass. The first thing Anlon noticed was the garment's assortment of bright colors. The main background was crimson, and its surrounding edges were trimmed with gold. Inside this border, numerous designs were interspersed throughout in gold, green, indigo, brown and orange. Toward one end of the shawl, the designs were obscured by a mottled stain.

"Well, my boy, what do you think of our little oddity?" Sinclair asked.

Anlon scratched at his head and said, "I'm a little out of my element, Elton. Tell me about it."

"Jonesey, why don't you do the honors," Sinclair said.

"Right. I'll give it a burl," she said, adjusting her glasses as she leaned over the case. Fanning her hand along the length of the shawl, she said, "Dr. Sinclair discovered this last year at Huaca Prieta. It was found rolled up inside a sealed pot in a chamber about fifty meters from the main excavation site, roughly ten meters below the surface."

An excited Sinclair interrupted. "We chose the dig site because it's farther back from the ocean. You see, there is evidence of a great disturbance in excavations closer to the beach."

"Disturbance?" Anlon asked. "Looters?"

"No, no," Sinclair said. "A natural disturbance of some kind. Most likely a tsunami. Many of the artifacts found underneath the mound are displaced, meaning they were found amid a swirl of different sediments. Some of the pottery, for instance, was smashed by the force of the waves and pieces were found scattered in the sediment layers."

Cesar leaned in and said to Anlon, "The mound was not always near the beach. In fact, there is evidence to suggest it was built several miles inland. The tsunami swallowed the land in between."

Jonesey said, "Right. Dr. Sinclair's site was chosen hoping to find a layer less disturbed by flooding. If you imagine the mound itself served as a breakwater, taking the brunt of the tidal waves, then the area directly behind the mound might have avoided the full force. At least, that was the theory. A hunch that proved an ace."

"Oh, I can't take all the credit," said the blushing archaeologist, removing his Fedora again and bowing. "Others theorized the same, years before me. I was just fortunate to get funded before they did."

"You're too modest," Jonesey said, wrapping her fingers around his with a light squeeze. Sinclair blushed deeper red, giving his face the full Santa Claus effect. Directing her gaze back to Anlon, she said, "The initial layer showed the same mix of sediments, but five meters down, it started to settle out. Ten meters down, they found remnants of a stone wall. Then they found a real corker: a walled room full of artifacts, including the shawl."

While Anlon listened, he studied the shawl more closely. Cesar noticed him examining the cloth and maneuvered one of the magnifying lamps in his direction. Peering through the illuminated glass, Anlon studied the fabric. The dyed threads were incredibly thin and tightly woven. The designs were of objects, animals and humanlike figures with headdresses. They seemed ordered, as if they told a story. There was another curious feature. The gold stitching around the borders sparkled. Anlon adjusted the focus of the magnifying glass and whispered, "Would you look at that."

"Eh? What's that you say?" Sinclair asked.

"The border, there are small gold beads on the threads," Anlon said.

"Exquisite, aren't they?" Sinclair said with pride.

"More like extraordinary," Anlon said. Turning toward Cesar, he said, "I'm not a textile expert, but even I can tell this piece is far more sophisticated than the ones you showed me downstairs."

Cesar nodded slowly, then said, "And far older. The cotton is twelve thousand years old, Anlon. More than nine thousand years older than the cotton used to weave the ones I showed you downstairs."

"A modern automated loom would have a hard time matching the complex weaving," Sinclair said. "How could such a garment be hand-sewn twelve thousand years ago? Let alone beaded?"

Jonesey pointed at the indigo-dyed piping on each side of the beaded border. "The same can be asked about the dye along the edge. The use of indigo does not appear on textiles again until the Egyptians started using it eight thousand years later...seven thousand miles away."

"Incredible," Anlon said.

"Oh, that's not all, not by a long shot," Cesar said. "The weaved pattern is identical to the imprint found on the Harappan copper shard I mentioned earlier. The imprint also has traces of indigo... and impressions of tiny beads."

"Then Devlin might have been right about the connection between Harappa and Huaca Prieta after all?" Anlon asked.

"So it seems," Cesar acknowledged. "Possibly in more ways than one."

"What do you mean?" Anlon asked.

"I'll tell you in a minute, but first I want you to look at something," Cesar said. He guided a pointed finger to one of the human figures depicted on the shawl. "You see this here? This is what first aroused my curiosity."

Anlon examined the figure. It appeared to be a man standing or dancing with arms upraised. He was smiling and wore a headdress that looked like a plume of feathers arranged around his head. In one hand, he held what appeared to be a serpent. In the other, a golden globe.

The background of the tapestry surrounding the man was full of wildlife and symbols. Above his head were dozens of round circles. Buzzing around his raised left hand were birds of various shapes. In the background surrounding his torso, an oddly depicted sun was positioned about halfway above the horizon. To the left of his body, the slice of visible sun seemed to be rising as rays projected outward. The sun slice on the right side, however, appeared to be setting, for it had no rays. To the left of his dangling feet were three creatures. One of the animals looked like a fox, another a butterfly or ladybug, and the last looked to Anlon like a lizard. To the right of the man's legs was nothing, although there was a spiky object just below his right foot that was obscured by the rusty stain covering the shawl at that end.

"Is it some kind of god?" Anlon asked. "He looks like he's floating down from the stars."

Sinclair slapped him hard on the shoulder. "Not a bad guess. Tell him, Cesar. It's your theory."

Cesar looked at Anlon and said, "You asked earlier whether there was any mythology tied to Huaca Prieta. I've found none, but elements of this shawl do suggest a connection with a specific Incan legend. A legend which might sound familiar.

"A great cataclysm destroys the Earth, and from across the water, or sky, depending on interpretation, arrives Aramu Muru. He carries a golden globe and other objects that have special powers. He uses these powers to help survivors of the cataclysm and helps them create great cities in the Andes."

"That does have a familiar ring," Anlon said.

Turning his attention back to the textile, Cesar said, "When I look at the shawl, I see a man descending from a starry heaven at a crossroads in time. The left side shows a thriving world before his arrival. The right side shows a barren world. The golden globe in his hand is suggestive of the disc of Aramu Muru legend, as is the serpent in the right hand. He is sometimes referred to as a serpent deity.

"Devlin was aware of the myth, of course, but he discounted it because of the 'space aliens' hysteria that seems to have taken over the legend," Cesar said.

Anlon frowned. "Aliens?"

"Yeah," Jonesey said. Rolling her eyes, she waved her hands in a spooky fashion. "The stargate legend. The portal of the gods."

Anlon stared at her, expecting her to continue. When she didn't, he said, "Afraid I don't know that one. What's it about?"

"Oh, it's just some nonsense dreamed up by wackadoodles," Jonesey said with derision. "There's a legend that says Aramu Muru used the globe to open a portal to communicate with the gods and to transport back and forth between the heavens. Some conspiracy theorist in the seventies wrote a book claiming the myth was a story about ancient aliens. Then, in the nineties, the supposed portal was found."

"Really?" Anlon said. "What does it look like?"

Cesar said, "It is an interesting site, with little in the way of explanation for its location or purpose. A partial doorway, large enough for a person to stand in, cut a few feet into the sheer face of an Andean boulder near Lake Titicaca. Most archaeologists believe it is simply an unfinished structure, probably carved by the same people who built Tiahuanaco."

"Devlin was interested in Tiahuanaco, as I recall," Anlon said.

"Yes, he was. There are many unexplained mysteries about Tiahuanaco. Who built it? When? How did they do it? What was its purpose? There are many theories, but little proof to declare any one of them conclusively the frontrunner."

Sinclair said, "One of the more prominent features at Tiahuanaco is the so-called Gateway of the Sun. It's an archway with a carving at its center point. The carving is purportedly of Viracocha, the creator god in Incan mythology. Some believe there are parallels between stories about Viracocha and Aramu Muru. In fact, some believe the Gateway of the Sun is Aramu Muru's portal."

"So, you're interested in the shawl because of the possible connection with Tiahuanaco?" Anlon asked Cesar.

"Partially," Cesar said. "Remember, my specialty is discerning history from mythology. I'm interested because the shawl significantly predates the rise of the Incan civilization, and yet it seems to include a central figure in Incan mythology. Then there is the craftmanship. It is far superior to any textile discovered in this part of the world, and it's several thousand years older than the earliest comparable weaving. And the striking similarity to the Harappan imprint is another mystery. Not just the pattern, but the use of indigo and beading. These things suggest the two were made by the same culture. One that could travel across oceans...twelve thousand years ago. A culture whose mythology — or history — made its way into Incan lore. A culture that might, therefore, be responsible for the creation of Tiahuanaco and the portal structure."

Anlon listened to Cesar's theory while he stared back at the cloth. When Cesar originally asked for his help to investigate a mysterious artifact, Anlon had told Cesar he was a bit surprised by the request. After all, Anlon was a biologist, not an archaeologist. Cesar had smiled at him and assured him that he would find the artifact fascinating. Therefore, Anlon had assumed Cesar's mystery relic must have something to do with the Munuorians, and while there now appeared to be a loose connection from a legend standpoint, nothing Cesar had described seemed to suggest a direct link.

The myths about the Munuorians were all "fish-men" legends, stories about men who came by sea, not deities who descended from the heavens. Plus, the garment was made from cotton two thousand years before the Munuorian civilization was annihilated, so how could the scene it depicted be linked to the same cataclysm that wiped out the later culture? Presumably the cotton didn't sit around for two thousand years waiting for someone to weave it into a shawl after the Munirvo catastrophe. No, the shawl's age suggested it depicted an earlier, albeit similar, catastrophe. Finally, the Munuorians' prowess had been with magnetism and stone, not weaving.

Well, that wasn't entirely true, Anlon thought. He recalled the visit to Malinyah's tomb, and Pebbles showing him Malinyah's beaded burial cloak. He cautiously ventured a question. "Cesar, are you thinking the shawl is somehow connected to Devlin's work?"

"Until you showed me his black stone, I didn't think so," Cesar said.

"The *Sinethal*? Why did that change your mind?" Anlon asked.

"The Cinn-a-what?" Sinclair asked.

"In a moment, Elton. If you please," Cesar said. "Anlon, come take a look."

Cesar repositioned the magnifying lamp over the shawl once more. He gently guided it to the right and adjusted the focus. Then he stepped back and gestured for Anlon to look through the glass. When Anlon gazed through the viewer, a chill ran through his body. He turned and stared at Cesar. The magnifier was aimed at the spiky object below the god's right foot. Although the stain obscured the object to the naked eye, there was no mistaking the woven symbol under the magnifier: a circle with six evenly-spaced rays.

"Whoa," Anlon said. "I wasn't expecting that!"

"Yes, you see now why I asked for your help?" Cesar asked.

Elton frowned and stepped forward to look through the magnifier. With his head perched over the shawl, he said, "You're talking about the symbol? You've seen the star symbol somewhere else? On a stone?"

"Yes. My uncle had a stone in his collection with a similar symbol," Anlon said.

"How interesting," Sinclair said. "Have you dated the stone?"

"Not formally, but we believe it to be in the neighborhood of ten thousand years old," Anlon said to Sinclair.

"May we see the stone?" Jonesey asked, edging close to Anlon.

"Uh, I don't have it with me. I can show you a picture of it, if you'd like," Anlon said, pulling his cell phone out. Once he located the picture in his photo library, he handed the phone to Jonesey. She moved to one of the table's other magnifying lights and studied the picture closely. Her face flushed as Sinclair sidled up beside her and looked over her shoulder.

While the two archaeologists examined the *Sinethal's* magnified image, Anlon turned back to Cesar. "You want me to ask her about the shawl, don't you? That's why you wanted me to see this. You think Malinyah might help you figure out who made the shawl, how it was made."

Cesar flashed a wry smile just as Jonesey returned with Anlon's phone. Handing it over, she thanked him and sighed. "Pity you didn't bring it with you."

4

Autopsy

Burlington, Vermont
September 26

I t was after 9 p.m. when Jennifer arrived at the University of Vermont Medical Center. Entering through the main pavilion entrance, she spied the lobby reception desk. It was staffed by a cheery, elderly volunteer who eagerly offered to provide assistance.

When Jennifer asked for directions to Dr. Ishikawa's office, the elderly woman's smile quickly faded into a somber, concerned expression. In a soft voice, the volunteer provided the directions. As Jennifer thanked her and turned to leave, the woman patted her hand and offered condolences. The gesture initially surprised Jennifer, but then she realized the impetus behind the show of sympathy. Late-night requests for directions to the medical examiner's office were likely only made by loved ones arriving to identify the bodies of deceased relatives. Jennifer thanked her again and went in search of Dr. Ishikawa.

The instructions seemed simple: Take the elevator down one floor and proceed through the emergency department to a door marked "Restricted Access." Ring the bell and wait for someone to trigger the door to unlock. Then follow the corridor until reaching the medical examiner suite door. There, ring another bell and someone would let her in. Simple.

Not! Whether the volunteer misspoke or Jennifer misheard, the emergency department was two floors down, not one. And the emergency department waiting room had two doors marked "Restricted Access," not one. Of course, Jennifer picked the wrong one to try first and was greeted by a frazzled emergency room nurse who rolled her eyes when Jennifer asked for Dr. Ishikawa. The nurse pointed across the room to the other door without a word and then disappeared back into the emergency room.

When Jennifer finally made it through the correct door, she spotted a thin Asian man dressed in scrubs at the end of the hall. Holding open the secure entry door of the M.E. suite with his foot, he waved to Jennifer. "Hello there. Detective Stevens?"

She waved back as she paced down the shiny linoleum-floored corridor. "Yep, that's me. Sorry about the delay. Got my directions a little mixed up."

"Don't worry. Happens all the time. I think they make it hard to find us on purpose," Ishikawa said with a smile. When she reached the door, they shook hands. "Brett Ishikawa. Good to meet you."

"Likewise," she said.

With the entry door closed behind them, they walked down a corridor. They passed a kitchenette and Ishikawa stopped in to pour a cup of coffee. He offered to pour Jennifer a cup, but she declined. When they reached his small office, he motioned for her to occupy the sole guest chair while he stifled a yawn and slid into his desk chair. Propping his sneaker-clad feet on the desk's edge, he took a quick sip and then said, "So, you're here about the Simpson case, eh?"

Looking at his mussed hair, stubbled face, bloodshot eyes and wrinkled scrubs, Jennifer suddenly felt bad for wrangling the late-night meeting. "Yes, thank you again for making time to meet with me. I'm sure you'd like to get out of here, so I'll try to make it quick."

"No worries. I'm glad you reached out. You knew the deceased, right?"

"Uh-huh. Anabel, er, Ms. Simpson, was connected to some cases I worked earlier in the year."

Ishikawa eyed her warily and took another sip. "I read about them online earlier today. The kidnapping and the murders. You took out the killer, if I'm not mistaken."

"Um, something like that," Jennifer said. She managed to maintain a casual demeanor, but she could feel the warmth rise on her face and neck. If he'd read about Stillwater Quarry, then he surely read about her suspension. And if he'd read about that, then it wouldn't have taken much research to learn of the Indio Maiz shooting that ended her police career. So much for the "Detective" Stevens cover.

"Sounds like it was a pretty hairy sitch," he said.

She nodded. "It was tense, that's for sure."

"I also got a chance to read the police report, *your* report about the kidnapping incident," Ishikawa said.

"Did you, now?" Jennifer said, crossing her arms.

"Yeah, cross-departmental courtesy," he said with a smile. "Paints a very different picture than what the press reported. Something tells me you know more about what happened to Ms. Simpson than I do."

Jennifer looked away. "Uh—"

He placed the half-empty cup on the desk and bluntly asked, "It's got something to do with the stones, the ones mentioned in your report, doesn't it?"

She slowly moved her eyes to meet his and nodded.

"Stones that can lift a grown man above the treetops and slam him to the ground?" Ishikawa rhetorically asked, his voice thick with skepticism.

Jennifer had hoped to avoid discussing the Stones until she knew more about Ishikawa's findings, but now that he had broached the subject, that plan was dashed. As she readied a comment, Ishikawa lifted a file from his desk. "If not for the severity of her injuries, and the bits of stone embedded in her body, I would never have believed such an irrational thing. But there's nothing rational about Ms. Simpson and what happened to her."

Leaning forward, Jennifer asked, "What do you mean?"

"I've been an M.E. for a decade, here and down in Baltimore, and I've never seen anything like this," he said, waving the file. "Up here, we don't get a lot of murders, but when we do it's usually cut-and-dried stuff. Gunshot wounds, stabbings, occasionally someone gets bludgeoned during an argument. Now, Baltimore was a different animal. There we saw lots of beyond-the-norm killings. Poisonings, drownings, arson. You name it, we saw it. But this right here, this is *X-Files* kind of shit."

He slapped the file on the desk and pushed it toward Jennifer. She took the thick folder and rested it on her lap. "I hear you. The crime scene photos were bizarre. I take it the autopsy was, too."

With a short laugh, Ishikawa said, "Oh, yeah."

Tapping the folder, Jennifer said, "This looks like it'll take some time to go through. Can you give me the highlights?"

He nodded and folded his hands on his lap. "Sure, let's start with what I don't know. I have no idea who killed her, what weapons were used, when it happened or where it happened."

While he spoke, Jennifer reached into her tote bag and retrieved her notebook and pen, careful not to tip over the file's contents. Ignoring the sarcastic tone of Ishikawa's overview, she opened the pad and jotted down a shorthand summary of his comments. When she was finished, she looked up and said, "Okay. Got it. So, then, what *do* you know?"

Ishikawa held up the index and middle fingers of his right hand. "Two things."

With a waggle of the index finger, he said, "I know she was killed outdoors. Some place with a stone surface. Granite, to be precise. Granite with moss on it."

He paused while Jennifer scribbled away. When she stopped writing, he waggled his middle finger. "And I know the cause of death: blunt force trauma to her heart."

Jennifer frowned and lowered her pen. "Really? I thought she was electrocuted."

"Oh, she was electrocuted, all right," Ishikawa said, shifting his hand to lift the coffee cup. "But that was just part of the torture she endured."

"Torture? She was tortured?"

Ishikawa nodded. "Brutally. Hard to believe she withstood it as long as she did, given her condition."

"Her condition?"

"Yeah. During the autopsy, we found tumors in her liver, lungs and colon. I doubt she had more than a few months left," Ishikawa said.

The quick burst of unexpected news momentarily shook Jennifer. Torture? Cancer?

"Of course, her entire physiology was unusual. Very unusual," Ishikawa said. He lightly hummed a few bars of the *X-Files* theme song while wiggling his fingers.

Jennifer frowned. Though Ishikawa's gesture was intended as comic relief, it came off a little creepy given the context of the conversation. She asked, "What did you find?"

"Impossible things. Like, bone density similar to a teenager's. Yet, at the same time, there was significant deterioration in the cell structures of her organs, the kind of deterioration one would find in a centenarian. Except the brain. It showed almost no signs of aging or disease. And her blood was all wrong, too. There was a free-floating enzyme I've never seen before, and very high amounts of another enzyme rare to humans called—"

"Cryptochromes," Jennifer said.

Ishikawa's eyelids fluttered. He lifted his crossed feet off the desk and lowered them to the floor. Scooting his chair closer to the desk, he said, "Yes...exactly. I'd like to believe that was a lucky guess, but it wasn't, was it?"

Jennifer closed her notepad atop the autopsy file and placed both on the desk. "No, it wasn't."

"What the hell is all this about?" he asked.

"I don't know...exactly," she said. "There are several possibilities, but I'm not sold on any of them yet. Given what you've just told me, there may be other possibilities I hadn't considered."

"Some of the detectives here think it was some kind of cult sacrifice, given the way the body was laid out in the garden. A few think it's a twisted serial killer. But I gotta tell you, to me, the torture aspect makes it look more like a revenge killing. There's a very personal level of violence about the torture. The kind of thing you'd see between rival gangs or in a crime of passion," he said.

Revenge? A crime of passion? Jennifer thought of the locket. "Hmmm. If it was a revenge killing, how do you see that fitting with the house break-in?"

"I'm not sure I follow you."

"Well, we believe Anabel had a valuable art collection. The killer may have been after one or more pieces from the collection. Anabel might have resisted telling the killer where to find the art. So, maybe the killer tortured her to get her to talk rather than seeking revenge?"

Ishikawa propped his elbows on the table and clasped his hands together. Shaking his head, he said, "No disrespect intended, but the torture Ms. Simpson suffered wasn't conducive to her talking. Screaming, yes. Talking, no.

"Whoever killed that poor woman wanted to inflict some serious pain. Her legs were broken, well, more like pulverized. The wounds to her torso look like someone stabbed her with an electrified implement like a cattle prod."

The medical examiner went on to explain how he envisioned the murder unfolding. From the forensic evidence, he said, it appeared her legs received the first attack, shattering the tibia and fibula of both legs. From the striations of the scrapes on her jeans and knees, it appeared to Ishikawa as if she had then tried to crawl away or was dragged across a stone surface. The front of her sweatshirt, jeans and sneakers had traces of granite dust and moss. The first stab entry wound went through her back at an upward angle, suggesting she was still in the act of crawling, or lying on the ground facedown, when attacked by the killer pursuing her from behind. She must have rolled over at some point, Ishikawa had surmised, because the next stab wound was in her chest. The final use of the prod went the deepest into her chest and was held in long enough for her right lung to catch fire.

The blow by blow sickened Jennifer. She closed her eyes and held a tightly balled fist beneath her nose. Her other hand gripped her knee, the fingernails digging deep into the denim fabric. When he finished the description, all she could say was, "Poor Anabel."

Ishikawa cleared his throat to attract Jennifer's attention. She opened her eyes and looked up at him. "That's not all, unfortunately."

The tone of his voice and the look in his eyes made Jennifer feel queasy. It's one thing to have an M.E. describe the murder of a stranger. It's another thing entirely when it's someone you know, someone you might consider a friend.

"At some point between the second and third stab, something exploded in her hands," he said.

Jennifer recalled Anabel's mangled hands in the photos of the crime scene. Ishikawa ran his hands down his neck, chest and legs. "She had hundreds of shards lodged in her tissue from the neck to her thighs, not to mention what was left of her hands. The trauma to the hands and the shard pattern in her body was very similar to what one would see from a hand grenade explosion. Only the shards weren't metal, they were stone. Well, two different types of stone."

Jennifer stared at him and whispered, "Olivine basalt and kimberlite."

He nodded. "I don't know what to make of it. There was no residue of explosives on the shards or in the wounds, just bits of stone. I don't think she was forced to hold the stone object; there was no sign her hands were bound. From what I can tell from the shrapnel pattern, when the stone exploded, she was lying on her back on the ground, looking up with her arms extended about waist high. The grenade, or whatever, was grasped in both hands. She could have been trying to throw it at her torturer, but what made it explode beats me."

"What color was the stone?" Jennifer asked.

"Huh?"

"The olivine shards, what color were they?"

"Why?"

"Humor me."

"Pinkish."

Of all the Munuorian *Lifintyls*, there was only one *Tyl* with a pink-gray tint. She mumbled, "A *Terusael*?"

"A what?" Ishikawa asked.

A ghoulish thought crossed Jennifer's mind. Were they looking at the physical evidence all wrong? She asked Ishikawa, "Are you positive about the timing of when the stone exploded? Is it possible it happened before any of the stabs?"

"No, I'd say not. It definitely happened between the second and third stabs. There was shrapnel embedded in the surface area of the second stab wound, but not in the third. If it had happened before the first stab—"

Jennifer interjected. "Did she have any burn marks on her head or the back of her neck? They would be small, probably laid out in a line or a pattern."

Ishikawa's face reddened. "What? No. What makes you think that?"

Lost in thought, she didn't answer right away. A frustrated Ishikawa said, "Look, if you know what happened to this woman, you have an obligation to step forward and share what you know!"

Jennifer leaned back and calmly said, "Hey, Doc, we're on the same side. I don't know for sure what happened to her, but I'm starting to get a clearer picture."

"Well, make it clearer for *me*. My ass is getting chapped by everyone up the chain for answers, and I don't have any!" he said, rapping his knuckles on the desk.

"All right, all right. Simmer down. I'm here to help in any way I can. Promise," Jennifer said, placing a hand over her heart. "Why don't we take a break and grab some fresh air. I could use a few minutes to organize my thoughts, and you're gonna need a clear head for what I tell you."

After shutting down his office for the evening, Ishikawa led Jennifer out the main entrance of the medical center. It was now past 10 p.m. and quite chilly outside, but Jennifer welcomed the brisk air, though she was ill-dressed for the nighttime stroll.

Their path initially led them past Converse Hall, a circa-1900 stone building that still served as a student dormitory. With high-pitched roofs and corner spires, the dorm took on an eerie appearance in the dark. It was rumored, Ishikawa told Jennifer, to be haunted, having been the site of a student suicide in the 1920s — a rumor that had grown into a full-blown mythology over the past one hundred years. A perfect setting for their talk, Jennifer thought.

A few minutes later, with Converse Hall behind them, they approached the center of the university's campus. At the late hour, there weren't many people out and about, but there were small groups of students here and there, trundling between buildings surrounding the quad.

Jennifer found it hard to find the right place to begin the story. There was still much to absorb from their earlier conversation and she wasn't sure how each piece of information from Ishikawa fit into the story. Separately, she worried how the medical examiner would take the fantastical elements of the story and what he might say to "higher-ups" and Detective Hall. Although Ishikawa had rightly pegged Anabel's death as having spooky qualities, Jennifer wasn't sure whether he'd buy into the Munuorians, their special Stones and Muran.

After several minutes of silent walking, she said, "So, what I'm about to tell you will take an open mind. A *very* open mind."

"Understood," he said.

Oh, I'm not sure you do, she thought. She zipped her jacket all the way up to her chin and took a deep breath. "I'm pretty sure Anabel's murder is connected to some rare, ancient artifacts. They're, sort of, Stone-Age tools, but they have some, um, unusual properties. They're very valuable, valuable enough that several people have already been killed over them.

"Anabel had knowledge of the Stones and their properties. How much she knew, I don't know, but I'm confident she knew more than she told me. And I know she had at least two of them in her possession. She may have had more. Matter of fact, given what's happened, I'm pretty sure she had more. But I didn't see any in the house when I walked through it with Detective Hall yesterday, and he said the forensics team didn't take away any stones or art pieces as evidence. So I presume the killer snatched them, or they're hidden in the house or somewhere off-site."

"Ah, the keys," Ishikawa said. "That's why Detective Hall asked me to take another look at the keys they found."

"Yeah, it's possible she had a storage locker or safe-deposit box somewhere. She supposedly had other artifacts that were worth quite a bit, and none of those were in the house, either. Anyway, I truly don't know who the killer is, but I think I've got a better handle on the motive. She was either killed by someone who wanted the Stones she had, or she may have known something about the Stones the killer wanted to know. For example, if she didn't have more of the Stones herself, she may have known where more of the Stones were held. I know for a fact that, at one point, she was holding a map that led to more of the Stones."

"A map? I see," Ishikawa said. "Possibly the missing document the police think was taken."

"Yep. But the brutality of the murder is disproportional for either motive," Jennifer said. "And none of the other murders connected with the Stones involved torture. You said it yourself, the torture seemed personal. That's what makes me wonder if there's another motive at play here." She shivered as a gust of wind funneled down the quad.

Ishikawa, bundled in a heavier coat, shivered as well. He suggested they head for Davis Center, the on-campus student social center.

Several minutes later, they huddled over hot coffee in a popular pub in the building. Over the din of students imbibing a different kind of refreshment, Ishikawa asked, "You said earlier, the Stones have unusual properties. I take it your police report didn't exaggerate what you saw at Stillwater Quarry?"

"Uh, no. Exaggerations don't go over well in police reports. If anything, I downplayed what I saw," she said.

"So, you're telling me the kidnapper, this Pacal Flores, literally lifted the Cully fellow in the air by blowing on a stone?"

"Open mind, remember, Doc?" she said with a slight smile. After a sip of coffee, she explained, "The Stones, they're magnetic. Magnetic in ways that give them special capabilities. The one that was used at Stillwater produces sound waves that allow a person to move heavy objects through the air. Anabel had one, in fact. It's a bowl that kind of looks like a speaker-woofer. You put your lips against the backside of the bowl and hum on it. It projects sound waves at the object you want to lift or move. It works. I have one myself. I'm pretty handy with it, too."

"You're joking," he said with a dismissive flourish of his hand.

"I shit you not," she replied, a deadly serious look on her face. "I could lift any car out in the lot above this building in less than twenty seconds."

He frowned and crossed his arms. She said, "Tell you what. If you let me come back tomorrow and make a copy of Anabel's file, I'll bring my *Breylofte*, that's what it's called, and show you in person."

"I can't do that. It's against the law," he said.

"I won't tell if you don't tell," she said.

"Not a chance. I'll pretend I didn't hear you suggest it."

"Not even if I agree to tell you why Anabel's physiology was so weird? Why she had that special enzyme and cryptochromes in her blood?" she said.

Ishikawa didn't flinch.

"Sounds like a pretty good trade to me, Doc. You'll dig the explanation. It's all *X-Files*-ey."

The stoic medical examiner maintained a steady stare, though Jennifer did notice him squirm ever so slightly.

Jennifer relented. "Okay, okay. As a sign of good faith, I'll give you a hint. Go back to her house. Look in the refrigerator. You'll find a pitcher with a pink fluid in it. Test it, see what you come up with."

"You're suggesting whatever's in the fluid altered her physiology," he said.

It was Jennifer's turn to display a stoic expression.

"All right," he said. "I'll test it. But tell me, where did she get it?"

"I'll tell you if you tell me something in return," she said. "In your office, you said Anabel died from blunt force trauma to her heart, not from the torture."

"Yes, that's right. She would have eventually died from the torture injuries, but the killer didn't wait for that," Ishikawa said.

"So...what happened to her heart?"

"You first. Where did she get the fluid?"

"She made it, using two of the Stones and flowers from her garden," Jennifer said. "She crushed up petals and ground them up with the Stones. The friction of the Stones electrified the enzymes in the flowers' juices. The fluid has...healing properties."

"She had cancer; her organs were very diseased," he said.

"That I can't explain. But you'll find the same enzyme in both her blood and the fluid. You'll find cryptochromes in both, too. Now, your turn. What happened to Anabel's heart?"

Ishikawa leaned forward and lowered his voice. "The killer reached into her chest and crushed her heart with a bare hand."

Dr. Ishikawa's words replayed in Jennifer's mind as she laid in the dark hotel room. "Crushed her heart with a bare hand..."

Revenge. Cancer. An exploding *Terusael*. Crime of passion. Torture. Jennifer had hoped the meeting with Ishikawa would help winnow her three possible crime scenarios, but the evidence he'd shared suggested at least one other scenario she hadn't previously considered: the murder was about payback. But payback for what? By whom?

As she tossed and turned, one of her prior scenarios seemed out of the running. Anabel had not been Muran. In her mind, the torture aspect ruled it out. Even the Foucault-kills-Muran scenario seemed less plausible. While Foucault certainly had some emotional energy tied up in bringing Muran to justice on behalf of Mereau, Jennifer couldn't imagine the smallish man using his bare hands to crush Anabel's heart. Maybe his associate, Christian Hunte, could have pulled that off, but not Foucault.

That left two viable scenarios. Either someone tortured and killed Anabel for her *Tyls*, or other artifacts, or someone tortured and killed her because of some unknown dispute. If the latter, Jennifer thought, it must have been one helluva dispute.

5

Opening Volley

Middlebury, Vermont
September 27

Pulling the bank's heavy glass door open, Aja stepped into the lobby. To her left, she spotted an elderly lady with a walker. She was chatting with the lone teller, who listened attentively with a smile. To her right, a young man in suit and tie spotted her from behind a glassed-in cubicle. He popped out from behind and said, "Good morning, ma'am. May I help you?"

"I'm here to see the bank manager, Ms. Bailey. I have an appointment."

"Sure, no problem. Your name is…?"

"Warwick. Evelyn Warwick."

"Okay, just have a seat, Ms. Warwick. I'll let her know you're here," he said with cheer before he loped off.

Shortly thereafter, he returned to escort her to Debbie Bailey's office. As they entered the office, Debbie smiled and rose to greet Aja, but there was no mistaking the malice in her eyes. Before departing, the young man asked Aja, "Cup of coffee?"

"No," she said.

"How about your coat? Can I hang it up for you?"

"No. I won't be long."

The young man bowed and left. As soon as he was out of earshot, Aja said, "Let's do this quickly. Remember what's at stake."

Debbie, red-faced, dutifully led the way to the vault. At the security door separating the lobby from the vault's anteroom, she miskeyed the code to enter. After flexing her shaking hand, she tried again. This time, the door sounded a click and they entered the anteroom. Debbie paused and turned toward Aja. "You have the keys?"

"Of course I do," Aja said with irritation. "Keep moving."

Once inside the vault, Debbie asked, "Which ones?"

Aja rattled off the box numbers. Debbie scanned for the numbers and located the two large boxes on the bottom row. She glared at Aja and said, "Pick one. Your key goes in first."

Leaning over, Aja removed a ring with two keys from the pocket of her slacks. She inserted the key to the box on the left and turned it. Debbie knelt down and inserted the bank's key. When it turned, the door opened and she slid out the box. It was heavy, and she almost dropped it when she tried to stand. The items inside shifted and clanged against the box. Instinctively, Debbie apologized.

She carried the box from the safe to a small privacy cubicle in the anteroom and placed the box on the table inside. Debbie exited and stood aside. Aja glared at her. "Quickly, now the other box."

Debbie hesitated. Aja snapped, "Do it! Now!"

"It's not the way it's done," whispered Debbie.

"I don't care. You have the keys. Get the box. Bring it to me."

While Aja settled in the cubicle, Debbie obeyed and retrieved the second box. Aja then commanded Debbie to step inside the cubicle and shut the door. Above the cubicle, a security camera captured every move.

Aja stared at the two boxes and her pulse quickened. In a moment, she would be reunited with her long-lost treasure — treasure that had been nicked by the ungrateful bitch seventy-six years ago. As Aja thought of that fateful night, she was overcome by a flood of memories.

The air raid sirens began to wail throughout London just before midnight. The date: May 10, 1941. Ensconced in the drawing room of the Notting Hill hideaway of a charming member of parliament, Aja had been enjoying an evening of conversation, cigarettes and brandy. While the rakish M.P. regaled her with tales of his adventures in Egypt, Aja had gazed at him with feigned wonderment, and for much of the evening he had seemed mesmerized by her attentiveness. But as soon as the first claxon sounded, the M.P. had abruptly stopped his storytelling, extinguished his cigarette and called for his valet.

Although the M.P. had offered his sincere apologies with a smile, Aja's more prominent memory was his grip on her arm as he ushered her out of the drawing room. In gentlemanly fashion, he had given her directions to an air raid shelter in the neighborhood while escorting her to the rowhouse's back door. He hadn't offered a reason for choosing the rear exit, but Aja had understood. Parliament members were not keen on being seen in public with their mistresses, and the street outside the front door had been flooded with neighbors on their way to the shelter.

Evelyn Warwick, Aja's handmaiden, had followed close behind, escorted by the M.P.'s stoic valet. Evelyn had barely finished draping a mink stole over Aja's bare shoulders before the pair had been rushed out the door and into the alleyway behind the rowhouse. Aja remembered the sight of people scurrying past the alley and their own hurried gaits to join them. There had been a raid two nights prior that had inflicted heavy casualties on the Kensington neighborhood, and everyone, including Aja, feared a repeat. Despite their haste, however, they found the shelter fully occupied by the time they arrived.

Evelyn had been very edgy, looking up at the skies constantly. When it became clear they would not find a place in the shelter, Evelyn had shivered with panic. Aja had tried to calm her, suggesting they turn back and head for the Holland Park Underground station. Evelyn had pressed to keep in the same direction, arguing the Latimer Road station was closer. Shortly after agreeing on Latimer, they had been intercepted by a bobby as they rushed along Bomore Road. Aja could still recall the drone of the bombers' engines as she replayed the memory of what happened next.

The bobby called to them and a group of others caught on the street. He urged them to follow him down a set of steps leading to the basement of a rowhouse. He kicked in the door and waved them into the dark cavern just as the bombs began to land. Thunderous explosions shook the building above them, growing louder and more violent with each successive blast. Aja and Evelyn found an empty spot against a wall and huddled close together. With eyes closed and arms wrapped around each other, they teetered with each concussion.

Aja didn't recall the blast that cratered the building above them. She remembered Evelyn squeezing her tightly, and then nothing else until she awoke to discover herself buried beneath a mountain of rubble. In the blackness, she had been unable to see or move. Badly wounded, Aja had called out for Evelyn, but there had been no answer. The only sounds had come from the rubble settling around her and intermittent moans. Throughout the long night, while a rescue brigade dug through the debris to reach the survivors, Aja beseeched Evelyn to say something, anything. But Evelyn never said a word. And her body was never found.

Aja placed her hands on the box lid as she recalled mourning Evelyn. Her fingers trembled as she relived the discovery of Evelyn's true fate…and her betrayal. Shunting aside the bitter memories, Aja threw open the box lid and looked inside.

A short while later, the cubicle door flung open. Aja pushed Debbie aside and left the anteroom. She hoisted her satchel over her shoulder as she stomped down the hallway and spewed a stream of epithets. She continued to curse as she pounded through the lobby, completely unaware it was now vacant of employees and patrons. Blinded by fury, she pushed through the bank's double-glass doors with a scowl on her face — a scowl that vanished when she heard guns cocking and a voice to her left shout, "Freeze!"

Paralyzed with shock, Aja teetered to a stop.

"On the ground. Hands up!" yelled another voice, this one coming from the right.

Aja blinked rapidly and swiveled her head in the directions of the voices. Instinctively, she shoved her hands into her coat pockets.

"Hands out of your pockets! On the ground, now!" screamed the advancing police officer on the right, gun pointed at Aja.

"There must be some mistake," she frantically said.

"Down! Down! Get those hands out where I can see them."

"Okay, okay," she said. Lowering to her knees, she slowly slid her hands from her pockets. In each, she gripped a Stone...

Incline Village, Nevada

Legs dangling from the dock, Pebbles watched tiny droplets of rain dance on the water's surface, blurring the reflection of the dreary clouds above. Closing her eyes, she listened to the comforting pitter-patter of rain on the hood of her anorak and thought of Anabel.

She wanted to mourn for her but found it difficult. She wanted to believe Anabel had been the sweet, smiling woman in the pictures with Devlin, the woman who'd shared a long, exotic love affair with the cantankerous archaeologist, the woman with a garden full of butterflies and a kitchen full of Holstein cow knickknacks.

But she just couldn't embrace the images. Instead, when she thought of Anabel, her mind filled with thoughts of Malinyah. Of her loss of Alynioria. Of what Muran had done to the both of them. Pain, emptiness, rage. Those were the feelings that crept into Pebbles' mind. Malinyah's emotions. Though they weren't as sharp as when she was bonded with Malinyah's *Sinethal*, they were still there, and Pebbles expected they would linger for a very long time.

Opening her eyes, Pebbles unzipped her coat and stroked her fingers along the thin, gold necklace holding Malinyah's medallion. When her hand reached the medallion, she clutched it and held it against her breast. The gesture always had a calming, soothing effect, one that chased away Malinyah's sorrowful memories and the loneliness that accompanied them. She sighed and let go of the medallion. It was unfair to speculate Anabel was Muran, she thought. Not yet. They needed to know for sure.

Pebbles shivered as the intensity of the rain picked up. While her coat was waterproof, her leggings were not, and they were now soaked. The thin garment offered little protection from the icy mountain air when dry, and no protection when wet. Shivering again, she abandoned her dockside vigil and headed toward Anlon's house. As she walked along the dock, she looked up at the sky, rain splattering her face, and wondered when it would end. The morning weather report had suggested it would clear by ten, but it was nearly nine now and there was no sign of it letting up.

An hour later, Pebbles stood in the kitchen, bundled in flannel pajamas, robe and thick socks, and waited for the Keurig to perform its brewing magic. Outside the kitchen window, she watched the pine needle–covered yard sparkle as the sun finally began to poke through the cloud cover. She mumbled, "Huh, I guess the weather forecast was right after all."

Thinking of the weather forecast caused Pebbles to recall her visit to Sydney's Bistro earlier in the week. She had stopped by after returning from Nicaragua to say hello to Sydney and visit with the off-season "regulars" at the bar, and quickly found herself engaged in an hour-long discussion about the winter weather forecast. Most of the talk had been about the prospects of another deluge of snow over the winter, a welcome development for a community that depended as much on a robust ski season as it did on summer lake lovers. For several years in a row, during the worst of California's severe drought, Tahoe had barely seen a flake of snow. But last year, nearly six hundred inches had fallen in the mountains surrounding the lake, and the regulars had been downright giddy speculating snow totals for the coming winter.

Her reminiscence was interrupted by the sound of liquid gold gurgling from the Keurig's spout into her insulated travel cup. While she watched the cup fill, she caught a glimpse of movement outside the window. Looking up, she spotted Griffin "Bones" Taylor striding toward the back patio in a T-shirt, shorts and sandals. Griffin, their next-door neighbor, was the lead guitarist for a metal rock band and, more recently, a frequent companion of Jennifer's.

Pebbles cracked open the door leading from the patio to the kitchen and called out, "Hurry up, it's freezing out there."

Griffin smiled and waved as he mounted the slate steps to the kitchen door. "Hey there, Pebbles! Good to see you."

"Same here," she said as he reached the door. "Coffee? Just take a sec to whip up a cup."

"Sounds great," he said, shivering.

"What the heck were you thinking going out like that?" she asked, pointing to his out-of-season choice of clothing.

He laughed and said, "Heading to Maui this afternoon. I guess you can tell I'm excited to go."

"Maui? I'm jealous. Jen will be, too. Does she know?" Pebbles asked, as she refilled the coffeemaker's water tank.

"Yeah, I told her. Even invited her to come along, but she's tied up with stuff in Vermont. I promised her a rain check. That seemed to soften the blow...a little," he said with a sheepish smile.

Pebbles held up two K-cup pods. "Breakfast Blend or Medium Roast?"

"What? No Dark Roast Kona?"

"Um, no...and we don't have battery acid blend, either."

"Okay," he said, feigning disappointment. "I'll go with the Breakfast Blend."

"Good choice," she said, placing the pod into the coffeemaker. They sat at the kitchen table while the machine hummed and gurgled. "So, what's up?"

"Jen called last night and asked that I check in on you before I go," he said. "She seemed kinda worried about you."

Typical, but sweet, thought Pebbles. While Jennifer was a good friend and colleague, she also had a motherly side to her that could be annoying at times. Don't walk too close to the ledge, Pebbles! Careful, the monkey might bite you if you get too close! Look out for falling rocks! Yada, yada. And since Anabel's murder, Jennifer's safety-conscious henpecking had grown exponentially.

"Well, as you can see, I'm doing just fine," she said, rising to fetch Griffin's coffee.

"Thank you," he said, receiving the mug. "She'll be glad to hear it."

He raised the cup and sniffed the aroma drifting up from the mug. Standing by the refrigerator, Pebbles asked, "Cream or sugar?"

"Yes to both, please."

Pebbles grabbed creamer from the refrigerator and a sugar bowl from the counter and returned to the table. They sat together in silence while Griffin stirred in his preferred mix of the additional flavors. The silence was awkward to Pebbles, made even more awkward by the fact that Griffin wouldn't look up at her.

"So, are you headed to Maui for business or pleasure?" she asked.

"A little of both. There's a drummer there I'm going to see. We need a fill-in for Nicky for a little while."

"Oh, no. What happened to him?"

"Rehab."

"Ah, sorry to hear that."

"Don't be. The numb-nut's forty-two but parties like he's twenty-one. Hopefully the rehab will stick this time." Griffin sipped his coffee and looked off into space.

"I'm sure it's hard," Pebbles said. "I imagine there are a lot of temptations."

"No doubt. We try to keep as much of the craziness away from him as we can, but he always seems to find a way around us. You know the expression, trouble finds him? Well, that's Nicky." Griffin paused to sigh while swirling a spoon in his coffee. "Anyway, enough of our band blues. Are you back for a while?"

"Just a couple days. I'm meeting Anlon and Jen in New York on Friday, then I'm headed back to Nicaragua the week after that."

"Cool."

"Why? Need me to do something for you while you're gone?" Pebbles asked.

"Nah, I'm good."

Griffin scratched at his goatee-covered chin during another awkward pause. There's something on his mind, Pebbles thought.

Something he's brooding over. She sipped her coffee while he fiddled with his spoon, waiting for him to speak. Was it to do with Jennifer, she wondered. Or was he just bummed out about Nicky?

"Everything okay, Griffin?" she finally asked.

"Huh?"

"You seem…I don't know…like you're lost in thought."

He nodded and let go of the spoon. "Yeah, sorry. I'm just trying to think of the right way to tell you. It's about Jen."

Pebbles' heart fell. Oh my God! she thought. He's breaking up with Jen! Reflexively, she raised a hand to cover her mouth.

Griffin glanced up at her timidly. "She wanted me to check the locks while I'm here. And to remind you to turn on the alarm, even during the day."

Pebbles frowned for a moment, then broke out laughing. "You're shitting me!"

"Like I said, she's worried about you."

"Holy crap! You scared me so bad. I thought you were going to say you two broke up!" she said, patting her chest to still her heart rate.

"What? No. No way. We're good. Great, in fact," he replied.

"Then why all the drama? You looked like you were going to choke on your words."

"Well, don't take it personal," Griffin said with a relieved smile. "Jen said you might not take it too well."

"Am I that bad?"

He shrugged. "Not to me. Jen said you get angry when she reminds you of stuff."

"Oh, I'll take it out on her later, you can count on that! But you're in the clear. Messengers get a free pass." With a dramatic arm wave, she said, "Go ahead, be my guest, feel free to check the locks."

Ten minutes later, after finishing their coffee, Griffin verified the front door was locked and after he secured Pebbles' promise to lock the kitchen door after his departure, they exchanged a friendly hug and he left. As she closed the door, she shouted out, "Mahalo! Safe travels."

He walked away without looking back, fist raised above his head with thumb and pinky extended, Hawaiian for "hang loose."

Pebbles shut the door and dutifully turned the lock. She picked up her cell phone from the table and snapped a quick picture of the locked door, which she then texted to Jennifer. The accompanying caption read, "Happy, mother?"

While cleaning up the kitchen, Pebbles received Jennifer's reply. "I won't be happy til you and Malinyah safely arrive in NYC."

Jennifer had not been thrilled when she learned of Foucault's request to bring Malinyah to New York. In fact, Jennifer had made it clear to Pebbles and Anlon that she viewed the request as a ploy by Foucault to take the Stone. Given his status as a suspect in Anabel's murder, Jennifer had argued, it was better to keep the *Sinethal* under lock and key. To support her point, she had itemized Foucault's deceitful actions at Indio Maiz.

"Let it go, woman!" Pebbles texted back on her way upstairs to shower and dress. Antonio was due to arrive around midday with Malinyah's *Sinethal*. As she walked through the master bedroom she slid out of her robe. After turning on the shower, she leaned against the bathroom counter and whisked off her pajamas and socks. She stuck a tentative hand in the spray from the showerhead, shivered and stepped in. The glass door was almost closed when she heard the doorbell chime echo from the hallway.

Pebbles stood motionless for a moment and debated whether to answer the door. It might be Griffin, she thought. He might have forgotten to bestow another caution from Jennifer. Or it might be Antonio, arriving earlier than planned. She stepped out of the shower and wrapped a towel around her torso just as the chime pealed again. She mumbled, "Gah! Hold your horses."

She padded to the guest bedroom that overlooked the front of the house. As soon as she neared the window, she spotted the large brown truck in the driveway. It was Reggie, their UPS deliveryman. Holding the towel in place with one hand, Pebbles cranked open the casement window and called down. "Hey there, Reggie."

Reggie appeared from beneath the covered doorstep and looked up. "Oh, hi, Pebbles. Sorry to disturb you. Got a few packages for the good doctor."

"Just leave them on the step, please. I'll get them later," she said.

"Okay, no problem," he said, waving his hand. "Have a good one!"

"Thanks, Reggie. You too! See you soon."

Covered in goosebumps, she quickly cranked the window shut and wound her way back to the master bath and the now-steaming shower. She unclamped the towel from beneath her arm and let it drop to the marble floor. Her cell phone, resting on the bathroom counter, sounded out with a xylophone ringtone. Pebbles retrieved the phone and looked at the lock screen. It was a text from Jennifer. "Send me a pic of the alarm key pad with the red light on. Then I'll be happy!"

"Haha," Pebbles replied before placing the phone back on the counter and sliding into the shower. While she stood with her head and neck bowed under the jet of hot water, the xylophone tone sounded out again. Jennifer had sent another text. It read, "Not joking!"

It was noon before Pebbles picked up her phone again. Dressed in a fresh pair of leggings and an oversized sweater, she stood before the bathroom mirror applying the finishing touches to the spiked upward swoosh of her purple bangs. When the xylophone trilled again, she lifted the phone and saw two message notifications on the lock screen: the earlier text from Jennifer and a new one from Antonio.

She read Antonio's first. "Delayed. Won't be there til 2. Sorry."

"No prob. See u then," she answered.

When she opened Jennifer's text, she laughed. Lowering the phone to the counter without a reply, she looked at her reflection in the mirror and mumbled, "Geez, Louise. I hope Griffin knows what he's getting into."

Satisfied with her hair, she draped Malinyah's necklace over her head and rested the medallion on her chest. As she turned to leave the bathroom, the door chime rang. Pebbles retraced a path to the guest bedroom and looked out the window. In the driveway was an idling sedan with a car topper sign for Benny's, a pizza delivery service in nearby Seal Beach. She hadn't ordered any pizza, and Benny's wasn't a pizza place they frequented. She rolled open the window a few inches and called out, "Hello?"

A cheery young man with a yellow Benny's baseball cap appeared from beneath the stoop. In his hands he held a pizza box. "Hi, there. Got your pizza."

"Um, think you've got the wrong address," she said.

"This is 24 Lakeshore, right?"

"Yep."

"Cully residence?"

"Yep, again."

"Well, someone here ordered a large sausage pizza."

"Don't know what to tell you. I'm the only one here and I didn't order anything. Sorry."

The delivery man sighed and shook his head. "Well, that sucks."

"Sorry!" she called out again as he descended the steps.

"No worries. Happens sometimes." As he opened the car door, he turned back and said, "By the way, you've got packages at the door."

"Oh, that's right, I forgot," she mumbled to herself. To the deliveryman, she called out, "Thank you!"

Pebbles wound the window closed and watched the man turn left out of Anlon's driveway, heading back in the direction of Seal Beach. When he was out of sight, she headed downstairs to the main level of the lodge-style home and unlocked the front door.

On the slate landing were two packages. One was about the size and shape of a book. The other had the dimensions of a cake box. Crouching to pick them up, she said, "What have you ordered this time, A.C.?"

The smaller package did indeed feel like the weight of a book. Pebbles crooked this one under her arm and picked up the second box with both hands. It was relatively light given the size of the package, but there was something bulky inside that shifted when she lifted it. Curious, Pebbles squinted at the shipping label, but the lighting under the front stoop was poor and she couldn't read the tiny print. She stepped back inside the house and shut the door with her foot.

Walking toward the kitchen, she raised the larger box closer to her face to study the label more closely. The smaller package wedged beneath her arm began to slip. Pebbles was too late to tighten the clamp of her elbow against the box and it slid free. It landed on the floor with a loud clap. Pebbles cursed and halted by a small table in the foyer. Onto this, she deposited the larger package and then bent down to retrieve the other.

As she stood up, a floorboard creaked behind her, followed by a metallic click. Pebbles whirled in the direction of the sounds. In the doorway leading from the kitchen into the foyer loomed a hooded figure, gun in hand.

"Don't move a muscle," a stern voice commanded.

Pebbles gasped and wobbled back a step, unconsciously enveloping Malinyah's medallion with her fist. She darted a look toward the alarm keypad by the front door and then back at the man.

"Don't do it," he said. "I will shoot you."

It took another second before Pebbles felt the weight of the book package in her other hand, but when she realized she was still holding it, she heaved it at him and took off for the front door. It was a stupid idea, she realized later, but in the heat of the moment it seemed like the best thing to do.

When the gun fired, two booms echoed through the house. Pebbles tumbled to the floor and grasped her left calf. The burning sensation was so intense, she was unable to cry out for several seconds. When she finally did make a sound, it was a mix of a scream and an extended groan.

She could feel the warm wetness seep between her fingers as she rocked on the floor. The man now stood over her and cocked the gun again. This time, it was pointed at her head. Pebbles curled into the fetal position and held up her blood-streaked hands. Through pained gasps, she pleaded, "Don't shoot! Don't shoot!"

The man bent over her and ripped the medallion from her neck. Pebbles reached up to stop him and he hit her on the forehead with the butt of the gun. He yelled, "Where is it?"

"What? What?"

"The Stone! The *Sinethal*," he said. He raised his foot and stomped on Pebbles' wounded calf. She screamed, blood dripping from her trembling hands onto her face.

"Where the f— is it?"

Between moans, she said, "It's not here. It's not here."

"Where, then?"

Despite the terror of the man screaming at her while aiming the gun at her head, Pebbles couldn't bring herself to answer. Frustrated, the man changed tactics. He began kicking her in the back, demanding an answer between each wallop to her ribs.

Pebbles begged for him to stop between gasps for air. The man knelt beside her and began pounding her head against the hardwood floor. Woozy and nauseated, Pebbles closed her eyes and passed out.

The burning pain in her leg stirred Pebbles awake a little while later. She quickly discovered her hands were bound behind her back and her legs tied at the ankles. The man was no longer in the same room, but she could hear him moving about the house, slamming drawers and throwing things about. It sounded to her as if he were rummaging in Anlon's office on the far side of the house. As her vision focused, she realized she'd been moved to the living room. Lifting her head, Pebbles could see a trail of smeared blood leading from the hallway to where she now lay. She craned her throbbing head to look at her calf and saw that her assailant had bandaged it, though blood was soaking through the dressing. The sight of all the blood on the floor and her body made her throw up.

The man, attracted by the sound of her retching, returned to hover over her. Placing the gun barrel against her temple, he demanded, "The safe in the bedroom. Combinations. Both of them. Now."

Pebbles closed her eyes and blurted out the two sets of combinations. He left without a word and pounded up the stairs. While he was gone, Pebbles tried to wiggle her hands free. If she could pull them free, she could drag herself to the front hall. Once there, she thought she might be able to pull up on her knees and reach the alarm pad. But it proved to be a pipedream. Her wrists were too tightly bound, and the man came bounding down the stairs before she had made any progress.

He grabbed her by her blood-streaked hair and dragged her back across the floor to the front hall. Pebbles cried out and squirmed, causing the man to bump into the hall table, knocking a package and a few pieces of mail onto the floor. He rolled her on her back and placed the gun barrel to her forehead. "One more chance. Where's the Stone?"

With the barrel pressing into her flesh, Pebbles began to cry. It was a no-win situation. If she told him that Antonio was due to arrive at any minute, and that he had the *Sinethal* with him, she feared he would kill her and then ambush Antonio. If, instead, she tried to stall, hoping Antonio's arrival would scare him off, she felt certain the end result would be the same. If she continued to deny knowledge of the Stone's whereabouts, there was no doubt in her mind he would pull the trigger. Pebbles' heart pounded furiously as she realized her life was about to end. Between sobs, she glared up at him and spat, "F— you."

With a cracking blow, he crushed her skull with the gun. Pebbles blacked out again, her body spasming as the cursing man stalked away.

6

Shockwaves

Incline Village, Nevada
September 27

The sun was low in the sky when Antonio guided the rental car into Anlon's driveway. He was in a bad mood, and the long drive up the mountain from Reno International Airport had only made it worse. Especially given Pebbles hadn't responded to his texts or answered his calls.

The first hitch in his plan had occurred when the armored vehicle carrying Malinyah's *Sinethal* arrived at his office an hour late. Then, there had been construction on the 101, which cost him another thirty minutes. When he arrived at the small aircraft terminal, he had been met by his sour-faced pilot. There was a problem with one of the jet's engines, the pilot had informed him, and he was awaiting the arrival of a mechanic to diagnose and fix the issue. Two hours and a faulty fuse later, they had finally taxied toward the runway only to discover they were twentieth in line for takeoff.

As he stepped out of the car and shut the door, Antonio shook his head in disgust. What had started out as a quick up-and-back trip had turned into an all-day affair, and it couldn't have come at a worse time. One of Whave Technologies' prized new inventions, a laser-toting stealth drone with an artificial intelligence–driven guidance system, had failed miserably in its first real-world test, and the Defense Department's project manager was royally pissed. As were several members of military brass up the food chain. I should have sent Katie to deliver the Stone to Pebbles, he thought. His assistant had in fact suggested it once the phone lines began to light up with calls from angry generals.

But Antonio had made a promise to Anlon to hand deliver Malinyah to Pebbles. Taking a deep breath, Antonio opened the car's back door and retrieved the steel briefcase. With the case at his side, he closed his eyes and tried to quell his frustration before mounting the front steps. It wasn't Pebbles' fault, after all. He was the one who was late. Way late. As he started for the steps, he uttered a silent prayer that she hadn't left on an errand; otherwise he was in for yet another delay.

Antonio had ascended the first step before he noticed the trail of rust-colored splatters on the steps above.

Burlington, Vermont

Jennifer sat on the edge of the hotel bed clutching the television remote. She switched from news station to news station until she found one showing the incredible video footage again.

It began with a view of the entrance of the Middlebury Bank and Trust. The quality of the video was sketchy, having been recorded through the coffee shop window across the street. The college student who made the recording was speaking in the background to the news anchor while the video rolled.

"I was just sitting there with my coffee, when all of a sudden I see half a dozen cops come sprinting down Main Street. So, I got out my phone and started recording."

Jennifer watched the recording pan to the right. In it, two officers dashed toward the bank, while four others fanned out and started clearing the street of pedestrians. A police cruiser could be seen in the background blocking Main Street to the north. The video then rotated to the left side of the bank. Another police cruiser was shown blocking the bridge at the end of the strip of shops. While the video continued to play, the student said, "I wasn't sure what was going on, but it looked pretty serious."

The recording refocused on the bank entrance. On the street in front, two police officers crouched behind vehicles parked outside the bank. Two more took positions at the side corners of the free-standing building. All had their guns drawn. The video wavered up and down for a moment, and excited voices could be heard in the background as other people in the coffee shop started to crowd around the window. Then, a loud voice called out over the din: "Everybody down. Take cover. Stay away from the window."

The student's video quickly shifted toward the voice. A police officer stood in the coffee shop doorway, motioning the people inside to duck down. The video angled toward the floor as the student moved away from the window. Shortly after, the video once again retrained on the bank entrance, though the image was farther away.

When the woman appeared through the bank's double doors, she looked angry. Jennifer was stunned at how casually she strode out of the bank, completely oblivious of the officers surrounding the bank. The video quality was awful, but Jennifer could tell the woman was slim and professionally dressed. The image was too far away to accurately judge her age, but Jennifer guessed the woman to be somewhere between thirty-five and forty-five.

What happened next was spellbinding. Officers at the corners of the building came out from hiding, pistols aimed at the woman. They gestured gruffly for her to get down. The woman paused, looking confused as she snapped her head to the left and right. The officers cautiously approached, their gestures becoming more animated.

The woman started to comply. She slowly removed her hands from her pockets and raised them above her head. Then, with military precision, she ducked, turned left and slapped her hands together. The officer on that side immediately flew backward, out of the camera's view. The sound when her hands collided was so loud, it could be heard on the video over the gasps inside the coffee shop. The officer to the woman's right fired his gun. Inexplicably, he missed. The woman spun in his direction and crashed her hands together again. The policeman tumbled from view. The woman did not wait for the next shots to be fired. She clasped her hands together and, in a swooping motion, shot a bright light that cut across the street in an arc, shattering car windows and setting others on fire. The image on the television became a blurry jumble of movements. The panicked reactions in the coffee shop could be heard in the background. On the television screen, a small inset popped up next to the blurry image. It showed the student videographer talking to the reporter. "When she did the laser thing, I freaked. Everybody freaked."

The television screen cut away to the news anchor. "Truly terrifying footage from earlier today in Middlebury, Vermont. We'll take a quick break here. When we return, we'll have more hair-raising accounts from eyewitnesses to the brazen bank robbery, plus an update on the condition of the officers injured during the face-off."

The newscast camera panned out and a second anchor chimed in. "All that, and we hope to bring you live coverage of the Vermont State Police press conference at the top of the hour."

Jennifer toggled the remote as the screen cut to commercial. This time, she landed on a local Burlington station, where a grandfatherly anchor was shown on a split screen next to a perky blonde standing on the street outside the bank. It was nighttime, and the bank was aglow with lights from the dozen news crews doing similar standups. Police crime scene tape cordoned off the area around the bank, and inside it, several crime scene technicians could be seen as they gathered evidence and conferred.

"I understand you have some breaking news, Jessica?" asked the anchor.

"That's right, Ted," said the reporter, her friendly demeanor turning somber. "And I'm afraid it's sad news. We just spoke to a police official, off the record, who told us some chilling new information. Apparently, the lead-up to the robbery began yesterday, when the robber kidnapped the bank manager and her teenaged daughter. The robber threatened to kill the daughter unless the manager helped her steal items from the bank vault. A threat she apparently carried out. We have confirmed with officials that the body of the teenaged girl was found a little over an hour ago. No word on where she was found or how she was killed, but we do know she was dead when they found her."

"Heartbreaking," Ted said, lowering his gaze and shaking his head. After a pause, he looked back into the camera. "Add murder and kidnapping to bank robbery and assault. Have you learned anything more about the woman who perpetrated these crimes?"

"Very little, Ted. At this point, the police are still scrambling to put a name to the face."

At the bottom of the screen, a scroll appeared. "Breaking: News conference from Vermont State Police to begin any minute. Stay tuned for live coverage."

Jennifer muted the television and picked up her cell phone. Thus far, she'd received no reply to her earlier texts to Anlon and Pebbles. Texts that read: "Find a TV! Right now! Bank robbery in Middlebury, VT. On all the news channels. Muran!"

She had a strong urge to call Detective Hall, but she was reluctant to distract him, as she was sure he was engaged in the hunt. On the other hand, she believed it was critical the police know more about what they were up against. She decided to call Nickerson for his advice.

"Nickerson," the voice said on the other end of the line.

"Hey, Dan, it's Jen. Got a minute?"

"Sure, anything for you. What's up?"

Jennifer stood and paced in front of the television. "You watching the news? About the bank robbery in Vermont?"

"I'm not, but believe me, we're on high alert about it."

"I think it's the same person who killed Anabel Simpson."

"Thought crossed my mind, too."

"She's crazy dangerous, Dan."

"Obviously. You heard about the girl?"

"Yeah, just did. Pisses me off," Jennifer said through clenched teeth. "Look, I need your advice. I'm thinking of calling Tim Hall at VSP. Let him know who and what they're hunting."

"Do it. I know their heads are spinning. If you've got info that could help them, I'm sure he'll be all ears."

"I'm worried he'll think what I tell him is crazy, far-fetched."

"Jen, after that video, I can't see how."

"Yeah, I guess that's true," she said, slumping down on the bed.

"Listen, gotta run," Nickerson said. "I'm heading to a roadblock we've set up on Route 7, just in case she tries for Massachusetts. Call him. The worst he can do is blow you off."

"Okay, thanks, Dan. Be safe."

"Will do. Any parting words of advice in case we run into her?"

"Yeah, shoot first, ask questions later."

When Jennifer looked up, the press conference was about to begin. She exchanged her phone for the remote and unmuted the television. There were several people on the platform behind the uniformed man standing at the podium. The caption beneath the picture identified him as Colonel Richard Springer, Commander, Vermont State Police. After he introduced the others, including the mayor of Middlebury and the Vermont attorney general, Springer cleared his throat and read from a prepared statement.

"At approximately 11:34 this morning, 911 operators received a call from the Middlebury Bank and Trust branch on Main Street. The call was initiated by the branch's security guard, who noticed unusual activity on the bank's video surveillance feed and was concerned a robbery might be in progress. The guard was immediately patched through to the Middlebury Police Department barracks, and after a brief discussion, it was decided to send officers to the scene."

The commander paused from his reading and looked up at the flashing cameras. "I know there have been some questions as to why the local police did not come blazing in with sirens blaring, instead of the cautious approach evident in video footage of the incident. I think it's important to note it was unclear to police what was happening inside the bank; even the security guard was unsure. Though he told officers the bank manager appeared to be acting under duress, the suspect did not appear to have a weapon and did not act in a threatening manner."

He returned to his statement. "Out of an abundance of caution, officers elected to treat the situation as a potential hostage situation and first sought to secure the perimeter and safeguard citizens in the area. Inside the bank, the security guard rounded up and sequestered bank employees and patrons, all except the branch manager who was with the suspect in the bank's vault.

"At approximately 11:49 a.m., the suspect exited through the lobby entrance alone. Officers outside the entrance confronted the suspect and demanded her surrender. Instead, the suspect attacked the officers and fled the scene. Three of the officers sustained non-life-threatening injuries. They were taken to the hospital and released earlier this evening. Two other officers were killed during a confrontation with the suspect as she fled the scene. Their names will be released once family members have been notified. At this hour, the suspect remains at large. A massive search is underway, led by the Vermont State Police. Given the suspect may attempt to leave the state, the state police in New York, New Hampshire and Massachusetts are also engaged in search efforts.

"We believe the suspect departed the scene in a silver Honda CR-V with New York license plates. Officers located an abandoned vehicle fitting the description approximately seven miles southwest of Middlebury, near the Ticonderoga ferry crossing. Efforts are underway to identify the vehicle and suspect, but at this time, we have no additional information. The suspect should be considered armed and dangerous. If anyone watching or listening to this broadcast encounters the suspect, call 911 immediately and take shelter. Do not — I repeat, *do not* — attempt to engage the suspect.

"We have distributed two images of the suspect to all police departments involved in the search and have posted the images on the Vermont State Police website."

As the commander continued to speak, the television screen placed the press conference in an inset. The main screen showed the two images, side by side. Across the bottom of the screen, a scroll read, "Suspect at large. Last seen near Ticonderoga ferry. Contact 911 immediately if you see suspicious activity. Suspect considered armed and dangerous."

Jennifer studied the images while the commander continued to speak. "The first image is a photograph taken from video surveillance inside the bank. The second is a composite sketch developed from conversations with the branch manager."

The woman in the surveillance screen capture appeared closer to forty in Jennifer's estimation, though the video quality was still poor. In the sketch, however, the woman looked younger. She had feathery, long black hair. Her jawline was chiseled, and her olive-toned skin was wrinkle-free. The shape of the eyes, nose and lips gave the woman a touch of an exotic look. As Jennifer compared the sketch with the screen capture, she realized her perception of the woman's older age was influenced by the woman's ponytail, glasses and generously applied makeup.

"In addition to grand theft and assault charges, the suspect is also wanted for kidnapping and murder. We are still gathering evidence, but it appears this crime began yesterday with the kidnapping of the branch manager's daughter, and then the branch manager herself. The suspect used the threat of harm to the daughter to compel the branch manager to assist her in the robbery. Both were held captive overnight. This morning, the suspect drove the branch manager to work and returned approximately two hours later to rob the bank.

"Her target was an item or items in two safe-deposit boxes stored in the bank vault. From security camera video taken while the suspect examined the boxes, we know the suspect removed a rectangular, black stone and placed it in a briefcase she brought to the bank. Afterward, the suspect continued to search the boxes for another item or items and became agitated when she could not locate the additional piece or pieces, and then left the vault area."

While the commander provided additional details, a snippet of the security video played on a split screen opposite the press conference. Jennifer watched Muran extract a *Sinethal* from one of the boxes and rummage through the second. When finished, Muran combed through both boxes again, halting several times to pound her fist on the cubicle tabletop. She then knocked the boxes to the floor, grabbed her satchel and disappeared from the camera's view.

Jennifer's attention returned to the press conference when she heard the commander pause and utter an extended sigh. The split screen vanished and the newsfeed zoomed in on the commander as he slowly looked around the room of reporters. "Finally, it is with a heavy heart that I tell you we located a deceased teenaged girl earlier this evening fitting the description of the branch manager's daughter. Out of respect for the family, we will not divulge the names of the manager or her daughter at this time. We ask the media to refrain from intruding on the grieving mother or other family members. At the appropriate time, we will release a statement with more information."

His eyes teared. "It's been a hard day, folks. And it's gonna be a harder night. But we will catch this woman and bring her to justice, I promise you that."

The final words were barely out of his mouth when the room erupted with questions from reporters in the room.

"What kind of weapon did she use?" shouted one reporter.

The commander frowned. "Your guess is as good as mine. She had something in her hands, but it wasn't a gun."

Another reporter piped up. "Was it a laser?"

"If it was, it was unlike any laser I've seen or heard of."

From the back of the room, another question: "How did she escape?"

The commander turned to another uniformed official on the small stage and they engaged in a whispered exchange. The other official stepped forward and identified himself as the chief of the Middlebury Police. "The suspect disabled the officers on scene and fled on foot toward the south side of town."

"Is that where the two officers were killed?"

The Middlebury chief nodded. "Yes, they were stationed behind a police cruiser blocking the Otter Creek bridge. They exchanged fire with the suspect and were killed."

In the front row, a coiffed reporter from a national news channel stood up. "Chief, eyewitnesses tell us the police cruiser was shot with a laser beam and the car flew over the side of the bridge and into the creek. And that the suspect mowed down the officers while they sought cover. Can you confirm that?"

The commander nudged the chief from his place before the microphones. "We're still gathering evidence."

"We have video of the car being pulled from the river," said the undaunted reporter. "What kind of weapon could do that? Are we talking something military?"

"No comment."

The reporter fired another question. "Is the FBI involved? Have you contacted the Defense Department?"

The commander ignored the questions and pointed to a rival network reporter who'd risen to stand by his competitor. "Commander, where was the dead teenager found? How did she die?"

"We're still securing the scene. I don't have anything more on that right now."

"We've heard reports of a large police presence at Fort Ticonderoga, across the river from where the suspect's car was found. Is that where the girl was found?"

"No comment."

Jennifer muted the television. Shortly after, the commander waved off another question and motioned for the group of officials to depart the stage. The network feed switched to a live helicopter view of a dozen police cars and several emergency vehicles. The helicopter's spotlight illuminated a star-shaped stone structure. Beneath the image was a caption. "Unidentified body found at Fort Ticonderoga."

Reaching for her cell phone, Jennifer saw no replies from Anlon and Pebbles. She briefly weighed calling each again, but she'd already left two messages. Instead, she dialed Detective Hall. He did not answer, either. Jennifer left a message. "Hi, Tim. Jennifer Stevens here. Please call me. I have some information about the suspect in the Middlebury incident today. It's important. Call me when you get a chance."

She typed out a similar text to him and laid back on the bed. With a forearm covering her eyes, she said, "What should I do? What should I do?"

Middlebury was only about forty miles from Burlington, but Jennifer imagined it would take more than an hour to get there, especially if roadblocks were set up along Route 7, the most direct route between the two cities. Was it better to try for Ticonderoga? She uncovered her eyes and checked her cell phone map app for the distance to Fort Ticonderoga — twenty miles past Middlebury.

That settled it. Anything was better than sitting in the hotel room. She hoisted herself off the bed and grabbed her tote bag from the dresser. Rustling through the bag, she pulled out the rental car keys and dropped them on the bed. Digging deeper in the bag, she felt for the scratchy Stones at the bottom. She found one, then the other, and placed them next to the keys. She crossed her arms and she stared at the Stones. Would they believe her? Or would she have to provide a demonstration?

New York, New York

In a not-so-quiet corner of the midtown steakhouse, Anlon patiently waited for the wine steward to finish pouring before continuing his conversation with Cesar. The topic was their visit the prior day to see Elton Sinclair's shawl, and Anlon was excited to learn more from Cesar.

"I'm still blown away by the symbol," Anlon said.

Cesar raised his wine glass to toast his enthusiasm. "I'm so glad I wasn't the only one who noticed the similarity. I was unsure at first, given the symbol doesn't carry the *Lifintyl* icons. But your reaction was as strong as mine when I first saw the *Sinethal.*"

"There's no doubt in my mind. It's definitely the same symbol," Anlon said, as he clinked glasses with Cesar. He sipped some of the wine, then asked, "But I'm puzzled by the time gap. What do you make of it? It seems too big a gap for the Munuorians to have made it."

"I don't know, but the archaeological record of human development shows us that nearly all cultures are built on preceding ones in one fashion or another," Cesar said.

"So, if it wasn't made by them, you're thinking it was made by an earlier society? One that influenced the Munuorians?" Anlon asked.

"Yes, one or the other," Cesar said.

Anlon thought of the many examples of Munuorian artistry he'd witnessed in visions with Malinyah. Beyond their mystical Stones, he thought of the unusual styling of their ships, the precision with which Malinyah carved volcanic rock, and the wall of unusual seashells. Then there was the fine feel of Malinyah's tunic and the intricacy of her beaded burial cloak. "I remember Pebbles saying Malinyah claimed the Munuorians had watched the stars for 'years beyond count.' I've never asked her to quantify how far back their ancestry goes. Maybe it stretches back two thousand years prior to Munirvo."

"It's certainly a possibility, but the other imagery on the shawl is so different from anything else we've seen from the Munuorians. Wouldn't you agree?" Cesar asked.

"Yeah, that's true," Anlon said.

"Either way, it will be fascinating to explore," Cesar said with a smile.

Their conversation was interrupted by the delivery of their appetizer, a raw bar platter featuring shrimp, lump crabmeat and oysters. As they each selected a few pieces, Anlon asked, "What do you think of Sinclair?"

"Elton? He's theatrical, but the man has a knack for finding gems others miss. Huaca Prieta's not his only big hit," Cesar said.

"How well did Devlin know him, you think?"

"I'm sure they crossed paths, but I don't really know. Why?"

"I don't know. He made it sound like they were chums."

"That's your uncle's doing. He made everyone feel like they were dearest friends. Speaking of Devlin and Elton, the shawl may help resolve another mystery Devlin and I grappled with over the years."

"Really? In what way?" Anlon asked, spearing another shrimp from the platter.

"Well, if we discover it was made by a society predating the Munuorians, it will lend greater credence to the theory we put forth in our book," Cesar said.

"Let me guess, the mystery in question is the one about the Mayan calendar you guys found in a Mexican jungle," Anlon said. He knew the two men had written two books and several articles together about their discoveries, of which the unusual Mayan calendar had garnered the most interest in archaeology circles.

"Spot on. We called it the 'Calakmul Star Clock,' given we found it in the jungle near the ruins of the Mayan city Calakmul. But, technically, it's not a Mayan creation, or so Devlin and I believed," said Cesar.

"Interesting. What's the connection with the shawl?" Anlon asked.

"There are several features that intrigue me. For instance, the clock used animal figures as symbols for various constellations. Some of those symbols are on the shawl," Cesar said. "Did Devlin ever talk about the expedition where we found it? It was quite an adventure."

"No," Anlon said. "Can't say that he did. But you've got me interested now."

"Oh, it would take all of dinner, plus some, to give you the full tale. Perhaps another time," Cesar said with a twinkle in his eye. Staring down at his reflection in the wine glass, he softly said, "Poor

Devlin. He was so angry we had to cut so much out of the book. But our editor thought it too 'Indiana Jones' for an academic tome."

Anlon urged him to share the tale, but Cesar demurred, claiming it was best told under the glow of a campfire rather than a crowded restaurant. "Besides, I'd rather talk about the shawl. The potential connection with the clock is more intriguing."

"How so?" Anlon asked.

"It is a question of time," Cesar said. "The ages of both pieces are out of place with known history. And both pieces have characteristics beyond the animals that seem out of place, too."

"You mean like the beading on the shawl?" Anlon asked.

"Yes, exactly," Cesar said.

"What's out of whack with the clock?" Anlon asked.

"On one hand, it is an amazing demonstration of astronomy and mathematics," Cesar said. "On the other, it's a bit off in its precision...maybe."

Nearly all ancient cultures, Cesar explained, seemed to have been obsessed with a need to mark time. Specifically, the cycles of the sun and moon. To wit, he explained, most ancient calendars measured time by tracking the movements and positions of the sun and moon. The cycles of these bodies helped ancient societies learn how to predict the change in seasons, which, in turn, allowed them to prepare for changes in weather and helped them to better manage their food and water supply.

"In this way, early clocks and calendars were mandatory survival tools," he said.

Ancient peoples marked the changes in seasons using similar methods, he continued. They used fixed objects, natural or ones they placed, with unobstructed views of the horizon. Then they recorded the rising and/or setting of the sun and/or moon each day in relation to the fixed objects.

"After a few years of recording their observations, they would have grown confident in their capability to predict the seasons. If their observations were off a little bit here and there, it made little difference. With enough history under their pelts, as it were, they would have had ample time to adapt to shifts in climate and precipitation.

"As history progressed, sun and moon calendars became more sophisticated and precise, leading to the development of clock-type devices, which gave them the ability to track the length of each day and night. This allowed for greater organization and coordination of efforts. People were able to gather at precise times to accomplish coordinated tasks. Clocks provided a leap in efficiency," Cesar said.

The waiter stopped by to clear their appetizer plates and motioned for the wine steward to refresh their glasses. After informing Anlon and Cesar that the arrival of their dinner was imminent, the waiter breezed to the next table.

"All that makes sense, so far," Anlon said. "But how does that apply to your clock?"

"Like Mayan calendars, it doesn't mark time in terms of hours or seasons. It marks time in blocks of months and years. In fact, much like Mayan calendars, the clock we found allowed its makers to project out time for thousands of years. Now, the only way to construct such a calendar, at least the only way we've surmised it could be done, is to watch the stars. Specifically, the alignment of constellations as they wheel through the sky."

"So, I take it you think the clock's makers influenced the development of the Mayan calendar," Anlon said.

"Yes, it's incredibly complex…and reasonably accurate. To create it, the makers would have had to know the curvature of the Earth and the angle of its rotation. And they would have had to watch the stars for a very, very long time. You see, even though a given constellation appears in the sky in the same general area on a given day in one year versus the same day in the next year, it isn't exactly in the same spot. Because of the Earth's angle of rotation, constellations shift slightly, each day, each month, each year. All told, it takes about nineteen thousand years for a constellation to return to the exact point it occupied on the day one first began to track it."

"Are you telling me whoever built the clock watched the stars for nineteen thousand years?"

"No, I don't think they did, and no one thinks the Mayans did. I think they took some shortcuts. They knew enough from watching the small shifts in constellation position from year to year to project out the full nineteen-thousand-year cycle. But, it would have taken easily a thousand years to see enough shift to calculate out the full cycle. It's a mystery how they did it, but to me, the biggest mystery is *why* they did it."

"I see what you mean," Anlon said. "What practical purpose would such a clock serve?"

Two porters descended on the table, one carrying their entrées, steak for Anlon, salmon for Cesar, while the other placed down family-style platters of grilled vegetables and the restaurant's signature hash browns. As Anlon and Cesar divvied up the side dishes, Cesar said, "The Mayans surely saw it as a means to attach specific dates in history to key events. That much is certain."

He took a bite of his salmon, then added, "But why they went to such elaborate lengths to do so is baffling. For an ancient culture, supposedly rudimentary in their technology, to create such a calendar is an inexplicable societal development. And truthfully, there were other older Mesoamerican cultures that produced similar calendars at earlier dates, including the Zapotecs and Olmecs. But the Calakmul clock predates them all by thousands of years."

"Suggesting that the knowledge to create the clock was passed on by the clockmaker's culture, just like weaving and beading in the shawl," Anlon said, cutting a slice of his steak.

"Exactly," Cesar said.

"Do you think the Munuorians were somehow involved with the clock?" Anlon asked.

"If they weren't directly, I think they may have known about the culture," Cesar said. "The missing piece, the answer I'd like to find is — what was so important about the movement of stars for thousands of years to relatively primitive people?"

Anlon thought of Pebbles' description of the Munuorian Fandis and their religious-like dedication to watching the *Breylif* constellation. "Maybe they weren't tracking the movement of constellations, per se. Maybe they were looking for something else?"

"Like what?" Cesar asked.

"Changes in constellations. Their shapes, the brightness of their stars, the spacing between their stars," Anlon said. "Maybe they were watching for asteroids? Maybe the clock served as their early warning system?"

There was a commotion behind them and Anlon turned to look. The maître d' had run into a waiter carrying a tray laden with someone's dinner, spilling the dishes of food onto two sets of diners. Anlon winced and said to Cesar, "Ouch."

As Anlon turned back around to concentrate on his dinner, he heard a voice call, "Dr. Cully?"

Surprised, Anlon looked up to see the maître d'. The man was out of breath, his suit coat covered in mashed potatoes, and his face looked like he'd seen a ghost. Before Anlon could speak, the man said, "I have a Dr. Wallace on the phone at the front. He says he needs to speak to you immediately. He says it's an emergency."

7

Eve of Destruction

Burlington, Vermont
September 27

Jennifer was only a mile outside Burlington when Detective Hall called back. She answered immediately. "Hi, Tim. Thanks for calling me back."

"Hey, Jennifer. How could I not? You know who our perp is?"

"Um, sort of. I know, well, I'm pretty sure she's the same person who killed Anabel Simpson. I think the weapon she used at the bank was the same one she used to torture Anabel."

Hall was silent for a moment. In the background, Jennifer could hear other people talking. Hall returned to the line and said, "Hold on a sec."

She listened to the muffled sound of Hall speaking to someone else. When he came back on the line, he said, "I'm going to put you on speaker. I've got my captain here and a couple other detectives."

A second later there was a click and he said, "Go ahead, Jen. Repeat what you just said."

"Okay, no problem." Clearing her throat, she said, "I'm pretty sure the Middlebury suspect is the same person who murdered Anabel Simpson. From the video, I think the weapon she used to escape today was the same she used to torture Anabel. They're called *Dreylaeks*."

"This is Captain Bennett," said a gravelly voice through the phone. "Tell me about the weapon. You called them dreadlocks?"

"No. They're pronounced 'dray-locks.' They are two magnetic stones, each about the size of drink coasters and roughly the thickness of a cookie. When you slam or rub them together, they can create different effects, say, a blast of air or directed electrical charges. They are only effective at close range — no more than thirty feet.

At least, that's as far as I've seen them work. She might be able to do more with them; she's got a lot more experience using them than I do," Jennifer said.

"You've used these things?" Bennett asked.

"Uh-huh. I've got a pair with me now. I can show them to you, if you want."

"Where are you?"

"Um, driving south on 7, right now. Looks like I'm coming up on a town called Charlotte."

There was more low-voice conversation on Hall's end of the line before Bennett spoke again. "Hall tells me you used to be a detective with Mass PD."

"Yes, lieutenant detective, to be accurate. Worked out of the Berkshire Detective Unit in Pittsfield."

"For Bruno Gambelli?"

"Yes. You know him?"

"I do indeed. He's a good man." Bennett paused, then asked, "He'll vouch for you?"

The question surprised Jennifer and she hesitated before answering. Her resignation from the force had occurred under controversial circumstances, a fact Hall must have learned and passed to Bennett. "I believe he will. I'm on good terms with him."

After a few seconds' delay, Bennett said, "All right, Stevens, get down here as fast as you can. I'm going to give you back over to Detective Hall."

"Yes, sir," she said.

Through the phone, Jennifer heard Bennett speak to Hall. "Give her directions to the station. Make sure you alert the team at the junction with Route 17 to let her through. Tell her to use my name."

A moment later Bennett came back on the line. "One question before Hall jumps back on. You said you know the suspect?"

"I don't know her personally, but I know a bit about her backstory," Jennifer said.

"What's her name?" Bennett asked.

Jennifer had hoped to delay the conversation until she could do it in person, but she understood the urgency to discover the suspect's identity. "The only name I know her by is Muran, but I'm sure she's using an alias."

"Spell it," Bennett said. Jennifer gave her best guess on the spelling. He asked if Muran was a first or last name. She told him she thought it was her first name, but she couldn't be certain. He followed with a question about Muran's last known address. Jennifer said she didn't know and told him it was her understanding that Muran moved frequently. Finally, Bennett grumbled, "All right, get a move on, Stevens. Every second counts."

Middlebury, Vermont

When she arrived at the Middlebury police headquarters, Jennifer couldn't help but recall her days as an army M.P., for the small-town station had been converted into a battlefield command post. While armed officers guarded the cordoned perimeter, other officers hustled between the main HQ building and temporary tents erected in the station's parking lot. The air was filled with sounds of radio chatter and conversation, and everyone in Jennifer's view wore stern, intense expressions.

A patrolman led Jennifer inside the headquarters and into a conference room where a dozen officials were gathered in three different groups. One group was positioned in front of a wall map while the other two groups engaged in separate conversations at opposite ends of the conference table. Jennifer spotted Detective Hall at the wall map and waved to him. He immediately tapped the shoulder of the white-haired man standing next to him, and they both broke away from the map group. Hall gave a brief introduction. "Jennifer, this is Captain Bennett. Captain Bennett, Jennifer Stevens."

While Hall spoke, Bennett eyed her up and down. Jennifer, clad in jeans and sweatshirt, suddenly felt underdressed in the room full of besuited and uniformed officers. Yet, if Bennett disapproved of her appearance, he didn't show it on his face. "Good to meet you, Stevens."

"Thank you, Captain. Wish it were under different circumstances, but same here."

The captain nodded and turned to address the others in the room. "Folks, attention, please."

The groups silenced and all eyes turned toward Bennett. Jennifer recognized three of the people from the televised press conference. Colonel Springer, the VSP commander, was one of them. The other two were the Middlebury Police chief and the VSP public relations officer. Bennett placed a hand on her shoulder and said, "This here is Jennifer Stevens, a former detective from Mass PD. She's got knowledge of the suspect's weapon. She's also the one who gave us the lead on the suspect's name earlier."

To Jennifer, he said, "Under normal circumstances, we'd go around the room making introductions, but we don't have time for that. We need your help and we need it fast. We think we've found the suspect. Before we try to nab her, we need to know more about the weapon she has. You brought it with you? The dray-locks, right?"

"Yes, that's right," Jennifer said. Her heart racing, she asked, "You found her? Where?"

"Later. The weapon — please show it to us."

"Okay, understood."

She reached inside her tote and retrieved the two Stones. She held them up for the group to see, then placed them on the table in front of her. The other people in the room converged around the *Dreylaeks*.

"Williams," said the Middlebury chief. "Do those look like what you saw?"

A short, stocky uniformed officer stepped closer to the Stones. Leaning over the table, he said, "Can't say for sure, Chief, but they look pretty damn close. Same color, about the same size, but I didn't get much of a look at them before she attacked."

The chief looked unconvinced. Jennifer directed her gaze at him while pointing at the Stones. "I'm one hundred percent certain she used *Dreylaeks*."

"You said they're stone?" Bennett said, recalling their earlier conversation.

"Yes, magnetized stone."

"Is it military?" asked Colonel Springer, lifting the Stones.

"They're not necessarily intended to be weapons, but they can be used that way," Jennifer said, wary of getting into too much detail about their lineage.

"You ever seen anything like this, Bobby?" Springer asked, handing the Stones to a man dressed in a gray camouflage uniform. His black baseball cap read "S.W.A.T."

"No, sir. Never," answered the man, turning one Stone over in his palm. He cast a skeptical eye at Jennifer. "These look more like skipping stones than a weapon to me. You're telling me these stones can slice a car in two? Send it flying over a bridge and into the creek?"

"Easily," she answered, maintaining eye contact with the SWAT team leader. "I'm not very experienced using them, certainly nowhere near as experienced as Muran, but I've seen what they can do firsthand."

"Show us," the SWAT leader said, exchanging "she's full of shit" glances with Springer.

"Um, here?" she asked.

"Yeah," the smirking officer said, handing the Stones back to Jennifer.

"Not a good idea. I can do it outside, but it'll cause a fire if I demonstrate in here." Jennifer motioned for the group to follow her outside and started for the conference room door.

The SWAT leader held up a hand. "Hold up. We don't have time for that. Do it here."

Jennifer turned to Bennett. "Captain?"

"Time's a-wasting, people," Springer interjected.

"Go ahead, Stevens," Bennett said.

"Okay, but can someone please get a fire extinguisher?" Jennifer asked.

She heard the SWAT leader chuckle as an officer left to retrieve a fire extinguisher. Jennifer had only been in the man's presence for five minutes, but already she'd had enough of "Bobby." With a smile, she asked him, "Want to be the test dummy?"

"What?"

Before the word finished spilling out of his mouth, Jennifer pointed her aim at his midsection and smashed the two Stones together. The gunshot-like sound caused everyone to flinch. Everyone but Bobby. He was otherwise occupied, flying backward over the table and crashing into the wall next to the map. He uttered a loud "oof" at impact and slid down the wall with a bewildered expression.

Jennifer didn't wait for reactions from the others in the room. She quickly began to rub the Stones together in her hands. When she felt them beginning to warm, she aimed at a chair at the end of the table and slapped the *Dreylaeks* together again, this time grinding them against each other long enough for a bolt of electricity to shoot forth and pierce a hole through the chair's backrest. The bolt continued through the wall, catching both the chair and the wall on fire. She released the hot Stones onto the table. The glowing *Dreylaeks* wobbled to a standstill while the gaping onlookers stood frozen in place.

"Holy shit!" Springer blurted out.

Bennett yelled for the fire extinguisher just as the officer ran into the room with it. He doused the small blazes with two gushes of white foam while the woozy Bobby was helped to his feet. Springer pointed at Jennifer. "You're coming with us. Come on, people, let's roll."

Ticonderoga, New York

The police motorcade raced along two-lane roads, headed for the northern shore of Lake George. They initially proceeded northwest from Middlebury and crossed into New York over the Lake Champlain Bridge. From there, they turned south on Route 9N and continued on to the city of Ticonderoga.

During the thirty-five-minute drive, Jennifer learned more details from Colonel Springer and Captain Bennett. They confirmed that the car Muran used to escape Middlebury was indeed found at the parking lot of the Ticonderoga ferry. Unfortunately, they told her, the discovery had not been made until two hours after the robbery. Bennett explained the robbery and aftermath had unfolded so quickly, Muran slipped away before Middlebury police recovered from her attacks and gave chase.

"They knew she went south, across the bridge, and ran down a side street. Two patrolmen chased after her, but, by the time they reached the street corner, she was gone," Bennett said.

According to Bennett, it took officers an hour to search the area around the side street, during which time other officers interviewed eyewitnesses who were near the bridge when Muran had run across. By then, the Middlebury police had also alerted VSP and other departments in the neighboring towns about the robbery, but Bennett said the alerts hadn't been very helpful. "The description of the suspect they provided was too generic. They couldn't tell us if she was holed up in town or if she'd taken off. But then we got a couple breaks."

The first one came from a teenaged waiter for a café two blocks from the bridge. He had been on a smoke break out back of the café, sitting on steps leading to a public parking lot, when he noticed a woman sprint into the lot. Bennett told Jennifer the waiter hadn't been able to provide a better description of the woman, but he had noticed the car she drove off in. "Turns out the young man has a passion for cars."

"Anabel Simpson's Honda CR-V?" Jennifer ventured.

Springer and Bennett looked at each other with mild surprise before Bennett confirmed Jennifer's guess. He told her the waiter had said the Honda turned onto College Street and away from town.

"We weren't sure it was our suspect at first, but it was the best lead we had, so we put out another alert. The teen didn't get the license plate number, so it was a total crapshoot, but then we got our second break," Springer said.

With the vehicle description in hand, police in the area had canvassed roads and neighborhoods surrounding Middlebury,

including two VSP patrol cars that were dispatched to the Ticonderoga ferry. Upon arriving at the ferry, the officers had noted
a silver CR-V in the small parking area. They called in the license plate number and discovered the plates were stolen. They
traced the VIN number and determined the vehicle belonged to
a Miss Anabel Simpson of Bennington. The commander said the
officers also questioned the ferry operator, who told them he was
pretty sure a woman fitting the suspect's description had taken
the ferry across the river earlier in the afternoon.

"Once we ID'd the vehicle, we realized we were probably deal-
ing with Miss Simpson's killer," Bennett said.

Jennifer had made the connection between the robbery and Anabel as soon as she'd seen the newscast video of Muran obliterat-
ing the police dragnet outside the bank. That supposition was confirmed by the later broadcast of the bank security camera footage
that had shown Muran removing a *Sinethal* from the safe-deposit
box. At least, that's what the grainy image had looked like to Jennifer. Whose *Sinethal* was it? Jennifer had pondered. At Indio Maiz,
Foucault had told them he believed Muran was seeking a *Tuliskaera*,
a *Taellin* or possibly both. He'd said nothing about a *Sinethal*. Was
it Muran's? Or possibly another Munuorian's?

And what else had Muran expected to find? At the earlier press
conference, the bank security cam video showed Muran had continued to search the boxes after she removed the *Sinethal*. When she
had finished searching, her mannerisms on the video implied she
was upset. If that interpretation was correct, it implied she had expected to find something else. Given the *Taellin* was a helmet, Jennifer thought it too large an item to fit in the boxes. That left open
the possibility of a *Tuliskaera*. The cone-shaped Stone was about
the length of a *Sinethal*, so Jennifer was confident it could have fit
in one of the boxes. Another thought crossed her mind as she pondered the conundrum. If she wasn't after a *Tuliskaera*, maybe she
had been looking for a *Naetir*. After all, she thought, the hockey-
puck-shaped Stone was needed to activate a *Sinethal*.

Regardless of the answers, it seemed a safe bet to Jennifer that the safe-deposit boxes had been Anabel's. With this supposition in mind, Jennifer had stitched together a scenario on the drive to Middlebury — Muran had tortured Anabel to get her to divulge where the Stones were located. Given the degree of torture and the condition of her house, Anabel had died before revealing her secret. After killing Anabel, Muran had then combed through Anabel's possessions looking for clues to the Stones' whereabouts. Somewhere she found the safe-deposit box keys, and somehow, she had figured out that the keys were meant for the boxes in the Middlebury bank.

"Why did Anabel have safe-deposit boxes in Middlebury? It's ninety miles from Bennington," Jennifer mumbled.

"The boxes aren't registered to Anabel Simpson. They belong to a woman named Evelyn Warwick," Bennett said.

"Huh? Who?"

"We're in the dark, too. We're trying to track her down right now."

At that moment, Springer received a call, ending their conversation. As they passed through the city of Ticonderoga, Bennett said, "Command post is up ahead."

Jennifer looked out the window and spotted a horde of flashing lights in the distance. As the procession of Vermont police vehicles began to slow, she asked, "How did you find her?"

"She stole a car after getting off the ferry. Knocked some poor old biddy unconscious and took her car," Bennett said.

"Oh, no. Is she okay?"

"Yeah, I think so. I know she was able to give the local PD a description, so I assume she wasn't hurt too badly. But she was out cold for a good hour."

"No one noticed her?"

"Nope. The perp dragged her behind a dumpster near the lot."

"Geez," Jennifer said, shaking her head.

Springer frowned and squeezed his hand into a fist. "Too bad no one noticed. Carla Bailey might still be alive if someone had."

Looking at Springer, Jennifer thought it obvious he was in anguish over the teenager's death. He must have daughters, she thought. As she pondered a delicate way to ask about the killing, Bennett changed subjects. "I'll tell you what, this Muran is crafty. First, she wipes out the Middlebury PD with precision in a very public firefight. After that, she slips out of town undetected, and then takes out an old woman and steals her car like some kind of ninja. She must have a military background."

"She may be military, but she's not that crafty," Springer said. "She should have ditched the car after killing the girl. Lucky for us she didn't."

Jennifer didn't understand the meaning behind his comment and her face must have shown it. Before she could ask Springer to explain, Bennett said, "The car has OnStar."

"Ah," Jennifer said. "So, you were able to track the car."

"Yep, we've got the place surrounded. Helicopter's got the house all lit up," Bennett said.

"She picked a terrible place to hole up," Springer said. "House is in a cul-de-sac. Butts up against the lake. Crafty, my ass."

The VSP SUV came to a halt at a makeshift command post in a Denny's parking lot. Jennifer fished in her tote for the *Dreylaeks,* then followed the Vermont officers as they exited the vehicle and assembled with a contingent of New York state troopers, two FBI agents from the Albany field office and an ATF agent who'd just arrived from the Boston field office via helicopter. Given the multiple jurisdictions involved, Jennifer wondered who would take the lead. Her question was answered in short order. In the middle of the group was a gray-haired African American in a dark blue uniform with more brass and insignia than Jennifer had ever seen on a police uniform. On his lapel was a name tag: Supt. Dunsmore. He shook Springer's hand and nodded to the rest of the group.

"Jack," Dunsmore said to an officer standing nearby. "Let's go through it one more time for the new folks."

"Yes, sir," said the gung-ho officer. He stood before a map laid out on the hood of a police cruiser. "This is a map of the cul-de-sac. Our perp is in this one here."

Jennifer peeked over the shoulder of an officer. There were six houses in the cul-de-sac and Jack was pointing to the one farthest to the right.

"We've cleared the other houses. We've got SWAT guys in position on all three sides of the perp and more in a boat in the bay. Helicopter overhead, a dozen units blocking the road into the court. The house has two entry doors, one in the front, the other in back. We've got snipers locked in on both."

Jennifer could hear the helicopter in the distance, though it was not visible from the command post. Jack continued to speak. "We're going to send in a negotiator with a SWAT escort. The negotiator will try to coax our perp out, but if shit goes south, we'll storm the house and take the perp out."

Springer asked, "Do we know if she's alone in the house?"

"Yes, sir," Jack said. "We've got heat seekers on-site. Best we can tell, only one person inside."

"Has anyone tried to talk to her?" Bennett asked.

"No, sir. But she's aware of what's going down. No way she couldn't know. We've got the whole perimeter lit up with spotlights."

"Damon," Springer said to Superintendent Dunsmore, "I know it's your show, but before you send in your negotiator, we brought someone you should talk to. Jennifer, come here, please."

Jennifer politely asked the officers standing in front of her to make way. When she stepped into the inner circle, Springer said, "Damon, this is Jennifer Stevens. She's a former Massachusetts State Police detective. She has some knowledge of the suspect, and more importantly, she knows what kind of weapon the suspect used in Middlebury. You shouldn't send in your team until you see what the weapon can do. Jennifer, show him."

In anticipation of the request, Jennifer was already holding up the *Dreylaeks* she'd taken from her bag back in the SUV. She handed them to the superintendent and ran through the same description of the Stones as she had in Middlebury. When she finished, she said, "I know it's not my place to question your plan, Superintendent, but I don't think she's coming out without a fight."

"I'm inclined to agree with you given everything that's happened today. But, we've got to try to resolve this peacefully, if at all possible," Dunsmore said. He handed the *Dreylaeks* back to Jennifer. "I've seen the video from the robbery. You're telling me these little things did all that damage?"

"Yes, sir," she said, holding the Stones in her open palms for others in the group to see. "Together, they're like a stun gun on steroids, but they have a limited range. I'd say as long as your guys are more than thirty feet away, she can't do much damage with them. But, up close, they're lethal."

Major Jack Sterns, the SWAT leader, asked to hold them. As he weighed them in his palms, he asked, "They have to be used together?"

"That's right. They interact magnetically. She needs to build up friction between the two Stones, heat them up, before she can shoot," Jennifer said. "I can demonstrate."

"Please do," Jack said.

She took the two Stones from him and scratched them against each other in the palms of her hands. Using a circular motion, she quickened the pace of the scratching. In the darkness, the group standing around her could see the *Dreylaeks* start to glow.

"Wow, they heat up fast," Jack said.

Jennifer pulled the Stones apart and looked around for something to shoot. There was a trash bin on the sidewalk outside the Denny's entrance. She asked officers to move it to an empty spot in the parking lot. They positioned it about fifteen feet away and then cleared from the area. As the group backed up, the Ticonderoga fire chief stepped forward and told Jennifer to hold her fire until two of his men could empty the bin. "If what you say is true, and there's something flammable inside, it'll go up like a bomb."

After the container was emptied and two firefighters were positioned with extinguishers at the ready, Jennifer aimed at the bin and slapped the heated Stones together, causing a bright beam to shoot forth. Her aim was off and the crackling bolt missed the target. Grinding the *Dreylaeks* together, she guided the bolt through the air until it struck the bin. When it did, the aluminum container blew apart into two flaming pieces. The top piece spun through the air before landing on the lot surface twenty feet back from its original spot. The bottom piece shot sideways and tumbled a few feet away. As the firefighters ran to douse the molten heaps, a chorus of whistles and murmured expletives sounded from the group around her. Jennifer dropped the glowing Stones to the ground and blew on her singed palms.

An EMT noticed her hands and rushed forward to administer aid. While he layered a cooling salve on her hands, Jack asked, "You okay?"

"Yeah, I'll be fine. I didn't hold them long enough to do real damage," she said, wincing as the EMT wrapped her hands with gauze.

"You should use gloves when you fire those things," said the EMT.

"Wish I could. The hands have to feel the Stones vibrate to know when they're ready to fire. Gloves mask the vibration," Jennifer said.

"The vibration's that subtle?" Jack asked.

"Yeah, and you don't want to miss the vibration. *Dreylaeks* explode if they get too hot. I'd rather have burned hands than missing hands," Jennifer said.

"Jesus, I've seen a lot of weapons in my day, but nothing like that," Jack said. "Where did you get them? Is it new tech?"

Jennifer hesitated before answering. There wasn't time for an extended discussion on the topic, so she kept her explanation brief. "Um, no, it's old tech that kind of got shelved for a while."

"I can see why," he said, looking down at her bandaged hands. "If they get that hot, she can't use them for very long without burning her hands."

"Oh, I wouldn't count on that. She's a lot more experienced with them than I am," Jennifer said.

"You know the suspect well, then?" he asked.

"No, not at all."

"Then how do you know her name? How do you know she's experienced with the Stones?"

"I've heard stories about her, about some of the things she's done."

"You're not shooting straight with me, Stevens. I can see it in your eyes," Jack said.

Jennifer bit her lip. She wanted to be helpful, but there was no chance the SWAT leader would react favorably if she said, "She's an evil, ten-thousand-year-old woman from a lost civilization." So, instead, she said, "I know enough about her to know she's very dangerous."

"No shit," he responded. Stepping closer, he locked cold eyes on hers. "Look, I'm about to send my team in. If you know anything about her, anything that can help me prevent bloodshed, you better start talking."

She looked away and crossed her arms. "Trust me, Major, anything I could tell you about her you wouldn't believe."

Jack moved to stand in her line of sight. "God damn it, Stevens. Give me something more than that. I've got men with families I'm sending in there."

Jennifer suddenly regretted the decision to get involved, but telling him what she knew about Muran was asking for a one-way ticket to Crazy Town. She could see only one way out of the situation. "Let me go in with your negotiator."

"What?"

"Let me go in with him."

"Why in f—'s sake would I do that? You're a civilian."

"Listen to me, she's not going to surrender, Major. She's going to fight her way out or die trying."

"All the more reason you shouldn't go."

Jennifer was about to plead her case when a deafening explosion occurred. Instinctively, everyone at the command post took cover. Out of the corner of her eye, Jennifer saw a ball of fire in the sky. All around, she heard a frantic stream of chatter burst from the first responder radios surrounding her.

"Chopper down! Chopper down!"

"Take cover!"

"Open fire!"

In the distance, the popping sound of firearms filled the night air, followed by another massive explosion. Jennifer saw the halo of another fireball rise above the tree line.

"Boat just blew up!"

"Officers down! Need immediate assistance!"

Jennifer turned to see Jack running for an armored BearCat vehicle. As he ran, he shouted commands into the microphone attached to his flak jacket. Jennifer picked up the *Dreylaeks* and raced after him. She climbed into the back of the truck along with two other SWAT officers. If Jack had noticed her board the truck, he said nothing. His focus seemed solely devoted to the radio reports of the battle raging a few miles away.

8

Old Terrors and New

Route 395, Mammoth Lakes, California
September 27

For hours, Pebbles had faded in and out of consciousness. Each time she would stir, all she could hear was the high-pitched whine of the car's tires and all she could feel was the vibration of the trunk floor against her curled body. The sensations were hypnotic and had lured her back to sleep on several occasions. But some time ago, Pebbles could not be sure how long, the grogginess that had held grip on her began to wane.

Fully awake now, she shivered uncontrollably. It was freezing inside the trunk, and to make matters worse, she was sweating profusely. Yet, these discomforts paled in comparison to the burning pain in her calf. Earlier, she had tried to warm herself by tucking her bound legs closer to her chest, but it caused stabbing twinges along her battered rib cage. It had been painful enough that she cried out, but the cloth wedged in her mouth muted the sound. She had also tried to raise her head and look around, but it had proved a wasted gesture. Her eyes were covered and the movement produced sharp throbs on the side of her head where her captor had bashed it into the floor.

She had cried for a while as she relived the savagery of the attack. He had warned her not to move, but she had foolishly believed she could outrun his bullet.

What was I thinking? Pebbles thought. Lying in the dark cargo hold, she came up with a half dozen ways she could have talked her way out of the situation, including waiting for Antonio to arrive and simply handing over the Stone. But instead she'd acted impulsively and paid a dear price. She had no way of knowing how badly she was injured, but she was in enough pain to realize the injuries were serious. She didn't know where she was or where the car was headed, but she doubted it mattered much. Whenever they arrived at her captor's intended destination, she expected to be on the receiving end of more brutality. This time, however, she would tell him anything that would help keep her alive.

Pebbles thought of Anlon. She reasoned he had to know by now. Antonio would have arrived at the house and discovered she was not at home. She imagined Antonio would then have tried to text and call her. When he received no answer, would he have suspected something was amiss? Would he have called Anlon? She had to hope he reached Anlon and that Anlon gave him the garage door code to get into the house. If Antonio had managed to get in the house, he would have quickly discovered the blood in the hallway. He would have searched the house and found her gone. He would have immediately contacted Anlon, before or after alerting the police. She was certain Anlon would have contacted Jennifer, too.

If that were all true, then there were now a bunch of people searching for her. It was a comforting thought to Pebbles, but only if she could stay alive long enough for them to find her, or for them to negotiate her release. For that was the only reason she wasn't dead already, Pebbles realized. Her captor wanted Malinyah's *Sinethal*, and now the only way for him to get it was to use her as his bargaining chip. How he expected to accomplish that without getting captured himself, Pebbles didn't know, but her game plan for the time being was simple — cooperate and survive.

It would be easier to cooperate if she knew the identity of her captor, Pebbles thought. But she hadn't recognized his face or voice. Was he on his own or was he acting on behalf of someone else? If he was someone else's stooge, then there was one obvious string-puller that came to mind: Klaus Navarro. Pebbles knew he was searching for a *Tuliskaera* and had tried before to steal Malinyah's

Sinethal. She also knew he was partial to letting others do his dirty work for him, a la Margaret and Kyle Corchran. And she was sure Navarro hadn't forgotten or forgiven her for bludgeoning him with a lamp in Devlin's office.

Another long stretch of time passed before Pebbles felt the car finally begin to slow. Soon after, it came to a brief stop and turned. They were on a gravel or dirt road, given the grinding sound coming from the tires. A few minutes later, they stopped again. This time, the car's engine went silent.

By now, not only was Pebbles numb from the cold, but she also had an urgent need to pee. Given all the other indignities of the day, the thought of urinating where she lay didn't faze her. At least it'll warm me up for a little while, she thought. But she ultimately decided against it, reckoning that wet clothes would only make matters worse once the fluid cooled. Plus, she didn't think her captor would take kindly to her befouling the car. She hoped he would allow her to take care of business before resuming his interrogation.

She heard the car door push open and felt the vehicle jiggle as her captor stepped out of the car. Then came the crunch of footsteps in her direction, followed by a click and then the squeak of the trunk's hinges moving. Immediately, a blast of icy air filled the chamber. Pebbles' whole body shuddered from the unexpected gust. With her eyes shielded by cloth, she could not see either her captor or her surroundings. A hand touched against her forehead. Pebbles flinched and turned her head away.

"Easy, now. Be still," the man said. The hand returned, this time cupping her forehead. The hand was cold, very cold. The hand lifted off and came to rest against her cheek. A moment later, the hand lifted and she felt it wrap around her ankle. She jerked her leg to pull away, but he clamped her ankle firmly. "Stop. I need to check the dressing."

Pebbles nodded, relaxed her leg and tried to speak. Restricted by the fabric inside her mouth, all that came out was a muffled, "Okay."

She felt a tug along her calf, and then his cold hand touched the skin beneath the bandage. A moment later, he adhered it back in place and asked, "Want water?"

After a quick nod, her captor removed the tape covering her mouth and fished out the bunched cloth inside. Pebbles licked her dry lips, closed her mouth and wiggled her jaw. His hand gripped her head and lifted it a few inches. "Open up."

Pebbles did as he instructed and felt water dribble in her mouth. She swished it around and swallowed. She quickly opened her mouth again and he poured in some more. This time she swallowed it directly. It was cold and soothed her parched throat as it passed through. Finally, he placed the bottle against her lips and let her gulp down more. When he pulled it away, she said, "I need to pee."

"Tough. Hold it 'til we stop again," he said.

She shook her head. "Been holding it. Can't any longer."

Pebbles heard his feet shuffle on the gravel, but he didn't reply. She said, "It's either out there or in here."

He let out a protracted sigh and cursed. Five minutes later, he maneuvered Pebbles back in the trunk. She was pliant as he re-wrapped the binding around her ankles. When he barked at her to open her mouth, she thanked him as sweetly as she could, hoping it would diffuse his hostility. But it seemed to only irritate him more. He shoved the rag in deeply, causing Pebbles to gag. Seconds later, a fresh strip of tape was pasted over her mouth and the trunk lid slammed shut.

Requesting the bio-break had proved to be one of those "be careful what you ask for" moments for Pebbles. Even though he'd agreed to her request, it hadn't been an easy task for either of them. Given the extent of her injuries, and the hours-long incarceration in the trunk, it had been a painful and awkward process to remove her from the cramped chamber — a process made more difficult by his refusal to remove her blindfold or the binding around her wrists. This same refusal also meant a rather humiliating joint effort had been required for her to accomplish the rest of the deed.

But she had learned a few valuable tidbits from the experience that might prove useful later. The first and most important — she had been able to put some weight on her injured leg, enough weight that she could stand when she leaned against him or the car. She also learned she was taller than her captor, and he wasn't as strong as she expected. He'd had difficulty balancing her weight when he helped lower her into a squatting position. She hadn't been pleased with how long he'd left her leggings rolled at her ankles after lifting her back up, but at least he hadn't groped her.

Back onto the road they went. Soon, the drone of the tires lulled Pebbles back to sleep.

Ticonderoga, New York

It took four minutes to reach the perimeter roadblock…or what was left of it, for the gauntlet of police vehicles was now a burning heap of twisted metal. Jack told the driver to halt. He flung the passenger door open and jumped out. In the back of the vehicle, one of the SWAT officers opened the rear gate, and Jennifer followed the two men out the door and into the street. Jennifer hid by the side of the vehicle while Jack sent the two men ahead.

As Jack instructed the driver to hold the road, Jennifer dashed past him. The movement caught his attention and he shouted after Jennifer. "Hey, where in the hell do you think you're going?"

Jennifer didn't answer. She just kept running. Ahead, the scene she encountered was surreal. With the exception of two cars parked on the street, fires raged everywhere in the cul-de-sac. Anything that could be ignited had been ignited — trees, houses and cars left in driveways were all ablaze. Even the house Muran had supposedly occupied was engulfed in flames. Jennifer followed the two SWAT officers as they took cover behind a vehicle that had escaped Muran's fury. Jennifer could hear urgent cries for medical assistance coming from the blackness beyond the fires. Just as Jack arrived at the vehicle, the rat-a-tat of automatic gunfire sounded out. Over his radio, a voice called out, "Suspect's on the move. In pursuit."

"What direction? Which way is she headed?" Jack demanded, yanking the chest protector microphone close to his mouth.

"South. Into the woods at the edge of the lake. To the right of the house she came out of," answered the voice.

For the next few minutes, Jack took control over the chaos. He told the small force trailing the suspect to hold in place while he sorted out the situation. He called up the armored vehicle and stationed it in the center of the cul-de-sac's circle and instructed his team members scattered around the perimeter to rally to him at the armored vehicle for a quick debrief.

One of Jack's team leaders was the first to arrive. Jennifer could see the hardened veteran was badly shaken as he relayed the details of the encounter. "Everyone was holding in position, then bam! Lightning bolt comes shooting out of an upstairs window and blows the helicopter out of the sky. I gave the order to fire...and then all hell broke loose. Boat blew up, and then lightning was shooting everywhere...Jesus, Major, it was a total clusterf——!"

As the team leader recounted his story, Jennifer realized Muran had more than *Dreylaeks* at her disposal. There was no way a pair of *Dreylaeks* could do the kind of damage described. She had a Flash Stone, a *Tuliskaera* as the Munuorians called it.

When the man finished his summary, Jack laid out a plan of action. He organized the dozen men who made it to the armored vehicle into three teams. Two of the teams, Alpha and Beta, he sent to take positions at the edge of the woods. Once there, they were to await his arrival, and then together with team Gamma already hunkered at the woods, they would fan out in sectors and scour the woods. Jack denoted the last group of men gathered at the BearCat as team Delta. He instructed Delta to secure the perimeter, search for wounded and missing officers and evacuate them from the area.

After giving the assembled teams the order to move out, Jack radioed back to the command post and gave a terse rundown to Superintendent Dunsmore. He requested another helicopter to aid the search, and more boats. The superintendent told him they were en route already. They discussed bringing in fire and rescue personnel, but Jack told him the situation was too fluid at present. Jack said they would triage their own wounded as best they could while they worked to secure the perimeter. Once cleared, they would call in fire and rescue.

Jack ended radio transmission, dipped his head down and wiped his brow. Looking back up, he turned to Jennifer and said, "Guess she's got more range with the Stones than you thought."

"She didn't do this with *Dreylaeks*," Jennifer said. "She's got another weapon with her. One you don't want to f— with."

"I don't care if she's got a f—ing rocket launcher, we're going after her." Jabbing a finger into her shoulder, he said, "You need to get out of here. When the wounded get evac'd, you go with them. Until then, get inside the BearCat and stay put."

"Listen to me! If she's in those woods and she uses it, you're toast. It's a trap. Don't do it."

He turned and ran to join his men without a reply. Jennifer swore under her breath, climbed into the armored vehicle's driver's seat and slammed the door shut. While she gripped the steering wheel and peered through the bulletproof glass for signs of activity, she listened to updates over the BearCat's police scanner.

She heard the command post inform Jack that two helicopters were expected on scene within minutes, and the Lake George Marine Patrol had four more boats on the way. In a near whisper, Jack advised the command post of his search plans. "I'm sending team Alpha southeast along the shoreline to cut off an escape to the lake. Team Beta will go southwest through the woods in case she makes for Route 9N or tries to double back to the cul-de-sac. Team Gamma will head due south through the center of the woods."

Jennifer spied a map the driver had left on the dashboard. She opened it to follow along with the coordinated search plan.

She listened again as the command post acknowledged Jack's search plan and relayed that troopers had been dispatched to surveil a ten-mile stretch of Route 9N. They also proposed devoting one of the choppers to support team Alpha's search of the shoreline until the boats arrived, while directing the other to concentrate its searchlights on the woods. Jack agreed with the proposal and suggested dedicating two of the incoming boats for search and rescue of survivors from the earlier helicopter and boat explosions. He proposed platooning the remaining two boats to monitor the lake and shoreline.

Jennifer saw on the map that they'd covered all the possible exit routes. If Muran went east, she'd hit the lake. Without a boat, she'd be a sitting duck in the water. If she tried to double back to the north in a direct line or by curling to the west first, she'd run into one of the SWAT teams. If she tried to cut through the woods to reach the only other road in the area, Muran would be squeezed between the SWAT teams and the troopers on Route 9N. With helicopter support above and boats on the water, Muran was trapped.

She won't surrender, Jennifer thought. If they corner her, Muran will kill anyone and everyone she can before they put her down. Leaning back against the headrest, Jennifer put aside the map and closed her eyes. She flexed her bandaged hands, aware of the stinging appendages for the first time since leaving the command post. She tried to remember if she had a bottle of *enjyia* in her tote bag or if she had left it in her Burlington hotel room.

"Crap!" she said, remembering her tote bag was sitting in Colonel Springer's SUV. Her cell phone was in the tote as well, she realized, along with her *Breylofte*. "Double crap!"

The *Breylofte* would have come in handy if she had run into Muran. The woofer-shaped Stone had a longer range than the *Dreylaeks* and an air blast from it would have been harder to detect in the darkness. Opening her eyes, Jennifer stared out the window at the orange glow from the surrounding fires and reconsidered the thought. The *Breylofte* would have been useless in a fight against a *Tuliskaera*, she concluded.

Focusing her eyes on the scattered fires around the cul-de-sac, Jennifer noticed they were close to linking up into one sprawling inferno. A blaze that would soon spread to the woods, cutting off Jack and his men's retreat if confronted by Muran. She glanced at the side mirrors and realized the fires would also soon cut off the road into the court, making it difficult to rescue Jack's wounded men. The thought caused Jennifer to wonder why team Delta hadn't returned with any injured officers yet. The houses ringing the lakeside cul-de-sac were no more than a hundred yards from the BearCat, so it should have been a quick round-trip for at least a few of the searchers.

Jennifer exited the BearCat and looked toward the houses, shielding her eyes from the glare of the fires. Inside the SWAT truck she had been insulated from the heat of the fires, but now that she was standing outside, she felt their full intensity. Panic rose within her, as did the sense of urgency to leave the cul-de-sac.

With Jack occupied in the woods and no other officers on-site, Jennifer debated using the BearCat's radio to request a status update from team Delta and to request fire and rescue assistance from the command post. She knew Jack would be pissed with her interference in his operation, but she wasn't keen on roasting alive either. She climbed back in the BearCat and grabbed the scanner microphone. "Team Delta, this is BearCat One, what's your status?"

There was no answer, just static. "Repeat, Team Delta, this is BearCat One, what's your status? Fire's getting out of hand here. We need to evac ASAP."

Jack's voice sounded over the intercom. "Gamma leader to Delta leader. Sit rep."

Again, no answer. A queasy feeling formed in Jennifer's stomach. Had Muran slipped back through the SWAT teams' line? She anxiously scanned the cul-de-sac again, as she heard Jack more forcefully demand an update from team Delta. When none came, Jennifer popped the BearCat into gear and turned the truck around. The road leading out was now blocked by a wall of fire.

"Just frickin' great!" she said. With one hand on the steering wheel and the other clutching the scanner microphone, Jennifer revved the engine and announced, "Gamma leader. Fire's out of control. Team Delta unresponsive. I am out of here."

As she started down the lane, Jack answered, "Ten-four, BearCat One."

Gritting her teeth, Jennifer tossed aside the microphone and floored the accelerator. As she sped toward the wall of fire, she spat out, "This thing better be fireproof!"

With a loud whoosh, the armored truck pierced through the fire. Inside the truck, Jennifer gasped and shut her eyes as blinding flames coated the hood and windows. Though it only took three seconds for the BearCat to punch through, the roaring sound of the fire seemed to last an eternity. As the back end of the truck cleared the fire, the rear wheels hit something hard enough to cause the truck to lurch to the right. Jennifer's eyes flew open as the BearCat bounced over the curb. She slammed on the brakes, but not fast enough to avoid clipping a tree on the side of the road.

In her haste to escape, Jennifer had neglected to strap into the seat harness. When the truck hit the tree, her body launched forward. Her abdomen slammed into the steering wheel just before her face hit against the windshield. The truck spun to a stop on the side of the road. Jennifer, dazed and bleeding, slumped onto the center console and passed out.

Back at the command post, a muffled ping sounded from inside Jennifer's tote bag. She wouldn't see the message until the following day, when she would be reunited with her bag at the hospital. The text was the first in a series of frantic messages Anlon would leave. It read, "Call me ASAP. Pebbles is missing! Police think she was shot. I'm on my way back to Tahoe."

Ludlow, California

Pebbles awoke to a hand squeezing her shoulder. "Wake up!"

As her senses stirred, she noticed the aroma of fried food and the sound of music nearby. She felt the man's hands jerking at the binding around her feet. He whispered, "Time to get you out. No funny business, understood?"

She nodded and he continued with his instructions. "We need to do this quick. It's less than ten feet to get inside. Do *not* — I repeat, do *not* — attract any attention. Got it?"

The command nearly made Pebbles laugh. Here he was, pulling a bruised and bloodied woman from a trunk. A woman restrained, blindfolded and gagged. And he was worried about her attracting attention?

Standing beside her with his arm around her shoulder, he guided Pebbles up onto a curb, then across a small sidewalk, over a door sill and into a carpeted room. To Pebbles' bare feet, the carpet felt coarse and greasy. She heard him shut and lock the door, and then he led her to a bed and eased her onto it. It creaked in several places as she stretched out on it. Though the mattress was thin and lumpy, it was heavenly compared to the trunk. The aroma she noticed outside was stronger in the room. It was a familiar smell. Fried chicken, perhaps? Whatever it was caused her mouth to water.

The music she had heard moments earlier had apparently come from a television in the room. It had been a cheery commercial jingle that had since ended and had been replaced by a voice-over promotion for a news broadcast. "The latest on today's bizarre robbery in New England coming up at the top of the hour. Stay tuned for live coverage from—"

The television clicked off. She heard a bag rustle and the creaking of what she supposed was another bed. Her captor said, "Hungry?"

She nodded.

He maneuvered her legs to the floor and raised her torso into a sitting position. After he unpeeled the tape across her mouth and removed the rag, he hand-fed her strips of fried chicken and french fries. In between portions, he held a straw to her lips through which she sipped cola. Pebbles ate and drank with gusto, and the carb-dense meal quickly filled her empty stomach. When he deemed her feeding complete, he told her to lie down.

"If it's all the same, I'd rather sit," she said.

"Suit yourself," he said. The bag rustled again, and Pebbles heard him start to chew.

While he ate, Pebbles remained silent and took stock of her injuries. The burning sensation in her calf had been replaced by a dull throb, which struck her as odd, given that her lower leg felt numb. Her ribs were still very sore, but so long as she limited her movement and breathed in shallow increments, the pain was manageable. The lump on the side of her head still ached, but the earlier wooziness had tapered off, likely helped by the meal.

She worried about the bullet wound, though. While it was obvious her captor had bandaged her leg, it was less clear whether the wound was still bleeding. The bandage didn't feel wet against her leg, but Pebbles wondered if the numbness in her lower leg masked the sensation. Yet, he'd checked the wound when they stopped by the road and didn't administer any new aid. She risked a question. "My leg is numb. Am I still bleeding?"

"No," he said, his speech obscured by a mouth full of food.

His chomping and sipping went on for some minutes, during which time Pebbles rallied the courage to make an appeal. "Look, I'll tell you whatever you want to know. I'll help you get the Stone you want. Just no more rough stuff, okay? I won't give you any trouble. I prom—"

"Quiet!" he snapped.

Pebbles dutifully closed her mouth. So much for being cooperative, she thought. A moment later, she heard him clean up the food containers and stuff them in the bag. After plunking the bag in a trash can, he said, "Lie down so I can check your leg."

Pebbles rolled facedown on the bed and waited for him to uncover the wound. He sat down next to her, his thigh touching hers. He peeled off the bandage and examined her leg. He lifted off the bed and she heard him walk across the room. She heard water running, and a minute later he returned to her side. She felt him wipe her calf with a warm, wet cloth, then he dabbed the area with a dry one.

"Looks okay," was all he said. She heard him walk away, and the gurgle of the running water was replaced by the spray of a showerhead. When he returned, he rolled her on her side. "Get up."

He helped her off the bed and led her toward the running water, his arm around her shoulder. When they reached the bathroom, he removed her blindfold. The fluorescent light was blinding and Pebbles clamped her eyes shut. He gripped her wrists and cut away the binding.

Pebbles massaged the raw skin on each wrist while fluttering her eyes to adjust to the light. Only one of them would fully open. Through this, she looked around the tiny bathroom. She stood facing a mildew-bordered tub, into which the showerhead sprayed. To her immediate right was a toilet without a lid or seat, and to her left was a sink with a dripping faucet and a rusty water stain around the drain. The lime green walls were as dingy as the off-white tile on the floor. Pebbles peeked up at a small mirror above the sink and caught a partial glimpse of her reflection. She immediately turned away from the gruesome image and came face to face with her captor.

Her earlier deductions about his build had been accurate. He was short and relatively thin. He wore a black turtleneck and matching black slacks. They looked expensive and tailored to fit his slim frame. While the look on his face was not friendly, his features did not strike Pebbles as particularly sinister. Yes, there was a thin layer of stubble on his face and his hair was mussed, but with a quick brush of his hair and a clean shave, Pebbles thought he could easily pass for a "corporate casual" businessman. Except, that is, for the gun in his hand, pointed at Pebbles.

"Undress," he said with a stern voice.

"Uh…"

He pointed the gun toward the tub. "Undress and in you go."

Pebbles backed up a step and propped her thigh against the sink. "I'd rather not."

"Do it, or I'll do it for you."

She looked past him to the bedroom. She could see the door leading outside, but to reach it she would have to navigate around the beds or climb over them. Even if she managed to push past him, she wouldn't reach the door before he shot her again.

"Don't even think about it," he said, wagging the gun.

Pebbles tried another tack. She twisted the sink spigot and reached for a folded washcloth on the shelf between the mirror and sink. "I can clean up here."

With her head turned, Pebbles didn't see the snarl on his face, nor his boot-covered foot shoot forward. The blow struck her injured calf and down she went, her head knocking against the sink as she crumpled to the floor. While she writhed on the floor with her hands wrapped around her calf, she felt a hand tug down the waistband of her leggings. Pebbles cried out, "Stop! I'll do it myself!"

He let go and stood over her. Pebbles raised herself into a seated position, propping her back against the tub. Raising her knees up, she leaned her elbows against them and crossed her forearms. She bowed her head, took a deep breath and began to disrobe. After guiding her leggings the rest of the way off, she reached for the bottom hem of her blood-covered sweater. She froze for a second. Malinyah's medallion was gone! Darting a frantic look up at her captor, she said, "Where is it? Where's my necklace?"

"Keep going," he said, nudging her bare thigh with his foot.

After stepping into the shower, Pebbles kept her back turned to him as she lathered and rinsed her hair and body, but there was no way to prevent providing her smug captor with a peep show when she tended to her legs and feet. She tried to ignore his invading gaze while she appraised her injuries. The sight of the swollen, discolored holes in her calf made her nauseous, but she managed to hold down her fast-food dinner. She couldn't see the bruises on her back from his kicks, but her soapy fingers could feel the tenderness along her rib cage. The lump on the side of her head was prodigious, as was the cut bisecting it. The hot water stung everywhere Pebbles had an abrasion or cut, and while it also soothed her weary muscles, it did little to calm her mind. What had happened to Malinyah's necklace? Pebbles tried to recall the last time she was aware of its presence around her neck, but she drew a blank. Had it fallen off at Anlon's or had her captor taken it?

Pebbles was so lost in thought, she didn't notice her captor had turned the shower off until he nudged her arm with a bath towel. Pebbles wrapped it around her body, tucking a corner under her arm, and stepped out of the tub. Holding one hand against the wall for balance, she grabbed another towel from the rack above the toilet and limped out of the bathroom. After returning to the bed, she used the second towel to dry her hair and face, then her legs and feet. As she raised up, the towel around her torso came loose and landed around her waist. She quickly pulled it up, aware that he was standing by her side, peering down at her. Before she could re-anchor the towel, he reached down and snatched it off.

"What are you doing?" she spat, turning to shield her body from his view. "Give me the towel."

"Lie down so I can put a fresh bandage on your leg."

"Give me the towel."

"Lie down."

Pebbles reached for a bed pillow, clamped it between her arms and hunched forward. He grabbed her by the hair and shoved her face against the mattress. She tried to squirm free but he jabbed the muzzle of the gun against her bruised ribs.

"Be still!" he growled as he jabbed her a second time. She yelped and pulled away. He hopped on the bed and straddled her, pushing her face deeper into the mattress. "Be still, damn it!"

The command was delivered with a livid tone — the same harsh edge that spewed from him during the attack in Tahoe. Pebbles went limp. As much as she wanted to struggle, she didn't want to risk another full-scale beating. She held up her hands to signal her surrender. He jabbed her with the gun once more, then pulled her hands behind her back. After ordering her to stay put, he crawled off her and left the bed. Pebbles turned her head from the pillow and panted to regain her breath.

When he returned, he roughly retied her wrists. Afterward, he patted her calf and applied a fresh bandage. A moment later, he slid the blindfold into place and retied her legs at the ankles. There was a pause and then Pebbles felt his hand stroking her body. A flash of anger welled inside her. "Get your hands off me!"

She heard the arrogant bastard snort, seemingly amused by her outburst. His hand slid toward her pelvis. Pebbles rolled away to prevent his hand traveling further south. He grabbed her by the jaw and pried her mouth open. After stuffing the rag back in her mouth, he resumed exploring her curves, this time with both hands. Pebbles protested and squirmed, but restrained as she was, there was little she could do to prevent his invasive probing. His touches grew progressively intimate, despite Pebbles' angry grunts.

9

Narrow Escapes

Lake George, New York
September 27

B y the time the new helicopters arrived on scene, Aja was already halfway across the thin sliver of the lake between Coates Point and Black Point. She quietly surfaced from beneath the water and turned to look back at the roaring blaze she left behind. As she treaded in place, she scanned the lake in every direction. No searchlights were trained on the water, and she heard no motorboats in the area. Confident her underwater escape had gone undetected, Aja turned her gaze to the eastern shore. There were lights on in several of the houses dotting the Black Point peninsula, and she could see a gaggle of onlookers huddled in one yard, peering across the water at the bonfire. As far as she could tell, however, there were no police among them.

She took a deep breath and disappeared beneath the icy water. Turning her back to Black Point once again, she raised the bowl-shaped *Breylofte* to her lips and hummed against its underside. The sound waves emanating from the bowl pushed against the water and propelled her closer to Black Point. On the lake's surface, a barely perceptible wake marked her progress.

When she neared the rocky shore, Aja surfaced again and looked for a dark place to come on land. Numb from the frigid lake temperature, she nearly dropped the *Breylofte* as she tried to slide it into her backpack. With shaking hands, she held the backpack above the water and kicked her legs to swim the last stretch of open water.

An hour and two more dead bodies later, Aja motored down Route 22 in the stolen vehicle belonging to the murdered couple whose home Aja invaded after coming ashore. Her soaked back-pack sat on the floor of the passenger seat. On the seat itself was a *Tuliskaera* and *Naetir*, ready to be engaged at a moment's notice.

Aja shivered from head to toe. Despite a quick change into dry clothes she had purloined from the dead couple's home, her body temperature was still well below normal — a circumstance made worse by the night air pouring through the car's open windows. She briefly considered closing the windows but decided it was more immediately important to detect approaching helicopters or sirens than it was to be warm. She turned the car's heat up to its highest setting and activated the heated driver's seat. If that didn't help, she could use the two flannel blankets she had snatched from the home as well.

The farther she drove without signs of police pursuit, the more Aja relaxed. In so doing, her thoughts began to shift from escape and survival to planning her next steps. The first order of business was to find another car before she traveled much farther. She had to count on the discovery of the dead couple by sunrise, and that meant more police would be on her tail. Aja was still mystified how the Ticonderoga police found her at the Lake George rental home, but she guessed it had to do with the car she'd nicked from the ferry. There must have been a surveillance camera I didn't notice, Aja thought.

It was another sobering reminder of how fast the pace of technology continued to change in the modern world, a pace that Aja still struggled to cope with. For thousands of years, she had dominated her surroundings and the people within them. Armed with the Munuorian *Tyls* and her ability to take over new bodies, she had always been able to stay one step ahead of rivals and enemies. Although her name had changed many times over the millennia, the result had always been the same — she conquered and ruled.

But since reawakening after a thousand-year exile in stone, Aja discovered her ability to control people and her environment had diminished. *Gensae* was now rare among Terra's population — too rare. And the mindset of humans had drastically changed after the passing asteroid, Munirvo. This, Aja had seen even before her exile...

Before the asteroid reset the development of mankind, people had relied on the natural world around them. Pre-Munirvo, the planet had spun around on a balanced axis. This had produced milder seasonal changes and more arable land. As a result, plant-based food was more abundant, and animal and sea life thrived to an extent unimaginable today. This had meant less conflict among peoples. With bountiful resources, wars over territory or natural resources were virtually nonexistent. It was a tranquil world, one in which human senses were more in tune with the planet's rhythms, an age of harmony between nature and mankind that was then ravaged by a cyclical extraterrestrial flyby.

Yet, by the time Aja had been forced to store her mind on her *Sinethal*, the human race had regained much of its footing, even though they lived in a harsher world. The asteroid close encounter that flipped the planet upside down had left Earth with a wobbling tilt, and that tilt had produced more pronounced swings in climate. This had made it harder for survivors to find shelter, plant crops and hunt animals, leading to a world where competition for land and resources dominated the thoughts and actions of humans. War became common, and the concept of survival of the fittest rose to supremacy.

Humans learned one other important lesson from Munirvo, Aja had observed. They no longer believed in harmony with nature. Instead, they embraced conquer over nature. And, honestly, Aja couldn't blame them. Munirvo and its aftereffects had been so horrendous, no survivor could look upon Terra as the stable, nurturing environment it had once been. Instead, human existence for thousands of years after the asteroid's passing had morphed into a constant struggle to overcome the unforgiving world Terra had become. And humans had carried those memories with them from generation to generation, each new generation building upon the progress of those before them, with one goal in mind — to conquer the untamable planet.

By the time Aja had fled the invading Tikal army in an ill-fated attempt to escape across the Atlantic, war had become so endemic that nearly all societies had become warrior cultures. None more so than the fractious Mayans she had once ruled from her seat in Naranjo. In that age, brute force had been the primary method of acquiring resources and territory. Hence the reason, Aja, with the aid of her technologically advanced *Tyls*, had risen to power after taking the body of the young bride pledged to the prince of Naranjo. In that body, she had unleashed her weapons and ruthless temperament on the surrounding Mayan cities and became the mighty warrior princess, Wak Chanil Ajaw.

But during her long sleep, technology had leapt to the forefront as the dominant way to acquire resources and control populations. And since reawakening, Aja had seen her fellow humans make technological advancements with dizzying speed, a speed that had seemed to accelerate over the past one hundred years. In this new world, she had struggled to regain her former glory. Aja, in the early days of her rebirth, had quickly discovered that when she wielded her *Tyls*, people did not revere her as a goddess to be feared and worshiped. Instead, she had been treated as a pariah. A witch. A criminal. A freak. So, Aja had been forced to adapt, to use the *Tyls* more selectively and bide her time as she searched for a relic that would help her revolutionize the technology forged into a new generation of *Tyls*. It was a task that had twice been sabotaged by the treacherous Evelyn Warwick, and once before her by the naïve Malinyah.

As Aja drove onward, she glanced at the car's digital clock and smiled. Midnight had come, and that meant she was one step closer to her long-awaited dream. She had reacquired one of the three *Sinethal*s taken by Evelyn, and by the end of the new day she might be reunited with the remaining two, plus the relic that had eluded her for more than ten thousand years. Then, she would reawake Omereau, and the world would never be the same.

Ticonderoga, New York
September 28

Jennifer stood at the bathroom sink and stared at her reflection in the mirror. The person looking back was unrecognizable. The right side of the reflection's face was bruised and puffy, the eye swollen shut. Across her forehead, adhesive tape held a bandage atop a stitched gash. Wrapped around her neck was a padded brace. Another bandage covered abrasions on her chin.

She was afraid to lift the hospital gown to see the bruises underneath, and even if she wanted to, it would have been a painful exercise. Though her ribs were not broken, her chest felt as if it had been pounded mercilessly by a baseball bat. And, at the moment, she could not move her neck from side to side.

When the doctors authorized the move from ICU to the general hospital ward, they had told her she had avoided damage to her vertebrae, but her neck muscles were inflamed enough that they advocated restricting the mobility of her head. She also had a honking headache, a lingering effect of the concussion that had landed her in the ICU in the first place.

From outside the bathroom, Jennifer heard Nurse LeShana call to her. "Are you all right, sugar? Do you need any help?"

"I'm fine," mumbled Jennifer, her speech impaired by the painkiller dripping through the IV inserted in her hand and the muscle relaxant she had somehow managed to swallow. She slowly shuffled her feet to turn away from the sink. With one hand, she guided the wheeled rack holding the intravenous solutions toward the bathroom door, while she used the other hand to help balance her stilted steps. "Coming out now."

Nurse LeShana opened the door for Jennifer and helped her back into the hospital bed. She adjusted the incline of the bed so Jennifer was half sitting, half lying. The nurse propped pillows behind her back and neck and layered the bed's sheet and blanket over her legs. When all was set, she offered Jennifer water. While Jennifer sipped through a straw, LeShana asked, "Are you sure you're up for this? I can have the doctor tell them to come back later."

"No, I'm fine. Let them in," she said.

"Okay, sugar," LeShana said. "If you need me, just press the red button."

Jennifer thanked her and waited for LeShana to escort the police entourage into the room. As much as she rued the coming interrogation, she was desperate to know what had happened after crashing the BearCat. From the insistent police requests to "interview" Jennifer as soon as possible, she assumed Muran had escaped.

The door opened and LeShana ushered in Dan Nickerson, Captain Bennett and Detective Hall from the Vermont State Police, as well as New York troopers Jack Sterns and Superintendent Dunsmore. An Asian woman who was with them tersely introduced herself as FBI Special Agent Elizabeth Li.

Before LeShana left the room, she told the officers that Jennifer couldn't move her head much, so it was best if they stood at the foot of the bed instead of spreading out around the room. On her way out, she turned one last time to remind Jennifer to press the button if she needed anything.

When the door closed, Nickerson was the first to speak. "Hey, Jen. How are you feeling?"

Jennifer raised a hand and waggled it. "I feel like I look."

"Yeah, I imagine so," he said with a soft smile.

"Good to see you. Thanks for coming," she said.

"No problem. Wanted to make sure you were okay," Nickerson said.

Jennifer smiled at him and then turned to Jack and said, "Sorry about the truck."

"Nah, truck's okay. It'd take a lot more than a tree to knock it out of service. I'm just glad you made it out when you did."

"Please tell me Team Delta made it out, too," Jennifer said.

Jack lowered his head and sighed. "Unfortunately, Muran got them. She must have doubled back between our lines."

Agent Li interrupted the conversation. "I'm sorry. We don't have a lot of time to chitchat. We need some answers from you, and we need them fast. We have a dangerous fugitive on our hands."

"Understood," Jennifer said.

Agent Li forged ahead. "Major Sterns and Captain Bennett say you know the woman who robbed the bank by the name Muran, but they say you were evasive when they asked for details about her.

We need you to be totally candid about everything you know about her. Right now."

Captain Bennett, adopting a less antagonistic approach, said, "Jennifer, she killed twelve officers and two civilians last night. Not to mention torching an entire neighborhood. That's on top of Carla Bailey's murder, the officers she killed during the fiasco in Middlebury and possibly Anabel Simpson. We need full disclosure from you."

"I understand, Captain. I want her caught, too," Jennifer said.

"How well did you know her?" Agent Li asked.

"I don't know her. Never met her, never seen her until the video yesterday."

"Then how did you know the person on the video was Muran?" Li asked.

"The weapon she used, the *Dreylaeks.*"

"Ah, yes. The little cookie stones," Li said, with a mocking tone. She held up an evidence bag with the Stones taken from Jennifer's jeans pockets. "I saw your demonstration in Ticonderoga. Impressive little weapon. Compact, portable, lethal. Did you get them from her? From Muran?"

Jennifer frowned. "No."

"Where did you get them?"

"Excuse me?"

"You heard me. Where did you get your 'dray-locks'?"

"Um, Nicaragua. At an archaeological dig site."

"Indio Maiz, right? The place you shot an unarmed man?" Li asked.

The unexpected mention of Christian Hunte's shooting stunned Jennifer, as did the tone of Agent Li's question. She looked to Nickerson, who shrugged his shoulders as if to say, "She didn't hear about it from me."

"I'm not sure what you're getting at," Jennifer said to Li.

"Did Muran show you how to use them?"

"Look, I told you. I've never met her."

"Then who showed you how to use them?"

"One of the people at the dig," Jennifer said.

"Name?"

"Jacques Foucault," Jennifer said.

"Address?"

"He lives in France, don't know his address," Jennifer said.

"I have it, I'll get it to you," Nickerson said. Jennifer stared at him with a puzzled look, but then remembered she had asked Nickerson to run database queries on Foucault and Hunte after the Indio Maiz shooting.

"Did this Foucault know Muran? Is that who you first heard the name from?"

Jennifer recalled the first time she heard Muran's name. Pebbles had screamed it during a turbulent session with Malinyah's *Sinethal*. But the next time she heard the name, it indeed came from the lips of Jacques Foucault at Indio Maiz. She was not about to drag Pebbles into the situation, but she saw no reason to protect Foucault. "Yes, the first time I heard the name Muran was from Foucault. I don't think he knows her personally, but I can't say for sure."

The assembled officers exchanged a fresh round of silent looks. Li asked Nickerson, "Did you get a photo of Foucault in your search?"

"Yes, I have an image of his passport," Nickerson said. "But you can pull him up on your phone right now. He's a somewhat public figure. I found lots of pictures of him on the Internet during my search."

Li slid her phone from her jacket pocket. Opening the device's web browser, she typed in Foucault's name. Jennifer could see her flicking her thumb to scroll through multiple screens. She handed the phone to Dunsmore. "I don't think that's him. Too old."

Dunsmore agreed and passed the phone to Bennett. With Detective Hall looking over his shoulder, the two officers examined the pictures and handed the phone back to Li. Bennett said, "Definitely not our guy."

The confused look on Jennifer's face was met by a clarifying comment by Li. "Our perp didn't act alone. She had help."

"What?" Jennifer asked.

Li's phone began to buzz. After glancing down at the screen, she looked to Dunsmore and said, "Superintendent, can you fill her in? I need to take this call."

"Of course," Dunsmore said. He waited until the door closed behind Li and then said to Jennifer, "We found Carla Bailey's body at the fort. She was laid out on the parapet facing the lake. According to Detective Hall, she was posed in a similar manner as the Simpson woman. The body was obviously brought to the fort after it closed for the day, but its placement looked purposely staged, so we considered the possibility the suspect had previously visited the fort to pick the staging spot. So, we had detectives review footage from the park's security cams for a period covering the past several days. And we came up big."

Two days before the robbery, Dunsmore explained, video of a woman fitting Debbie Bailey's description of Muran was captured by a security camera in the museum café. Further analysis of footage around the fort taken the same day showed the woman bundled under disguising clothes in the fort's courtyard, and on two separate occasions she lingered at the very spot where Carla's body was found.

Before Dunsmore could say it, Jennifer guessed his next comment. "There was someone with her. A man."

"Correct. A man met her in the courtyard and they went to the café together," Dunsmore said, just as Agent Li returned to the room. Having overheard Dunsmore's comment, Li reached into her briefcase and withdrew an eight-by-ten blowup of the café security cam image. She walked around the bed until she stood by Jennifer. She held the photograph in front of Jennifer's face and asked, "Recognize him?"

A butterfly wing would have knocked Jennifer over. As she stared at the pompous man's smile, her face turned scarlet. "I'll be damned! Chuck f—ing Goodwin."

As soon as Jennifer identified Charles Goodwin as the man in the photo, all the officers scurried out of the room, phones in hand. The Chuck-hunt was on. As she examined the photo some more, Jennifer wondered aloud, "What have you got yourself mixed up in, Chuck? Accessory to murder, grand theft, kidnapping. Damn, your ass is grass."

She recalled sitting in the stuck-up curator's office. Well, it was less of an office and more of a shrine to Goodwin's brilliance and celebrity, as Jennifer remembered it. She had arranged the meeting in the hopes of discovering where Devlin Wilson had acquired Malinyah's *Sinethal* and the two unusual statuettes in his collection. At first, Goodwin had treated her like a peon, a messenger unworthy of his time. She had quickly dispelled his perception, causing only a small shift in his dismissive demeanor. It wasn't until she had threatened to leave without handing over Anlon's donation that Goodwin's level of cooperation improved. But even then, he had still seemed aloof and, in spots, combative. This latter attitude had ultimately fizzled when Jennifer threatened to involve the police.

As she replayed the conversation in her mind, she began to reconsider the shifts in his behavior over the course of the meeting. He never really shed his holier-than-thou disdain for her as they parried back and forth, but Jennifer now wondered if her interpretations of his combativeness and indifference had been faulty.

She remembered Goodwin initially wouldn't look at the photograph of Malinyah's *Sinethal* when Jennifer had tried to show him. When she badgered him into taking a quick glance, he'd just as quickly denied any knowledge of it. His instantaneous reaction had seemed odd and she had pressed him about it. With great irritation, Goodwin had emphatically stated that his museum had not sold the *Sinethal* to Devlin. When she probed him again about whether he'd ever seen it before, his answer had been patently evasive. The conclusion she had reached at the time: Goodwin was lying. He had seen the Stone or was at least aware of its existence.

It would have been a simple matter for him to examine the photograph with some depth and then say, "I've seen similar pieces, but I don't think I've ever run across this one." But he had treated the photograph like radioactive waste. He didn't want to touch it, look at it or talk about it. There definitely had been a panicked quality in his denials, a "move along, nothing to see here" kind of vibe, Jennifer thought. She had interpreted his reactions as a tacit admission that he had seen the Stone before but had been unwilling to tell her where or when he had.

Now, however, she considered his reactions in a different light. If Goodwin was connected with Muran, as the Ticonderoga video capture implied, maybe he reacted to Jennifer's questions for the opposite reason — not because he had seen it before but because he had been looking for it on Muran's behalf.

Yet, Jennifer had told Goodwin that Anlon had the *Sinethal* and that it was a piece from Devlin's collection. Presuming Goodwin passed those tidbits to Muran, why had Muran gone after Anabel instead of Anlon? And how had that ultimately led her to the Middlebury bank and the safe-deposit boxes registered to someone else? Also unexplained was the surveillance video of Muran removing another *Sinethal* from the safe-deposit box and her angry reaction to a missing piece, or pieces.

There was another aspect of Goodwin's behavior that Jennifer now believed she had misinterpreted. He had fought her hard when she requested the catalog records pertaining to three Munuorian *Aromaeghs* in the museum's archives. He had only relented when she threatened to tip the police of her suspicions that there might be something connected to Devlin's death hidden in the records. She had made the threat betting on Goodwin's desire to protect the museum from potential scandal. Anyone who looked at the framed pictures on the "wall of fame" in Goodwin's office would have concluded the man was image conscious beyond the norm. Her bet had paid off and Goodwin had provided the records.

Later, when Jennifer had been in Villahermosa to visit the curator of the La Venta museum, she had learned Devlin's "fishman" statuette was a replica of larger statues originally discovered on the Nicaraguan island of Zapatera. The name of the island had triggered Jennifer's memory; Goodwin's catalog records had shown two of the museum's *Aromaeghs* had been discovered on Zapatera. Jennifer had put two and two together and concluded that Goodwin's reluctance to share the records was likely an attempt to hide the connection between the *Aromaeghs* and the picture of the statuette she had shown him, for he had denied knowledge of the statuette, too.

But, now, Jennifer wondered if there had been something else in the records. Something pointing toward Muran. Something Goodwin hadn't wanted the police to sniff out. She made a mental note to call Pebbles to ask her to pull the records from Anlon's office and email them to her. She laid down the photo of Goodwin and Muran and said, "My phone!"

Jennifer pressed the call button to summon the nurse. She waited a few minutes for LeShana to appear, but the nurse did not. Reluctantly, Jennifer pulled back the sheets and maneuvered out of bed. With her IV cart in tow, she shuffled to the room door and pulled it open. The hallway outside the room was vacant, but Jennifer could see the sprawling nurse's station down the corridor. It seemed too far a distance to shout, and she was not thrilled with the idea of trying to walk to the station, as she didn't feel particularly stable on her feet. Plus, she was self-conscious of her battered face, not to mention the loosely tied opening in the back of her flimsy hospital gown. She hovered in the doorway, hoping to catch the attention of a nurse or doctor exiting one of the rooms, when she saw Nickerson turn into the hallway. He didn't see her at first, so Jennifer stepped out into the corridor and called to him.

Nickerson looked up and immediately quickened his pace in Jennifer's direction. As he approached, he said, "Are you all right? Do you need something?"

"My bag. I left my bag somewhere at the command post last night. My phone's in it. I wanted to call Anlon and Pebbles. Let them know what happened."

Nickerson hesitated and looked back toward the nurse's station. He wavered in place for a few seconds, then turned to Jennifer and motioned her to turn around. "Um, okay. I'll go ask Tim Hall about it in a sec. Let's get you back in bed first."

Jennifer agreed to return to the room but asked Nickerson to precede her, explaining, "Not much covering my caboose."

As he assisted her into bed, Nickerson seemed awkward, averting his eyes away from her. At first, Jennifer thought he was making a demonstrative effort to avoid catching a glimpse of her bare backside, but his manner didn't change once she was safely under the bed's coverings. He stood with his hands in his pockets, looking at his shoes, deep in thought.

"You're acting weird," Jennifer said. "Why won't you look at me?"

"Huh?" he said, finally raising his eyes to meet hers.

"Something's the matter, isn't it?" Jennifer asked. "Did they lose my bag?"

"No," he said. "I'm pretty sure Hall has it."

"Then, what?"

"Um, I'm not sure it's my place to tell you, Jen. I think Captain Bennett said he would talk to you about it."

"I'm in trouble, aren't I?"

He shook his head. "No, I don't think so, not now. When I first got here, Agent Li was ready to throw the book at you, but when you identified Goodwin, she simmered down."

"Then, what's going on, Dan? The look on your face is starting to scare me."

Nickerson sighed and approached the bed. He sat down on the edge and reached for Jennifer's hand. Peering into her eyes, he softly said, "It's about Pebbles."

10

The Longest Flight

Reno, Nevada
September 28

T he six-hour flight had been excruciating. Trapped in the Gulfstream as it zoomed across the country, Anlon had spent the
entirety of the red-eye journey in a whirlwind of phone calls
and texts.

Early in the flight, he'd used the chartered plane's satellite phone
to speak with Carl Emerson, the Nevada State Police detective leading the investigation into Pebbles' disappearance. Emerson had
pummeled him with question after question about Pebbles, the
state of their relationship, their neighbors, Anlon's business dealings
and potential enemies. Antonio had evidently told them about the
Lifintyls, because Emerson also posed questions about their value,
where they were kept, who knew about them and the like.

This latter part of the conversation had led Anlon to tell Emerson about his murdered uncle and the cast of villains who'd been
involved in multiple attempts to steal the Stones, including Margaret Corchran, her brother Kyle, Klaus Navarro, Thatcher Reynolds and even Jacques Foucault. He told Emerson he thought one
of them, directly or indirectly, was behind the home invasion. The
detective had thanked him for the information, then ended their
call with a request to meet Anlon as soon as he landed.

For all his candor answering the detective's questions, Anlon
had received precious little information from Emerson, other
than receiving confirmation that Pebbles had been shot during
the home invasion. This frustrating imbalance in cooperation

had been somewhat mitigated after Anlon learned the chartered plane had a Wi-Fi connection. Once online, he had immediately texted Antonio, who was at the house with the police. In one of their exchanges, Antonio shared a piece of hopeful news. He had overheard the medical examiner speaking with Emerson, and the M.E. didn't think Pebbles' injury was life threatening.

Then had come a text from Dan Nickerson, informing Anlon of Jennifer's accident. Until that moment, Anlon had been very angry with Jennifer. He had tried to reach her on the restaurant's landline immediately after taking Antonio's emergency call, but she hadn't answered. Once he had left the restaurant and his cell phone reception returned, he had tried to call her again. But while he waited for the call to connect, his phone had buzzed with a flurry of message notifications. He ditched the call and quickly scanned the notifications for any calls or messages from Pebbles. Seeing none, he had ignored the others and hailed a taxi.

It wasn't until Anlon was in the taxi, speeding toward the Westchester County Airport to catch the hastily arranged charter, that he finally had read Jennifer's text messages imploring him to find a television, telling him Muran had surfaced. Upon reading the last of her texts, Anlon had messaged her back to call him immediately. While he awaited her reply, he asked the driver to tune the taxi's radio to a news station. That's where Anlon first learned the details of the Middlebury bank robbery and the stand-off near Ticonderoga. After boarding the plane, he had called Jennifer once more. Frustrated at his inability to reach her, Anlon had ripped off a terse text telling her to get her ass on a plane to Reno as soon as she got the message.

The moment he read Nickerson's text about Jennifer's accident, Anlon had used the satellite phone to call him. That's when Anlon learned Nickerson was at the hospital awaiting an update on her condition. "Jennifer is going to be okay," Nickerson had said, "but she's sustained a concussion and is in intensive care for observation. They're keeping her overnight." The conversation had continued for several more minutes, but Anlon remembered little of it. He knew he had told Nickerson about Pebbles, but his mind had been filled with such turmoil that the rest of the conversation was beyond recall.

In between the calls and texts, Anlon had used his phone's Internet browser to cycle through a slew of articles and video clips of Muran's exploits in New England. The charter's flight attendant noticed Anlon's overall air of distress and stopped by twice to ask if he wanted a stiff drink. Anlon declined, the second time a bit gruffly, and the attendant had retreated for the remainder of the flight.

Toward the end of the flight, Anlon had called Jacques Foucault. When Anlon asked him if he was aware of the happenings in Middlebury and Ticonderoga, Foucault had said he had been following the news reports for several hours. Anlon then told him about Pebbles and Jennifer. Foucault expressed his dismay. Though spoken with sincerity, the show of sympathy hadn't been convincing to Anlon, especially given the two questions Foucault had asked right after offering his condolences. The bugger had wanted to know if Malinyah was safe! And then he had asked about the damn necklace! Anlon had managed to control his temper because he needed Foucault's assistance. After answering Foucault's questions, Anlon had asked Foucault to shift the location of their previously planned meeting from New York to Reno and implored the Frenchman to get underway as soon as possible. Foucault had swiftly agreed, indicating he was of the same mind.

Shortly after the call ended, Anlon dozed off until the Gulfstream's wheels hit the runway and jolted him awake. Immediately, the pilot came on the intercom to offer his apology for the rough landing. Once the G500 had taxied to the terminal, the pilot opened the cockpit door and apologized to Anlon again.

"Don't worry about it," Anlon said, shaking the pilot's hand. "I owe you big time."

"Just doing my job," the pilot said.

"Seriously, thank you for treating my emergency like it was your own. Both of you," Anlon said, turning to also thank the bleary-eyed flight attendant.

"You're welcome," said the young woman. "I hope everything works out."

"God, I hope so, too," Anlon said, crossing his fingers as he deplaned.

Antonio was the first to greet Anlon when he reached the tarmac. After exchanging a brief hug, Antonio said, "I'm so sorry, buddy. If I'd only gotten there sooner, none of this would have happened."

Anlon brushed off the suggestion. "Don't be ridiculous, you couldn't have known."

"Well, I still feel badly. I just hope she's all right," Antonio said, lowering his head.

"Me, too," Anlon said. Looking past Antonio, Anlon spotted a police SUV fifty yards away. Next to the vehicle stood a man in a brown suit. His tie hung loose beneath an open collar. As the man stifled a yawn, Anlon asked Antonio, "That Emerson?"

Antonio turned to follow Anlon's gaze. "Yep, that's him. He's anxious to talk with you."

"Then let's get to it," Anlon said. As the two men walked toward Emerson, Anlon patted Antonio's shoulder. "Thanks for sticking around, Skipper. Appreciate it."

"Of course. No way I'm cutting out till she's back safe and sound," Antonio said.

Detective Emerson stepped forward and Antonio introduced him to Anlon. Moments later the three men hopped in the waiting SUV. Emerson sat in front with the driver. Anlon and Antonio were in back. Before the vehicle had traveled a hundred feet, Anlon asked Emerson, "Any news? Have you found her?"

"No, not yet," Emerson said. "We've got lots of people working it, but so far we don't have much to go on. We've set up a tip line. The media is helping get the word out. Hopefully, we'll get some credible leads."

"I assume you've talked with my neighbors," Anlon said.

"Those we could track down, yes. But we're still trying to get in touch with a couple of them," Emerson said.

"I can't believe no one heard a gunshot," Anlon said.

The detective agreed, then handed Anlon a photograph of Pebbles taken from the house. "Dr. Wallace helped us choose a picture of Miss McCarver to circulate internally. It's the same one we've passed to the media. Is this the best one you have?"

Anlon stared at the head shot. In it, Pebbles smiled broadly for the camera. Her hair, styled in a bob cut and colored royal blue, whipped in the wind. She wore a nose ring through one nostril, and several smaller rings lined the opposing eyebrow. Her head was turned slightly, making the hummingbird tattoo on her neck plainly visible. A beach towel was wrapped around her bare shoulders. On one of them, another of her six tattoos could be seen — the Japanese symbol for strength.

The picture had been taken on Anlon's boat on a beautiful summer afternoon. Pebbles and Jennifer had just finished a water-skiing contest in which Pebbles emerged victorious. Anlon, still recuperating from the injuries he had sustained at Stillwater Quarry, had snapped the pic while the two women exchanged good-natured barbs as Jennifer captained the boat back to his dock in Crystal Bay. The memory brought a brief smile to his face. Handing the picture back to Emerson, he said, "Her hair is shorter now, and the last time I saw her, it was purple. But, otherwise, it's a good picture of her. I'm sure I have more recent ones on my phone, but I'm not sure they show her neck tattoo as good as this one does."

"If you've got something more recent, we'll take it, with or without the tattoo," Emerson said.

"I'll look in a sec, but first, I'd like some answers," Anlon said, tired of the continued one-sided flow of information. "Tell me what happened, what you think happened."

"All right, I can give you a quick rundown," Emerson said. "We think a male intruder entered your house through the patio door into the kitchen. It looks to us like Miss McCarver came upon him in the hallway between the kitchen and living room. There was a confrontation and he shot Miss McCarver as she tried to run away, at least that's what the evidence suggests. After the shooting, the intruder searched the house, and, at some point, treated her leg wound before they left the house."

"Leg? How do you know where she was shot?" Anlon asked.

"There were women's shoes, socks and a piece of spandex in the hallway," Emerson said. He paused, then added, "Without getting too graphic, they had blood on them, and the spandex had pretty obvious bullet holes in it, one where the bullet entered, the other where it came out. We also found two slugs in the wall by the front door, about a foot off the ground."

"She was shot twice?" Anlon asked.

"No, we don't think so. One of the slugs was completely clean," Emerson said.

Anlon cringed. He knew the detective was trying his best to avoid getting into gory details, but it was impossible to shut off the mental image of Pebbles lying in the hallway in pain, blood pouring from the gunshot wound.

"I know it doesn't offer much comfort," Emerson said, "but the evidence suggests the bullet that hit Miss McCarver passed through soft tissue and exited in one piece. It means the shooter didn't use hollow-point ammo. If he had, the bullet would have fragmented on contact and caused a lot more trauma."

"You're right, it's not comforting," Anlon said in a sarcastic tone.

The detective nodded and turned to look out the window. For the next several minutes, no one spoke. Anlon felt woozy from stress and lack of sleep, a condition that wasn't helped by the road's winding twists as the car climbed Mount Rose Highway. His mind replayed the scene that Emerson described: Pebbles walking through the house, coming upon a stranger, turning to run, and then, bam. Anlon buried his head between his hands. "Christ, I don't believe this is happening. It's insane!"

During the detective's recap, Antonio had been silent, but Anlon's anguish led him to offer encouragement. "Hang in there, buddy. We'll get her back."

"F—ing Stones!" Anlon said. "God damn it! I wish I'd never heard of the effing things."

Ludlow, California

As dawn broke over the desert horizon, Charles Goodwin sat in the car outside the motel room. For the better part of an hour, he'd been listening to the radio and surfing the Internet on his tablet. From the on-air and online reports, he was pleased to discover limited mention of his prisoner's disappearance, but he realized it was only a matter of time before news spread and an intensive manhunt commenced. That made it imperative to speak with Aja as soon as possible, for if they didn't connect soon, he would have no choice but to kill the girl and dump her body in the desert. Aja would not like it, but Goodwin reasoned there were other ways to gain Cully's cooperation, and Aja had no intention of letting her live anyway.

He was tempted to break from the plan and call Aja, but he knew it was not advisable under the circumstances. She'll call once she links up with Kora, he thought. He also considered calling Kora directly, but refrained. She was diligent enough to reach out if there was a problem on her end. It was better to stick with the plan, for now.

"Who am I kidding?" he mumbled. The plan was already in shambles. Its success had hinged on speed, stealth and synchronization, and they'd failed on all counts. Aja's catastrophic attempt to recover her "lost" relics from the bank had been enough to ruin the plan on its own, but she had made matters far worse at Ticonderoga. He could only hope the news reports were right and that Aja had eluded capture.

If she had escaped with the "square, black stone" taken from the bank, as the news reports speculated, then part of their plan was still possible — the part that mattered most to Goodwin. On the other hand, thought Goodwin, the part dearest to Aja was in greater jeopardy, despite his success in nabbing the girl and the *lyktyl*.

He wondered whether his prisoner, Little Miss Tattoos, realized how foolish it had been to wear the medallion in the photograph accompanying the announcement of Cully's Indio Maiz discovery. And how asinine it was for her to share the name of the foundation Cully established to manage the preservation of the site and artifacts. When Aja had seen the photograph and Alynioria's name, she had become enraged.

Aja had viewed both as taunts from Cully and the girl. Their slights led Aja to squash Goodwin's gentle coaxing of Evelyn Warwick and pursue a more aggressive strategy to recover her lost items. He had tried to dissuade Aja from the slash-and-burn solution she formulated, rightly pointing out the inherent risks in forcing matters to a head — risks that were now unpleasant realities.

Yet, as Goodwin scanned the motel parking lot, he knew it was his own fault. He shouldn't have contacted Kora so quickly after Cully's minion visited him at the museum. He should have taken the time to learn more about Devlin Wilson's murder before alerting Kora. Instead, he told her of the visit from Jennifer Stevens, and, in turn, Kora had told Aja.

Goodwin angled the rearview mirror to spy the diner across the parking lot and then nudged it to check out the gas station/minimart beside the diner. He observed no signs of anything out of the ordinary and returned to ponder the chain of events that had led Aja to throw caution to the wind.

It all began with the persistence of Devlin Wilson, Goodwin mused. Everyone in the archaeology community had known about Devlin's "wacky" pursuit of the elusive "fish-men." Even Aja had been amused by his determination to find proof of the mythical men who *came up out of the sea* to help survivors of the biblical great flood.

Her tune had changed, however, when she learned Devlin had put out feelers searching for *Aromaeghs*, *Breyloftes* and later a *Naetir*. Although Devlin hadn't referred to the *Tyls* by their given Munuorian names, the fact he'd zeroed in on them as part of his investigations had caused Aja to view Devlin as a potential problem. Goodwin still remembered her biting comment after he told her of Devlin's inquiries: "Not *another* worm. Isn't one enough?"

It had been a reference to Jacques Foucault, the French archaeologist who had become an ardent bidder for the rarest of *Tyls* and a frequent visitor to dig sites where new *Tyls* had been unearthed. Goodwin had tried on many occasions to dispel Aja's fears about Foucault. "He also buys meteorites, my Queen. He shouldn't be taken seriously."

"You should not dismiss him so lightly. He may be using the meteorites to build his *gensae*. What if Evelyn has already sold him my *Tyls*? He may *know*!" Aja had fretted.

"If she did…if he knew, my Queen, why would he still be hunting for *Tyls*?" Goodwin had countered.

Aja had conceded Goodwin's point but had remained skeptical of Foucault, worrying that he might eventually cross paths with Evelyn. Aja had even talked of killing him, but Goodwin had convinced her that it was better to let Foucault nose around. "He might lead us to her."

Goodwin laughed as he checked the tablet for messages. He found it ironic that Aja had worried so much about Foucault and Evelyn stumbling across each other, only to discover later that Devlin had been the one who connected with the handmaiden — and Evelyn had fueled his wild theories and investigations, ultimately bestowing some of Aja's relics upon him.

Thinking back, Goodwin recalled how stunned he was when Stevens showed him the pictures of Malinyah's *Sinethal* and the statuette of Aja wearing her *Taellin*. Goodwin had heard of Devlin's murder, of course, but the news stories about his death hadn't roused Goodwin's or Aja's suspicions. The articles had depicted a murder driven by the greed of his research partner, Matthew Dobson, and several coconspirators. Among the coconspirators, only Klaus Navarro's name had been familiar to Goodwin, and although Navarro was a collector of some repute, his interests were limited to Mesoamerican art, or so Goodwin had thought at the time.

But, the visit from Stevens had changed everything. At first, Goodwin had been confused by her statement that Cully didn't know where Devlin acquired either the *Sinethal* or the statuette. But the fact that Devlin had the pieces meant Evelyn had parted with them. It wasn't until Goodwin had done more research into Devlin's death that he made the discovery that led him to Evelyn's, a.k.a. Anabel Simpson's, doorstep.

The discovery had been an article about Anabel's kidnapping. Goodwin had read it months before but had not paid attention to a thumbnail-sized picture of Anabel included with the story. He supposed he had glossed over it given the poor quality of the photograph and the fact that Evelyn had aged significantly compared to the photos of her shared by Aja. But when he read the article again, looking closely for clues of Evelyn's involvement, he had examined the photo with greater scrutiny and concluded it might be Evelyn.

Aja had been bloodthirsty when Goodwin shared his suspicions. "I will rip her heart out!"

"My Queen, revenge is meaningless unless we recover the *Tyls*. Let me try to get them back first. Then you can have your revenge," Goodwin had said. Aja had reluctantly agreed.

He remembered how courteous Evelyn had been when he showed up at her home. When Goodwin told her why he had come to pay a visit, however, her polite manner had vanished. She had denied his assertions in no uncertain terms and demanded that he leave. But the look on her face when he said the name Evelyn Warwick betrayed her indignation. As he stood to depart, Goodwin had given her his business card and said, "Look, I came as an emissary. Return what you took and no harm will come to you. Otherwise, she knows where you live now, and she *will* come for you."

He had given her a week to think on it, and then visited again. By then Evelyn had dropped all pretenses and told him she had destroyed the *Tyls*, so there was nothing left to hand over. When he informed her that he knew she had given at least two of the pieces to Devlin, and that Aja was aware the pieces were now with Cully, Evelyn had told him to leave Cully alone, saying, "He doesn't have what she wants."

"Then give it to me," Goodwin had advised. "You know she can't do anything with it, anyway. Not until she finds the *lyktyl*. In all likelihood, it'll never turn up."

But then the Indio Maiz article had been published, and once Aja saw the *lyktyl* dangling from his prisoner's tattooed neck, it was the beginning of the end, leaving Goodwin at the edge of the Mojave Desert, with the girl, the *lyktyl* and a busted plan.

Goodwin turned off the radio with a sigh and stepped out of the car. Yawning, he checked his watch and contemplated next steps. As there was nothing else he could do but wait for Aja's call, he decided to grab a few hours of sleep. If he still hadn't heard from Aja by noon, he would drown the girl in the bathtub and make his way back east. With that revised plan decided, he unlocked the room door and tiptoed inside, placing the privacy placard on the outer doorknob before closing the door. Inside, the room was still relatively dark. He could see the girl was still asleep, huddled under the blanket he had draped over her. He collapsed on the room's other bed and drifted off to sleep.

Incline Village, Nevada

When the SUV neared Anlon's home, he could see the entrance to his driveway was cordoned off with yellow tape and blocked by a police cruiser. Next to the cruiser stood an officer, who directed the

SUV's driver to pull off the narrow, two-lane road and park on the shoulder behind another cruiser and Antonio's rental car.

As they readied to exit the SUV, Emerson turned to Anlon. "Look, there's no way to sugarcoat it: the crime scene is going to upset you. I wish I didn't have to ask you to go inside right now, but I need you to go through every room in the house with me. Something might stick out to you that didn't to us. Something missing, something out of place. Anything out of the ordinary."

"I understand. I'll do whatever I can to help," Anlon said, sickened by Emerson's description of his home as a crime scene.

Together, Antonio, Anlon and Emerson walked along the macadam path separating the property lines of lakefront homes from the road. When they reached Anlon's driveway, Emerson turned to Antonio. "Dr. Wallace, I'd like you to stay here until Dr. Cully and I finish going through the house. Shouldn't be too long."

"Sure, no problem," Antonio said. Resting a hand on Anlon's shoulder, he said, "I'll be here as long as you need me."

"Thanks, Skipper," Anlon said with a shaky voice.

After Emerson instructed Anlon to avoid touching anything inside the house, he raised the tape for him to pass. In the driveway, they stopped by an evidence cone which marked the end of the blood trail leading from the house. Emerson pointed at the drops and said, "We think our suspect carried Miss McCarver from the house and put her in a vehicle at this spot."

"I thought you said he treated her wound," Anlon said, scanning the line of droplets on the front steps.

"He did. You'll see what I mean when we go inside."

They were met at the bottom step by a crime scene technician who handed the two men disposable jumpsuits, gloves and shoe covers. After layering on the protective garb, and before they climbed the steps, Emerson said, "The front hallway and living room are the worst of it. Unfortunately, they'll be the first things you see."

The strained look on Emerson's face made Anlon queasy. He took a deep breath and said, "Let's get it over with."

On the way up the steps, they passed a few more of the mini fluorescent cones. With Emerson leading the way, they walked through the open front door. Anlon froze. As much warning as the detective provided, Anlon was not prepared for what he saw. Blood was everywhere. It was smeared on the floor, splattered on the walls and streaked on the furniture. There was a crisscross of bloody footprints to and from the kitchen and others that crossed the hall and led to the front staircase. Blood-covered towels were strewn about the floor. Among them, Anlon spotted Pebbles' shoes and socks, their surfaces coated a rusty color. On the hallway table next to a small stack of packages was an uncapped bottle of rubbing alcohol. There were a few packages on the floor, two closer to the living room and the other near the kitchen doorway. Scattered among them were half a dozen envelopes. By each piece of evidence was a numbered cone. Anlon turned away. Inside, he felt the urge to barf.

Emerson drew Anlon's attention away from the grisly scene to look at the wall where the slugs had been found. Higher on the wall was the alarm keypad. "The bullets lodged here and here. We think Miss McCarver was either trying to get to the front door or to the alarm keypad."

Anlon looked at the keypad, then back at the packages. "What time did this happen, you think?"

"Best we can narrow it, somewhere between 11 a.m. and 4 p.m. yesterday," Emerson said, following Anlon's eyes to the packages. "Two of the packages on the floor were delivered yesterday morning, right around eleven, according to the UPS deliveryman."

"Reggie?"

"That's him. He said he spoke to Miss McCarver. Said she was upstairs, talked to him through an open window above the front door. She asked him to leave the packages on the front step, said she would get them later," Emerson said.

"That was at eleven?"

"Yes, eight after eleven to be precise. Why?"

"Just trying to make sense of the boxes," Anlon said, crouching down to examine the book-sized package near the kitchen entrance. An edge of the cardboard mailer was dented, and unlike the other two boxes on the floor, it was free of any bloodstains. "Pebbles is a bit of a late riser, so it doesn't surprise me that she was upstairs when Reggie came by. I doubt she would have come down right away to get them off the step, but she obviously brought them inside at some point."

"Would she have put them on the table like the others?" Emerson asked.

"Hmmm…maybe. Sometimes she'll leave them on the kitchen counter or in my office," Anlon said, rising to scan the living room. "Do you think it's possible the intruder was already in the house when the packages were delivered?"

"Your guy Reggie said there were no other cars in the driveway when he dropped off the packages, and he said Miss McCarver seemed her normal, friendly self. But it's possible. We found damp towels in the master bathroom. He might have entered the house while she was showering and waited for her to come downstairs," Emerson said.

Pointing down at the book package, Anlon asked, "What do you make of the dent?"

"Looks like she threw it at him," Emerson said. "We asked Reggie if either of the packages was damaged when he delivered them. He said no. So, the dent happened after the fact."

"Right, like she threw it at him," Anlon said, imagining the confrontation. "She brings in the packages, notices the intruder, throws this one at him, drops one of the others and runs for the door."

"That's how we see it. If all the boxes on the floor had been on the table with the other mail, and she grabbed one to throw, it's hard to believe just two of the other boxes and a few pieces of mail would have fallen off. It's a small table. Most of the other mail would have been knocked off. But the majority of it's stacked as if nothing ever happened. So, unless the intruder neatened up the stack afterward, the most logical explanation seems to be she had the boxes that were delivered yesterday in her hands when she encountered him. At some point later, the other pieces on the floor were knocked off," Emerson said.

Anlon joined Emerson by the table and leaned over to study the packages more closely. The bottom one he identified from the shoe company logo on the side of the box. It contained a new pair of hiking boots Anlon had ordered after returning from Nicaragua. The middle one was harder to size up, as he couldn't see the shipping label without moving the top box. It had the word "Fragile" stamped on each side that Anlon could see, and it looked big enough to contain a basketball. The top package was the size and shape of a child's lunch box, and the sender's name on the shipping label was from the San Diego Zoo. Anlon recalled he'd ordered Pebbles a small, stuffed howler monkey from the zoo's website — a joke gift that didn't feel that funny now.

"We thought maybe the intruder had gone through the mail and then stacked it all back up after he searched the house, but given how much of a mess he left everywhere else, it doesn't seem likely," Emerson said. "Come on, let's start upstairs and work our way down."

The first place Anlon searched was the gun safe in his bedroom's walk-in closet. Tall and black, the four-hundred-pound safe was anchored to the floor with heavy-duty bolts in the closet's back corner. It featured dual locks and was large enough to hold an array of rifles, but there was only one firearm stored inside, Pebbles' Glock.

The safe door was ajar when they entered the closet, and Emerson gently nudged it further open with a pen he removed from his shirt pocket. "We found it like this. It doesn't appear forced, so we assume Miss McCarver either had the safe open when the intruder came in, she opened it for him, or she gave him the combination… assuming she knows the combination."

As Anlon looked among the safe's contents, he said, "She knows it, but I've never known her to leave it open."

The Glock rested on the highest of five shelves inside the safe, along with two spare clips and a few boxes of ammunition. Ironically, they were hollow points. The next shelf down held miscellaneous valuables, including Anlon's passport, some jewelry belonging to Pebbles and a stack of emergency cash, among other items. The third shelf was devoted to a small sampling of *Lifintyls*, including two *Breyloftes*, two pair of *Dreylaeks* and a *Terusael*. The bottom two shelves were empty. As best as Anlon could tell, nothing was missing. "Someone clearly went through it, but I don't see anything missing. Kind of surprised the gun and cash didn't get taken."

"Surprised us as well," Emerson said. "Reinforces the premise the intruder wanted something very specific."

"Yeah, like I said earlier, I'm pretty sure he was after the artifact Antonio had intended to give to Pebbles yesterday, or the map he's also storing for us."

"The black stone with the carved design?" Emerson asked.

"Yeah. It was made by the same culture that shaped these stones. I have a few more in my office downstairs," Anlon said, his eyes riveted on the third shelf. "The black one's more valuable than all of them put together. That's why I asked Antonio to hold it for me. His security is way more elaborate than this."

"How valuable is it? The black stone, I mean."

"Haven't had it appraised, but fair to say it's close to priceless."

"Give me a ballpark. Are we talking millions?"

"Easily," Anlon said, squinting at the items on the second shelf again. "You know, I think I was wrong. I do see one thing missing. Pebbles has a necklace; it's gold with a medallion made of a black stone set in gold. She wears it a lot, but when she doesn't, she keeps it in here."

The detective scribbled down the description, asking Anlon a few more questions about the necklace as he wrote. The last one tripped Anlon. "Do you think she wore it yesterday?"

"Maybe," he said. "Matter of fact, she probably did. She likes to wear it when she talks with Malinyah."

"Huh? Malinyah?" Emerson asked.

"Oh, sorry," Anlon said, embarrassed by his slip. "She's one of Pebbles' friends."

"Was she expecting to talk with Miss McCarver yesterday?"

"Um, couldn't say," Anlon said. He felt bad for the lie, but he could tell where the detective was headed.

"Well, we ought to check with her just the same. If they did talk, it might help us narrow the time window. Is she a neighbor? Do you know how we can reach her?" Emerson asked.

"No, she's not a neighbor. I think she's an old college friend," Anlon said, looking away. "Uh, hmmm...you know, I'm not sure I have her number in my phone. Let me check."

After pulling the phone from the back pocket of his jeans, he made a show of thumbing through his contacts directory. Standing beside him, the detective waited with poised pen. Anlon uttered a couple of thoughtful "hmmms" and then said, "Nope. Don't have it. Sorry."

Emerson then asked for her last name. Anlon said he only knew her as Malinyah. It was the one truth among the string of lies. If the detective was suspicious, he didn't show it, but he didn't let the matter drop, either. "Oh, well. Maybe Miss McCarver has it on her phone. I meant to tell you we found it on the bathroom counter. You wouldn't happen to know the passcode? We can get the record of her calls and texts from the carrier, but I'd like to see if there's anything else on it that might help us."

"Um, yeah. I do," Anlon said. He recited the code and Emerson jotted it down. Anlon realized the Malinyah mention was likely to come back to bite him once the police scrutinized the phone, but he knew it was far more important to do everything he could to help them find Pebbles and bring her home safely. If worst came to worst, he'd introduce the detective to Malinyah.

When they finished in the bedroom, the two men went through the rest of the house. Anlon noticed the intruder had searched every room but hadn't trashed the place like Margaret and Kyle Corchran trashed

Devlin's house in Stockbridge. Nothing was broken, smashed or torn. The only damage he observed were partial bloody boot prints on some of the carpets. They were too big to be from any boots of Pebbles', leading Anlon to realize how the police surmised the intruder was male, and how they reached the conclusion there had only been one other person besides Pebbles in the house.

When they reached his office, Anlon slowly circled the room. It was amazing how spacious the office seemed to Anlon now that most of Devlin's artifacts and papers had been moved to Antonio's storage facility along with Malinyah's *Sinethal* and the Waterland Map. Gone also was the horrid smell emanating from his "bilge" collection, as Pebbles had dubbed it. The fish tanks containing lichens, algae and the spritely zebrafish had all been banished from the house as soon as they returned from Nicaragua.

There were some holdovers that Anlon refused to pack up and store, and these items seemed to have attracted great interest from the intruder. Behind his desk, Anlon kept three boxes of Devlin's papers, documents that he intended to revisit someday. On one of the built-in bookshelves lining the far wall, Anlon had cleared two shelves that now exhibited some of Devlin's smaller artifacts. There were clear signs that both the boxes and the shelves had been searched, and four items had been moved from the shelves to his desk.

There was the ornate "fish-man" statuette depicting a man wearing a *Taellin* upon his head. Behind it stood the comparatively plain statuette of a faceless man brandishing a *Tuliskaera*. Also on the desk sat a hockey-puck-shaped *Naetir* and an *Aromaegh* which told the story of the approaching asteroid, Munirvo. The reddish, square stone was facedown, revealing the center slot and carved handholds on the back surface. Curiously, there was a ballpoint pen resting against it.

"Now that's odd," Anlon said, facing the desk from the middle of the room.

"What's that?" Emerson asked.

"These pieces were moved from the shelf," Anlon replied as he approached the desk. He maneuvered between the two guest chairs facing the desk and looked down at the pieces.

Emerson came up and stood beside him. "They look arranged, don't they?"

"They do," Anlon said. Spaced equally apart, the *Naetir* was closest to Anlon, followed by the *Aromaegh*, then the fish-man statue and finally the *Tuliskaera* statue farthest back. Anlon said, "It's a message. Question is, did Pebbles leave it or did the intruder?"

"What kind of message?" Emerson asked, stepping behind the desk to view the pieces from another angle.

"It tells me who did this," Anlon said. The *Naetir* clasped to the back of a *Sinethal*, held in the hands of one wearing a *Taellin*, while an accomplice stands behind and jolts the *Sulataer* on the helmet's crown with a blast from the *Tuliskaera* — the recipe for transferring a mind from the wearer of the *Taellin* into a *Sinethal*.

"Who?" Emerson asked.

Anlon didn't answer for a moment. He stared down at the desktop diorama, his attention focused on the pen. Why was it left on the desk? It wasn't an accident; the pen wasn't one of Anlon's. Again, Emerson pressed for an answer, this time more forcefully. "Dr. Cully, tell me who!"

As Anlon studied the pen more closely, he mumbled a reply. "You been watching the news?"

"What?" Emerson asked.

While the detective frowned at him, Anlon raised his eyes to look at the lineup of Stones. They were arranged in a row, but the angle of the row was odd. They hadn't been plucked from the shelf and haphazardly placed on the desk. Instead, they were arranged diagonally across the desk, angled toward the office door. Anlon studied the angle and asked for Emerson's opinion. "Why do you think they're diagonal across the desk?"

"Beats me. We weren't sure if the intruder put them here or if they were here beforehand."

"Understood. But now that you know I didn't place them here, does their positioning suggest anything to you? Not necessarily which piece comes before which piece, but the overall alignment? The fact they're diagonal with the desk?" Anlon asked.

"Hmmm..."

In the current lineup, the *Naetir* was closest to the office door. Both men circled the desk, staring down at the Stones. When Anlon stood behind the *Tuliskaera*, a thought occurred to him. Even though the objects seemed aligned with the door when Anlon had been on the opposite side of the desk, from his new position they seemed to be aimed to the right of the door. On that side of the door was a large world map pinned to the wall. Anlon had his answer. He quickly moved to the map.

It was barren of the pins that had earlier marked the Maerlif locations Anlon had decoded from the Waterland Map. Thank goodness for that, he thought. But his relief was short lived. The map still bore notes he had scribbled in various places and if one looked closely, the holes where the pins had been anchored were clearly visible. That's when he saw it.

"Son of a bitch!" he said, pounding a fist against his thigh.

"What? What's the matter?" Emerson asked.

Anlon angrily pointed to the map. His gloved finger hovered over Ometepe, the small island in the middle of Lake Nicaragua. Just above the lake, nestled between the map's labels marking the town of Granada and the country's capital, Managua, was a scribbled note. "Malinyah for the girl."

11

Pézenas Parlay

Pézenas, France
September 28

Foucault stepped onto the terrace and lit a cigarette. Inhaling deeply, he looked toward the garden. In the darkness, it looked eerier than usual, for a thick layer of mist hovered over the grounds of the entire estate, including his cathedral of oleanders. He was tempted to take a quick stroll through the garden, hoping it would help him find the right words to say. But there were no right words for the conversation to come.

He sighed, flicked ashes from the cigarette and headed for the observatory. When he descended the terrace steps, his feet disappeared into the mist. Unable to see the path, Foucault directed his gaze at the silo-shaped structure in the distance and walked toward it across the dew-covered lawn. With each step, the watery film coating the grass splashed onto his shoes and slacks. Soon, even his socks were soaked. Yet, Foucault didn't notice. He trudged forward, dragging on the cigarette, with bleary eyes riveted on the observatory.

From the moment Foucault had seen the woman in the grainy video slap her hands together and slice through the police car with a beam of light, he knew Muran had finally emerged from the shadows. Evil as ever, Muran had unleashed her accursed powers for the whole world to see. Powers she had used again and again with cold-blooded effectiveness in Middlebury and Ticonderoga.

As much of a shock as it had been, Foucault was relieved she was finally out in the open. Yet, he was also devastated. Despite all his meticulous planning, he had miscalculated — Muran had not been as powerless as he had believed. Desperate, yes, but not powerless.

The only measure of solace Foucault had found while watching the American news reports came when the video capture from the Fort Ticonderoga café was shown. The clear picture of the undisguised face was indeed the same woman he had tracked since finding Muran's Maerlif, a woman whose trail had grown cold as time passed until she seemed to vanish altogether. Foucault had been surprised how young she looked. Given the diminishing effects of *enjyia* within his own body, Foucault had expected Muran's current body to have aged. Maybe not as much as he had aged, but more than was apparent in the photo.

"Imbecile!" Foucault seethed, as he reached the observatory. Before he entered, he dropped the cigarette butt and crushed it beneath his soggy shoe. No wonder she evaded my trap for so long! he thought. She had not needed a new body. And she already had a *Tuliskaera*! Foucault cursed again. He felt like a fool for having laid breadcrumbs to a trap she had no need to follow.

Inside the observatory, Foucault paused and looked up the spiral staircase at the telescope above. Again, he felt a desire to linger. It was the last night of a new moon, and the sky would be dense with stars. He clenched his fist and shook his head. *"Non!* No more delays."

He stepped around to the back side of the stone staircase. Hidden from view was a steel door protected by a security system and separate cypher lock. Foucault entered the necessary passcode into the alarm's electronic keypad, then the secondary code into the cypher lock's mechanical face. A click echoed up the silo as the door opened and revealed a well-lit staircase leading below. As Foucault descended the stairs, he patted the cement wall with affection. "You have served me well, *ami*."

The bunker had been built long before Foucault bought the estate and erected his observatory over it. Local lore claimed it was originally constructed by a court advisor to the Count of Montpellier in the eighteenth century. With the French Revolution in full swing and nobles under siege, the Count's advisor had hastily built the bunker to hide the family's wealth from plundering mobs. Over the ensuing centuries, it had been enlarged and reinforced and served different roles for different masters. At one time, it had been a wine cellar for a Languedoc vineyard. At another point in its history, the bunker had been a secret meeting place for *La Résistance* during the Vichy occupation of southern France. And now it served to house Foucault's collection of Munuorian artifacts.

When Foucault reached the bunker's landing, he opened another cypher-protected door and entered the Munuorian-style chamber. The furnishings were replicas he had commissioned based on rooms he had seen during visits with Mereau.

Lavish rugs made from silk and metallic beads graced the bunker's marble floors. Atop the rugs were sturdy tables and cushioned armchairs made from the wood of ceiba trees. The tables were topped with stone and wood sculptures shaped by later cultures to honor the Munuorian saviors who rescued their ancestors from the horrors of Munirvo. Upon the marble walls hung framed murals depicting iconic images of the Munuorians. In one, an armada of ships cut through ocean waves. In another, a glowing sunrise coated the cliffside Seybalrosa monument. A third paid homage to the volcanos where the *Lifintyls* were forged.

On the bunker's far wall were three tall safes containing *Lifintyls* he'd excavated or bought over the centuries. The most important of all, Mereau's *Sinethal*, was stored in the center safe — the safe that Foucault now opened. Uncharacteristically, his hands trembled as he reached for the squarish black stone. It had been many years since he last visited with the valorous Munuorian captain, and tonight's visit would not be a pleasant one.

For long stretches of time, Foucault had regularly used the *Sinethal* to meet and learn from Mereau. From the onset of his first meaningful visit with the captain, he had been drawn to Mereau's commanding, yet compassionate personality. An hour in his presence had filled Foucault with soaring confidence. It was the kind of self-assurance that had enabled Foucault to accomplish many things that would otherwise have been out of his reach. Mereau had also been an able teacher whose bullish spirit made Foucault desire to exceed his expectations in every way imaginable. However, that standard had proved beyond his capabilities when it came to Muran. Ashamed of his failures to fulfill his promise to bring *The Betrayer* to justice, Foucault had suspended his visits with the great man.

It had crushed him to disappoint Mereau, for Foucault owed the Munuorian everything. With Mereau's guidance and encouragement, Foucault had become an educated and wealthy man. Under different names and personas, he had used these assets to cultivate favor among European aristocrats for hundreds of years. In so doing, he had been an eyewitness to many of the continent's most extraordinary historical events over the past four centuries. In some cases, Foucault had been far more than an eyewitness, shaping some of that history himself.

But now Foucault's magic was nearly spent. The life-extending effects of *enjyia* had deteriorated precipitously over the past decade, causing him to rapidly age. At his current pace of decline, Foucault didn't anticipate surviving more than another five years.

A moot concern, thought Foucault. And a selfish one. He'd enjoyed six lifetimes of the average man, and he'd made the most of each. There was only one thing that mattered now, and that was ending the curse of *The Painted Lady*…whatever the sacrifice.

Foucault lowered Mereau's *Sinethal* to the stone table with reverence. Retracing his steps to the safe, he retrieved a *Naetir* and returned to the table. Seated in an armchair, he wasted no time maneuvering the *Naetir* to the center slot on the back of the *Sinethal*. Before he slid his fingers into the side notches, Foucault took a deep breath and closed his eyes.

The vision began as it always did with Mereau. The captain stood on the bridge of his ship as it pushed through sparkling waves made silver by the sun above. While Foucault gazed up at Mereau from the main deck, groups of crewmen moved about performing their appointed tasks. As Foucault started for the bridge, a sea breeze rose up. It ruffled his tunic and peppered his face with a spray of saltwater. The familiar taste prompted a smile. Also familiar was the feel of the ship's vibrations on his bare feet. They emanated from belowdecks, where a dozen men rhythmically hammered on a bank of enormous *Breyloftes* embedded in the aft hull. The pulsing sound waves produced by the Stones powered the ship forward.

When Foucault stepped onto the bridge, he bowed and spoke in the Munuorian tongue. *"Halas, Mereau, fryael ut visi."* Greetings, *Mereau, captain and master.*

"Ut aeh, Mathieu!" replied Mereau, invoking Foucault's birth name. *"Vean ut fereau."* And you, Mathieu! Friend and countryman. Continuing the conversation in Munuorian, Mereau looked into Foucault's eyes and his brow furrowed. "Your spirit is heavy, my friend, I can feel it."

"Aye, it is indeed," Foucault said.

Mereau studied Foucault's weathered face and gray hair. "And you are much older than you were when you last journeyed with us."

Foucault nodded. He knew Mereau would quickly notice his aged appearance. He also knew the captain would deduce the cause of his aging just as fast. The disappointment evident in Mereau's reply hit Foucault in the gut. "How long has it been, Mathieu?"

"Eighty years, give or take," Foucault said.

"Eighty?"

"I am sorry."

"Why, Mathieu? Why so long?"

Foucault turned away from Mereau's punishing gaze. A sudden craving for a cigarette rushed through his body. "There is no excuse. I should have come earlier. I grew weary of the search. I didn't see the point in visiting unless there were new developments."

Mereau's eyes widened. "You have found her?"

"Aye, my captain. Though it is more accurate to say she has made an appearance. An unmistakable public appearance."

A large wave slammed against the starboard side of the ship, causing the hull to shudder. Mereau stood with eyes transfixed on Foucault as another swell pummeled the boat. Mereau shouted instructions to the crew to make ready to dive. He took Foucault by the arm and led him down the bridge steps to the main deck. Around them, Mereau's men pulled the curved sections of the boat's inner hull from their retracted slots in the port and starboard gunwales. They guided the two arching halves toward the deck's center. When they met at the center, the main deck became fully enclosed. From the outside, the encased ship looked like a dolphin swimming on the surface.

Inside the enclosed ship, the crew on deck rapidly split into two teams. One focused on sealing the inner hull with a long, rubbery band that they fastened from bow to stern. The other team rubbed pairs of *Dreylaeks* together until their inner surfaces glowed, providing dim amber lighting for the darkened chamber. They clamped the Stones into iron sconces around the gunwales. The clamps applied pressure on the Stones, thereby maintaining the friction responsible for their radiance. With both missions complete, the crew braced themselves against railings lining the gunwales. Mereau gave the command to dive and the rudderman edged the bow downward. The crew manning the *Breylofte* engines belowdecks increased the rhythm of their pounding, and in less than a minute the ship was submerged beneath the pummeling action of the waves.

Foucault had observed Mereau's men perform the maneuver thousands of times over the past four centuries, and on many of those occasions he had lent his own hands to those of the crew. Yet, he still marveled at the speed and efficiency of their teamwork and at the amazing prehistoric technology built into their hybrid ships. He often wondered how historians would react if they ever found one of the Munuorian vessels, for the ships predated the first manned submarines by nine thousand years. Would they still view the fish-man legends as fanciful parables, or would they treat them as factual accounts? *They literally came up out of the sea.*

As the ship glided underwater, Mereau led Foucault to his cabin. As soon as the door closed behind them, he asked, "Tell me of Muran. What has happened?"

"It is a long tale, I'm afraid. You will not be pleased with most of it," Foucault said.

Mereau sat in a chair by his map table and motioned for Foucault to join him. "Come, tell me all, good and bad."

Foucault lowered into a chair next to Mereau and bowed his head while he gathered his thoughts. During the silence, Mereau poured a glass of *enjyia* and handed it to Foucault, telling him the drink would settle his spirit. Foucault sipped the Munuorian concoction and savored the silky fluid coating his tongue and throat. Its sweet, earthy taste was richer than any batch Foucault had ever made on his own. He thanked Mereau and placed the glass on the table. "I suppose it's best to start with Malinyah."

"Malinyah?"

"Yes, her *Sinethal* resurfaced within the last year. It found its way into the hands of an archaeologist, a man named Devlin Wilson."

"Malinyah...," whispered Mereau, blankly staring at the pile of rolled maps. "I am happy to hear her mind still lives. Have you talked with her?"

"I have not, but I've met with the man who now has the *Sinethal*. His name is Anlon Cully, and he is the nephew of the archaeologist. Cully and his female companion have visited with her. Malinyah is well, but still very angry with Muran," Foucault said.

"Understandably so," Mereau said with a sigh. "Poor Alynioria."

Foucault watched Mereau bow his head and close his eyes as he honored the memory of Alynioria. The murder of the teenaged girl's mind had hurt him deeply, and Foucault had always suspected Mereau's obsession with Muran stemmed from a desire to avenge Alynioria's untimely death rather than punish *The Betrayer's* other misdeeds. After the impromptu moment of silence, Mereau raised his head. "Forgive me, Mathieu, but I don't understand. Many years ago, you told me you believed Muran had destroyed Malinyah's *Sinethal*."

"That is true. I knew for certain Muran had removed it from Malinyah's tomb. It seemed likely to me that she destroyed the Stone and Malinyah's mind along with it," Foucault said.

"If she didn't destroy it, she has had it with her all these thousands of years?"

"I cannot say for certain," Foucault said.

"Did Muran give it to this man Devlin?"

"It is a good question," Foucault said. "For much of the past year, I would have said yes. But there are things that have happened more recently that seem to suggest she did not."

"Such as?"

"As you can imagine, when Malinyah's *Sinethal* was rediscovered, it spun me about. Of course, I tried to find out where Devlin had acquired it, believing the answer would lead me to Muran. Before I made much progress, I learned Devlin had figured out how to activate Malinyah's mind-keeper and that he'd used it to make a map."

Foucault paused and watched Mereau absorb the comment. The captain stared down at his map table and mumbled, "A map?" Then his head lifted and his eyes lit up. "The Munirvo Maerlifs!"

"Precisely. This made me believe Devlin was acting for Muran. I reasoned she had given him the *Sinethal* to coax the Maerlif locations from Malinyah. I should have gone to Devlin directly, but I was concerned it would cause Muran to act. Instead, I hired someone close to Devlin to learn the truth without alerting Muran to my presence. I tasked him to get a copy of the map so I could find and destroy any *Tuliskaeras* still left in the vaults." Foucault's voice trailed off. He shifted his eyes from Mereau to the maps stacked on the table.

"I don't understand. Why would Muran want a *Tuliskaera*, Mathieu?"

"Because her own was destroyed, along with her *Sinethal* and *Taellin*."

"What? How do you know this?"

"I found Muran's Maerlif."

Mereau popped up out of his chair, his hip bumping the table. Several of the coiled maps rolled over the edge and fell to the floor. "Her Maerlif? She died?"

"Yes, she died. But someone found her crypt before me. A woman, I believe," Foucault said. "A portion of the Maerlif's wall had broken free, as happened with yours, and she must have climbed in to investigate. And just like I figured out how to activate your *Sinethal*, and Devlin did with Malinyah, this woman activated Muran's. I believe Muran convinced her to lure another young woman to the Maerlif, and together they moved Muran's mind from her *Sinethal* into the unsuspecting girl's body."

"How do you know all this? How do you know it was Muran's Maerlif?"

Foucault explained. "There are tributes to Muran painted on the inner walls of the Maerlif. Well, tributes to the last persona she assumed before dying. She went by the name Wak Chanil Ajaw. She was the ruler of a great city called Naranjo. According to the tributes, she held power for almost sixty years before a rival city overthrew her and her son. The son was captured and executed, but she managed to escape on a ship. The tributes claim 'Ajaw' was injured in the final battle and died shortly after."

"Was Muran mentioned by name in these tributes?" asked a skeptical Mereau.

"No."

"Then, how can you know for sure it was Muran's tomb?"

"My captain, there is no other explanation. It is clearly a Munuorian burial Maerlif. I have seen enough of them over the last four hundred years to know."

"Could it not be the tomb of one of our people who survived Munirvo and resettled near this city you mentioned?" Mereau asked, rising from his chair.

"No. Please let me continue. I will explain," Foucault said. Mereau crossed his arms and glared at Foucault.

"First of all, the Maerlif is on an island very far from Munuoria — the farthest away I've ever found one of your people's tombs. It is also a great distance from the land where Ajaw ruled."

"Show me," Mereau said, reaching for one of the fallen maps. He unfurled it and spread it on the table. It was a crude drawing of Earth's current continents drawn by Foucault during a *Sinethal* session with Mereau many years prior. The great captain had commissioned the map so he could better understand the full scope of changes to the world's geography caused by Munirvo.

"Right here, off the continent of Africa," Foucault said, pointing to a bay directly below what is now Nigeria. He then ran his finger to the west across the Atlantic Ocean until it reached the east coast of Guatemala. He tapped the map. "This is where Ajaw ruled."

"That is very far, but it doesn't prove the Maerlif is Muran's," Mereau said.

With his finger poised over Guatemala, Foucault said, "There are monuments to Ajaw at the ruins of Naranjo. They date her reign. She came to power twelve hundred years ago. Unless another Munuorian violated your sacred laws and used a *Sinethal* to switch bodies, how could the Maerlif belong to anyone else besides Muran? The rest of your people died out thousands of years beforehand."

"Were the bones of this Ajaw inside the crypt?"

"They were."

"Did she wear a Munuorian burial cloak?"

"No, she was adorned with the finery of the Maya, the people Ajaw ruled."

"You say her *Sinethal* was destroyed?"

"Pieces of her *Sinethal* were scattered everywhere inside. The same was true for her *Taellin* and *Tuliskaera*."

"Were the rest of her *Tyls* inside?"

"No. I know what you are thinking. The tomb was looted. I considered it, especially since her *Sulataers* were missing, as were the diamonds from her *Tuliskaera* and *Taellin*. But, my captain, her *Sinethal* wasn't just broken. It was obliterated. All three *Tyls* were obliterated.

"There was only one explanation that made sense. Someone had tried a mind transfer, and something went wrong. Don't you see? Muran's accomplice did not use the *Tuliskaera* correctly and the *Tyls* exploded once the transfer was complete. Muran or her accomplice must have come back later to remove the remaining undamaged *Tyls* and the diamonds from the debris of the destroyed *Tyls*."

"But, Mathieu, if the *Tyls* exploded, Muran would have been killed. They both would have been killed," Mereau said.

"Muran was badly injured, not killed. I know this for a fact," Foucault said.

Mereau stalked the cabin to quell his anger. "Mathieu, you should have told me this as soon as you learned of it!"

Foucault sighed. Standing to face the ire-filled captain, he said, "I know, but I wanted to catch her and bring her to you on my own. I thought she would be easy to hunt down. You see, I discovered the identity of the woman whose body she assumed."

Foucault went on to explain. He told Mereau he had found two bonnets in the Maerlif, one made from silk, the other from straw. He surmised one had been worn by the woman who facilitated the transfer of Muran's mind, and the other by the woman whose mind was replaced. "They would have left in quite a hurry after the explosion, especially if one or both had been injured. In their haste, I assumed the bonnets were forgotten."

The silk bonnet, Foucault explained, had a distinctive floral pattern that helped him date the head covering to the mid-nineteenth century. With that information, Foucault researched the history of Fernando Pó, the island where the Maerlif was located. During that time period, he told Mereau, the island had been a Spanish territory, so Foucault focused his research on old Spanish newspapers and looked for mentions of unusual occurrences on the island.

He discovered the island had been used as a port by slave ships ferrying captured Africans off the continent. Later, British authorities leased ports on the island to moor ships used to intercept slave ships and free their prisoners. Therefore, most of the Spanish articles Foucault found described events related to the slave trade, including stories about naval conflicts between the slavers and the British navy. In turn, Foucault started to examine old British newspapers as well.

One day, he found an article describing an incident involving the daughter of the top British naval officer on the island, an explosion that gravely injured the teenaged girl. Foucault sought out other articles about the incident, the naval officer and his daughter, and found many. He told Mereau the officer had been a prominent member of British society and, as a result, the newspapers took great interest in the story.

"Some of the articles included photographs of the daughter, before and after she recovered. It is the same woman who reappeared yesterday and killed many people with *Dreylaeks*. She looks a little older now but otherwise is identical. Understand, Mereau. The incident that injured this woman occurred over one hundred seventy years ago. It can be no one else. It is Muran."

"If you knew this woman was Muran, why didn't you kill her?"

"I discovered the Maerlif sixty years ago, long after she disappeared."

"Disappeared?"

"Yes. It's a long story, one we don't have time to discuss now, but I believe she moved about as I have over the centuries, changing her name, taking on new personas. The last mention I found about the daughter was an article written eight years after the Fernando Pó incident." Foucault pointed at Australia on the map and continued his story. "She had married a British tycoon and they had settled here, on this continent."

"You said she disappeared. Did you follow her to this place?" Mereau asked, his finger on Australia.

"I did. And I tried to find what became of her. I learned after some digging that the tycoon, his wife and their only child had gone missing on a safari and were never heard from again."

With head lowered and hands clasped behind his back, Mereau paced back and forth while absorbing Foucault's tale. He looked both angry and confused. After several minutes, he stopped pacing and turned to Foucault. "You said you thought she was seeking a *Tuliskaera?*"

"I thought so, but I was wrong," Foucault said.

"Explain."

"Once I knew she'd been revived and that her *Sinethal* had been destroyed, I thought she would go in search of replacements. Otherwise she would never be able to switch bodies again and would eventually die. I changed the focus of my search and began hunting for other *Sinethals*. I also searched for *Tuliskaeras* and *Taellins*, but I found none. After a time, I confess I gave up.

"But when Malinyah's *Sinethal* resurfaced, I took it as a sign Muran was afoot. At first, I could not understand why she would give it to Devlin, but when I learned Devlin had interacted with Malinyah and had drawn a map of the Munirvo Maerlifs, it convinced me she was after a *Tuliskaera* and was using Devlin to tap Malinyah for the information. As there were no *Taellins* or *Sinethals* stashed in the Munirvo Maerlifs, that left *Tuliskaeras* as the only viable target of her search."

"A reasonable deduction," Mereau said.

"But yesterday, when Muran emerged from hiding, she used a *Tuliskaera* to aid her escape after taking a *Sinethal* from a modern vault, so she already had a *Tuliskaera*. She was never looking for one! I was wrong."

"Then, she is searching for a *Taellin*?"

"I do not think so. I believe her target is more ambitious than that," Foucault said.

Foucault told Mereau about the bank robbery and Pebbles' kidnapping and shared his suspicions that Muran had engineered Pebbles' abduction to acquire Malinyah's *Sinethal* and the *lyktyl*. Mereau understood the implication immediately. "You should have never passed the medallion to the girl," he said harshly. Foucault tried to explain his reasoning, but Mereau called his explanation naïve and the decision reckless.

Mereau's disposition soured further when Foucault made it clear that Muran was operating with an accomplice. It was most likely the woman who helped her secure a new body, he speculated, as there was no way Muran could have been in two places on opposite ends of a continent at the same time. Foucault could feel the great

Munuorian's anguish flow through the Stone into his own mind. When he finished speaking, Foucault apologized for his sins. "I am sorry, Master and Captain. I disgraced the trust you placed in me."

"It is not for me to judge you, Mathieu. I am disappointed, of course, that you did not consult me earlier, but dwelling on that will not help our cause," Mereau said, leaning forward to clasp a hand on Foucault's shoulder. His grip was strong yet reassuring. Foucault could sense his anger ebbing. "It is my fault. I should never have asked you to carry this burden for me."

"Nonsense," Foucault said. "It has been my privilege to serve you. To know the splendor of Munuoria through your memories has been a blessing, not a burden," Foucault said.

"I feel your sincerity, Mathieu. And I believe you," Mereau said, squeezing Foucault's shoulder firmly. "You could have taken the knowledge I passed to you and used it solely for profit's sake. You could have used the *Tyls* to conquer, to control the lives of others. You could even have tried to cheat death, following in the footsteps of *The Betrayer*. But you did none of these things. You have not been perfect, but no man ever is."

Mereau released his hold on Foucault and rose from the table. He headed for the cabin door and called for Foucault to follow. On the main deck, Mereau gave the command to surface the ship. Several minutes later, the craft rose from beneath the waves. When the crew retracted the boat's hull-shell, brilliant rays of sunlight showered the deck. Foucault turned his head away from the sky to allow his eyes to adapt to the sudden change in radiance. Strong swells still buffeted the ship, but Mereau seemed not to care. He dashed up the planked steps to the quarterdeck. "Come, Mathieu, let us make ready a plan. If your speculation is right, we have little time to waste."

When Foucault released his hold on Mereau's *Sinethal*, the *Naetir* dislodged and both Stones dropped onto the table with soft thuds. His eyes opened and slowly his blurred vision cleared. He was very thirsty and chided himself for not bringing water or *enjyia* to replenish his body after visiting Mereau. The intensity of the electromagnetic exchanges between the *Sinethal* and the brain triggered electrolysis within the body, a fact Foucault should have remembered.

But his annoyance was short-lived. Though his body was weakened by the visit, his mind was energized. It would fortify him long enough to reach the chateau, rehydrate, roust Christian from bed and return to the observatory to gather the items needed for their trip.

He braced his hands on the chair's arms and slowly stood up. Despite the effort to cautiously rise from the seat, a rush of dizziness caused Foucault to teeter. He leaned his thighs against the edge of the table and waited for the woozy sensation to pass. Once it had, he maneuvered between the chamber's furniture and reached the door. Before ascending the stairs, Foucault turned to look at the room. Mereau's *Sinethal* and the *Naetir* still rested on the table, and he noticed the safe door was still open. Though his body beseeched him to find water, his mind called for discipline. Foucault retraced his steps, wobbling here and there, until he restored both Stones to the safe. As he prepared to close the door, he glanced at the glittering gold object on the top shelf and thought of Pebbles. He said a silent prayer for her safety and locked the safe.

By the time he made his way out of the observatory, the knee-high mist had transformed into a London-worthy fog. As he staggered toward the chateau, he was surprised to see the lights on the main level were out. Foucault then noticed the patio door was propped open. He halted and scanned the patio more closely, squinting through the hazy darkness.

His body tensed. Caught halfway between the house and the observatory, he had no hope of outrunning the figures racing toward him. Instinctively, he reached into the pockets of his blazer. He cursed and withdrew his empty hands.

12

Pressure Cooker

Incline Village, Nevada
September 28

"It's good to hear your voice. I was worried about you," Anlon said.

"Good to hear yours, too," Jennifer said. "I literally just heard about Pebbles from Dan. I'm so sorry, Anlon. I should have had my phone with me."

As Anlon listened to Jennifer, Detective Emerson entered the kitchen. He looked at Anlon with an expectant expression. Anlon shook his head and held his hand over the phone. "It's a friend."

Emerson nodded and turned to leave the kitchen. On his way out, he looked back at Anlon and whispered, "Make it quick."

"Anlon?" Jennifer asked.

Removing his hand from the phone, Anlon said, "Yeah, I'm here. Sorry about that; police are still here. They want me off the line. And don't apologize. Neither of us could have done anything to prevent it."

"I'm sorry still the same. Is there any news? Is she all right?" Jennifer asked.

Anlon stared down at his coffee cup and idly spun a spoon on the kitchen table. At his side was Antonio, who silently offered to brew a fresh cup. Anlon waved him off and said to Jennifer, "No news. It appears she's being held for ransom. We're waiting for a call. How are you feeling? Understand you took a pretty good bonk to the head."

"I'm fine, just sore," she said. "Dan said Pebbles was shot. Is that true?"

"Yeah, looks that way," Anlon said, massaging his forehead. "Police think she tried to run and got shot in the leg."

"Jesus," Jennifer said, her voice trailing off into a sigh. "Well, Dan's driving me to the airport as we speak. I'll be there as fast as I can, hopefully late this afternoon."

"What? I thought you were in intensive care?"

"Uh, yeah...I was."

"Jen, come on, now. I appreciate you wanting to help, but you should—"

"But, nothing," Jennifer said. "It's about the Stones, isn't it?"

"Yes. A note was left. 'Malinyah for the girl.' Pretty much points the finger at Muran, wouldn't you say?" Anlon said. "Though if it is Muran, it means she has an accomplice, a male accomplice."

Emerson reentered the kitchen with a frown on his face. Circling his hand, he whispered to Anlon, "Wrap it up."

Anlon pulled the phone from his ear and covered it with his hand again. "Be done in a sec."

The detective scowled and left the kitchen. Anlon turned to Antonio. "Guy's starting to get on my nerves."

As Antonio voiced his agreement, Anlon heard Jennifer speaking. The pitch of her voice was raised, and she was talking rapidly. He replaced the phone to his ear in time to hear her say, "...they're trying to track him down, right now!"

"Sorry, Jen. Missed that. Who's tracking who?"

"Charles Goodwin! The guy from the museum in New Haven. The one who lied about Devlin's statue!"

"What about him?" Anlon asked.

"He was with Muran! At Ticonderoga...three days ago!"

Anlon popped up off the chair, knocking it over. "What?"

Antonio was in mid-sip when the chair crashed onto the floor. He flinched, startled by the sound, and spilled coffee down his chin and onto his clothes. Holding the dripping cup away from his body, he reached for a napkin and frowned at Anlon.

"Emerson! Get in here. Now!" Anlon shouted, lowering the phone to his side. Glancing down at Antonio dabbing his shirt, he said, "Sorry, Skipper. My bad."

As Emerson appeared in the doorway, Anlon raised the phone and pushed the speaker icon. "Jen, I've put you on speaker. I've got Detective Emerson from the Nevada State Police here. Antonio's with me, too. Tell them what you just told me."

"Um, okay. Sure. I think your perp might be a man named Charles Goodwin."

For the next several minutes, Jennifer ran through the events in Middlebury and Ticonderoga, shading the fantastical elements of Muran's exploits in order to focus attention on the bank robbery and the photo of Muran and Goodwin. When she finished, Emerson said, "Can you get me a copy of the photo?"

"Hold on," Jennifer said. Through the speakerphone, Anlon and the others heard a muffled conversation. When Jennifer returned to the line, she said, "We'll get you a copy ASAP, but check online. FBI's planning to put out an alert on him, might be out already."

"I'll get someone to check right away," Emerson said, leaving the room.

"Anlon?"

"Yes, Jen."

"I should let the FBI know about Pebbles."

"Do it. We'll take whatever help we can get."

"Agreed. Probably means I won't make it to Tahoe tonight, though. Depending on how mad the agent in charge gets, I might need your help posting bail."

"What?"

"Don't have time to explain, just keep your phone handy."

"Okay, will do."

"And call me if there's any news about Pebbles, will you?"

"Of course."

"Thanks. I'll check in with you later," Jennifer said.

"Sounds good. Thanks, Jen. Take care," Anlon said.

"Oh, I almost forgot. You ever heard the name Evelyn Warwick? Ever see the name in Devlin's papers?"

"Doesn't ring a bell. Should I have?"

"I don't know. Remember when you said Anabel had a collection of artifacts Devlin had given her, as gifts?"

"Yeah."

"I think that's what's in the safe-deposit boxes in Middlebury, only the boxes were registered under the name Evelyn Warwick, not Anabel Simpson."

"Hmmm…an alias Anabel used?"

"Could be. Probably was. Only, there are pieces of evidence that don't fit."

"I'm not sure what you mean."

"I don't have time to go into all of it now, but the coroner found some strange things during Anabel's autopsy. And there was an odd assortment of clothes and jewelry in her house. Together with the safe-deposit boxes, it makes me think 'Anabel Simpson' was an alias."

"You think her real name was Evelyn Warwick?"

"No. I think that was an alias, too. Sort of…"

"You lost me."

"It's going to sound crazy, but I think she might have been—"

A double beep from the speakerphone overrode Jennifer's comment. Anlon looked down to see "Unknown Caller" on the screen. Two icons below prompted Anlon to either accept or ignore the new call. "Hey, Jen. Call coming in. Gotta go," Anlon said. Turning to Antonio, he said, "Go get Emerson."

Anlon's shaking thumb hovered over the screen. He took a deep breath and pressed the "Accept Call" icon. As the call connected, Antonio returned to the kitchen with Emerson and two other officers in tow.

"Anlon Cully."

There was just static at first. Anlon increased the speaker's volume and set it on the kitchen's center-island countertop. The four men stood around him as he said, "Hello? Anyone there?"

A long sigh echoed through the phone, and then a woman's voice said, "The police are with you."

The statement was delivered as an accusation rather than a question. Anlon, eyes glued on the phone, leaned forward and nodded. "Yes, they are."

There was a pause, during which Anlon heard car horns and the sound of moving traffic over the speaker. When the woman spoke again, there was a tired quality to her voice, as if she was annoyed by a perceived inconvenience. "Unfortunate, but not unexpected. You know why I'm calling?"

"Yes, I saw the note," Anlon said. "You are Muran, I presume?"

Three short puffs sounded from the phone. To Anlon, they came across as an amused laugh, a perception reinforced by the syrupy-superior tone of her reply. "My, I haven't been called that for a very, very long time. It's strange to hear the name spoken in your tongue."

Anlon's jaw tightened. "Honestly, I wish I'd never heard the name. I just want Pebbles back."

A cackling laugh filled the kitchen. "Pebbles? What a dreadful pet name!"

If Anlon could have reached through the phone, he would have choked the life out of her laugh, and Muran with it. He bowed his head and gripped the edge of the marble counter with both hands. Antonio placed his hand on Anlon's shoulder, causing Anlon to look up at him. Antonio mouthed, "Easy," and mimed a deep breath.

"You have some things of mine. I want them back," Aja said, her voice now icy.

"Things? The note said you wanted Malinyah," Anlon said.

"At the time I did not know you had Omereau, too."

"Omereau? Do you mean Mereau?"

"Don't play games with me. You know of whom I speak. I want his *Sinethal*. I want it back."

"I don't know what you're talking about. I only have one *Sinethal*. Malinyah's. And I will give it to you in exchange for Peb—"

Aja's retort was swift and venomous. "Liar! Don't deny it!"

Anlon glanced at Emerson and Antonio and shrugged his shoulders. Leaning back over the phone, he said in a raised voice, "I'm not lying, Muran. I don't have Mer—"

"You lie! Your woman wore the *lyktyl*!" Aja spat.

"The what?" Anlon asked.

"Enough!" Aja shouted over Anlon's question. In the ensuing silence, all that could be heard over the speaker was Aja's labored breathing. In almost a whisper, she said, "You will give me both, or she will be sacrificed."

Anlon pounded the counter. "Look! I'll give you every f—ing Stone I have. I'll give you Malinyah's map. I'll f—ing gift wrap the damn things. But I don't have two *Sinethals*! Pebbles must have told you that already!"

"I will strip her naked and paint her blue…" Aja taunted. "She will resist, of course, but it won't be hard for my *chacs* to pin her down..."

"If you f—ing harm her, I wi—"

With the conversation spinning out of control, Emerson grabbed Anlon by the arm and pulled him away from the phone. "Cool it. This isn't helping, Cully."

Anlon fought against his grip and yanked his arm free. His face was deep red as he listened to Aja continue to needle him. "She'll cry and plead, like they all do. But I'll make sure to take my time… make her suffer for as long as it entertai—"

"F— you, Muran!"

Emerson directed his two officers and Antonio to lead Anlon from the room. "Get him out of here!"

Aja laughed.

"Look, Miss Muran, let's all take a step back, here," Emerson said. "I'm certain we can talk this out without threats or further injury to Miss McCarver."

Anlon pushed away the officers and yelled, "So help me God, if you touch her, I will smash Malinyah's *Sinethal* to rubble! Do you hear me, Betrayer?"

"Betrayer? Betrayer?" Aja yelled back. "I tried to save my people! And for that I'm called Betrayer? Malinyah has poisoned you with lies."

With a click, the phone call ended.

Pézenas, France

Klaus Navarro strolled around the chateau parlor with a smile on his face and gloved hands clasped behind his back. As he approached the fireplace, he stopped to admire the array of Egyptian figurines lining the mantel. Picking up a statuette of a woman, he closely examined the carved features. "What dynasty is this?"

"Eighteenth," Foucault said, kneeling in the room's center under the watchful eyes of Navarro's bodyguards. The two men, dressed in all black, aimed semiautomatic pistols at Foucault and Christian Hunte, who knelt beside him.

"The gold leaf is in excellent condition. Who is the woman?" Navarro casually asked.

"Queen Tiye, wife of Amenhotep the Fourth," Foucault said.

"Did you acquire it through Van der Berg?"

"*Non.* It was a gift."

"A gift? Is it a reproduction?"

"*Non.*"

"A three-thousand-year-old statue in near-original condition? It must be worth a great deal. Who would give such a gift?"

"An old friend," Foucault said. The sight of Navarro handling the priceless statuette disgusted him. Other than Foucault, the last person to touch it had been Napoleone di Buonaparte. The renowned French general had presented it to Foucault as tribute for his service during Napoleone's Egyptian campaign.

"Well, it will be a beautiful addition to my collection. In fact, all of these pieces will look splendid in my gallery," Navarro said, sweeping his arm the length of the mantel.

Over my dead body, thought Foucault, as Navarro replaced the figurine and sashayed his way around a gold, scroll-backed sofa. When the smarmy Argentinian reached his kneeling prisoners, he briefly hovered over Foucault before taking a seat on an armchair facing the two men. He crossed one leg over the other and brushed lint from his olive Armani slacks. Then, from the pocket of his matching suit jacket, he removed a thin, black-bladed knife. He held it up for Foucault and Hunte to see. "A nasty little devil, this one. It nearly decapitated my poor cousin, Nicolás. Where did you get it? I've never seen one like it. Another old friend?"

Foucault glared at him. The fool didn't know it, but his arrogance only served to strengthen Foucault. Dehydrated and weary from his earlier visit with Mereau, Foucault had been in no position to put up a fight against Navarro's armed men as they stormed toward him outside the chateau. He offered no resistance as they dragged him inside the house and dropped him next to Christian. Dizzy and confused by the surprise intrusion, Foucault had leaned against Christian and asked for water. Navarro's men had laughed and mocked him. Foucault had lolled, nearly fainting. But then Navarro had entered the room, and Foucault's ire began to stir. And the more Navarro gloated, the angrier Foucault grew, melting away his weariness. To see Mereau's blade in the snake's hand was too much. Foucault answered Navarro's question by imploring him to kiss his ass. *"Va te faire foutre!"*

The outburst caused Navarro to titter with laughter. When he quieted down, he wiped faux tears from his eyes and said, "How rude. But I guess I should expect as much from the man who sent a whore to assassinate me."

His face strained as he leaned forward and slapped Foucault across the face. "You are a coward, Monsieur."

Foucault slowly raised a hand and massaged his jaw, while Christian spat on Navarro's Ferragamo loafers. The gesture earned Christian a blow to the side of the head from one of the bodyguards. Christian slumped onto the floor. Foucault bent down to help his friend up, saying, *"Calmer, ami.* This nonsense will be over soon."

"Uh-uh. Not so, Monsieur," Navarro said, twirling the knife in his hand. "I plan to take my sweet time with the both of you, just like I did with your pathetic whore. Just like poor Van der Berg."

Foucault sighed. He knew, of course, that Navarro had escaped Margaret Corchran's assassination attempt. Shortly after leaving Anlon Cully and his party at Indio Maiz, Foucault had called Margaret's cell phone again. Unlike his previous attempts to reach her while awaiting Henri to arrive by helicopter, this time the phone was answered. Upon hearing the male voice on the other end of the line, Foucault had quickly ended the call, presuming the worst. But there had been no time in the immediate aftermath to sort out what had happened at the Finca 6 museum. Foucault had been more focused on retrieving Christian from Greytown's clinic-hospital and escaping Nicaragua before either the police or Navarro tracked them down.

After returning to his Pézenas estate, Foucault had learned of the murder and kidnapping at Finca 6 on the day in question. The accounts he read indicated the kidnap victim had been a woman, and that she had killed a man before being abducted by three other men. But Foucault could find no mention of Navarro as the murder victim in any of the articles.

From these reports, Foucault assumed Margaret had been intercepted by Navarro's security detail before she could strike down the troublesome collector. But he had not known whether Navarro himself had been present at Finca 6, nor whether the Argentinian knew about Foucault's role in the scheme. With Christian bedridden while he recovered from his gunshot wound, Foucault had limited resources to discreetly ferret out the answers to these questions. From Navarro's jibes, he now knew the answer to both.

"Of course, I can be persuaded to be merciful," Navarro said, sliding the knife back into his jacket's pocket. "Give me the Serpent's Tooth and your bootlicker here will die swiftly. Deny me the Stone, and watch him suffer alongside the whore before I turn the blade on you."

"Excusez-moi?"

"Oh, how thoughtless of me. Tomas, bring in what's left of *la puta*," Navarro said. As the bodyguard left the room, Navarro stroked his ponytail and smiled at Foucault. "You are surprised, I see. Good, good. I hoped you might be."

Tomas returned shortly with a limp figure draped over his shoulder. At Navarro's command, the bodyguard dumped Margaret onto the floor. She rolled onto her side, facing away from Foucault. He stared at her visible wounds with remorseful eyes. Navarro had used Mereau's knife to slice off her ear, and Foucault could see her thumbs were also missing. From the burn marks dotting her shaved head and the bruises on her arms, it was evident Navarro's torture had gone beyond employing the knife.

Navarro kicked at her shoulder, causing her to roll on her back. Foucault winced when he saw Margaret's disfigured face. She was conscious, but she stared vacantly at the ceiling. "What do you think of her necklace? I think it turned out well."

Navarro tugged down the collar of Margaret's T-shirt. Below the jagged scar left by Navarro during his machete attack on Margaret in the Amazon, the bastard had carved a snake into Margaret's upper chest that extended from shoulder to shoulder. Foucault closed his eyes and cursed Navarro.

"Don't curse me, it is your own fault. Had you been a man and faced me yourself, none of this would have been necessary," Navarro said.

"You call yourself a man? Only a monster would do such vile things," Foucault said, fists clenched.

"Ha! What does that make you?" Navarro spat back. "I don't know you. We've never met. And yet, you try to assassinate me! For what? Did I best you in some mining deal? Was I competing for the same piece? What reason did you have to order my death?"

"I did it for you own good!" Foucault shouted.

Navarro laughed maniacally. "My own good? You are insane!"

"The *Tuliskaera* in your hands would have been a beacon to Muran," Foucault said. His voice trailed off, "At least, I thought so at the time…"

"Tool-a-what? Muran?"

Foucault stood. "*Tuliskaera, imbecile!* Your Serpent's Tooth. The Flash Stone. Whatever you care to call it! Come, I will show it to you. I will show you what it can do!"

"Back on your knees!" Navarro commanded.

"*Non!* I have no more time for you. Do you want the Stone or not?"

Navarro grabbed the gun from Tomas. "On your knees or your man is dead."

Christian jumped up and stepped in front of Foucault. Spreading his arms, he shouted at Navarro, "Do it! Do it!"

Navarro's other man, Manuel, ran up from behind and grabbed Christian around the neck, holding a pistol to his temple. Christian grabbed Manuel's hand and the gun went off.

In the small parlor, the sound was deafening. Christian and Manuel fell to the ground, smoke hovering in the air. As the two men struggled for control of the gun, Navarro stood frozen, his gun at his side. Tomas, who had ducked beside Navarro when Manuel's gun fired, now moved to help subdue Christian.

As Foucault pleaded with Christian to stop fighting, Manuel seized control of the weapon and fired twice. Christian moaned once and collapsed next to Manuel. Forgotten as nothing more than a catatonic heap on the floor, Margaret reached up and flailed her maimed hands at the gun in Navarro's hand, knocking it loose. Turning to Foucault, she shouted, "Run!"

The command shocked Foucault into action. He took off through the parlor door and into the hallway while Tomas and Navarro scrambled for the gun Margaret had knocked away. Snarling like an animal, she charged at Navarro and knocked him to the floor, leaving Tomas free to collect the weapon while Manuel took off after Foucault.

Tomas turned to see Margaret straddling Navarro, raining blow after blow on his face and head. He did not hesitate. At point-blank range, he fired three shots into Margaret's back. Her lifeless body fell onto Navarro.

"Get her off me," cried Navarro, wiggling underneath the dead woman.

Tomas heaved Margaret's body to the side to find Navarro covered in blood and shaking. Navarro screamed at him, "Kill him! Find him and kill him!"

Tomas nodded and ran off through the parlor door.

Incline Village, Nevada

Antonio and Anlon sat together on the edge of Anlon's dock. The cloudy sky gave the water a steely hue, one that masked the lake's natural deep blue beauty. It had been fifteen minutes since Antonio had dragged Anlon from the house, and his friend had yet to say a word.

He had never seen Anlon so angry, so filled with animus. He was sure Anlon's behavior on the phone was primarily driven by frustration with the whole situation. It was an emotion that Antonio shared. If he'd only been on time, none of it might have happened. Although, he was smart enough to realize there was an equal chance his presence would have made matters worse. The invader might have taken Malinyah's *Sinethal* and then killed them both on the spot.

Antonio reached into his coat pocket and retrieved a cigar. Before lighting it, he put an arm around Anlon. "Hang in there, buddy. We'll figure this out. We'll get her back."

Anlon's eyes remained focused on their dim reflection on the water's surface. "I don't know, Skipper. Think I just cocked up our best chance of getting her back."

"I'm not so sure. I think she'll call back," Antonio said, puffing on the lit cigar. "Think about how bad she must want these Stones.

All the trouble she's gone through the last few days to get them. Do you really think she'd risk losing out when she's this close to getting what she wants?"

"No, probably not. But I can't give her what she wants," Anlon said.

"I wouldn't be so sure about that," Antonio said.

"What do you mean?"

"I assume you're going to talk with Malinyah, right? To find out about Omereau and the other thing she mentioned, the 'lick-till.'"

"Yeah. I wanted to cool off first, but, yes, I'm going to visit with her when I go back inside. I think I already know what the *lyktyl* is. She said Pebbles 'wore' it. If I'm not mistaken, she was referring to Malinyah's medallion. And I know who Mereau is, and who has his *Sinethal*. What I don't know is why Muran wants it so bad."

"Good. Talk with her, find out what you can — especially about the *Sinethal*," Antonio said.

"Why?" Anlon asked.

Antonio smiled and chomped down on his cigar. "Dylan and I've been working on something I think you'll find very interesting."

Footsteps pounded along the dock behind them. Turning, they saw a police officer running toward them. He stopped and called out, "She's on the phone!"

Antonio turned to Anlon and smiled again. "Told ya."

"Come," the officer said, impatiently waving his hands. "It's Miss McCarver! She's on the phone."

Anlon jumped up so fast, he nearly knocked Antonio into the lake.

As Anlon dashed down the deck, Emerson came out from the kitchen door with Anlon's phone to his ear. He descended the steps and then race-walked toward the dock, curving around the stone firepit on his way. They met midway along the path leading from the patio to the deck. Both men were out of breath. Emerson reached the phone toward Anlon. "Here…we're trying to track her down."

Anlon grasped the phone, leaning on a nearby pine. "Pebbles?"

"Anlon? Thank God someone answered your phone!" she said in a whisper.

The sound of her voice, even as a whisper, melted away every ounce of weariness weighing upon Anlon. "I've been so worried about you. Are you okay?"

"I'm scared to hell right now, but I'm okay," she said, her voice fading in and out.

"Where are you?"

"California, I think. Could be Arizona. Somewhere in the desert. Motel called Mojave Palms. Hold on…shit!"

The line went dead.

"Pebbles? Pebbles?" Anlon pulled the phone from his ear and said to Emerson, "Lost the call!"

He cycled through his phone app to find the last call. He pressed the number to reconnect the call. Busy signal. "She said she's at a motel called Mojave Palms."

Emerson said, "I know. We've got people on it."

An officer stuck his head out the kitchen door. "It's in California. CHP is already on the way. She called 911 before she called here."

Antonio came up beside Anlon and tugged him by the arm. "Come on. Let's go. I'll call my pilot on the way down the mountain. You coming, Detective?"

"Uh, yeah. Let's do it," Emerson said.

The three men ran around the corner of the house to reach the driveway. Emerson commandeered one of the police cruisers and they piled in the car. Just as they were about to take off, Anlon said, "Hold on. Be right back."

He sprinted up the steps and through the front door. He stopped in the kitchen to grab the steel case holding Malinyah's *Sinethal*, then bounded up the stairs to the second floor. In the master bedroom, he tossed the case on the bed and went to the closet. From the open safe, he grabbed a *Breylofte*, a pair of *Dreylaeks* and a *Naetir*. He also snagged Pebbles' gun and a loaded clip. After loading the collection in the case, he dashed downstairs, out the front door and into the waiting car. With lights flashing and siren blaring, the cruiser took off down Lakeshore Boulevard.

Pézenas, France

The *Dreylaeks* were in their normal storage spot in Foucault's dressing room, stacked between his Patek Philippe timepiece and cuff links. Foucault snagged the Stones and instantly began to scrape them against one another. Three shots echoed from the parlor below as he raced back through the bedroom. Quickening his grinding, Foucault emerged into the hallway above the main staircase.

Below, he saw Manuel charging up the stairs, gun raised and pointed in his direction. Foucault slammed the two Stones together and whipped his arms in a slashing motion. A bolt shot forth and cut Manuel in half, his gun tumbling harmlessly down the steps.

Enraged, Foucault pounded down the stairs, kicking Manuel's torso out of his way on the descent. Tomas came into view through the parlor entrance. He, too, had his gun ready to fire, but his eyes weren't on Foucault. They were locked on the two halves of his severed colleague. Foucault fired the *Dreylaeks* again, slicing off the man's hand that held the gun. Tomas screamed, but it didn't last long as another jolt from Foucault ended his life.

By the time Foucault burst into the parlor, Navarro was already gone, having scurried out the patio door. Foucault spied Christian and he fell to his knees beside him. One look at his injuries told Foucault there was nothing he could do for his friend. He glanced at the blood surrounding Margaret and concluded the same. Rising, Foucault shouted Navarro's name and gave chase, grinding the Stones as he ran toward the patio door.

Emerging onto the terrace, Foucault looked around and screamed for Navarro to show himself. It took but a second to see the oleanders to the left of his garden swaying furiously. Foucault sped down the steps and down the garden's center aisle. He caught a glimpse of Navarro's ponytail through the sea of flowers and smashed the

Dreylaeks together. The arc of the bolt severed the oleander bushes providing cover for Navarro. A shriek echoed around the bocage bowl formed by the roots of Foucault's ceiba trees.

Foucault followed the sound and found Navarro, arm missing, cowering on the ground. Without thought or word, he burrowed a bolt through Navarro's head. Deed done, Foucault turned and fired the *Dreylaeks* at the remaining oleanders, turning his precious garden into a hellish bonfire.

13

Roller Coaster

Ludlow, California
September 28

The ringing phone jolted Goodwin awake. Grabbing it from the nightstand, he hopped out of bed, glanced over at his sleeping prisoner and quickly exited the room. The midday sun bounced off the car's windows, attacking Goodwin's eyes as soon as he stepped outside. Turning his head away from the glare, he approached the car and answered the call. "Hello?"

"You have the girl?" Aja asked.

Goodwin slid into the driver's seat. "Yes, I have her."

"What about Malinyah?"

"No. Her *Sinethal* wasn't in the house. The girl said Cully keeps it off-site," Goodwin said, shutting the car door.

"Where?"

"She said she didn't know."

"Pah! The girl wears the *lyktyl*. She knows about Alynioria. You can't seriously believe she doesn't know where Cully stores the Stone."

"Why does it matter?" Goodwin asked. "We have her. We can trade her for Malinyah."

"I'm tired of waiting!" Aja said. "Make her tell you where it is. I'll send Kora to take it."

Goodwin chafed at Aja's directive. Did she not realize the seriousness of their situations? Did she not realize that every law enforcement agency on the Eastern Seaboard was searching for her? And that, soon, he would likely face the same on the West Coast?

To him, their number one priority at present was to seek refuge beyond the reach of the American police, just as they had planned. "Look, we need to get across the border. It's too risky to try to do anything else at this point."

"Pah! You are too weak!" Aja growled. "Force it out of her!"

"It's not that simple, my Queen," Goodwin said.

"Cut her hand off. She'll talk," Aja said. "If that doesn't work, cut her other hand off. And then her feet. Sooner or later, she'll talk. They always do."

The suggestion stunned Goodwin. Was she insane? Cut her hands off? What good would come from that? Had torture been effective with Evelyn? God, how the old woman had screamed and begged for Aja to stop. It had been horrific. And she never did reveal where she hid the safe-deposit box keys. Aja had lost control and killed her, and as a result they'd had to search the house anyway. And after all that, she had lied about Omereau!

What was to say Little Miss Tattoo wouldn't lie, too? He'd beaten her savagely at Cully's home, but she'd repeatedly denied any knowledge of Malinyah's whereabouts. Granted, his abuse had convinced her to finally reveal the safe combination, but even when he threatened to shoot her again, she'd not wavered about Malinyah.

"Did you at least get the *lyktyl*?" she asked, interrupting his thoughts.

As Goodwin poised to answer, Aja began to cough. He waited until the fit was over, and said, "Yes. I have it."

"How ironic," said Aja, her voice thick with sarcasm. "Finally, we have the *lyktyl*, but now no Omereau. It wasn't in the boxes. Evelyn lied to us!"

"Yes, I know. I saw the video from the bank," Goodwin said.

"Have you asked the girl about it, then?"

"Not yet."

"Why not?"

"My Queen, if she wouldn't tell me where Malinyah's mindkeeper is, there's no chance she would give up Omereau's. Besides, I'm not convinced Cully has Omereau." Aja did not reply. Only her labored breathing could be heard over the line. He asked, "You sound ill. Are you all right?"

"I will be fine after some *enjyia*," she snapped back. "Now, listen to me! Evelyn must have given Omereau's *Sinethal* to Devlin Wilson when she gave him Malinyah's, which means Cully has it now."

"Maybe, maybe not. It wasn't in the house. I would have noticed it."

"Don't be stupid. He has it wherever Malinyah is stashed."

"Look, there is nothing we can do about it now," Goodwin said. "Right now, we need to get to safety. Then we can negotiate for both *Sinethals*. Has Kora picked you up yet?"

"No. I sent her on an errand."

"What errand?"

"Nothing that concerns you."

"Any deviation from the plan concerns me, my Queen. Improvisation has not served us well," he said.

"Enough! We will meet you at Needles, as planned. I will text you when we are in flight," she said. "You find out what the girl knows about Omereau's *Sinethal*. Hurt her until she tells you everything."

A click signaled the end of the call. Goodwin cursed and pounded the steering wheel. What was on her mind? Even if the girl told him everything he wanted to know, what could they do with the information at this point? Aja was coming unhinged, acting more like a bloodthirsty tyrant than the benevolent Queen she espoused to be. He would have to find a way to temper her rage, or what little was left of their plan would disintegrate.

Albany, New York

"Weakling!" Aja said, tossing the phone aside. "I should have sent Kora!"

He was incapable of acting like a warrior, she thought. He'd shown that when he threw up during Evelyn's confessional! And he had *no idea* how important it was to get Malinyah now that it was clear Cully also had Omereau. Malinyah would ruin everything! Cully would tell Malinyah that "Muran" was alive and that she wanted Omereau. Malinyah would order Cully to destroy Omereau rather than risk his mind-keeper falling into Aja's hands.

Oh, Malinyah had been clever to hide Omereau's *Sinethal* separate from the *lyktyl* after the revolt, Aja thought. She knew Aja would try to take them again. And while Aja had quickly discovered where Malinyah re-entombed Omereau and his *Tyls*, the *lyktyl* had remained hidden for thousands of years. Yet, despite Aja's failure to locate the medallion, she was certain Malinyah hadn't destroyed it; otherwise, there would have been no purpose in hiding Omereau's *Sinethal*. No, Malinyah had been too pure to erase the Munuorians' link with their ancestors, Aja had often reasoned during her fruitless search.

After all, she mused, Malinyah and the other Andaers had expected to rebuild Munuoria once the aftereffects of Munirvo had waned, and after their men had returned from Mereau's pitiful mission of mercy. And Omereau would have figured prominently in their rebuilding plans. But the haughty Andaers had completely misjudged the impact of scattering their people and *Tyls* at a time when self-preservation of their race should have been paramount.

Indeed, Aja had tried to warn them. There was only one way to save the devastated Munuoria: devote every surviving resource to find a new homeland and rebuild their society as quickly as possible. But they hadn't listened. Instead, the fools sent off their best men and most of their scarce *Tyls* to help woebegone foreigners! Riffraff! All because of Mereau and his bleeding heart.

Aja wondered if Malinyah now rued her role in the decision. She surely had interacted with Devlin, Cully and the girl. Otherwise, they would not have found the Indio Maiz Maerlif. They would not know the name Alynioria. They would not have the *lyktyl*. Poor Malinyah must have been crushed to learn that the Andaers' selfless decision had resulted in the annihilation of their own people, leaving the planet populated by lesser men and women. People who warred constantly over stupid things. Selfish mongrels who raped nature. Idiots who were totally unprepared for the next Munirvo, paying more attention to the search for little green men than they did to protecting their own planet from the inevitable assault from another star-washer.

Aja fumed. How could they look at the cratered surfaces of other worlds and not see their peril? How could they examine their own planet's geological and biological record and not grasp the implications? It nauseated Aja to know Munuoria had sacrificed itself for these pathetic animals.

But she would change all that. With Omereau's *Sinethal*, she would chart a new path for humanity. She knew the old man would be enraged to discover Malinyah, Mereau and the others had frittered away his precious gifts. She knew he would favor returning balance to nature, to reestablishing a global society built on his guiding principles. And Aja would be his instrument, his voice and his enforcer. Yes, billions of people would be sacrificed in the cleansing, but in the end, humanity would be set on a more sustainable course, with its priorities and ambitions properly aligned with nature and the stars.

But if Cully got to Omereau first...

Ludlow, California

Goodwin lowered the car windows, hoping the fresh air would help clear his head. As he weighed Aja's command to torture the girl, competing images of Aja filled his mind. There was the Aja with whom he had fallen in love, the sweet, caring woman who sought to end humanity's self-inflicted suffering. Then there was the fire-breathing despot who craved vengeance and power.

He was not blind. He'd read enough legends about her past personas to know she had an evil side to her personality, but in the time he'd known her — nearly eighty years — she'd never resorted to the barbaric tactics the legends ascribed to her. That is, until Malinyah's *Sinethal* resurfaced, sparking the possibility of her recovering Omereau's *Sinethal*.

His thoughts drifted back to the first time he laid eyes on her at Naranjo. It had been the summer of 1942, and Goodwin had gone to the ancient Mayan city as part of a university-funded excavation to learn the ropes of archaeological fieldwork. In the back of his mind, Goodwin had also hoped the excursion would help extend his student deferment a little longer.

The work had been tiresome, as the Mayan ruins there were ravaged by erosion and the creeping tentacles of the jungle, and most of the Mayan treasures hidden there had been looted long ago. He spent most of the summer doing little more than clearing debris. Yet, as mundane as it had been, Goodwin had constantly reminded himself that it was preferable to digging foxholes in Africa, Asia or Europe.

He remembered kneeling at the base of the central pyramid one day toward the end of summer, brushing debris from its stone blocks, when a shadow blocked his light. He looked up, expecting to see a passing cloud, but instead saw a young woman standing on the grass-covered mound at the pyramid's peak. The sight had surprised him for two reasons. One, the expedition's lead archaeologist had made it clear that no one was to mount the pyramid for fear of damaging the crumbling structure. And, two, it was extremely unusual to see an Anglo woman in the Guatemalan jungle in 1942. Reaching Naranjo today is still no easy task, thought Goodwin, and back then it was nearly impossible. Because of the hardships associated with the trek and remote location, women had been strongly discouraged from expeditions to the site.

He had shouted up to tell her to move, but the woman had paid no attention. Thinking back now, Goodwin wondered how different his life might have turned out had he simply ignored her shadow and continued working. Instead, he had climbed a bit farther up the ruin and shouted for her to get down from the top. When Aja turned in his direction, her eyes had blazed into him. When told she was blocking his light, she had huffed and returned to surveying the jungle-covered complex.

Goodwin had shrugged her rudeness off and moved to a section of the base unaffected by her shadow. He was busily brushing away when the shadow returned. He had looked back to find the woman hovering over him. In the sweetest of British accents, she had said, "Pardon me. I wonder if I might ask for your assistance?"

Little did Goodwin know that the "assistance" he would provide would entail helping her excavate a cache of *Lifintyls* buried in the jungle, halfway between Naranjo and another set of Mayan ruins at Yaxha. *Tyls* that Goodwin later learned Aja had stashed during her escape from the invading Tikal army.

He remembered thinking the woman was crazy when she suggested the remote dig site, but she overcame his objections by telling him tales of an enormous trove of gold hidden during the first-century battle between Tikal and Naranjo. She had been an effective manipulator, using her feminine charms to seduce him while filling his mind with dreams of treasure. Before he knew what had happened, he had fallen completely under her spell.

After several failed attempts, they finally found the buried trove, but there had been no gold. Just dozens of stones stacked inside a chest. He had been so disappointed, and equally confused by the woman's reaction. She had been jubilant, parading around the dig, singing in a strange language with a cone-shaped stone in one hand and a hockey-puck-shaped stone in the other. As she had continued to celebrate, Goodwin recalled that she seemed to forget he was there. At one point, she halted her dance and raised her head to the sky, gripping the stones above her head. With a loud shout, she slammed them together and Goodwin's life changed forever.

With a fire raging all around them, she had declared herself Wak Chanil Ajaw, longest reigning ruler of Mayan Naranjo. After rattling off various other titles and names she had ruled under, she finished by announcing herself the last living descendant of the great Munuorian empire. Goodwin recalled she had seemed oblivious to the fires closing in on them. In fact, she had seemed to revel at the specter. She ordered him to bow before her, to recognize her as his Queen. Frightened, Goodwin had ignored her ridiculous command, opting to search for a way through the blaze encircling them.

"Bow," she had demanded, "and I will make the fire vanish. Stand, and I will burn you alive."

She pointed the cone-shaped stone in his direction and readied to strike it with the other. Goodwin fell to his knees, fear in his eyes, hands raised in surrender. Aja, pleased by his submission, had dropped the two stones and reached in the chest for a bowl-shaped stone. Twirling in a circle, she had huffed against the bowl's base and within seconds had extinguished the fire.

He still remembered her words as she approached him and stroked his hair: "Be loyal and your Queen will always protect you."

When Pebbles heard a man's raised voice outside the room, she hung up on Anlon and crawled to the door. Heart thumping, she reached up to verify that the chain lock and deadbolt were secured before turning around and crawling toward the bathroom. As she neared the bathroom door, she stopped and listened. Other than the rattling from the room's climate control unit, she heard nothing.

She directed her gaze upward toward the small windows on each side of the room's entry door. The curtains were drawn over the windows, but they were thin enough for light to filter into the semi-dark room. Pebbles watched for shadows, expecting her captor to approach the door at any second. When none appeared, she dropped back to the floor and crawled into the bathroom. She pushed the door until it was within a few inches from closing and continued to watch and listen for her captor.

While she waited, she patted her hands on the tile floor of the windowless bathroom, searching for her clothes. She found her sweater first and quickly pulled it on. The tag rubbing against her throat signaled the sweater was on backward, but before she could adjust it, Pebbles heard the raised voice again and she froze in place. The voice was closer this time but still too far away for Pebbles to make out what was said. She grabbed the doorknob and kept her eyes glued on the windows. Was it the police? Had they gotten there that quickly? She'd not heard any sirens.

The third time the voice called out, Pebbles was finally able to make out the man's words. "Out of the car. Now!"

She heard a car door creak open, followed by an angry exchange of threats, and then a gunshot boomed out. She slammed the bathroom door closed and depressed the knob lock. Crawling into the tub, Pebbles whispered, "Please be the police!"

Pebbles had made a tough choice after she managed to wiggle her wrists free. Every cell in her brain had urged her to bolt from the room and run for the nearest sign of life, but she had been worried he would see her and chase her down before she could summon help, or worse, shoot her again. So, she had opted for the only other viable alternative: use the room phone to call 911.

After Pebbles had described her situation, the 911 operator cross-referenced the phone number from which Pebbles had called and dispatched the police. After he told her the police were on the way, Pebbles had asked him what she should do until the police arrived. In a calm, firm voice, the operator had told her to lock the doors and barricade herself in the bathroom. Pebbles had asked whether it was a better idea to make a run for it, and the operator unequivocally recommended staying put.

"But what if he gets in before the police get here?" Pebbles had asked.

"Look around the room, find something to defend yourself with," the operator had suggested.

Pebbles had already done that, and the best she had been able to come up with was the bedside alarm clock. It was no bigger than a shoe and hardly heavy enough to do any serious damage, but it was better than nothing. The only problem — Pebbles had left it on the bed after hanging up on Anlon. As she rued the lack of a weapon, Pebbles heard the entry door violently rattle. Her captor hollered, "Open the f—ing door! Now!"

The command was followed by several heavy blows on the door. Shaking uncontrollably, Pebbles lifted her head above the tub ledge and yelled, "I called 911! Cops are com—"

Her retort was cut short by the sound of shattering glass. She ducked back into the tub and cursed again. There was a loud thump, accompanied by a groan, and then the crunching of glass. Oh, Jesus! thought Pebbles. He's in the room! Come on, where are you, sirens?

With one kick of the bathroom door, it flew open and crashed against the commode. The light flicked on and Pebbles buried her head between her hands. Frantic, she began to scream for help with all the force her lungs could muster. She continued to scream as he delivered blow after blow with the butt of the gun against her arm-covered head.

"Shut the f— up!" he shouted repeatedly.

He swung wildly enough that most of the blows glanced off her arms and hands, but then Pebbles shifted her arm to shield her face, exposing her head above the ear. When the gun stock collided against her skull, the force of the blow bounced her head against the tub floor and knocked her out cold.

Unconscious, Pebbles didn't sense him hauling her out of the tub. Nor did she feel the shards of glass slice her legs as he dragged her through the room. As he stuffed her in the trunk again, she was unaware of the dead motel manager sprawled on the sidewalk outside the room, shotgun at his side. Pebbles did stir briefly when the car peeled out of the parking lot. In the distance, she heard the wail of sirens before she faded into unconsciousness.

Reno, Nevada

The police cruiser careened around the sharp curves of Mount Rose Highway as it sped down the mountain. In the backseat, Antonio was on the phone with his pilot, making sure all was ready to go for immediate liftoff upon their arrival at Reno International.

Anlon sat next to him with the case of *Tyls* on his lap, anxiously awaiting an update from Detective Emerson, who was on the phone with the California Highway Patrol. Anlon became alarmed when the detective dropped his head and began to massage his temples. Clearly, something had gone wrong. When the call was over, he turned to face Anlon. His stoic expression did little to alleviate Anlon's uneasiness. Emerson's expression also caught Antonio's attention, leading him to end his own phone call.

"CHP is on-site right now," Emerson said. "Unfortunately, Miss McCarver was gone by the time they got there. Evidently, CHP alerted the motel manager about what was going down, and the idiot tried to rescue her on his own and got himself killed. Two witnesses heard the gunshot and saw a man load a woman into the trunk of a car and take off. CHP has a description of the car. They're searching for them now."

"Damn it," Anlon said.

"I know it's not the news you wanted to hear, but CHP is pulling out all the stops to find them. Road checkpoints, helicopters, you name it," Emerson said.

"Was it Goodwin?" Anlon asked.

"Don't know. CHP didn't get a positive ID from the witnesses," Emerson said.

"Do they know which way he headed?" Antonio asked.

"No, but his options are limited. The motel's in a pretty remote area."

"Where is it? The motel?" Anlon asked, opening the maps app on his cell phone.

"Near a podunk little town called Ludlow. Not much larger than a truck stop, really," Emerson said.

Anlon typed in the town name and the app zeroed in on its location. Antonio leaned over and watched as Anlon used his fingers to zoom out on the map's image. Ludlow sat astride Route 66, a spur off I-40, an east-west highway that led toward Flagstaff, Arizona, to the east and Barstow, California, to the west. To the northside of Ludlow was the Mojave National Preserve. To the south was Joshua Tree National Park. As Anlon zoomed out further, he discovered there were several other wilderness preserves to the west and south, and all were accessible from roads near Ludlow. That meant there were escape route options in every direction.

"Looks to me like he has lots of options," Anlon said, holding up the app for Emerson.

"Less than it looks. The terrain in the area is mostly desert scrubland, according to CHP, and he had a ten-to-fifteen-minute head start, at most. Once the choppers are overhead, it'll be hard for him to hide," Emerson said.

"I know the area," Antonio said. "We do a lot of our military testing near the Mojave. Like you said, lots of desert. But lots of mountains, also. The car won't be so easy to spot from the air if he gets into the mountains."

"We'll see. Hopefully, they catch him before he has time to come up with a plan," Emerson said.

"Do you think he'll kill her?" Anlon asked.

"Let's hope not," Emerson said, holding up crossed fingers.

14

Clearing Fog

Albany, New York
September 28

Jennifer paced the security holding room waiting for Agent Li to reenter. As she had suspected, Li was upset to discover Jennifer's departure from the hospital. Li had been even more angry to learn that Nickerson had helped her slip out. Li had taken the position that Jennifer skipped out before she finished questioning her. Jennifer had countered by saying she thought the questioning was over when they left the room after she identified Goodwin. Li had summarily dismissed her explanation, calling it "total B.S." On her way out of the holding room, Li declared Jennifer a person-of-interest and said she would be held for further questioning.

Li then dressed down Nickerson in an adjoining room. They were still going at it as Jennifer paced her room. She could hear their heated exchange through the thin wall. Jennifer had never heard Nickerson raise his voice before, and it shocked her to hear him boom back at Li as she badgered him with questions. Their parry and thrust went on for several minutes but abruptly ceased. Jennifer was unsure of the reason for the sudden end of their discussion, but right after the room went silent, she heard a third voice through the wall and then the door slammed.

Jennifer expected Li to barge into her holding room at any second with eyes afire and a snarl on her face, but it was a good twenty minutes before the agent came in. When she did, her manner was subdued. She approached Jennifer and asked her to sit at the room's small conference table. Li sat across from her and folded her hands on the table's laminate surface. She studied Jennifer's bruised face and said, "Your friend must mean a great deal to you."

"She does," Jennifer said.

"Then do yourself a favor and cooperate," Li said.

"I have cooperated."

"Not fully."

"Not true," Jennifer said. "Without my help, you wouldn't know who robbed the bank or what kind of weapons she used. I identified Charles Goodwin for you. I'm the one who brought Eleanor McCarver's abduction to your attention. I've answered every question asked of me by everyone involved in this madness."

Li patiently listened, nodding as Jennifer ticked off each of her contributions to the investigation. When Jennifer finished speaking, Li said, "I agree. You've been very helpful. It's the only reason I haven't arrested you for obstruction of justice, interfering in a criminal investigation, and aiding and abetting a fugitive — a fugitive wanted for a laundry list of felonies. But you haven't been completely honest. You've avoided answering certain questions and shaded your answers to others. And to be honest, there are incidents in your police personnel file you didn't mention upfront that concern me."

Jennifer crossed her arms. "What incidents? What are you talking about?"

"You seem to know a lot about the stone artifacts at the center of all these crimes," Li said.

"Yeah, so?"

"I'm concerned you are hiding something that might implicate you in criminal activity. I'm concerned that's the reason you won't answer my questions."

"What? You're out of your mind," Jennifer said, pushing back from the table.

In a level tone, Li said, "Your last case as a detective involved these same stones. A case in which you were suspended for destroying evidence — one of the stones, if I'm not mistaken. And then while you were serving your suspension you shot an unarmed man in Nicaragua. Again, these stones were involved. Then you showed up in Vermont, seeking to gain access to the Simpson murder investigation. You're not on the job anymore, but Detective Hall tells me you asked to tour the crime scene, and you met with the medical examiner."

Jennifer stood and leaned over the table. "You've left out some important facts, but all that's true. I don't deny any of it. How does any of it suggest I'm up to something criminal?"

"You found a rather large amount of gold coins back in May, didn't you?"

"Yeah. So what? They were collected as evidence."

"I ask myself, why won't this detective, excuse me, former detective, tell me where this Muran comes from? She tells me she knows the perp's name, but says she's never met her. She tells me Muran is after some stone artifacts, but won't tell me why. I ask her how she knows Goodwin, how she knew Simpson, she says she was doing research for a friend, this Anlon Cully. But, again, the research is about the stones. I ask how Miss McCarver is involved, I'm told she's another friend and that her abduction is connected with the stones.

"When I push harder for answers, I get pithy brush-offs; 'It'll sound crazy,' or 'It's a long story,' or my personal favorite, 'You'll think I'm a wacko.' So, I ask myself, why won't she come clean? I take a step back, and I wonder. Maybe's she's mixed up in it? Maybe she's after the stones herself? Maybe, just maybe, she got a taste of how much these artifacts are worth and wants another taste now that she's off the job. Her personnel file certainly paints the picture of a cop who doesn't always play by the rules. You know what I mean, more of an 'ends justify the means' kind of cop. Those kinds of cops tend to be vigilantes — and have been known to have sticky fingers," Li said, rubbing her thumbs against her fingers to emphasize the insinuation.

Glaring at Li, Jennifer said, "You couldn't be more wrong."

"Then prove it. Spill the whole truth."

Jennifer sighed and bowed her head. It was an impossible situation. If she told Li the "whole truth," there was a significant chance she'd never be able to work in law enforcement again. If they apprehended Muran or Goodwin, there would be a trial, and Jennifer's comments during the interview would be subject to discovery. The prosecutors would likely minimize Jennifer's testimony, but the defense counsel would seize the opportunity to destroy her credibility. She could see his opening question already. "Come now, Miss Stevens, do you really expect the jury to believe my client is ten thousand years old and that she routinely moves her mind from one body to another?" As sensational as the crimes were, the whole country, if not the whole world, would follow every moment of the trial. If she recanted her statements in court, she'd look like an attention-seeking liar. If she stood by them, she'd look like a loon. Either way, her professional reputation would be ruined.

On the other hand, if Jennifer didn't answer questions, she thought it likely Li would charge her with something that would allow the agent to detain her. Then, Li would try to wear her down into talking. Jennifer could lawyer up, but she realized it might take days to gain her release — precious days she would be unavailable to help Anlon rescue Pebbles or aid in the hunt for Muran and Goodwin.

Li tapped the table to draw Jennifer's attention. "Miss Stevens?"

Jennifer sat back down and locked eyes with Li. "If I tell you everything you want to know, am I free to go when we're finished talking?"

"No guarantees."

"Look, I'm on the same team, here. Truly, I am. I just don't think you'll find my answers credible, and I really don't think they matter at this point. What's important is tracking down Muran and Goodwin before they kill anyone else, including Pebbles, uh, Miss McCarver," Jennifer said.

"Wake up, Stevens. To track down Muran, we need to know a lot more about her than what you've told us. Her full name for starters. Where does she live? Where does she work? Does she have friends or associates she might turn to now that she's on the run? Does she have a criminal record? And so on. You know the drill," Li said.

"I've told you already, I don't know any of that information," Jennifer said. "I'd start by finding Goodwin. Not only does he seem to know Muran, he might know where Pebbles is."

"You may be right about that. His secretary said he left on vacation a few days ago but didn't say where he was headed. We have PDs in Nevada, California and Arizona on the lookout for him, just in case," Li said.

"Arizona? Why Arizona?" Jennifer asked.

"Your friend, 'Pebbles,' was able to make a phone call within the last hour," Li said. "She said she was at a motel very close to where Arizona, Nevada and Cali all touch."

"What?" Jennifer said, jumping up out of her seat. "Why didn't you say something earlier? Is she all right?"

"We don't know. She hung up before anyone could find out. We don't know if she escaped, or if she was able to sneak in the call before Goodwin noticed, assuming he's the one who abducted her. That's not a slam dunk until he's been found and we talk with him. Which would be easier to do if we knew more about his connection with Muran. There are two ways to get there. Start with Goodwin, get to Muran, or the other way around. You see why it's so important to me now?"

"Yes, I do. Just wish you'd led with that. It would have saved time," Jennifer said.

"I was hoping it wasn't necessary. I hoped you'd be straight up with me," Li said.

Jennifer sat back down and laid her hands on the table. "Okay, fine. What do you want to know?"

"Good decision," Li said. She opened a leather portfolio and readied to take notes. "First question — who is Muran?"

"She was a leader, like a council member, of a country called Munuoria."

"Was a leader?"

"The country no longer exists."

"And where was this country located?"

"I don't know."

"How's it spelled, the country name?"

"Couldn't tell you. I'd run it by your linguistics people."

"Okay, I'll have someone check it out. What's her full given name?"

"I don't know, but I'm pretty sure she is using an alias, so I doubt you'll find any trace of her under her given name. I think Anabel Simpson knew one of Muran's aliases, but I couldn't tell you if it was her current alias. I'd suggest having the Vermont PD go back through her papers, look through her computer. Look for a name with the initials C.A.," Jennifer said.

"C.A.? Where'd you come up with that?" Li asked.

This was a moment Jennifer had hoped to avoid, especially given Li's earlier dig about Jennifer not playing by the rules. It seemed so innocent at the time. The Vermont PD had already been through Anabel's house thoroughly and they'd missed it. But how could she blame them? They wouldn't have understood the significance even if they noticed it during their search. Hell, Jennifer hadn't grasped the significance until she saw the screen capture of Goodwin and Muran in the Ticonderoga café. Jennifer sighed. Li wouldn't be happy with her answer.

"There was a locket in Anabel's bedroom mixed in with her other jewelry. It had a picture inside of Anabel holding hands with Muran. I swear I had no idea it was Muran until you showed me the café picture," Jennifer said.

"What? Why didn't you mention it before?"

"Because I've been trying to work it out in my mind. It doesn't make any sense."

"What doesn't make sense?"

"Well, for one thing, there's an inscription on the outside of the locket. 'Forever One.'"

"Is that significant?"

"I don't know. Given the inscription, I expected there to be a man's picture inside."

"So, she had a 'close' lady friend. Big deal."

"Yeah, I know. It just was a surprise given what I knew of Anabel. But that's not all. The picture's puzzling, too."

"How so?"

"Well, Anabel is young in the picture. I'd say she was in her late twenties. Muran looks like the woman in the café. Literally. Hairstyle is different, but otherwise no difference."

"Hmmm…"

"And then there's another inscription inside. 'With all my love, C.A.' There's also a date below the inscription."

"Date?"

"Yeah. 1862."

"What? That can't be right. You said the locket's in the Simpson woman's bedroom? I want to see it."

"Uh, well, it *was* there," said a blushing Jennifer. "I sort of borrowed it. It's in my bag, wherever you've put it."

Li slid out of her chair and headed for the door.

In flight along the Nevada–California border

Upon reaching Reno International's general aviation terminal, Anlon, Antonio and Detective Emerson scurried through the building and out onto the terminal's apron where Antonio's Gulfstream was parked. As they approached the plane, Antonio's executive assistant, Kathleen "Katie" Kierney, appeared through the plane's door and welcomed them aboard.

While Antonio ducked into the cockpit to speak with his pilots, Katie led Anlon and Emerson into the main seating cabin. The compartment had four oversized leather seats, two facing forward, the other two facing aft. Anlon settled into a forward-facing seat and placed the steel briefcase housing the *Tyls* by his feet. As Emerson slid into an aft-facing seat across the aisle, Katie disappeared into the galley to prepare drinks.

Normally, a steward would have done the honors instead of Katie, but the steward had been left behind in San Francisco the day before, owing to Antonio's original plan for a quick out-and-back trip to drop off Malinyah's *Sinethal* with Pebbles. Once that plan was scotched, Antonio had sent the plane to San Francisco, a mere thirty-minute flight, to gather the steward and an overnight bag Antonio kept in his office. Katie, intensely protective of Antonio, took the steward's place, delivering the bag in person and declaring herself ready to assist Antonio and Anlon in any way possible.

Shortly after Katie emerged from the galley with a tray of drinks, Antonio exited the cockpit and took the seat facing Anlon. Katie distributed the drinks and then went forward to let the pilots know they were ready to go.

Once airborne, Antonio and Katie disappeared into the G500's middle compartment, an office-like cabin, for a brief conference. Antonio reappeared a short while later and said, "We should be landing at Twenty-Nine Palms Airport in about forty-five minutes. It's as close as the pilots could arrange on short notice. It's about seventy miles from there to Ludlow. Katie's going to take care of getting us a car. Should be there when we arrive."

"Right. I'll text CHP, see if they can send a cruiser to escort us to Ludlow," Emerson said.

Katie emerged from the office cabin, phone in hand, texting while she talked. "You're all set. Two SUVs from our lab in Palm Desert. Security detail included."

"Perfect. Thanks, Katie," Antonio said.

She nodded and took the seat opposite Emerson, continuing to tap on her phone's screen. "Anything else?"

"Not for me," Antonio said. "Anlon, you need anything?"

"No, I'm good for now." Turning to Emerson, Anlon asked, "Any updates?"

Emerson shook his head. Anlon downed the whiskey in his glass and lifted the steel case from the floor. "Well, then, I think it's time I paid a visit to Malinyah."

As Anlon rose from his seat, Antonio suggested he use the bedroom in the plane's aft cabin. "You'll have more privacy."

After Anlon had retreated to the bedroom, Emerson asked Antonio, "What did he mean, 'visit' Malinyah?"

Antonio exchanged looks with Katie before he responded. Katie had been present when Antonio first "visited" Malinyah, an encounter that ended up creating quite a public scene at the headquarters of Antonio's holding company, Whave Technologies. A scene that had petrified Katie, and one Antonio never fully explained to her.

"Yeah…well," Antonio began, "it's difficult to explain, but I'll try. Malinyah is the name of a woman who lived a long time ago. Her memories are stored on the Stone I brought to give Pebbles, the one Muran wants from Anlon. Even though it looks like a simple stone tile, it's actually a very complex piece of technology. The closest analogy I can think of is an artificial intelligence computer. You can talk with Malinyah, ask her questions just like you'd do with an AI app on your phone. She can answer you and ask questions back. That sort of thing."

"Didn't Dr. Cully say the Stones were ancient?" Emerson asked.

"They are. That's what makes them so valuable, particularly the one storing Malinyah's memories. They prove the existence of a Stone-Age, tech-savvy culture," Antonio said.

"If that's all it is, why did you have a seizure when you were holding the Stone?" Katie asked.

"Wait, what?" Emerson asked.

Before Antonio could answer, Katie said, "Oh, my God. You should have seen it! It looked like the Stone was electrocuting him."

Antonio laughed. "Well, there is electromagnetism involved, but not enough to harm someone. Let's just say it can be an overwhelming experience. It's hard for your mind to cope with what you see and feel. Sort of like the first time you try a virtual reality headset. Makes you freak out a bit, if you're not prepared for it."

"Huh. Sounds pretty 'out there,'" Emerson said.

"A good way to put it," Antonio said with a smile.

Emerson paused to ponder Antonio's description while swirling his glass of ice water. "So, this Muran wants the Stone because of its archaeological value or its technology value? Or both?"

"I don't think anyone knows for sure why she wants it, but she obviously wants it bad enough to kidnap and murder people," Antonio said. "Hopefully, Anlon can find out more from Malinyah, although it's a long shot. Would have been better if Pebbles were here to talk with her."

"Why is that?" Katie asked.

"Pebbles is the only one who understands Malinyah's language," Antonio said.

From the back of the plane came a sharp clap. Katie flinched, while Emerson jumped up out of his seat. "What the hell was that?"

"It's okay," Antonio said, motioning for Emerson to return to his seat. "It just means the conversation has started."

The first sensation Anlon noticed was the chirping of birds. Then a wisp of warm wind passed over him. As his vision cleared, Anlon found himself in a grove of fruit trees. Ahead, he saw Malinyah walking barefoot toward him, a smile on her face. In her hand, she held a piece of fruit plucked from the grove. It was round like an orange but had a bronzed rind. Malinyah was in the act of peeling away the rind when she stopped in front of Anlon. She raised the purple fruit inside to inhale its scent and then balanced it on a branch.

"Anlon," she said, leaning forward to lightly hug him. As he wrapped his arms around Malinyah, he was once again taken aback by the tactile sensations that followed. He felt the silkiness of her blond hair touching his face and the warmth of her body pressed against his. His hands could detect not only the sheer fabric of her tunic but also the movement of her shoulder blades and muscles as she patted him on the back. The sensory elements flowing from Malinyah's memories into Anlon's mind were incredibly vivid, down to the minutest of details — a leaf tickling Anlon's ear, her damp toes brushing against his feet, an insect buzzing by. And the colors! The fruit, the sky, the tan of Malinyah's skin, the glow of her blue eyes.

While Anlon believed he understood the scientific principle that made the transfer of memories and sensations through the *Sinethal* possible, the exchange of neural signals via electromagnetic stimulation, he was far from understanding the technology that made it possible. But his curiosity would have to wait for another opportunity; there were more pressing concerns to address with Malinyah.

He closed his eyes and concentrated on an image of Pebbles, letting his fear for her safety dominate his thoughts. Malinyah stiffened and withdrew from the embrace. Her eyes reflected Anlon's emotions. "Eleanor?"

Anlon nodded. He held up his right hand and said, "Eleanor." He clamped his left hand around the right and squeezed it tightly. "Muran."

Malinyah staggered back a step and covered her mouth with her hand. Swaying her head from side to side, she mumbled something in her native language. Anlon clasped his hands together in a praying position and said, "Anlon needs Malinyah's help."

It was pointless speaking to her. He knew she didn't know English, just as he was unable to interpret Munuorian, but he hoped she would understand his hand gestures better supported by the emotions communicated by the tone and inflection of his voice.

Malinyah's face grew stern. "Muran! *Sikaer!*"

Anlon didn't need a translation. The animus with which Malinyah delivered the epithet did the translation for him. *Sikaer!* Betrayer!

She stepped up and held out both hands, gesturing for Anlon to take them. When he took hold of them, she looked in his eyes and said, "Eleanor."

The grove disappeared, and Anlon's mind was filled with the image of Pebbles with Malinyah in a field of blue flowers. They held hands and watched a girl chase butterflies among the flowers. Anlon's heart ached seeing the happy look on Pebbles' face.

Malinyah abruptly pulled her hands away, ending the image and returning Anlon to the grove. She pointed to Anlon, then reached up and tapped his forehead, saying, "Eleanor."

She held out her hands again, encouraging Anlon to grasp them. He quickly understood the meaning of her gesture. Though they couldn't communicate with words, she could share images with him, and to Anlon's astonishment, Malinyah was trying to tell him he could do the same with her.

He wrapped his hands around hers and focused his thoughts on Pebbles. He filled his mind with an image of her injured and in pain. He had seen the photo of Muran in the café with Goodwin, so he presented Malinyah with an image of the two holding a struggling Pebbles. He said, "Muran. Goodwin. Eleanor."

Anlon then formed a mental image of the *Sinethal* and showed Malinyah a scene where he handed the *Sinethal* to Muran, and Goodwin let go of Pebbles. He felt a sudden blast of anger pass back from Malinyah before she let go of his hands. She spat the epithet again.

Okay, thought Anlon. Message transmitted and received.

The next part would be trickier. Anlon knew that Pebbles had told Malinyah about Foucault's discovery of Mereau's *Sinethal*. In that same conversation, Pebbles also had let Malinyah know that Foucault had given her the medallion and the necklace Malinyah had originally gifted to Mereau. So, it would be easy to show Malinyah a mental image of another *Sinethal*, saying the word "Mereau," and then an image of the necklace, saying, "*lyktyl.*" It would also be easy to depict a scene where Anlon handed the second *Sinethal* and necklace to Goodwin and Muran. The hard part would be asking Malinyah to explain why Muran wanted these pieces, and then interpreting her response.

Malinyah seemed puzzled when Anlon showed her the image of a second *Sinethal* and said Mereau's name. When he presented the image of the necklace with the medallion and said "*lyktyl,*" Malinyah gasped and tugged her hands free from his grip. This time, Anlon felt a sense of dread flow from Malinyah.

"*Eku Mereau,*" she said, with a downward slash of her arm. "Omereau!"

She grabbed Anlon's hands and filled his mind with a strange flurry of images while she chattered in an urgent tone. At first, the images made no sense, just a jumble of different memory snippets. But then Malinyah's voice slowed and her tone steadied. When she laced the snippets together in a more rational way, Anlon finally understood. "Son of a bitch!"

15

One Step Behind

In flight over the Atlantic Ocean
September 28

Foucault leaned through the cockpit door and tapped his pilot, Henri de la Roche, on the shoulder. "How much longer?"

Henri slid his headset off his right ear and turned to Foucault. "An hour, maybe less."

"*Bon.* The refueling arrangements have been made?" Foucault asked, sliding into the empty copilot seat.

"*Oui.*"

"How long will that take?"

"Depends. If we are first in line, we can be back in the air quickly, but if we're down in the queue, could be an hour or two," Henri said. "LaGuardia is always hard to predict."

"Let us hope we are near the front, then," Foucault said, looking out the cockpit window at the endless, grayish ocean ahead.

"Are we still heading to Reno after topping up?"

"I am still waiting to hear back from Dr. Cully," Foucault said, turning back to Henri. "If he doesn't respond by the time we are ready to go, then, yes."

Henri nodded and slid the headset back into place. Raising the headset microphone to his mouth, he responded to a command from air traffic control while Foucault returned his gaze to the ocean.

As he waited for the skyline of Manhattan to appear on the horizon, Foucault flexed his bandaged hands. Poor Christian, he thought. There had been no need for his rash act. Foucault had known Navarro would refrain from killing any of them until he had his prize, despite his threats to the contrary. If only Christian had heeded his advice to remain calm, both he and Margaret would still be alive.

Thinking back, Foucault rued his simple cue to Christian. "*Calmer, ami.* This nonsense will be over soon." He had hoped Christian would understand the comment was meant to communicate that Foucault had devised a plan, one that would have saved them from Navarro. He should have instead said, "*Calmer, ami.* We will give him the *Tuliskaera* and *Terusael,* and this nonsense will be over."

Said in that way, Christian would have immediately understood Foucault's plan. Navarro, unfamiliar with the *Tyls'* Munuorian names, would undoubtedly have demanded to know the meaning of the names. Foucault would have told him they were the Stones he wanted. Satisfied with the answer, Navarro would have sent one of his men with Christian to fetch the Stones, while Navarro and the other man stood watch over Foucault.

Foucault envisioned Christian returning with the cone-shaped *Tuliskaera* and the egg-shaped *Terusael.* He knew Navarro would immediately object to the *Terusael.* "This is not the right stone! Where is the other one, the one that looks like a tin?"

Foucault would have reassured him. "No, no. This is the right one. Let me show you."

The skeptical Navarro would have commanded him to stay put, but even so, Foucault knew Navarro would not be able to resist the impulse to try the device. The fool would have tinkered with the Stones with no success. "See, I told you. Get me the other one."

Foucault would have said, "You are not using them properly. Grind the egg on the bottom of the cone in a circular motion. It will heat the egg. When both Stones begin to glow, then hit them together, but be careful where you aim the tip of the cone. It will shoot out a deadly bolt. The hotter the Stones glow, the more intense the bolt."

It would have been glorious. Navarro, eyes twinkling with anticipation, rubbing the two *Tyls* together until they pulsed with light. Foucault was sure Navarro would have then aimed the *Tuliskaera*'s tip at him. In fact, he counted on it. The explosion when the two Stones collided would have ripped Navarro to shreds. The *Terusael*, a grenade when stimulated in this way, would have exploded on contact with the *Tuliskaera*, the force of the blast directed toward Navarro. The *Tuliskaera* would have shattered and crumbled to the floor. All but Christian and Foucault would have been paralyzed by the explosion, giving them the opportunity to disarm Navarro's men and end the stand-off.

Foucault sighed. If only Christian had remained calm. But he hadn't, and now Foucault's friend and confidant was dead, and there would never be a time to properly mourn for him.

Ludlow, California

By the time Anlon, Antonio and Emerson reached the Mojave Palms motel, a dozen police vehicles lined the road on both sides of the lot entrance. Emerson flashed his badge to a uniformed officer who flagged them to stop, and the policeman directed them to park at the end of the line of cars. While Emerson left to confer with the CHP detectives gathered by an unmarked cruiser, Anlon and Antonio stood at the lot entrance, looking beyond the police tape cordoning off the area toward the room where a forensics crew moved about collecting evidence.

The vision of tent cards marking evidence on the ground outside the room, including a large blood stain on the sidewalk, brought back unpleasant memories of Anlon's arrival at his home.

"Place looks like a ghost town," Antonio said.

Anlon looked around. Antonio was right. The strip motel shared a parking lot with a diner and a gas station/minimart. Outside of those structures, there was nothing to see but a lonely road, desert, scrubland and mountains in every direction. Each of the dusty buildings looked as if they'd been built in the 1950s. Aside from the few late-model cars parked at the diner, the three buildings did give the impression of being the last vestiges of a long-abandoned town.

"Certainly is remote," Anlon said. "Doesn't seem like a random choice, does it?"

"No, it doesn't," Antonio said. "Especially given all the escape routes."

As Anlon had seen in his earlier review of the map app on his phone, the motel was within a block of a four-way intersection and sat only a quarter mile from the entrance to I-40 and its parallel sister-road, Route 66. From the motel, Goodwin could have quickly hopped onto either road and headed east or west. If he hadn't wanted to risk taking the major thoroughfares, he could have proceeded north along a two-lane desert road that crossed several similar east-west roads and ultimately linked up with another major highway, I-15. If he opted to drive south on the desert road, he could have linked up with CA-52 at the city of Twenty-Nine Palms. Therefore, despite Emerson's repeated assurances, Anlon considered it quite possible that Goodwin was long gone. The question was — where?

"What do you think the game plan was?" Antonio asked.

"What do you mean?" Anlon asked.

"Well, I'm going to assume they didn't want all this police attention, right? So, they expected to sneak in and take Malinyah's Stone from you, likewise with the Stones from the bank, and then, what?"

"Oh, this has only a little to do with Malinyah. It's all about the necklace, and Omereau's *Sinethal*. Excuse me, Aramu Muru's *Sinethal*."

The moment Malinyah's vision revealed his *Sinethal* as a golden disc, Anlon recalled Elton Sinclair's tapestry and Diane Jones' description of the mythical Aramu Muru. When Malinyah flipped the disc over to show him the notch in its center and held up a gold medallion with a black stone in its center, he understood. The *lyktyl* was essentially the *Naetir* that activated Omereau's *Sinethal*.

The vision had gone on to show Anlon the great Omereau himself crafting the other *Tyls* in a volcanic foundry. While Anlon did not understand the narrative Malinyah provided along with the visions, the images told him enough. Omereau was the man who conceived the *Lifintyls*. The Einstein of their race. His *Sinethal* contained his memories and his consciousness. That meant whoever possessed his *Sinethal* had the means to tap his intellect and recreate the *Tyls*. At least, that's the implication Malinyah communicated through her vision.

To reinforce this latter speculation, Malinyah had shifted the vision to show Anlon a snippet of the post-Munirvo revolt, a scene where Malinyah and her guards surrounded Muran in a marble hall. In Muran's hands was Omereau's *Sinethal*, and on her chest swung a necklace with a gold pendant with a black stone. Muran screamed at Malinyah as the guards took both from her. It was Anlon's first view of Muran as she had been born.

She looked nothing like Anlon had expected. Based on the stories of her wickedness, his mind had conjured up an evil persona for Muran. Cold, unfeeling black eyes. A wizened, ugly face. Dark hair and a physique cut like a warrior's. The truth — she looked eerily like Malinyah. Beautiful, blond and tanned with lithe curves and penetrating blue eyes.

As Malinyah's snippet finished with Muran escaping from the guards, she displayed two follow-on scenes. One was familiar to him; a scene Pebbles had described on a few occasions: Malinyah stood on a dock and gave the medallion to Mereau before the captain and his men left on ships.

Unlike Muran, Mereau looked exactly as Anlon had expected. Tall, proud and chiseled, his bearing was commanding, yet his eyes were compassionate and his embraces with Malinyah were filled with tenderness. It was easy to see why Foucault had been so taken with the man. He looked virtuous, brave and caring, a hero the likes of which Anlon had never seen.

The final scene depicted Malinyah on a ship, approaching a lush island. Upon landing, she stepped off the boat with a cadre of men and women. Together, they traversed the island until arriving at a volcano. Up they climbed, until Malinyah and two others carved a cavern into the volcano's midsection. Into it they carried a sarcophagus and several boxes like the ones Anlon's team found in Indio Maiz. For Anlon's benefit, she showed the sarcophagus lid opened. Inside were the bones of a man draped in a crimson-and-gold robe. On his chest was the golden disc.

The implication was clear — Muran had used the revolt to sneak in and snatch Omereau's *Sinethal* and the *lyktyl*. Malinyah caught her in the act and relieved her of the booty. Fearing Muran might make another attempt to steal the precious pieces of their history, Malinyah first sent the medallion away with Mereau. Pebbles had misinterpreted the purpose of Malinyah passing the medallion to Mereau. It was never intended as a gift from one lover to another. The act was a precautionary measure intended to prevent Muran from accessing Omereau's memories. As a further safeguard, Malinyah then had hidden Omereau's remains and possessions, including his *Sinethal*, in a remote volcano Maerlif.

Anlon recognized the volcano from its three mounded peaks — Morne Trois Pitons, on the island of Dominica. And in that moment, Anlon realized the litany of lies and half-truths spewed by Jacques Foucault. They were fabrications that put Pebbles at the center of Muran's crosshairs. She had been the bait for his trap, a trap that Anlon feared had less to do with bringing Muran to justice and more to do with the ambitious designs of the crafty Frenchman.

However, his design included a faulty assumption. Foucault presumed Muran had Omereau's *Sinethal* already. Based on this flawed belief, Foucault had hoped to lure her out into the open with the *lyktyl*. On the surface, it seemed a ludicrous plan to Anlon. Why tempt Muran with the key to unlocking Omereau's memories? If she acquired it, and Foucault was unable to stop her, he would have literally handed her all she needed to create new *Tyls* and embark on a modern reign of terror.

Yet, Anlon had noticed something in Malinyah's visions that gave him the answer to the perplexing question. The *lyktyl*, the pendant that Pebbles wore so reverently as a physical reminder of Malinyah, was a fake.

Oh, it was a masterful replica, thought Anlon…with one flaw. During Malinyah's vision, when she showed Anlon how to insert the *lyktyl* into the slot on the back of Omereau's *Sinethal*, she did so with the medallion's face fitting into the slot, revealing the back side of the pendant. Etched into the gold surface was a circle with six rays; the back of Pebbles' medallion was devoid of any etching.

For the remainder of the flight, Anlon had pondered why Foucault had given Pebbles an imitation of the *lyktyl*, and why he had worn it himself. Once Goodwin delivered it to Muran, she would quickly discover it was a fake. What good would that do Foucault? It would only enrage Muran. And she didn't have Omereau's *Sinethal* to begin with. What had the conniving bastard been thinking? All he'd done was put Pebbles at extraordinary risk, and once Muran discovered the *lyktyl* was phony, she would take her anger out on Pebbles. Given what she had done to Anabel, and the carnage she left in New England, there was no doubt in Anlon's mind what she'd do to Pebbles.

Antonio shook Anlon by the shoulder. "Hey, buddy, you all right?"

"Huh? Oh…sorry. Got lost in thought. Did you say something?" Anlon asked.

"Yeah, I said a lot, actually. And you didn't hear a word of it, did you?"

"Uh…"

"Never mind, I'll tell you later. Emerson called us over. Come on, let's go."

Albany, New York

Jennifer watched Agent Li examine the picture and inscription inside the open locket. "I see what you mean. The woman next to Simpson does look like the same woman in the café."

As Li flipped it over in her gloved hand to inspect the locket's casing, Jennifer scrambled to come up with a believable story to satisfy the FBI agent. There was no more time to waste. She needed to get out of the holding room, check her voice messages, call Anlon and find a new flight. She said, "There's only one rational explanation I can come up with to explain the combination of the picture, inscriptions and date."

"And that is?"

"It's a stretch…"

Li lifted her head and frowned. "Come on, Stevens. Out with it."

"Okay, let's deal with the date first. 1862. The locket's a family heirloom. The picture —Anabel liked the locket and put her own picture in it. If it was taken when Anabel was in her twenties, the other woman in the picture can't be the woman in the café, right? Anabel was mid-fifty-ish when she died. So, maybe the other woman is a relative of Muran's. Her mother? An aunt?"

The agent nodded while she continued to study the locket. "Close, but you're off a bit in your generations."

"Excuse me?" Jennifer asked.

Li placed the locket on the table and grabbed her cell phone. After a few swipes and clicks, she slid the phone to Jennifer. "Take a look."

Before she picked up the phone, Jennifer could see a fuzzy, black-and-white picture on the screen. Even from a distance, she recognized Anabel. She reached for the phone and inspected the head shot more closely. It was Anabel at roughly the same age as in the locket photograph. Jennifer used her fingers to zoom out on the picture and discovered it was a thumbnail inside a newspaper article. The name Evelyn Warwick was printed beneath the photo.

Jennifer frowned and zoomed out further until the full article was visible. She noticed there were two other photos in the article, much larger than Anabel's. One was a professional portrait of a young woman in a ball gown. Beneath the photo, the woman was identified as Miss Clara Ambrose. The other photo showed a volcano surrounded by a jungle. The caption beneath the photo read, "San Carlos Volcano, Fernando Pó."

Jennifer read the brief article…

DAUGHTER OF ADMIRAL AMBROSE INJURED IN BRAZEN ATTACK BY SLAVER PIRATES

LONDON – April 17, 1842 – All of London society is in a state of shock upon news of the attack on Admiral Sir William Ambrose's daughter, Miss Clara Ambrose. The afternoon ambush took place last week on the African island of Ferdinand Pó, where Sir Ambrose serves as Governor of Her Majesty's anti-slavery outposts on the island.

According to Foreign Office officials, the precocious debutante was waylaid by a band of pirates while on a nature hike. Miss Ambrose was gravely injured in the attack, and only escaped due to the quick actions of her handmaiden, Evelyn Warwick.

Warwick told officials the two women were exploring a volcano on the island when the pirates surrounded them and took them as prisoners. Warwick said the pirates intended to sell them into slavery in retribution for the recent sinking of slaving ships by Sir Ambrose's fleet. Warwick managed to break free and ran to the outpost at San Carlos.

Sentries from the outpost were dispatched and came across the injured Miss Ambrose near the base of the volcano. They brought her to the San Carlos outpost, where she received medical attention. An extensive land and sea search to apprehend the pirates was ordered by Sir Ambrose, but they have yet to be captured.

No details were provided regarding Miss Ambrose's injuries; however, officials deemed them "serious," and indicated she will return to London within a fortnight for further medical treatment and rehabilitation. Sir Ambrose will accompany his daughter back to England and take a new post in the Royal Navy's staff offices.

When Jennifer finished reading the article, she looked up to see Agent Li using her finger to slide the picture from its frame inside the locket. Li turned it over, and Jennifer saw a note scribbled on the back. Li read it aloud. "C.A., E.W., 1862."

"That's crazy," Jennifer said, returning to view the newspaper article pictures. "Where did you get this?"

"We had HQ do a search on the name Evelyn Warwick. Bank records showed she listed her previous address in London. The account was opened in 1942, by the way. Safe-deposit box rental goes back that far, too. Though the bank's changed names and moved since the original account was opened," Li said.

"You had this the whole time we were talking?"

"Uh-huh," she said. "Had it this morning when we met in the hospital."

"I can't believe you didn't say anything," Jennifer said, pushing the phone back across the table.

"I'm in the information-getting business, Stevens. Not the information-giving."

"Nice," Jennifer scoffed.

Li smiled. "Take any other evidence from the Simpson house?"

"No," Jennifer said. "Are we done?"

"Not quite," Li said.

"Why? Sounds like you've got your answer about Muran. She's a descendant of Clara Ambrose. I'm sure you've got HQ researching her family members right now. What do you need me for? You've also got the connection with Anabel Simpson and Evelyn Warwick, and I'm sure it won't take long to track down links with Goodwin. I don't see what else I can do for you."

"Talk to me about Goodwin," Li said.

"There's not much to tell. I went to visit him at the museum where he works. He's an ass hat, by the way," Jennifer said.

"When was this?"

"Uh…about two months ago. Don't remember the exact date, but I can get it for you."

"Was your visit about the stones?"

"Yes, I went to show him some pictures of pieces in Devlin Wilson's collection on behalf of Anlon Cully. Anlon wanted to know if Goodwin was familiar with the pieces."

"What led you to Goodwin's museum in the first place?"

"They'd sold Devlin an artifact made by the same civilization. We were trying to find out where Devlin purchased the artifacts. It was a total flier. I visited a few other museums for the same purpose."

"What did you find out from Goodwin?" Li asked, flipping up a completed page of notes to continue on a fresh sheet.

"Very little. He said he didn't recognize the pieces. He showed me some others they had in their collection and gave me some background info on them. That was it. Lasted about thirty minutes. Haven't seen or talked to him since."

"Did this meeting happen before or after you first learned about Muran?"

"A few weeks before."

Li stopped taking notes and laid her pen on the table. With a blank stare, she looked toward the wall. A few minutes later, she returned her attention on the portfolio pad, flipping back several pages. She ran her finger along as she scanned the notes. Then her finger stopped, and she looked up at Jennifer. "Who is Malinyah?"

"Uh..."

"The Nevada police said Goodwin, or whomever abducted your friend Pebbles, left a note that said, 'Malinyah for the girl.' Who's Malinyah?" Li asked again.

How am I going to answer this one? Jennifer thought. "Um..."

"The detective in Nevada I spoke with said the name refers to a black stone that Cully owns. A stone that looks a lot like the one Muran took from the bank," Li interjected.

"Yes, that's right," Jennifer said.

"Is Malinyah one of the artifacts in the pictures you showed Goodwin?"

Jennifer's face twitched. "Oh, my God. I tipped him off."

Li nodded. "Looks that way to me."

The agent ran through her theory. There was a lingering dispute between the descendants of Clara Ambrose and Evelyn Warwick that went back a long way. Probably back to the two women in question. A dispute that had something to do with the artifacts — specifically, a dispute over ownership. Given that Evelyn was Clara's handmaiden, it seemed reasonable to assume that Evelyn had taken the artifacts from Clara or Clara's family. Li suggested that Muran, a descendant of Clara Ambrose, discovered that Anabel, a descendant of Evelyn Warwick, possessed the disputed artifacts and made a play to take them back. Li speculated Jennifer's visit to Goodwin was the catalyst that rekindled the dispute.

"The only thing missing to complete the picture is to sort out the connection between Goodwin and Muran," Li said. "How did they know each other? How did Goodwin know of the dispute? Why did he get involved in it?"

Before Jennifer could answer, Li stood. Holding up the locket, she said, "I'll be back in a minute. This is going into evidence."

Jennifer had listened attentively to Li's theory. While the agent was way off in her belief that Muran was a descendant of Clara Ambrose, the heart of her hypothesis was compelling. Jennifer didn't believe for a moment that Anabel was a descendant of Evelyn Warwick. She *was* Evelyn Warwick. She had taken Muran's *Tyls* and had gotten away with it. When she took them, and why she took them, Jennifer didn't know. But, at some point before or after taking the *Tyls*, Anabel met Devlin Wilson. And for some reason, within the last year, she decided to give him Malinyah's *Sinethal*. Why?

While Jennifer couldn't deny Li's speculation that her visit to Goodwin was the catalyst for the most recent events, Anabel's decision to give Devlin the *Sinethal* was really the first act that ignited the whole tragedy.

After Indio Maiz, Jennifer had strongly suspected Anabel was Muran. Even when she first learned of Anabel's death, she thought Muran had simply chosen a new body and discarded Anabel's. But the forensic evidence collected from Anabel's home and her body clearly showed she had been a victim of a callous murder, a murder steeped in revenge.

If Li was right, the reason for the revenge seemed clear: payback for taking *Tyls* from Muran. Yet, Jennifer wondered if it might even go beyond that. The locket's inscription and picture suggested Anabel's relationship with Muran was more intimate than servant and master. Muran crushed her heart, for heaven's sake, an act Jennifer now interpreted to mean, "You crushed mine, so I'm crushing yours." Personal. A crime of passion.

Jennifer allowed herself to consider a possible answer, one that had been bubbling in the back of her mind the past twenty-four hours. Was it possible Anabel had been a Munuorian herself? That, just like Muran, she had extended her life repeatedly by switching bodies? Had they been in it together? Forever one.

The root of her speculation? Anabel clearly had more than superficial knowledge of the *Tyls*, and she certainly had been using *enjyia* for a long time given the age of the photograph in the locket. If she had simply been Muran's handmaiden, why would Muran have shared the *Tyls'* secrets with her?

Further, whose *Sinethal* had Muran removed from the safe-deposit box? Had it been Anabel's? Foucault had given them the impression at Indio Maiz that all Muran lacked to switch bodies again was a *Tuliskaera*. If that were true, why had Muran taken the *Sinethal* from the safe-deposit box? And now that she had it, why was she determined to also acquire Malinyah's *Sinethal*?

And why had Muran been so upset when she finished fishing around in the boxes? Earlier, Jennifer had been sure Muran was upset because there was no *Tuliskaera* in the box. But then she unleashed the *Tyl* at Ticonderoga. So, what else had she expected to find?

Whatever the answers, Li was wrong. The key to solving the mystery at this point was not the link between Goodwin and Muran. It was the link between Anabel and Muran. Either way, in Jennifer's mind, solving the mystery ran a far second place to getting Pebbles back.

When Li reentered the room, Jennifer said, "Look, I can't help you with the link between Muran and Goodwin. I met him once, and I don't know any more about either of them beyond what I've told you. Now, can I please go? I need to go help get my friend back."

"Yes. But I'm coming with you," Li said.

Needles, California

Goodwin gripped the steering wheel and watched the descending airplane. As soon as he saw the crimson-and-gold trim on the plane's tailfin, he exhaled a sigh of relief. The escape from the motel had been harrowing, but Goodwin managed to get on I-40 without being spotted, and by the time police alerts began to broadcast over the radio, he had already pulled into the airfield and parked without incident. But the hour since then had been excruciating, especially after the alerts began broadcasting his name.

At first, he had been dumbfounded. How had the police discovered his involvement? As far as anyone at the museum knew, he had taken a few days off to "catch some fun in the sun." Kora had flown him to California on Aja's plane, and she had rented the car at the airport he used to transport the girl from Tahoe. He'd used cash when he checked into the motel. He was using a prepaid cell phone and a tablet registered to one of Aja's companies. The gun wasn't registered. He'd used gloves at Cully's house and had worn the hoodie while driving the car. Yet, despite all his precautions, the police had identified him as a person of interest.

When he later learned the reason from a news update on the radio, he seethed anew at Aja's recklessness. Why had she drawn their attention to the fort? Why couldn't she have just tossed the girl's body in the lake? Why did she insist on meeting at the fort in the first place?

Once the plane had landed and taxied off the runway, he grabbed his phone and rattled off a quick text. "Here, and ready to go."

"Good," Aja replied. "I will call you once we've parked."

The plane slowly rolled toward a large flattop area near the garage-sized building that served as control tower and terminal. When it came to a stop, Goodwin's phone rang. He pressed "answer" and held it to his ear. "Hi. Ready?"

"Not yet," Aja said. "Kora's coming out to check the plane and chat with the airport manager. We want to make this look like a normal turnaround."

"Okay, got it," Goodwin said.

"Where are you?"

"You see to the left of the building, underneath the trees? Near the junkyard of plane parts."

"Yes, I see you now. Where is the girl?"

"In the trunk. Tied and gagged."

"Get her in the front seat. We don't want the tower to see her pulled from the trunk."

"Okay. I'll do it when Kora's ready to go. Just let me know."

"It'll be a few minutes. I'll text you," Aja said, and she ended the call.

Goodwin spied the plane door open and the steps unfold. Kora exited the plane and casually walked across the tarmac, hands in her jeans pockets, baseball cap covering her head and aviator sunglasses perched on her nose. A man emerged from the building and approached her. They shook hands and conversed for several minutes. Her manner was so relaxed. She smiled, stretched her arms and yawned while the man spoke. They laughed about something and then she pointed at the plane. The man seemed to ask her a question, because Kora shook her head and then looked at her watch. A minute later, they shook hands again and she walked back to the plane.

"Time to go," said Aja's text.

Goodwin opened the backpack sitting on the passenger seat. He first checked to make sure the *lyktyl* was still inside and then retrieved the gun. Stepping out of the car, he opened the rear door and tossed the backpack inside. He looked around to make sure no one was watching before opening the trunk. With the gun in one hand, he popped the trunk with the key remote and pulled up the lid. The girl was awake. He leaned down and placed the gun against her head. She recoiled, her eyes wide and body trembling. Through the gag, she pleaded. He snapped, "Be quiet! I'm putting you up-front. Don't fight me or I will shoot."

Pebbles was complicit as he yanked her from the trunk and dragged her to the passenger-side door. After shutting the door and trunk, Goodwin hopped in and started the car. A two-hundred-yard drive later, Goodwin pulled the car beside the plane.

Kora stood waiting by the steps and opened the passenger door. Looking down on Pebbles, she said, "Jesus, what did you do to her?"

"Just get her on board," he said.

They quickly dragged Pebbles up the steps and into the cabin. Shortly after, Goodwin emerged. Kora followed moments later with a screwdriver in her hand. "Wait up."

"Huh?"

"Aja said I should go with you to park the car. She wants the license plates off," she said, holding up the screwdriver.

"Ah. Good thinking," Goodwin said. Reaching into the backseat, he pulled out the backpack and handed it to her. "The *lyktyl*'s inside. Give me the screwdriver, I'll take care of it. You get aboard and start the plane."

"Nah, it'll be quick. Come on, let's go," she said, sliding into the passenger seat, bag on her lap.

"All right. Fine," he said.

As Goodwin drove back to the small lot, he angled the car toward the spot underneath the trees he'd occupied before. Kora looked around and suggested they park among the junked planes instead. "It'll take them longer to find it."

"Okay, good idea."

With the car wedged between partial fuselages of old propeller planes, they got out and Kora held up the screwdriver. "You want to do the honors, or should I?"

"I'll do it. You stand watch." He took the tool and knelt down to remove the rear plate.

"Sounds good," she said with a cheery smile.

Goodwin had just finished removing the first screw when Kora grabbed him by the hair and slashed his throat.

16

Devil's Due

In flight over northern Arizona
September 28

She sat in an oversized, high-back seat toward the back of the plane. With a proud bearing, she looked down on Pebbles, her lips curled at one corner. She wore an ankle-length, white dress trimmed in crimson and gold. On the woman's chest rested Malinyah's medallion. The audacity of the gesture caused Pebbles' face to flush.

"Kora!" the woman shouted.

From behind, Pebbles heard a door open and the sound of approaching footsteps. She craned her neck to see a young woman strut past her head. It was the same woman who'd helped her captor hustle her onto the plane. The woman didn't stop to look at Pebbles. In fact, in Pebbles' estimation, the woman seemed to ignore her lying on the floor.

"Yes, my Queen," said the young woman.

"Untie her. Take the gag off. Get her *enjyia*," Aja instructed.

Kora swiftly retraced her path past Pebbles. A moment later, she returned and knelt behind her. She cut away the gag and bindings and then turned to leave.

"Put her there," Aja said, pointing to a window seat catty-corner across the aisle to hers.

Kora helped Pebbles stand and propped her up as she staggered to the seat. Pebbles slid onto the seat and tried to stretch her sweater down to cover for her lack of clothing below, but the fabric would not cooperate. Red-faced, she clamped her legs together and covered her lap with her hands.

She looked up to see Aja smiling at her, apparently amused by Pebbles' show of modesty. When Kora returned with a tall glass of *enjyia*, Aja instructed her to fetch Pebbles more suitable clothes from her bedroom in the back. Kora briefly resisted, reminding Aja she was supposed to be in the cockpit, flying the plane. After a sharp rebuke from Aja, Kora slapped down the glass on a tray by Pebbles' seat and disappeared into the aft cabin. A moment later, she returned with a beige garment that she tossed on Pebbles' lap on her way back to the cockpit. Pebbles quickly spread the dresslike piece over her waist and draped it down her legs.

"Go ahead," Aja said. "Put it on. It's impossible to take you seriously, half-naked."

Pebbles slowly pulled one arm from the sweater's sleeve and then the other. Each movement caused her to wince, as needling twinges stabbed along her ribs. With her arms underneath the body of the sweater, she leaned forward and scooped her hands up through the neck hole, lifting the sweater up and over her head in the process. Panting from the pain, she dropped the sweater on the floor and lifted up the dress. As she examined it, she saw it was more like a nightshirt than a dress. A few grunts and sharp pains later, the dress was on and Pebbles settled back into her seat.

"Now, drink the *enjyia*. It will lessen your pain," Aja said.

Starving and thirsty, Pebbles needed no further encouragement. She lifted the glass and downed the *enjyia* in four gulps. Lowering the empty glass to the tray, Pebbles wiped at her lips. She felt her tongue and throat begin to tingle. Within seconds, the restorative effects of the concoction began to take hold and she felt her weariness and dizziness start to melt away. Then, the stinging pains in her ribs, wrists and ankles began to fade, as did the throbbing from the bullet wounds. She closed her eyes and exhaled as a warm feeling coursed throughout her mind and body.

"Better now?" Aja asked.

Pebbles nodded. Despite the relief, she could not bring herself to thank Muran.

When Aja spoke again, she did so in her native tongue. "Do you know who I am?"

"You are *The Betrayer*," Pebbles answered back in Munuorian.

Aja smiled and clapped. "Impressive! Your pronunciation is perfect. I see my darling sister taught you well."

"Excuse me?"

"Ah! You are surprised. She did not tell you, did she? No, of course she didn't. I wonder what else she omitted from the memories she shared with you."

Pebbles was stunned, not surprised. Muran was Malinyah's sister? She wanted to lash out and call Muran a liar, but she held her tongue.

"There is a popular adage in your era," Aja said. "'History is written by the victors.' Many claim to have first uttered the phrase, but its roots go back much further than anyone would imagine. The same sentiment has been expressed for thousands of years, in many tongues and by many victors. The underlying message has always been the same — history is not the same as truth, and truth is not owned by any one person. Certainly not by Malinyah."

The sanctimonious tone of the lecture infuriated Pebbles. "You deny it, then? You deny betraying your people? Killing Alynioria? Breaking your oath as an Andaer? Leading a revolt against your own people?"

"What you call revolt, I call protecting those the Andaers abandoned. What you deem as a broken oath, I declare a necessity to ensure the survival of our race," Aja said, her voice level and calm. "Are the betrayers not the ones who put the welfare of strangers ahead of their own people? Are they not the ones who condemned the innocent by hiding the truth of what Munirvo would do?"

"But you used the *Tuliskaera* to kill your own people!" Pebbles said, pointing a shaking finger at Muran.

"Ha! How dramatic you are," Aja said. "A few hundred against thousands is not a fair fight, my child. Were we to be silenced and squashed without being heard? Could we shout our protests over the legions sent to suppress us? Legions armed with *Dreylaeks* and *Breyloftes*. You speak as if I used the *Tuliskaera* unjustly against cowering women and children. I merely used it to defend against the army sent to kill us. Has Malinyah shown you the conflict? Did she show you who attacked whom? No, I imagine not."

"But you killed Alynioria!" Pebbles said. "You wiped her mind. You took her body!"

"And what of my children?" Aja suddenly roared, lifting off her seat. The sudden motion caused the medallion to twirl. "What of their fate? Did sweet Malinyah tell you what happened to them? Answer me! Did she?"

The urge to leap up and charge at Muran swelled within Pebbles. She gripped the armrests and scooted toward the seat's edge. Through clenched teeth, she said, "No."

"Of course she didn't. Why would she?" Aja scoffed, tossing her hands in the air. "You have been misled and manipulated. Malinyah, my own sister, ordered the execution of my babies!"

"What?"

"She killed them to punish me...so I returned the favor," Aja said, slumping back onto her seat.

"I don't believe you," Pebbles said.

"I care not what you believe," Aja said with a wave of her hand.

It's not possible, thought Pebbles. Malinyah is incapable of such an act. She is gentle and kind, compassionate and considerate. Muran's a liar! She's just trying to toy with me!

Pebbles glared at her, wishing to strangle the deceitful bitch. Aja laughed at Pebbles' menacing glare, then reached down to flip the face of the medallion back into place.

Pebbles focused on the medallion as she fought to suppress her emotions. As her anger subsided and her strength improved, she turned her thoughts to the many questions that had been cycling through her mind since confronting the stranger in the hallway of the home she shared with Anlon. Why had Muran's stooge kidnapped her? Why did they want Malinyah's *Sinethal*? Why had they taken the medallion? Where were they going? Where was Muran's stooge? Who was Kora? Looking up at the smiling Muran, Pebbles asked, "Why am I here? What do you want from me?"

"I want what was stolen from me," Aja said.

"Stolen? I don't have anything of yours," Pebbles said.

"No, but your man does."

"You're talking about Malinyah's *Sinethal*."

"Yes. And Omereau's."

"Omereau? What is Omereau?" Pebbles asked. "Do you mean Mereau?"

"Don't play games with me!" Aja said. She held up the medallion. "You wore the *lyktyl*, you know exactly who Omereau is!"

"The lick what?"

"*Lyktyl!* The key."

"The key to what?"

"Omereau, you idiot!" Aja fumed. "His *Sinethal*!"

"I don't know what you're talking about."

"Bah! You spin the same lies as your man did!"

"Wait. You spoke to him? To Anlon?"

"Yes, I spoke to him. He was insolent."

A wave of relief passed through Pebbles. If Muran had spoken to Anlon, that meant he knew what was going on and who was behind her kidnapping. "Look, I honestly don't know anything about another *Sinethal*. Anlon only has Malinyah's. If you've talked to him, you know that."

"Enough lies. Do you think I'm a fool? You think I don't know how Devlin Wilson came by Malinyah's *Sinethal*?" Aja gripped the medallion again. "And you had this, which means Malinyah told you where to find it. Why would she have done that unless you had Omereau, too?"

"You've got it all wrong," Pebbles said, shaking her head. "First off, we don't know where Devlin found Malinyah's *Sine—*"

"Found? Found!" Aja spat, as she fished out a pair of *Dreylaeks* from her dress pockets. "Don't play games with me, or so help me, I will make you suffer."

Pebbles scowled, pointing to the cuts and bruises on her face. "Like your goon hasn't made me suffer already? He freakin' shot me!"

Aja began to grind the Stones together, her eyes narrowing to slits. "Obviously, he didn't do enough."

"Look, I don't know where the *Sinethal* came from! And Malinyah didn't tell me where to find the effing medallion! End of story."

Aja halted grinding. She stared at Pebbles, her expression wavering between disbelief and doubt. "If she didn't tell you where to find the *lyktyl*, then where did you get it? You can't expect me to believe you found it on your own!"

"A man named Jacques Foucault gave it to me," Pebbles said.

"Foucault!" Aja seethed, slapping down the *Dreylaeks*. She stared off into the distance and mumbled, "Foucault? How on Earth did it come to that little imp?"

The question had been rhetorical, but Pebbles provided an answer. "He found Mereau's Maerlif."

"What? He found Mereau! Where?" Aja demanded.

"I don't remember the island's name," said Pebbles. "It's somewhere in the Caribbean."

"Foucault has his *Sinethal*? His *Tyls*?"

"He has his *Sinethal* for sure. I don't know about the rest of his *Tyls*," Pebbles said.

Aja stood and paced. "So, Malinyah gave it to Mereau? How stupid of you, sister! How risky! What if Mereau's ship had sunk? Or if the pathetic savages had taken it from him?"

She stopped pacing and spun toward Pebbles. "Why would Foucault give it to *you*?"

"He said it belonged to Malinyah."

"Ha! Hardly," Aja said. "And does Malinyah know you have it?"

"Yes."

"And she approved of you wearing it about like party jewelry?"

"Look, we didn't talk much about it, okay? I told her I had it, that Mereau had returned it. She seemed happy. That was it. She didn't tell me it had a name, or that it was a key, and she never mentioned Omereau. For f—'s sake, who is Omereau anyway?" Pebbles asked.

Picking up the *Dreylaeks* again, Aja recommenced grinding them in a circular motion. "I will find the truth, even if it means you end up like Evelyn."

"Evelyn?"

Aja vaulted up and advanced a step toward Pebbles. "Last chance."

Pebbles grabbed the armrests of her seat and darted her eyes around the cabin. Aja held up the glowing Stones and smiled. "There's nowhere to run."

"Look, you have to believe me. I don't know anything about Omereau, I swear it!" Pebbles said, her voice quivering.

"Enough!" yelled Aja. She bounced the two Stones together for just a second, but it was long enough for a thin bolt to shoot toward Pebbles, hitting her in the right side of her chest, just below the shoulder.

Pebbles screamed and fell forward, clutching her shoulder. She rocked back and forth on the floor, grimacing in pain. In between groans, she screamed at Aja. "You bitch! I don't f—ing know!"

As Aja readied to zap Pebbles again, the cockpit door burst open and Kora came running into the cabin. Mouth agape, she glared at Aja. "What are you doing?"

Wild-eyed, Aja maintained her focus on Pebbles. Over her shoulder, she said to Kora, "Get out of here. Fly the plane!"

Kora stomped across the cabin until she stood between Pebbles and Aja. "Are you crazy? You can't use those in here!"

"Silence! Leave us!"

"Look at her, she's bleeding all over the place," Kora said, pointing down at Pebbles. "Let it go for now. You can slice her up all you want when we land, but not up here. You'll blow us all up!"

Kora knelt by Pebbles and reached for her discarded sweater. "Move your hand. Use this to put pressure on it. I'll be right back."

As Pebbles took the sweater, Kora stood and faced Aja. "No more. Not until we land. You go fly the plane, I'll take care of the burn."

Aja stepped back and lowered the *Dreylaeks*. Kora took her by the arm and escorted her to the front of the plane, taking the still-warm Stones from her as they walked. After shutting the cockpit door behind Aja, Kora disappeared into the adjacent galley. A moment later, she returned to Pebbles' side, carrying a glass of *enjyia* and a dish towel. She knelt back down and told Pebbles to move the sweater away. Placing the glass and towel on the floor, Kora leaned forward and stripped away the collar of Pebbles' dress, exposing the wound. As Kora inspected the injury, she said, "You're lucky. It's pretty shallow."

Kora then folded the towel into a square and poured a liberal amount of the *enjyia* onto it, squeezing the cloth to speed the tonic's absorption. When the towel was sufficiently wet, she pressed it against the wound, causing Pebbles to cry out.

"I know, it stings, but it'll stop the bleeding pretty fast. Just keep pressure on it. I'll bandage it up later," Kora said.

Panting through pursed lips, Pebbles nodded and closed her eyes.

"You know," Kora said, "it'll be a whole lot less painful if you just tell her what she wants to know."

Tears trickled down Pebbles' face as she shook her head. "But I don't know. I don't."

Kora gently wiped away a tear from Pebbles' cheek with her thumb. "Lie still. I'll be back in a few minutes."

She stood and walked to the cockpit, stopping at the galley to grab the *Dreylaeks*. Stuffing the Stones in her pants pocket, she looked back at Pebbles, then opened the door.

As Aja guided the plane forward, she mumbled an epithet in Munuorian, incensed by the thought of the tattooed waif bopping about with the sacred key swinging carelessly like some kind of bazaar trinket. She deserves to be cleaved into pieces! How could Malinyah have treated the *lyktyl* so cavalierly? Aja fumed. Did she care nothing for their heritage?

Her thoughts were interrupted by the squeak of the cockpit door. She turned to see Kora sliding into the copilot's seat. Looking through the open door behind her, Aja spied Pebbles lying on the floor, holding a towel to her shoulder. She said, "What are you doing? The girl should not be left alone."

"I'll go back in a sec. First, tell me what happened," Kora said.

"She lied to me," Aja said.

"About what?"

"She claims to know nothing of Omereau or the *lyktyl*! She said Foucault, of all people, gave it to her!"

"Foucault?"

"Yes. She said he found Mereau's Maerlif. Unbelievable! I have searched and searched for the blasted key for thousands of years, and that pipsqueak found it before *me*!" Aja said, looking back at Pebbles again. Unconsciously, she flexed her raw hands.

"Let me get you *enjyia*," Kora said, rising to leave.

"I'm fine," Aja said. "Come back and take the controls."

"I will in a little bit," Kora said, leaving the cockpit. She returned shortly with two soaked cloths. "Here, wrap these around your hands. While you cool down, I'll go talk with her. Okay?"

While Aja and Kora conferred in the cockpit, Pebbles held her hand against the towel and tried to ignore the pain. She briefly pondered making a run for the plane's aft cabin but quickly decided against it. There was no telling if the door had a lock, she reasoned, and even if it did, it wouldn't stand up against *Dreylaeks*. Besides, she thought, I'm zero-for-two trying to escape from these people. It'll only piss off Muran more than she is already.

Instead, she tried to concentrate on their earlier conversation. She first thought of Malinyah's medallion. If Pebbles understood Muran correctly, it was like a *Naetir*, allowing a person to access the *Sinethal* and memories of a Munuorian named Omereau, whoever that was! Had Foucault known it was a *Sinethal* key? Pebbles wondered. If so, why hadn't he said so? More important, why hadn't Malinyah said anything about the medallion or Omereau?

Turning her thoughts to Omereau, Pebbles wondered why Muran believed Anlon had the man's *Sinethal*. She said it had been stolen from her. She said the same of Malinyah's. Stolen by whom? She recalled Muran's angry reaction to the use of the word "found" when discussing how Devlin ended up with Malinyah. It was a reaction that implied Devlin had stolen it.

Pebbles heard a sound and opened her eyes. She twisted her head to see Kora in the galley, soaking two more towels with *enjyia*. When Kora disappeared back into the cockpit, Pebbles mumbled, "Serves you right, bitch."

Closing her eyes again, she refocused her thoughts on Devlin. Had he stolen Malinyah's *Sinethal*, or had he just been on the receiving end of the stolen property? Foucault, she recalled, had been adamant Muran had taken Malinyah's *Sinethal* from her Maerlif. He'd been equally passionate in his belief that Muran had given the Stone to Devlin so that Devlin might coax Malinyah to reveal where she'd stashed caches of *Lifintyls* before Munirvo. Although it now appeared to Pebbles as if he had been right about the former, Foucault had obviously been wrong about the latter.

So, where did Devlin get the Stone? Pebbles thought of Jennifer's suspicion that Anabel had been the one who passed the *Sinethal* to Devlin, a suspicion based on one of two premises. Either Anabel had been a cover identity for Muran, and under that cover, she'd given him the *Sinethal* directly, or Muran had used Anabel as a go-between and had encouraged her to give the *Sinethal* to Devlin. In both cases, Jennifer speculated the same motive as Foucault — to get Malinyah to reveal the map. But, so far, Muran had not asked about a map. Instead, she seemed far more interested in

Omereau's *Sinethal*. Which, as far as Pebbles knew, had nothing to do with the map.

The sound of a door closing caused Pebbles to open her eyes. Looking in the direction of the cockpit, she saw Kora walking toward her. When she reached Pebbles' spot on the floor, she crouched down and reached for the towel. Pebbles let go of the cloth and Kora pulled it back to reexamine the wound. "Good. The bleeding is almost stopped. I'll bandage it up and we'll get you off the floor."

Kora retrieved the plane's first aid kit and taped a gauze bandage between Pebbles' clavicle and breast. She then assisted Pebbles back into her seat and provided her with another glass of *enjyia*. As Pebbles sipped the pinkish fluid, she looked down at the tattered, bloodstained dress. God, she thought, please help me get out of this alive!

Kora sat in the window seat opposite Pebbles, crossed her legs and placed her hands in her lap. Smiling, she said, "Let's have a chat, shall we?"

Pebbles massaged her wrists and eyed Kora with suspicion.

"I presume you'd like to avoid any more bodily harm?" Kora asked.

"I think I've had my fill," Pebbles grumbled.

"Oh, believe me, it can get much, much worse," Kora said.

"Like what happened to Anabel, right?" Might as well throw all the chips on the table at once, Pebbles thought.

Kora nodded and smiled. "Yes, just like Anabel. Although, there was a bit more personal animosity involved in her situation."

"She stole it from Muran, didn't she? Malinyah's *Sinethal*."

"Right again. It was very disrespectful for Evelyn to steal from her queen."

"Hold up. You lost me. Who is Evelyn?"

"Evelyn is Anabel, or to be more accurate, Anabel was Evelyn before she was Anabel," Kora said, looking out the window at the darkening sky.

"All right, that helps fill in a blank."

"I thought it might," Kora said. "Now, you fill in a blank for me. Your friend, Dr. Cully. He has Devlin Wilson's entire collection, no?"

"As far as I know," Pebbles said.

"Does this collection include a statue of my queen?"

"A statue?"

"Yes. It's smallish. About yea high," Kora said, holding her hands a foot apart. "It depicts her wearing a *Taellin*. You know what a *Taellin* is, right?"

The fish-man statue! "Yes, I know what it is. And, yes, Anlon has it."

"And the other statue as well? The one of the man with the *Tuliskaera*?"

Pebbles nodded. "Anlon has both of the statues."

"Well, you can understand why my queen believes Dr. Cully also has Omereau's *Sinethal*?"

"I'm afraid I don't," Pebbles said. "Are you saying Anabel, um, sorry, Evelyn, took all of those things from Muran?"

"Those things and more. Like a thief in the night, she stole them and disappeared. She did it to hurt my queen," Kora said.

Pebbles thought of sweet, little Anabel. A thief in the night? Preposterous. Yet, there was nothing to be gained by arguing the point. Instead, Pebbles zeroed in on Kora's repeated use of "my queen." She asked, "Okay, another question. You keep referring to Muran as your queen. I thought she was an Andaer? The Munuorians didn't have a queen."

"You are correct, they didn't. But she has lived many lives since. And she has been a queen many times over," Kora said. "Now, it is only fair you answer my previous question. Do you see why my queen believes Cully has Omereau? You've confirmed he has Devlin's artifacts. You confirmed those artifacts include pieces taken by Evelyn."

"I can see why she might think so, but I'm telling you, Anlon doesn't have any other black stones. We've got *Aromae*—"

"Omereau's *Sinethal* is not like Malinyah's. It is made of gold, not stone. It is round, not square. It is marked with his symbol, the sun with six rays, but without the *Lifintyl* icons on other *Sinethals*," Kora said. "Have you seen a piece like that in Devlin's collection?"

"Absolutely not," Pebbles said. "Why is Omereau's *Sinethal* different? Was he a special Andaer?"

"Malinyah has not told you of Omereau?" Kora asked.

"No."

"Even though you have his key?"

"I swear, I just thought it was one of her necklaces with a medallion. She showed me a vision where she gave it to Mereau after Munirvo. I thought it was a gift. You know, something to remember her by."

"I see," Kora said, picking a speck of lint from her pants. "And Jacques Foucault gave it to you? Freely?"

"Yes. You know him?"

"I've met him once or twice. When did he give you the *lyktyl*?"

"Three, four weeks ago. It was spur of the moment. He knows I can communicate with Malinyah. He said it belonged with her. We were saying good-bye to each other and he took it off and handed it to me. He didn't call it the *lyktyl*. He didn't say anything about Omereau."

"He was wearing it?" Kora asked, her voice rising with surprise.

Pebbles nodded.

Anchoring her elbow on the armrest, Kora propped her chin atop her hand and stared blankly out the window. For several minutes, she remained in that position, her crossed leg bobbing back and forth. Then, without warning, she stood and started to walk back to the cockpit.

Pebbles held up a hand. "Hey, wait a minute."

Kora stopped and turned to face Pebbles.

"What's going to happen to me?" Pebbles asked. "Where are we going?"

"You'll see soon enough. If you want my advice, I'd try to get some sleep while you can. It's apt to be a long night," Kora said.

As soon as Kora disappeared into the cockpit, Pebbles replayed their conversation in her mind. So, Anabel stole Malinyah's *Sinethal*...

That certainly would explain why Anabel had been evasive when Jennifer questioned her about the Stone. As Pebbles mulled it further, she realized it explained another mystery they'd wondered about since Devlin's death. Why had Devlin been so afraid that he stored the *Sinethal* with George Grant shortly before he was murdered? Anabel had told Anlon that Devlin feared for his life. At the time, it had seemed a strange reaction to Pebbles. Yes, Devlin had discovered that Dobson had borrowed the Waterland Map and had swiped his Munuorian statues, and Pebbles could understand why that incentivized Devlin to hide the *Sinethal* and the map. But, as far as they knew, no one had threatened Devlin's life. Why, then, had he feared for his life? Was it possible Devlin had learned Muran was looking for the *Sinethal*? Had she discovered he had it and threatened to kill him unless he returned it? Or...maybe she'd threatened to kill Anabel and Devlin? But, if that had been the case, why had Devlin left the Waterland Map with Anabel? Why hadn't Devlin given the Stone and the map to Grant?

As Pebbles further played out the scenario in her mind, the less likely it seemed. The gap between Devlin's death and Anabel's murder was too long. If Muran had known Anabel had given Devlin the *Sinethal* back in May, it seemed impossible to believe she would have waited five months to go after Anabel and try to reclaim Malinyah. No, it seemed more likely Muran had discovered the connection recently. But how?

Another puzzling question invaded her thoughts. If Anabel had stolen both *Sinethals*, as Muran seemed to believe, why hadn't she given Omereau's to Devlin as well? Pebbles shook her head. It made no sense. Nor did it make sense why Malinyah had never mentioned the name Omereau, or why she had been silent about the medallion's true purpose. To Pebbles, the medallion had simply been a memento that made her feel close to Malinyah. If she had known it was more than just a piece of Malinyah's jewelry, she would have treated it differently…especially now knowing how precious it appeared to be to Muran. And it was precious to her. That much was obvious from her emotional outburst.

Yes, Muran wanted something stored on Omereau's *Sinethal*. Badly. What could it be? Pebbles cursed. It was yet another question that demanded an answer. Trying to clear her mind, she looked down at her bandaged shoulder. The gauze was spotted with a small amount of dried blood, and she noticed the stinging had stopped. She reached up and gingerly probed the bandaged area with her fingers. It was sore to the touch, but she could move her arm without too much discomfort. *Enjyia* was more than just a life-extending potion.

Leaning her head back against the seat, Pebbles closed her eyes and contemplated the meaning of Kora's parting words: "…it's apt to be a long night."

As Kora reentered the cockpit, she said, "I think we need to face facts, my Queen."

Aja looked up from the navigation screen. "What do you mean?"

"I don't think Cully has Omereau," Kora said. "I told you as much after I met him in New York. He didn't bat an eyelash when he saw the tapestry, nor did he flinch when I said the name Aramu Muru."

"Bah! That means nothing. He was just being clever, that's all. He has it. I'm sure of it," Aja said.

"I disagree, and I think we should consider the alternatives."

"Alternatives?"

"Based on what she just told me, I can think of three," Kora said.

"Well, what are they?" Aja asked.

Holding up a hand, Kora began to tick them off. "One — Evelyn gave it to Devlin and Devlin hid it somewhere without telling Cully. Two — Evelyn told us the truth. She never gave it to Devlin. Only, she didn't put it in the bank either. She hid it somewhere else. For example, it might still be in her house and we overlooked it. Or, another bank. Or a storage locker somewhere. There were a lot of keys in that house. Three — she gave it, or sold it, to someone else. She lied about putting it in the safe-deposit box to protect the other person. Jacques Foucault, perhaps."

"The first two are possible, but, Kora, why would Foucault give the girl the *lyktyl* if he had Omereau's *Sinethal*?"

"Why would he give it to her at all? Did you know he was wearing it himself? Our hostage says he took it off and gave it to her. Just like that." Kora snapped her fingers. "Like it was a toy, a trinket."

"What? That makes no sense. Mereau would never have sanctioned Foucault to wear it. He considered it holy."

"I know. You've told me a million times," Kora said, her eyes glued to the medallion on Aja's chest.

"Then I don't understand your point."

Kora reached over and lifted the medallion to inspect it. "How closely did you look at this?"

17

Musical Chairs

La Quinta, California
September 29

A cool breeze drifted into the courtyard. With eyes closed, Anlon listened to it rustle the flowers of the bougainvillea bushes lining the surrounding walls. The tranquil sound helped soothe his weary mind after a second sleepless night. There still had been no follow-up call from Muran, no news of Pebbles or any sightings of Goodwin. Throughout the long night, Anlon had stared at the ceiling of his suite, wondering where Pebbles might be and praying for her safe return.

Had Goodwin killed her? Had she died from her injuries? If she was still alive, how bad was her condition? Where was Muran? Had she linked up with Goodwin? Was Pebbles with the both of them now? If Pebbles was with her, had Muran discovered Pebbles' medallion was a forgery yet? Was she torturing Pebbles, like she had Anabel? The questions cycled endlessly in his mind, eating away at his energy and confidence. Yet, whenever his confidence flagged, he focused on Pebbles' toughness. Anlon knew if she was still alive, she would not give up hope, and so neither would he.

Another breeze pushed by. Anlon, sitting by the suite's pool, watched the water's surface ripple and thought of the last time he'd been with Pebbles. They had taken his boat out on the lake for a final excursion before dry-docking the cruiser for the winter. For most of the afternoon, they had lazed about in the early autumn sun, talking and laughing about anything and everything. Bundled in coats and long pants, a flannel blanket wrapped around them, they had watched the sun set and the stars rise. It had only been a week since their outing, but given how much had happened since, it felt as if it was a year in the past.

They had returned to the dock, walking hand in hand down its dark planks until they reached his patio firepit. With the fire aglow, they'd shared dinner delivered by Sydney's, accompanied by a little too much wine. The conversation had been light and flirty and had led to a sensuous coupling to cap the night. Afterward, he recalled lying with his body curled next to hers, tracing his fingers over her shoulders and back until she fell asleep. They had shared similar days in the past, but this one stood out to Anlon as one he would remember for a long time to come.

The sound of a doorbell stirred Anlon back to reality. Rising, he walked barefoot past the pool until he reached the courtyard door. When he opened it, a wide smile spread across his face. Jennifer had finally arrived.

Though her face sported abrasions and bruises, and a large bandage was plastered on her forehead, she still managed a smile in return. Anlon gently wrapped his arms around her, knowing her injuries included some rather sore ribs. "God, am I happy to see you!"

She squeezed him tightly, resting her head on his shoulder. "Same."

"How are you feeling?" Anlon asked as they separated.

"Rough, but I'll be okay," she said. "You?"

"Exhausted. Worried," he said, escorting her to the patio table by the pool.

"Any news?" she asked. She gingerly lowered herself onto one of the chairs.

Anlon sat next to her and shook his head. Jennifer laid her hand on his arm and said, "I'm so sorry this happened, Anlon. I feel like it's my fault."

"No, if it's anyone's fault, it's mine. I should have seen this coming, especially after what happened to Anabel."

"*We* should have seen this coming, I'm equally responsible," Jennifer said.

"Well, we are where we are. There's only one thing that matters now. Get her back. Alive."

"Agreed. So, what's the plan? What can I do to help?"

"Until we hear something from Muran or the police, we're in a holding pattern," Anlon said. "In the meantime, best thing we can—"

The suite doorbell chimed again. Jennifer rolled her eyes and said, "It's probably my new shadow, FBI Special Agent Elizabeth Li."

"Making new friends, are we?" Anlon smiled. "Actually, I think it's Antonio. Be back in a sec."

Anlon walked to the door. To his surprise, both guesses were wrong. It was Antonio's assistant. "Katie! Come in."

"Hi, just wanted to check to make sure everything was okay with the room," she said.

Anlon told her the accommodations were perfect and expressed his gratitude for Katie's assistance. She had stayed with Antonio's plane at the Twenty-Nine Palms Airport after Anlon, Antonio and Detective Emerson had disembarked for the road trip to Ludlow. When the prospect of finding Pebbles there faded, Antonio had called Katie to let her know they were on their way back to the airport and he asked her to arrange overnight accommodations.

By the time they had retraced their way to Twenty-Nine Palms to pick Katie up, she'd already booked rooms for all of them at a hotel in the town of La Quinta, about an hour's drive from the airport. Anlon had been puzzled by the choice of a hotel so far from the airport, but then overheard her telling Emerson it was the facility closest to Antonio's lab in Palm Desert.

Katie had spent most of the drive to the hotel on the phone, working out additional arrangements with the hotel manager. One such arrangement had been purchasing a set of fresh clothes for Anlon, as he was still clad in the clothes he'd worn to dinner with Cesar twenty-four hours prior. In addition, Katie had made dinner reservations for the group, coordinated the set-up of two conference rooms for the police to use as a makeshift command post, booked rooms for Jennifer, Foucault, Henri and Agent Li, and of course, continued doing her day job for Antonio.

"Come on in, I'd like you to meet a friend. Jen, this is Antonio's right hand, Katie Kierney."

The pert, blond-haired assistant marched into the courtyard and greeted Jennifer. Anlon watched her take in the sight of Jennifer's facial injuries and adopt an instant motherly demeanor. "What are you doing standing? Please sit. Can I get you anything? Do you need some ibuprofen? Water? Something stronger?"

While she spoke, she pulled out a pad and pen from her purse, ready to take orders and snap into action. Jennifer told her she was fine and thanked her for all she'd done already. Katie was not satisfied. She went into Anlon's room and returned with a pillow to prop behind Jennifer's back and said she'd get a doctor to come by and check on her. Jennifer said, "Really, I'm good. I look worse than I feel."

Katie rattled her pen against her chin, casting a skeptical look at Jennifer. "Hmmm...I don't believe you, but I'll back off...for now." She gave Jennifer her cell phone number and room number, then said, "Any hour, day or night."

She then turned to Anlon. "Count Foucault arrived a little while ago. Is noon still good for your meetup?"

"Uh, yeah...assuming we don't get some news before then."

"Of course," she said, jotting down a note. After she finished writing, she looked at both of them. "Have you eaten this morning?"

"No, not yet, at least I haven't," Anlon said. Jennifer indicated she hadn't either.

"Okay, I've had the hotel set up a breakfast buffet in one of the conference rooms. Tell me what you two want and I'll bring it over," Katie said.

"Nah, don't do that. We can walk over. Is Antonio up?" Anlon asked.

"Yes, he had a bunch of calls to make this morning. He asked if he could stop by when he's done."

"Absolutely. Tell him to come over any time. Jen and I are going to compare notes; it would be great if he joined us. You're welcome to come, too."

The offer seemed to startle Katie. "Oh, sure. That would be great, actually. Thanks. If Dr. Wallace doesn't need me to do something for him while you meet, I will be there."

Before she left she asked Jennifer again if she needed anything. "Clothes? Toiletries?"

Jennifer looked down at the cheesy T-shirt she had bought in the hospital gift shop to replace the shirt they cut away in the emergency room. "Well, now that you mention it…"

Katie seemed almost relieved for a new task. In less than a minute she was gone, in search of fresh clothes and some other necessities for Jennifer. When the courtyard door closed behind her, Jennifer said to Anlon, "Holy crap! She's amazing!"

"No kidding. Antonio's one lucky CEO."

"So, you want to get something to eat and then come back and talk?" she asked, rising out of the chair. "I feel like we should do it now, before my shadow reappears and locks us in an interrogation room."

The hotel's conference rooms were situated in two buildings separated by a long outdoor hallway. Above the hallway was an arbor covered with bougainvillea bushes, their snaking vines curling around the arbor's beams. As Anlon and Jennifer walked down the hallway, they noticed two police officers emerge from a conference room with bagels and coffee. They ducked in the room and discovered the buffet. As they moved through the lineup of breakfast dishes, selecting various items, Anlon could hear a woman's voice through the wall behind the buffet table. He stopped and listened as the woman delivered a briefing of the Ticonderoga incident.

"That's my shadow," Jennifer whispered, resting her plate on the buffet table while she poured coffee from an urn. When she finished, she handed the cup to Anlon and began to pour one for herself.

"She sounds intense," Anlon said.

"Oh, yeah. She's in it to win it. But that's good, right?" Jennifer asked.

"True. I guess I should be glad they're all taking the situation seriously," Anlon said, as they left the conference room and headed back to Anlon's room.

Several hotel guests passed through the hallway on their way to the resort's complex of shops and restaurants. Jennifer leaned close to Anlon and whispered, "Believe me, they are. Muran killed a bunch of cops and an innocent girl. They want Muran's ass."

"They can have her. I just want Pebbles back," Anlon said.

Back at Anlon's suite, they settled at the patio table and began to eat. In between bites, Anlon said, "So, I visited with Malinyah."

Jennifer, chewing on a cube of cantaloupe, said, "I thought you might. What did you find out?"

"That Foucault is a liar, that he put Pebbles in danger by giving her the necklace with the medallion," Anlon said. He went on to describe the visions Malinyah showed him. When he finished, he said, "So, he set her up. Set *us* up. We were part of his trap. I don't know how he got word to Muran, how she found out Pebbles had the medallion, but whatever he did, it worked."

Jennifer cringed. "I think I might have been the one that tipped her off, not about the medallion, but about Malinyah." She reminded Anlon that she had shown a picture of Malinyah's *Sinethal* to Goodwin. "I totally misread him. He'd been looking for it, and I led him right to it."

"You couldn't have known," Anlon said. "And even if you're right, it doesn't explain how Muran discovered Pebbles had the medallion."

"Maybe they started surveilling you and saw Pebbles with you, wearing the medallion?"

"I guess it's possible, but I think it's more likely Foucault led her to Pebbles," Anlon said, picking at a muffin. "Bastard."

The doorbell chimed. Anlon wiped his hands on a napkin and rose to answer the courtyard door. He opened it to find Antonio and Katie. While Anlon greeted Antonio, Katie breezed by with a shopping bag clutched in her hand. She presented the bag to Jennifer and the two chatted until Anlon and Antonio walked up. Antonio leaned to give Jennifer a quick hug and then joined the others seated at the table. Antonio said to Jennifer, "Saw the video of Muran's fire show. Don't know how you made it out of that inferno."

"If I'd waited much longer, probably wouldn't have." Waving her hand in front of her face, she said, "Just wish I'd buckled up before I tried to punch through it."

"Pretty damn brave, if you ask me," Antonio said. "Did you see her there? Muran?"

"No, never did. Kinda glad I didn't," she said. "I'm pretty sure I wouldn't be here right now if I had. She would have cut me in two with her *Tuliskaera*."

"Her what?" Katie asked.

Jennifer described the weapon and how Muran used it to neuter the police and aid in her escape. When she finished the description, Anlon said to Antonio, "Those diamonds I gave you to examine, the ones from Indio Maiz, they are the power source for the *Tuliskaera*. Couldn't tell you how they generate such a powerful beam, but obviously they can pack a serious punch."

"Yeah, I've been hoping to catch up with you about that. Dylan's made some progress analyzing the Stones you brought from Nicaragua. After we get Pebbles back, we should huddle with Dylan. Think you'll be very interested in what he's found," Antonio said.

"Really? Can you give me a quick snapshot now?" Anlon asked.

Antonio looked to Katie and laughed. "I knew I shouldn't have said anything." Turning back to Anlon, he said, "Let's just say Dylan learned an interesting lesson about them...the hard way."

"I'll say," Katie said. "He blew up the lab! Took out a whole wall!"

"What? Is he okay? Did anyone get hurt?" Anlon asked.

"Everyone's fine. Dylan was smart enough to wear protective gear. Military-grade stuff. And he cleared the lab before his experiment," Antonio said.

"So, what happened? What was the experiment?" Anlon asked.

"Don't we have more important things to discuss?" Antonio replied. "I know you, Anlon. Every time we talk shop, you can't let it go."

"Promise, no questions. Well, maybe one or two," Anlon said with a smile.

"Uh-huh," Antonio said, crossing his arms. "Okay, short version — the oblong shape of the diamonds. Very important. Concentrates the focus of electrical energy right down the centerline. Gives the diamonds incredible power...but also makes them susceptible to a disrupting force anywhere else along their surface. For example, hit the diamonds with an electrical charge from the side, they shatter...explosively. By the way, you have one less diamond now."

Anlon thought of Foucault destroying the three *Tuliskaeras* discovered at Indio Maiz. He struck the cone-shaped Stones on their sides, causing them to crumble, not explode. And the diamonds inside had remained intact. He shared the observations with Antonio.

"Dylan thinks the kimberlite and basalt mix surrounding the diamonds serves two purposes. It acts as an insulator when the Stone is used correctly, sort of helping to channel the diamonds' energy along its intended line. Since both types of stone are magnetic, they help pull electricity through the diamonds like a vacuum cleaner tube sucks in air.

"On the flip side, the stone mix seems to act like a shield, a protective covering that prevents the diamonds from being damaged from attack. Well, most attacks...as Dylan discovered."

"How did he do it?" Anlon asked.

"If the oblong diamond is struck with an electrical charge from an angle, while the diamond is building an electrical charge along its centerline...kaboom!" Antonio said, using both hands to simulate an explosion.

"The *Terusael*!" Jennifer said, gripping Anlon's forearm. "Anabel's hands. The medical examiner found bits of pink stone shrapnel. He said it looked like a stone grenade had exploded in her hands."

Antonio nodded. "We did a scan on all the Stones. All except Malinyah's. Don't give me that look, Anlon. I promise, we left hers alone like you asked. Anyway, the shapes of the diamonds inside each vary, but they all contain diamonds. They seem to channel the magnetic energy of the stone mix around them. Very ingenious."

The explanation caused Anlon to recall his experiment with the *Breylofte* and *Naetir* in Devlin's house and the strong polarity response they exhibited when stimulated in an incongruous manner. He also recalled his feeble efforts to fend off Pacal's *Breylofte* attack at Stillwater Quarry by holding a *Naetir* in the path of the soundwaves. Anlon considered the difference between these milder reactions and what Antonio described. The milder reactions, he realized, occurred when at least one of the Stones was in a resting electrical state, whereas in Antonio's example, both Stones, or to be more precise, the diamonds within both Stones, were in active, electrically charged states.

"That's very interesting," Anlon said. "It suggests a way to defend against the Stones."

"Exactly. Dylan's working on a prototype of a device that could be used to disrupt and destroy any of the Stones, but it'll only work if the Stones are in use. You might lose another diamond or two while he tests it," Antonio said. "Oh, one other interesting nugget Dylan found, if you pardon the pun. Guess what he discovered when he scanned the *Aromaeghs*?"

Anlon shrugged. The *Aromaeghs* were similar to the *Sinethal*, in that they held memories implanted by the Munuorians and they were activated and used in the same manner. Unlike the *Sinethal*, however, the *Aromaeghs* provided only one-way visions. There was no ability to interact with them. One could watch, listen and sense the "tutorials" provided by the *Aromaeghs*, but one could not ask questions or otherwise interact with the narrator.

"There's a gold disc inside. The damn thing looks like a rounded memory board in a computer. There are diamond styli inside the Stone that ring the notch where the *Naetir* is placed, and others are embedded in the handholds. They all touch the gold 'memory board' inside," Antonio said. "The *Naetir*, by the way, has styli that line up with the ones inside the notch of the *Aromaegh*."

The description led Anlon to recall Malinyah's vision of Omereau's *Sinethal*. At the time, he hadn't focused on its design. In light of Antonio's commentary, however, some thoughts immediately came to mind. Gold, he knew, is a common material used in computers and similar devices, but it's more often used to connect processing components with memory components, rather than as the core of memory storage units themselves. The reason? Gold is an excellent conductor of electricity and it doesn't tarnish or age when exposed to the elements. As a result, data stored on a gold-connected memory device is less prone to degradation. From what Antonio described, however, it sounded as if the Munuorians had discovered a way to use gold in combination with diamonds to store and interact with memories. If true, the two together were perfect choices for housing a culture's institutional memories for millennia.

Anlon was about to ask another question when the doorbell rang yet again. Over the courtyard wall, he heard a woman's voice call out. "Dr. Cully?"

Jennifer leaned over and said to Anlon, "It's my shadow. Either she's got news on Pebbles or you're in for it now."

"No, I don't have any updates," Agent Li said, pushing past Anlon into the courtyard. "But I've got plenty of questions."

She spied Antonio and Katie and rather rudely asked them to leave, explaining afterward, "I need to speak with Dr. Cully and Miss Stevens alone."

After they departed, Li occupied one of the chairs and pulled it up close to the patio table. She rested her elbows on the table's edge and clasped her hands together. "So, I'm going to talk. You're going to listen. When I'm done, I'm going to ask you questions. You're going to answer. No bullshit. No evasions."

She paused to inhale, forging ahead before Anlon or Jennifer could speak. "Anabel Simpson. Charles Goodwin. Jacques Foucault. What do these people have in common? None of them have birth certificates, at least ones we could find. Goodwin and Simpson have social security numbers, both issued in the 1940s. They both have driver's licenses. Simpson's says she was fifty-eight. Goodwin's, forty-eight. I'll save you the trouble of doing the math. Their driver's license ages are twenty-plus years younger than their social security records suggest. Foucault's passport claims he was born in 1932, yet his birth certificate says he was born in 1967. Not sure how that passed muster with the French, but it did.

"Fingerprints from items in Evelyn Warwick's safe-deposit boxes match prints on items from Anabel Simpson's home. I repeat, match. There is no record of an Evelyn Warwick emigrating from the UK to the US, either in our records or the Brits'. There's no record of an Evelyn Warwick ever having lived at the London address found in the bank's records.

"Clara Ambrose? She mysteriously disappeared in the Australian outback several years after returning to London from Fernando Pó. She was supposedly in her late twenties when she disappeared."

Anlon held up his hands to signal time-out. "Who is Clara Ambrose?"

Jennifer said to Li, "I haven't had the chance to debrief Anlon about the locket and the article." Turning to Anlon, she said, "Clara is the name of the woman in the locket photograph with Anabel, er, Evelyn."

"Ah," Anlon said.

Jennifer asked Li, "So, what's your point?"

"Come on, Stevens. You know my point. They're all impostors. All fake identities," Li said, slapping the table. "And there's more. Anabel — archaeology professor. Goodwin, same. Foucault? Make it a threesome. Your stones? Anabel-slash-Evelyn had some. Goodwin's museum has some, too. Auction records show Foucault has purchased a slew of them over the years.

"I've saved the kicker for last. Our villain, Muran? She left fingerprints everywhere, including the bank and Deborah Bailey's home. She left even more when she killed Bailey's daughter. I won't nauseate you with how she killed her; suffice it to say the crime scene photos make Anabel's murder look tame.

"Anyway, the fingerprints match two different women! A British national named Diane Caldwell. She was quite wealthy. She built a mining empire in the South Pacific. Only problem? She's quite dead. Or, at least, she was reported lost at sea in the 1980s."

Li paused and stared at Anlon, then at Jennifer. Reaching into the briefcase by the foot of her chair, she withdrew two pieces of paper, placing them facedown on the table. "Do either of you recognize the name?"

They both answered no. Li flipped over the top page. It was a photograph. "Diane Caldwell's passport photo."

Anlon looked at the photo while Jennifer said, "It's her. The same woman from the bank, the same woman in the locket picture with Anabel."

Li continued. "The second fingerprint match? A thirty-seven-year-old export-import executive based where? Wait for it...wait for it...New Caledonia. Name? Aja Jones."

She flipped over the second picture. Same woman, slightly older.

"Aja is still alive. And guess what. She owns a plane that entered the US about two weeks ago through JFK. Would either of you like to venture where it was hangared until a few days ago?"

Anlon shook his head from side to side, too stunned to speak.

"The airport at Lake Placid, New York. A sixty-mile drive from Middlebury and sixty-five miles from Ticonderoga," Li said, leaning back in the chair and crossing her arms. "Something very bizarre is going on here, and you two know exactly what it is. If you want my help to get your friend back, now's the time to talk."

The clock read eleven thirty-two. Foucault sealed the envelope and called for Henri. When the pilot stood beside him, Foucault asked, "Is everything ready?"

"*Oui*, Monsieur."

"*Bon*. You are to give this letter to Dr. Cully, do you understand?" Foucault asked.

"*Oui*."

"*Merci, ami*," Foucault said, hugging the man and then kissing him on both cheeks. "One last cigarette before we begin."

Foucault stepped from the bedroom of his suite out into a private courtyard similar to Anlon's. The air was much warmer than he expected. The sun reflected off the white walls surrounding the yard, causing Foucault to shield his eyes. He turned and found a shady spot beneath an arbor adorned with bougainvillea flowers.

He closed his eyes and enjoyed the flavor of the cigarette and the calming effect of the nicotine as it flowed through his brain. When he reopened his eyes, he looked around at the bright colors in every direction: a deep blue sky, tall palm trees with lush green canopies, the glowing pinkish-red of the bougainvillea and the brownish-orange of the mountains in the distance.

He thought of Christian, and Margaret, and the dozens that had preceded them in his service. Of their sacrifice, their loyalty. He recalled the great moments of his life and the simple pleasures he'd enjoyed most. Stargazing, Carignan, the spray of the ocean and the beauty of Munuoria through Mereau's memories.

Motion from the flowers caught his eye. Looking up, he spied a small butterfly flitting around the florets. A few inches away, a hummingbird hovered. He watched the two pollinators dance around each other until the butterfly conceded the flowers to the hummingbird and flew away. After one last drag of the cigarette, Foucault waved good-bye to the butterfly and rose to go back inside. *"Au revoir."*

Anlon returned to his seat and placed Malinyah's *Sinethal* and a *Naetir* on the patio table. He pointed at the Stones and said to Li, "These were made by a civilization that lived ten thousand years ago, a civilization called the Munuorians. They lived at a time when much of the human race was quite primitive, yet the Munuorians were anything but. They had an extra sense. An ability to detect and interact with the Earth's magnetic field. The Stones on the table might look like simple pieces of art, but they're actually sophisticated tools."

He picked up the *Naetir*. "This one is a key. It's magnetic, and when held against some of the other Stones in the right way, it activates the magnetic properties of the other Stones."

Lowering the *Naetir*, he lifted the *Sinethal* and flipped it to show Li the back side. "For example, if you place the key in the notch here, this Stone turns into a computer, of sorts. You put your fingers in these slots, and your brain receives electrical signals from the Stone, allowing you to access the data stored on the Stone."

Li listened, a serious expression on her face. As Anlon paused, she said, "Detective Emerson told me it contains the memories of a woman from the civilization, this Malinyah that our Muran-slash-Aja wants in exchange for Miss McCarver."

"That's right," Jennifer said.

"Malinyah," Anlon said, "was a contemporary of Muran's. They were part of the Munuorian leadership, ten thousand years ago."

Li didn't flinch. Anlon continued. "Muran and Malinyah had a falling out. Muran took revenge by killing one of Malinyah's children. Well, to be accurate, Muran erased the child's mind. Wiped out her memories. Then she did something against every law, every belief the Munuorians held sacred."

He pointed to the *Sinethal*. "This is called a *Sinethal*. Muran took one of these, and using some of the other Stones, transferred her memories from her brain into the *Sinethal*, and then transferred the memories from the *Sinethal* into the body of Malinyah's daughter. When she tired of the girl's body, she moved her mind to another body. And then another. And so on. For thousands of years, she's moved her mind from one body to another."

The frown on Li's face turned from skeptical to incredulous, as Anlon continued to speak. "So, you ask what's this all about?" Anlon asked. "Muran wants this Stone back. She wants Malinyah's memories back. I don't know why. She also wants a gold disc that holds the memories of a man named Omereau. He was the brilliant mind behind the creation of all these Stones. She also wants a medallion that Pebbles was given by Foucault. Muran calls it the *lyktyl*."

Anlon lowered Malinyah's *Sinethal* and picked up the *Naetir* again. "The *lyktyl* is a key, like this. It activates the gold disc with Omereau's memories. If I had to hazard a guess, I'd say that Muran wants to make more of these Stones but doesn't know how. She needs Omereau's memories to make them. She can't interact with his memories unless she has the key."

When he finished speaking, Li glared at him and then at Jennifer. "You really expect me to believe all that? Changing bodies? Moving minds onto stone and back?"

Anlon started to answer but was interrupted by the ringing of the doorbell. He turned to Jennifer and asked, "What time is it?"

"Noon."

"Perfect timing. Jacques Foucault is here. Don't believe me? Ask him. You'll get the same answers," Anlon said.

18

Captain Courageous

La Quinta, California
September 29

When the door opened, Anlon was greeted by Henri de la Roche, who introduced himself as Count Foucault's pilot and longtime associate.

"Yes, I recall meeting you at Indio Maiz," Anlon said. He then turned his attention to Foucault, who was standing next to Henri wearing sunglasses and holding onto his pilot's arm. To Anlon, Foucault looked unsteady, as if dizzy or drunk. Anlon said hello to him and offered his hand, but the Frenchman did not respond.

Henri said, "The Count is not feeling well. Perhaps we could go inside? Out of the sun?"

"Uh, sure. Of course. Follow me," Anlon said. He turned and walked toward the door of the cottage suite inside the courtyard. Henri followed behind, his arm wrapped around Foucault, guiding the man toward the cottage. Anlon directed his gaze to Jennifer and Agent Li, and said, "We're heading inside."

Jennifer grabbed the *Sinethal* and *Naetir*, leaving the shopping bag from Katie by the table. Li put the pictures of Muran in her satchel and followed Jennifer to the suite. Once inside, Henri lowered Foucault onto the living room sofa and then stood back in the corner of the room with his hands folded in front of him.

Jennifer sat beside Foucault, balancing Malinyah's *Sinethal* on her knees with the *Naetir* in her hand. Agent Li and Anlon carried chairs from the small dining table behind the sofa and brought them around to face Foucault. Anlon suggested Henri use the armchair in the corner of the room, but Henri indicated he preferred to stand.

Once all were settled, Henri cleared his throat. "*Docteur* Cully, Count Foucault asked that I give you this. He requested you read it before speaking."

Anlon received the envelope from a bowing Henri and then exchanged bewildered looks with Jennifer and Li. The envelope was embossed with gold initials, JMF. There was a letter inside with the same embossed initials at its top. Anlon opened the letter and read its contents.

> *Dear Anlon,*
>
> *I am very sorry for the trouble I have caused you and your companion, Miss McCarver. Please know that my intentions were honorable, though my execution was poor. If it is any consolation, and I doubt it is, I have suffered great loss as well.*
>
> *You seem, to me, a man of integrity, one who understands and appreciates the priceless nature of the gifts left by the Munuorians, and I don't mean the Lifintyls. I mean you, me and those fortunate to be here today thanks to the selfless acts of the people who gave their lives so that humanity might survive and begin anew.*
>
> *The greatest of whom sits in your presence now. I have given my life for his, so that he might aid in ridding the world of the accursed Betrayer, once and for all. I bid you a fond adieu, and know that together with the courageous captain, you shall defeat Muran and preserve the precious history of the star-watchers. If anyone can save your friend, it is Mereau.*
>
> > *Bon Courage,*
> > *Jacques Mathieu Foucault*

Anlon read through the letter twice, looking up at Foucault several times as he read. When he finished, he handed the letter to Jennifer and turned to Henri. The pilot nodded his head and wiped the corners of his eyes.

After the *Sinethal* session with Malinyah aboard Antonio's plane, Anlon had been ready to strangle Foucault. He believed the Frenchman had deceived them all in a greed-induced play to acquire Omereau's *Sinethal* himself, using Pebbles and the fake *lyktyl* as the bait to lure Muran to whatever trap he had set. While Anlon still believed Foucault purposely put Pebbles at risk, the letter now seemed to suggest a more gallant motive.

When Jennifer finished the note, she handed it to Li and said, "Wow."

Li quickly scanned the note and frowned. "I don't understand. What does this mean?"

"It means Jacques Foucault is dead," Anlon said.

"What are you talking about? He's sitting right in front of you," Li said, pointing at Foucault.

"It's Foucault's body, but his mind has been erased," Jennifer explained. She held up Malinyah's *Sinethal*. "Foucault had one of these. It held the memories of a man named Mereau. Foucault allowed Mereau to transfer his memories and consciousness into Foucault's body."

The FBI agent stood up, looked at Anlon and tossed the letter to the floor. "Okay, enough of this nonsense. I listened to your cockamamie story outside. People living hundreds, thousands of years. People moving their minds from one body to another. It's all horseshit!"

"No, it's not!" Anlon said, rising to confront Li. "I grant you, it sounds unbeliev—"

"Not *sounds* unbelievable, it *is* unbelievable," Li said.

"Excuse me," Mereau said, raising a hand. His voice was feeble, and it carried an accent, but Anlon noticed it wasn't Foucault's French accent.

"Quiet!" Li snapped.

"God damn it, Agent!" Anlon roared. "What's your explanation then? Explain the pictures you showed us. Explain how the same woman appears in pictures spread over, what, one hundred seventy-five years? Really good family genes? Plastic surgery? Smoke and—"

Jennifer interrupted Anlon's tirade and pointed to Malinyah's *Sinethal*. "Anlon, let her meet Malinyah. Let her see for herself."

"I agree," Mereau said. "I will join her, we can meet Malinyah together. Though, I will need someone to place the *Tyls* in my hands. I cannot see them."

"What?" Li asked.

Henri stepped forward and addressed the group. "I'm afraid *Capitaine* Mereau is blind. At least, for the time being. The *overtae*, the transfer, is not complete. The brain, it takes time to reestablish all the connections."

"Yeah, right. Save the hocus-pocus for someone else. You all are under arrest," Li announced.

"Oh, please," Jennifer said, popping up off the sofa. "On what charge?"

"Obstruction, making false statements," Li said.

"Good luck making those stick," Jennifer said. "Come on, Elizabeth! Get real! Pebbles is our friend, why would we put her life at risk by making false statements? Face it, you're just afraid."

"Of what?" Li asked.

"Look, all you have to do is hold the Stone like this, put your fingers in these notches. I'll hook up the other Stone, and you'll have all the proof you want…and then some," Jennifer said.

With arms crossed and foot tapping, Li watched Jennifer pick up the *Naetir* and move it toward the center notch. Jennifer said, "I'll do it with you. I've never met her. It'll be a first for both of us."

"What, exactly, will happen?" Li asked.

Anlon came up beside her and said in a softer tone, "You'll have a vision. You'll see Malinyah, the woman whose mind is stored on the Stone. Jennifer will be there, too. You'll be able to see and communicate with both of them. They'll be able to communicate with you."

He recalled trying to pry Pebbles' hands from the *Sinethal* during an earlier, turbulent session with Malinyah. As he struggled to pull the Stone away, his fingers had gripped the Stone's handholds at the same time as Pebbles', and he instantaneously had joined Pebbles' vision. Anlon turned to Mereau and asked, "All they have to do is have both sets of their fingers in the side holds, right?"

"Yes, that's right," Mereau said. "One of them should make the connection first. Then have the other join. I can do it with her if you wish."

"No offense, Mereau," Jennifer said, "this is a trust issue. Agent Li knows me better than she knows you. Come on, Elizabeth. What do you have to lose? If you're not convinced afterward, arrest us, then. What's a few minutes' difference going to make?"

"Fine. Let's get this over with," Li said.

Jennifer made room for Li on the sofa. Patting the cushions, she said, "Sit next to me. You don't want to stand for this."

"Jen, remember, it's intense at first. Try to keep your cool, don't freak out like I did," Anlon said.

"Oh, believe me, I remember!" she said. Without further delay, Jennifer snapped the *Naetir* into place. Almost immediately, her body stiffened and she gasped.

Anlon watched Li's stupefied facial expressions as Jennifer began to moan unintelligibly, her closed eyes darting back and forth. Sensing Li's resolve was beginning to wane, Anlon pushed her to take hold of the Stone. "Okay, Agent, you're up. When you're done, make sure to say *Kaeto* to Malinyah."

"What?"

"*Kaeto*. It means 'thank you' in Malinyah's language."

The first sensation Jennifer experienced was moisture on her feet. She wiggled her toes and felt something grainy between them. Then she became conscious of the sound of waves, followed by a spray of warm water that splashed her bare legs and arms. Behind her, she heard a woman's voice softly singing. A breeze whistled by, causing Jennifer's ponytail to flap against her shoulders.

At first, she saw only fuzzy colors, a mix of blues, greens and white. Attracted by the singing voice, Jennifer turned her head in the direction of the sound. Soon, the rough outline of shapes began to form. A sandy beach bordered by a thick stand of palm trees, a Caribbean blue ocean and two figures collecting seashells that had washed up in the surf — a tall blond woman and a little girl whose blond hair was nearly white.

Jennifer heard a gasp behind her and turned to see Agent Li. She reached out for the frightened woman's hand. "Hey there, it's all right. Come here. Hold my hand."

Li took a step and gasped again. "I can feel sand on my feet!"

"I know! Wicked cool, right?" Jennifer said.

"What am I wearing?" Li asked. Her navy pinstriped pantsuit had been replaced by a pinkish tunic. "Where did my clothes go? Where are yours?"

Jennifer looked down to observe her own tunic. It was tan and sleeveless and extended halfway down her thighs. From the effects of the breeze and the water splashing against her body, she could tell that was all she had on. She shrugged and said to Li, "Better than nothing, I guess."

Pointing ahead at the woman and child, Jennifer said, "I'm pretty sure the woman is Malinyah. I don't know who the little girl is, but I'm guessing it's Alynioria, one of her daughters. The one Muran killed."

Jennifer saw Malinyah look up. Her face was expressionless. She leaned over and whispered to the little girl, stroking her hair as she spoke. The child nodded and continued to hunt for seashells while Malinyah stood and walked through the surf toward Jennifer and Li. When she reached them, she spoke. The only word Jennifer understood was "Malinyah."

She held out a hand and touched Jennifer on the shoulder, then Li. The gesture caused the FBI agent to gasp again. "Jesus. She just touched me. I felt it."

Malinyah looked at her and smiled. "Jesus?"

Jennifer began to laugh.

"What's so funny?" Li asked.

"She thinks your name is Jesus," Jennifer said. "Let me handle this."

Pointing at herself, Jennifer said to Malinyah, "Jennifer."

The Munuorian's face lit up. "Ah! Eleanor, Anlon, Jennifer?"

"Yes, that's right!" Jennifer said, nodding. She reached out and touched Malinyah's arm. Her skin was soft and warm. Unreal, thought Jennifer. She turned and pointed to Li. "Elizabeth."

As Malinyah greeted Li, a large wave crashed on shore. Jennifer heard the child yelp just as the wave unceremoniously drenched the three women. Jennifer looked down and then at Malinyah and Li. If she had harbored any doubts before, the sight of their thin tunics plastered against their bodies confirmed Jennifer's earlier assumption about the simplicity of their attire. Li glanced at Jennifer with a shocked expression as the agent processed the same revelation. A second later, however, they both burst out laughing. The small child, soaked too, came running up and latched onto Malinyah's thigh. Malinyah spoke soothingly to the girl and began to laugh as well. Closing her eyes, she whispered something, and then, boom, the child was gone, the three women were in a marble hall, and they were perfectly dry.

"What the hell just happened?" Li asked, looking around the hall and then down at her dry tunic.

"We are in her memories. Pebbles said she can move between memories in an instant. She can show you objects, places, events. We must have intruded on a memory of a day at the beach."

The mention of Pebbles' nickname caused Malinyah to ask, "Eleanor?"

"Muran has Eleanor. She's taken her prisoner," Jennifer said, using her hand to clutch her own throat.

Although Jennifer was certain Malinyah didn't understand the words, she could tell the Munuorian understood the meaning. Her face twitched and she spat, *"Sikaer!"*

"What did she say?" Li asked.

"Don't know, but if I had to guess I'd say she said their word for 'betrayer.' It's sort of Muran's nickname," Jennifer said. "Let me try something."

She turned to Malinyah and said, "Mereau is here with me. With Elizabeth."

Malinyah frowned. "Mereau?"

"Yes, Mereau," Jennifer said. Turning to Li, she said, "Step away a little bit."

Once Li stepped aside, Jennifer pointed at herself, then the vacant spot between her and Li, and then lastly to Li. "Jennifer, Mereau, Elizabeth. Mereau is here. He's with us."

Confused, Malinyah asked again, "Mereau?"

Jennifer took Malinyah by the hand, gesturing for Malinyah to follow. "Come with me. Come meet Mereau."

Malinyah's eyes opened wide. "Mereau!"

"Yes, he's here!" Jennifer said. She looked to Li and asked, "Are you satisfied? Do you believe us now?"

"I…I…," stuttered a bewildered Li.

"I'll take that as a yes," Jennifer said. She looked back to Malinyah and held up her hand. "Wait here! We'll get Mereau."

Malinyah pulled her hand away and used it to cup her mouth. She backed away a step, whispering the great captain's name. Jennifer said to Li, "Come on, we're done here."

"Okay, how do we do it? How do we stop?"

"Good question. I'm not sure. I've never asked Pebbles or Anlon. Let's concentrate our thoughts on letting go of the Stone and see what happens," Jennifer said.

As soon as Li took hold of the *Sinethal* and joined Jennifer in the session with Malinyah, Anlon motioned for Henri to sit in the chair originally occupied by Li. "Please, Henri. I have questions for both of you."

"Yes, I imagine you do," Mereau said, shifting his head in the direction of Anlon's voice.

"Why did he do it?" Anlon asked.

"You mean Mathieu?" Mereau asked.

"Yes."

"He felt he would not be able to stop her on his own. It pained me to break the sacred laws of my people, and to lose Mathieu, but he convinced me it was the only way to defeat Muran," Mereau said. Henri nodded in agreement.

"I'm sure it was a difficult decision, but I don't mean that. I mean, why did he give Pebbles the bogus *lyktyl*? Why didn't he tell us what it was?"

"It was a rash decision, an impulsive one. I would have advised him against it, against the whole idea of using it as bait," Mereau said.

"Agreed. It was beyond stupid. But that doesn't answer my question," Anlon said. He looked at Henri. "You were there when he gave it to her. Why did he do it?"

"He was frustrated, I think," Henri said. "He had been wearing it himself for months, hoping Muran would take notice and come after him. He wore it everywhere he went — conferences, public dinners, private parties. He made sure he was photographed wearing it. He even tried to auction it, but nothing happened."

Henri went on to tell Anlon that Foucault had devised the idea shortly after the Maerlif on Dominica had been breached and the chest of *Sulataers* inside stolen. At the time, Henri explained, Foucault thought Devlin Wilson had broken into the vault. Anlon thought of Devlin's notebooks detailing his expeditions to Dominica, Guadeloupe and Martinique and recalled the stash of *Sulataers* found in Dobson's house.

"I don't understand," Anlon said. "Foucault told us he thought Muran was after a *Tuliskaera* or a *Taellin*. He never mentioned the *lyktyl*."

"Mathieu was mistaken," Mereau said. "He knew Muran's *Tuliskaera* and *Taellin* were destroyed along with her *Sinethal*. He assumed she would seek replacements."

"Destroyed? How did he know that?" Anlon asked.

"He found her Maerlif," Mereau said.

"What?"

"Yes, I was surprised, too," Mereau said. "I wish he'd told me when he first found it."

Muran had a Maerlif? Anlon thought. If that were true, it meant she had died...or had moved her mind to a new body, leaving the old one behind, as Foucault had claimed Muran had done with Alynioria and countless others. But why had she destroyed her own *Sinethal, Taellin* and *Tuliskaera*? He asked Mereau.

"Mathieu did not believe Muran destroyed them on purpose. He believed someone found her Maerlif and attempted to revive Muran, and broke the *Tyls* during the transfer," Mereau said.

Gasps escaped from the mouths of Jennifer and Li. Anlon turned to see them trembling. He watched as the shivering continued, wondering what was happening. Then, without any sort of transition, the quivering stopped and they both smiled. Turning away, Anlon refocused on Mereau's explanation.

At Indio Maiz, Foucault had said he suspected Muran sought a *Tuliskaera* and *Taellin* to change bodies again. Anlon remembered Foucault saying Muran was desperate to change bodies, that she was running out of time, that the life-extending effects of *enjyia* were fading for Muran, as they were for him.

But Foucault hadn't mentioned Muran was without a *Sinethal*, too. Ah! thought Anlon. Malinyah's *Sinethal*. Foucault must have believed Muran *loaned* Devlin the Stone to find the other *Tyls*. Then, once the other *Tyls* were acquired, he must have assumed Devlin planned to return the *Sinethal* to Muran and help her transfer her mind into a new body, erasing Malinyah's memories as an interim step. As a bonus, Muran would have also acquired the map marking the Munirvo Maerlif locations. With Malinyah's memories of the map erased, only Muran would have possessed the ability to find the Munuorian caches.

Given that mindset, Anlon could see why Foucault turned his attention to the *lyktyl*. Malinyah had expressly opted to send the medallion away with Mereau, keeping the key separate from the lock it was intended to open. If Foucault believed Devlin had opened Omereau's tomb on Dominica, Anlon could understand his logic in thinking that Devlin might also have been searching for Omereau's *Sinethal*. But, then a thought occurred to him.

"Mereau, there's something I don't understand. When I spoke with Muran, when she called to demand I turn over Malinyah's *Sinethal*, she also demanded Omereau's *Sinethal*. She said they'd *both* been taken from her."

"Yes, it seems she had both, though we never knew for certain," Mereau said. "You see, when Mathieu discovered Malinyah's and Omereau's Maerlifs, the *Sinethals* were gone from both. It seemed evident Muran had taken Malinyah's, as she left certain mementos in the Maerlif, but no such tokens were left in Omereau's. And unlike Malinyah's tomb, the rest of Omereau's tomb was intact, including his *Tyls*. That confused us," Mereau said.

Anlon recalled seeing the dusty remains of Alynioria's hair and tunic on Malinyah's burial cloak. Although he hadn't focused on it at the time, he now recalled her tomb was otherwise empty. It was no wonder, then, that Mereau and Foucault had been confused. If Muran had plundered Omereau's tomb, wouldn't she have also taken his *Tyls*, as it seemed she had from Malinyah's? Conversely, if Muran hadn't been the one who pilfered Omereau's *Sinethal*, why hadn't the looter also taken the other *Tyls*, including the chest of *Sulataers* that Dobson later discovered?

"Mereau, why did Foucault leave Omereau's *Tyls* in his Maerlif? Once he discovered it, why didn't he remove them all? If the tomb had already been looted once, weren't you both concerned it might happen again?"

"Omereau's *Tyls* are sacred!" Mereau answered. "Mathieu was instructed to seal the tomb so that no one could find the entry."

"But he left the beacon," Anlon said, recalling Devlin's notes.

"A false beacon. A trap for Muran, in case she returned for the *Tyls*," Mereau said. "If she had removed the entry stone where Mathieu placed the beacon, the surrounding stones would have collapsed as soon as she stepped through the entrance. She would have been crushed."

It's a good thing Devlin never found the entry stone then! Anlon thought. But Dobson had ...and escaped unscathed with the *Sulataers*. Foucault's trap had failed. Or had it? Thinking back to the confrontation with Foucault at Indio Maiz, Anlon remembered Foucault saying he had sent Christian to prevent them from opening the *Maerlif* because he thought they'd blast it open "like greedy treasure hunters." Had Dobson circumvented Foucault's trap on Dominica by blowing a hole through the *Maerlif* wall?

Anlon could see how that would have unnerved Foucault. He thought Devlin had done it, acting as a puppet for Muran. So, Foucault must have assumed Muran was somehow hip to the trap. It must have puzzled him, though. Why would Muran only take the *Sulataers*? If the rest of Omereau's *Tyls* had been inside, why wouldn't she also have snagged a *Tuliskaera* and *Taellin*?

He was about to ask Mereau that very question when he heard the telltale sound of the *Naetir* separating from the *Sinethal* and the thud of it landing on the floor. He turned to see the two woozy women slump against the sofa cushions and Henri scurrying into the suite's kitchen. As Anlon reached for the *Sinethal*, clutched precariously in Jennifer's right hand, Henri came alongside with two bottled waters. He handed one to Anlon to give to Jennifer. The other Henri prepped to give to Li. Jennifer's eyes fluttered open. Anlon asked, "Hey there, you okay?"

She smiled and whispered, "That was wild."

Li stirred too and looked around the room. To Anlon, she appeared very disoriented. Henri held the open bottle to her lips and encouraged her to drink. Anlon did likewise with Jennifer. She took a long sip, then pushed away the bottle. She pointed at the *Sinethal* in Anlon's other hand. "We told her Mereau is here. She wants to see him."

"And I, her," Mereau said, holding out his hands. Anlon reached forward and gave Mereau the *Sinethal*, then bent down to retrieve the *Naetir* from the floor. He watched Mereau smooth his fingers over the etched symbols. Mereau smiled and whispered, *"Ailta er-ill, ento ainfa."*

Anlon remembered the translation. "Ever apart, together always."

"You have a *Naetir*?" Mereau asked.

"Yes, here it is," Anlon said, resting it on Mereau's knee. A moment later, Mereau took the *Naetir* and guided it to the center notch. Unlike the sharp clap that occurred when Anlon and others used the *Sinethal*, Mereau gently nestled the *Naetir* into the slot. His fingers slid into the notches and he heaved a great sigh. It wasn't a pained sigh, Anlon noticed. The man had a smile on his face.

Even in Foucault's aged body, Mereau felt the energy of Malinyah's spirit flow into him. And he could instantly see. Malinyah sat beneath Seybalrosa under sunny skies. When she felt his presence, she stood and teetered, then came dashing down the hilly path.

Mereau ran to greet her, his bare feet slapping against the moist, red clay of the path as he dashed upward. The last time he'd seen her, she'd handed over Omereau's *lyktyl* with the understanding he was to protect it at all costs. It had been a dark and sad parting, one that tainted the many happy memories they had shared. But the emotions they exchanged now ranged from delight to relief. Their embrace was as real as any Mereau remembered sharing ten thousand years ago. The feel of her skin against his, the scent of her hair, the warmth of her touch — they were all the same. It was if they'd both awoken from a terrible dream to find themselves together once again.

And then other memories rushed forward, interrupting the joyous reunion. Images of Munirvo passed between them, as did a snippet of the smiling Alynioria, and another one of the sneering Muran cutting down her fellow countrymen with a *Tuliskaera*, and last, a vision of *The Betrayer* standing over the frightened, screaming Alynioria.

Mereau held onto Malinyah as she quivered. He whispered in her ear, "Ease your mind, my love. I have come to bring peace to our memories of Alynioria. I will avenge her, and then we will mourn the loss of our daughter, together."

While Mereau visited with Malinyah, Anlon led Jennifer and Li outside and they reconvened around the patio table. Anlon and Jennifer watched Li sip water while she stared at the pool with a blank expression.

"Well? What did you think of Malinyah?" Jennifer asked.

Agent Li gulped down some more water, then asked, "Did that really just happen?"

"It did," Jennifer said. "What an incredible experience. It seemed so real."

"Amazing, isn't it?" Anlon asked.

"Beyond amazing! It's weird, but I can still feel sand between my toes," Jennifer said, wiggling her feet.

"What about the wave?" Li asked Jennifer.

"Oh, my God! How real was that? I was soaked!"

As the two women engaged in a conversation about the range of sensations they experienced, Anlon thought of Pebbles. She often emerged from sessions with Malinyah with the same excitement in her voice and twinkle in her eyes. She could gab for hours about things she'd seen, or places Malinyah had taken her, or foods she'd tasted. Although Anlon didn't leave sessions with Malinyah with the same degree of excitement, he did retain equally powerful memories of the sensations and events he experienced.

How remarkable is that? What a way to preserve memories! Anlon thought of the modern phenomenon of online social media. Many people seemed to use the platforms to share memories, often in the form of pictures or videos. The implication was, "If I simply tell you about the great concert I attended, you can't imagine how fun it was. Let me show you instead. Then, you'll understand!" Yet,

Anlon found that the pictures and videos often fell short of conveying the richness of the events they chronicled. Much like murals and sculptures crafted by ancient cultures, these modern methods of sharing memories were often flat and uninspiring.

But here was a device that could share memories in their full context, including sensations and emotions associated with the memories. Sharing the full context seemed to ensure the memories were retained at a deeper, more personal level than storytelling or pictures ever could. What had led Omereau to imagine such a device? Why had the long-term preservation of memories been so important to him?

Anlon felt a hand tap his knee. He looked up to see Jennifer waving at him. "Hello, there. You still with us?"

He cleared his throat and shifted his posture. "Yeah. Sorry about that. What did I miss?"

"No worries. We were just talking about Muran. I was telling Elizabeth about *enjyia* and how Muran used it to extend her life span. You know, to explain how she looks the same in the locket picture," Jennifer said.

"Oh, right," Anlon said. "*Enjyia* apparently slows the aging process. Foucault told us the Munuorians could live as long as five hundred years."

"So, Anabel used it too?" Li asked.

"Yes, I know she did for a fact. She served me some when I last saw her," Jennifer said. "But, for some reason, it didn't last as long for her as it did for Muran."

"Or for Foucault," Anlon said.

"Well, as fantastical as most of this seems to be, at least the crime part makes sense to me," Li said. "I just wish I understood more about the dispute between Muran and Evelyn that spurred everything that's happened. I read the article and I walked away believing Evelyn saved Muran- slash-Clara's life. Twenty years later, Clara gives Evelyn a locket that seems to suggest they shared an intimate relationship. Fast forward one hundred fifty-five years later, Clara crushes Evelyn's heart with her hand."

"I think your earlier theory still stands," Jennifer said. "Somewhere between Clara giving Evelyn the locket and now, Evelyn took Muran's Stones."

"Can we step back a sec?" Anlon asked. "Evelyn saved Muran's life?"

"Oh, that's right. You don't know about the article," Jennifer said. She turned to Li. "You still have it on your phone?"

Several minutes later, Anlon finished reading the article for a third time. He still couldn't get over the photograph of Anabel. Although Anlon had not known Anabel when she was a young woman, he vividly remembered the framed pictures of her with Devlin scattered about her living room. Thinking back on it now, Anlon was surprised he hadn't noticed her persistent youthful appearance in the pictures. The pictures showed the two together at various archaeological sites and had been taken between the early 1980s and early 2000s. He supposed his mind had focused more on the age gap between Devlin and Anabel, rather than their absolute ages. It also should have dawned on him that she had aged significantly since the last of the pictures.

The article itself was very telling, especially in the context of Anlon's earlier conversation with Mereau and Henri. He relayed the conversation to Jennifer and Li. When he finished, he said, "This article seems to validate Foucault's story. Evelyn found Muran's tomb. She activated her *Sinethal*. Muran convinced her to find a body. Evelyn chose the lady she served. She helped Muran execute the transfer, but botched it up, destroying the Stones in the process. Muran survived and they concocted the pirate story to cover up what really happened."

"Right," Jennifer said. "Muran must have proposed a deal with Evelyn along the lines of the deal Mereau made with Foucault. Help me, I'll help you. I'll give you *enjyia*, you'll stay young and beautiful."

"It fits," Anlon said. "According to Mereau, Foucault said there were no other *Tyls* in the tomb, other than the ones that were destroyed during the transfer. Foucault believed it meant Muran had cleared out the undamaged *Tyls*. That means she would have had a *Breylofte* and *Terusael*, so she would have had what she needed to make *enjyia*. I wonder if Malinyah's *Sinethal* was in the tomb, too. Can you imagine how differently things might have turned out if Evelyn had connected with Malinyah instead of Muran?"

"Would have been totally different," Jennifer said. "But, whether Malinyah was in the tomb or not, Muran still had her *Sinethal* stashed somewhere, right? And she had Omereau, too."

"Yep. That's what Foucault told Mereau," Anlon said.

"I wonder what happened. Why did Evelyn steal them?" Jennifer asked.

"I've got two better questions: why did Anabel give Devlin Malinyah's *Sinethal*, and what the hell did she do with Omereau's?" Anlon asked.

19

Trojan Disc

La Quinta, California
September 29

Mereau emerged from the suite and walked to the patio table where Anlon and Jennifer awaited him. In his hands, he carried Malinyah's *Sinethal* and the *Naetir*. As he approached, Anlon noticed Mereau no longer wore sunglasses, and his earlier unsteady gait had disappeared. Instead, he came toward them with confident strides and steely eyes.

What an amazing transformation, thought Anlon. Though the man approaching him carried the physical features of Jacques Foucault, there was no mistaking the presence of entirely different mind and spirit. Gone were Foucault's elegant mannerisms and erudite style. In their places, Mereau projected the bearing of a determined, charismatic leader.

Anlon stood to greet him, followed shortly thereafter by Jennifer and Li. Mereau handed the ancient Stones to Anlon and thanked him for the opportunity to spend time with Malinyah's memories. "It was a gift to see and touch her again."

"I imagine she felt the same," Anlon said.

Mereau nodded and stared at the *Sinethal*. "I hope so. While we shared many joys in life, we also shared tragedies. Malinyah's memories of many things, including me, are tainted by those tragedies."

He sighed and looked up at Anlon. In his expression, Anlon sensed sorrow. Then, in the blink of Mereau's eyes, the sorrow vanished. He reached out and clasped Anlon's shoulder. With an unwavering stare, he said, "It is time to put an end to this curse. For all of us, including Malinyah."

The tenor of his voice and the firmness of his grip made Anlon want to shout out, "Oorah," and charge enemy lines.

"Amen to that!" said Jennifer.

"Tell me all that has happened and how the field stands," Mereau said. "Then we will devise a plan of action."

For the next hour, Anlon and Jennifer ran through the entire tale, beginning with Devlin Wilson's murder and ending with the information about Muran's recent identities provided earlier in the day by Li. At various points during the discussion, Mereau had asked questions, but he offered no insights or commentary. When Anlon finished the recap, Mereau said, "Our plan must accomplish three goals. The first, and most pressing, is the rescue of your friend, Eleanor. The second is the death of Muran. The third is to find and secure Omereau's *Sinethal*, if possible. All other matters are of lesser importance."

As Anlon listened to Mereau's goals, he was glad Agent Li had excused herself before Mereau stepped from the suite. She would not have taken kindly to the selection of murder as their number two goal, justified as it might seem. Instead, Anlon imagined Li would have prioritized solving the various crimes perpetrated by Muran and Goodwin, with an eye toward bringing them both before a judge and jury.

"So, I'm with you on goal number one, and I wouldn't shed a single tear if Muran died in the process, but depending on the situation, we might have to settle with capturing her," Anlon said.

"Killing her is the only way to stop her," Mereau said.

"Neither of us disagrees with you, Mereau. But in our country, it's a crime to kill another person unless you're acting in self-defense," Jennifer said.

"Don't delude yourselves. She will not surrender," Mereau said. "If she were surrounded by a hundred men with overwhelming weaponry and nowhere to run or hide, she would never yield."

As Mereau defended his stance, Anlon thought of Muran's actions outside the Middlebury bank and Jennifer's description of her later standoff with the police on the shore of Lake George. In both cases, Muran had acted like a cornered animal, lashing out at anyone and everyone who posed a threat. Jennifer must have been thinking along the same lines. Just as Anlon prepared to concede Mereau's position, she said, "Yeah, unfortunately, you're right. I had a front-row seat the last time she was surrounded. Trying to get her to surrender peacefully didn't go too well."

"So, what do you propose?" Anlon asked Mereau.

"It will not be easy. Muran has not survived ten thousand years by underestimating her opponents. She is shrewd and ruthless. She will seek to define the battlefield and set the conditions in her favor. We will have to outwit her," Mereau said. He rose from his seat and began to pace while he continued to talk. "We must assume she has discovered the *lyktyl* is a forgery. We must further assume Muran has already interrogated Eleanor to discover where the forgery originated. Whether Eleanor confessed freely or was induced to do so, we must assume Muran knows the forgery came from Mathieu."

"Question. Where is the real *lyktyl?*" Anlon asked.

"It is safe," Mereau answered.

"Does that mean you have it?" Anlon pressed.

"It is safe."

"As thrilled as I am to hear it's safe, I'd like to know where it is," Anlon said. "Pebbles, er, Eleanor's life may depend on it."

"Your friend's life is not tied to the *lyktyl*. Muran will be angry at the deception, yes, but she will be angry at Mathieu, not Eleanor," Mereau said.

"I wish I shared your confidence," Anlon said.

"So, you think she'll come after you, I mean, Foucault?" Jennifer asked, leaning forward with elbows on the table.

"It would not surprise me to learn she has already dispatched her confederate to Pézenas, assuming she did not kill him when she discovered the fake *lyktyl*," Mereau said. "But, I don't think she will go there herself. Not yet."

"How can you be so sure?" Anlon asked.

"You misunderstand me. I am *not* sure. She may focus on the *lyktyl* first. But…if I place myself in her shoes, I would concentrate on retrieving Malinyah's and Omereau's *Sinethals* ahead of the *lyktyl*," Mereau said.

"Why?" Jennifer asked.

"The *Sinethals* are unique. Malinyah's and Omereau's memories cannot be recreated," Mereau said.

"Hold up. Are you saying the *lyktyl* can be recreated?" Anlon asked. "I mean, I know Foucault created a forgery, so it's possible to make something that looks like the *lyktyl*. But I assume the forgery can't unlock Omereau's *Sinethal*, correct?"

"Correct. Mathieu's creation will not work," Mereau said. "But, it is possible to make a new *lyktyl*, if you have the right materials and know how to forge the materials together."

"You've lost me," Anlon said. "If what you say is true, and Muran had Omereau's *Sinethal* for, what, thousands of years, wouldn't she have tried to make her own *lyktyl*?"

Mereau nodded. "She may have tried, but it would have been very risky."

"Why?" Jennifer asked.

"If she had made the slightest error, she would have destroyed Omereau's memories," Mereau said.

Of course! Anlon thought. There must be a diamond inside the medallion's black stone. Assuming the design of Omereau's *Sinethal* is similar to the *Aromaegh* that Antonio scanned, the diamond inside its center notch acts as a stylus. It connects with the corresponding stylus inside the *lyktyl*. Unless Muran knew the diamond's shape and dimensions, she would be left to guess the right combination. And if she guessed wrong, the electrical charge between the two pieces might erase some or all of Omereau's memories.

"I see. She doesn't know the composition of diamond inside the medallion's stone," Anlon said.

"Yes. Exactly," Mereau said.

"Okay, let's assume you're right," Jennifer said, "and she wants the *Sinethals* first. We've got a slight problem there. We don't have Omereau's. Will she trade Pebbles for just Malinyah's *Sinethal?*"

Mereau shook his head, his expression stern. "She will not release her until she has both."

"What?" exclaimed Anlon.

"Muran would be a fool to release Eleanor without possessing both mind-keepers," Mereau said. "In fact, I doubt she will release her until she has the real *lyktyl*, too. Or makes a new one."

"Okay, time-out," Anlon said. "Why would she wait until she has all three pieces?"

"Until she has the *lyktyl*, she needs leverage," Mereau said.

"Leverage? What do you mean, leverage? Leverage with whom?"

"Malinyah," Mereau said, folding his arms across his chest.

Anlon tapped the table with his fingers while he mulled Mereau's comments. Why would Muran need leverage with Malinyah? The answer came to him as fast as the question had formed in his mind. "The *lyktyl*! Malinyah knows how to make a new *lyktyl*!"

Mereau's mouth formed a slight smile. Anlon jumped up from the table. Running his hands through his hair, he began to pace back and forth by the pool. As Anlon disappeared into thought, Jennifer and Mereau continued to talk.

Muran must have kept hope that she would find the real *lyktyl* on her own, holding onto Malinyah's *Sinethal* as an insurance policy in the event push came to shove, thought Anlon. A desperate circumstance that had apparently come to fruition. Anlon recalled Foucault's words at Indio Maiz: "She is running out of options. She needs to find one fast." While Foucault's comment had been intended to explain why he believed Muran was searching for a *Tuliskaera*, it could have equally applied to the *lyktyl*. Hence his decision to give Pebbles the fake *lyktyl* before departing Indio Maiz.

It must have grated on Muran to look at Malinyah's *Sinethal* for so long, knowing the key to her perpetual resurrection was but fingertips away. Had she given the *Sinethal* to Anabel after all? To have Anabel probe Malinyah for the *lyktyl's* location? Ah! thought Anlon. What if Anabel had visited with Malinyah and discovered who Muran really was? Had Malinyah encouraged Anabel to flee from Muran, taking both *Sinethals* with her? The scenario made some sense, but why would Anabel have then given Devlin the Stone?

A question from Jennifer brought Anlon back to the conversation with Mereau. "So, you're saying we need to tell Muran we have Omereau, hoping she will agree to meet."

"That's correct. You will arrange an exchange. Eleanor for the *Sinethals*," Mereau said.

"But a minute ago you said she wouldn't give up Pebbles unless she has the *lyktyl*, too," Jennifer said.

"True, but she will not say that. Muran is treacherous to the core. She will have no choice but to bring Eleanor to the exchange, knowing full well you will not agree to hand over the *Sinethals* unless Eleanor is with her when the trade takes place," Mereau said.

"Hold up," Anlon said, returning to his seat at the table. "Then what? What are we going to do when she asks to see Omereau's *Sinethal*?"

Jennifer nudged Anlon's shoulder. "You must have really zoned out. Mereau said he can translate for Malinyah. They can tell us how to make one."

"It only has to look like Omereau's *Sinethal*. You hold it up for her to see. Given Mathieu's attempt at deception, she will look closely for Omereau's symbol on the front and the cuts on the back. Don't let her handle it. Just show it to her for a moment, then put it away," Mereau said.

"Okay, I'm with you. What then?" Anlon asked.

"She will try to kill you…but I will kill her before she has the chance," Mereau said.

"What do you say? Can you help me?" Anlon asked.

"You know it," Antonio said. Turning to Katie, he said, "Send the plane to get Dylan. He'll probably put up a fuss, but tell him it's nonnegotiable."

Anlon recalled Dylan was not a fan of airplanes. He didn't mind designing them, but he didn't like riding in them. His phobia had proved an inconvenience during the Whave engine project, but they'd done their best to work around it.

Katie, clicking away furiously on her cell phone, answered Antonio without looking up. "Already gave the pilots and Dylan a heads-up."

"Any pushback?" Antonio asked.

She shook her head as she continued to type. "Nope."

"Huh! I'm surprised. He's usually such a baby about flying," Antonio said.

Katie looked up at Antonio with a devilish look on her face. "I told him what was up. He has a soft spot for Pebbles, if you recall."

"Ah! Good thinking," Antonio said, smiling broadly.

"Soft spot? What are you two talking about?" Anlon asked.

Katie giggled, then bit her lip. Antonio tried to suppress a laugh but failed to hold it in. "I'll tell you later. It's an inside joke."

Katie held up her hand. "Hold on. Dylan's typing back. He wants to know if you want him to bring the diamonds. He put two winking emoticons and a starburst at the end."

Anlon and Antonio exchanged puzzled looks. Then Anlon smiled. "Ah! Booby trap."

"Tell him yes," Antonio said. "Now where do we get enough gold bars to do the trick?"

"Already ordered a dozen," Katie replied. "There's a precious metals dealer in Palm Desert. I'll go pick them up as soon as we're done here and take them to the lab on Cook Street."

"Great. Now all we need is a smelter. We can spit out a mold in the lab, but we don't have a smelter to melt down the gold," Antonio said.

"Not a problem," Anlon said. "Mereau has a *Tuliskaera*. He can do the honors."

"Then let's hop to it," Antonio said. "Time's a-wasting."

Jennifer walked slowly toward the conference room, wondering how Li would react when she told her their plan. Would she co-operate and give them the space to make it work, or would she nix the whole idea?

Anlon had not been in favor of clueing in the police, but Jennifer had convinced him otherwise. If Mereau's plan A went wrong, they needed a plan C just in case Anlon's plan B failed, too. And the police presented their best option to put Muran down if the *Lifintyls* failed.

She imagined the police would not risk helicopters again after what happened at Lake George, but they'd put drones in the sky. They also wouldn't mess around with any sort of negotiator at this point. They'd use snipers and SWAT teams with armored vehicles. One wrong twitch from Muran and they'd bring the rain.

The only question was, would they stand by while Mereau did the deed, especially if he attacked first? This aspect of the plan would be the most delicate part of the conversation. Jennifer sighed, knowing she would have to shade the truth in order to get Li's buy-in.

When she walked into the conference room, she saw Li talking with two officers as they examined a map tacked to the wall. Jennifer approached from behind just as Li said, "Then we're screwed."

Jennifer froze in place, hoping to catch more of the conversation before interrupting. But one of the officers spotted her approach and said, "Can I help you, miss?"

Li turned around. When she saw Jennifer, she blushed and excused herself from the conversation with the two officers. Turning back to Jennifer, she said, "Come with me, we need to talk."

"Um, okay," Jennifer said, as she followed Li out the conference room door. "Everything all right?"

"Where is Anlon?" Li asked.

"I don't know, probably back in his room. Why?"

Li didn't answer. She walked briskly along the arbored hallway, ducking her head in each conference room she passed. At the third one, she looked back and said, "In here."

Inside the dark and empty room, Li paced back and forth, gathering her thoughts. Jennifer felt a pit form in her stomach. Something had gone wrong. "Is it Pebbles?"

"What?" Li asked, stopping suddenly.

"Has something else happened to Pebbles?" Jennifer timidly asked, afraid to say the words, "Is she dead?"

"No," Li said, as she began to pace again. "Not to my knowledge."

"Then what's up? You're freaking me out," Jennifer said, stepping to block Li's path.

"We found Goodwin. He's dead. His throat was slashed," Li said.

"What? Where?"

"Small airport on the border between California and Arizona. Place called Needles. We alerted FAA, gave them Muran's plane's ID. We asked them to help us locate the plane. Unfortunately, we were a little too late. By the time they loaded the information in their system, the plane was already airborne and they'd turned off the plane's transponder. No way to know where they went," Li said, shaking her head. "We sent CHP to the airport. They talked to the guy who runs the control tower. Showed him a picture of Muran. Said he'd never seen her, but…he said he'd talked with the plane's pilot. Another woman. Young woman. They're working on a composite sketch now, but I'm not sure how helpful it will be. She wore sunglasses and a baseball cap when she talked to the controller."

"What about Goodwin?"

"Controller said he saw a white car pull up next to the plane before the plane left. He said he saw a man get out of the car and help the pilot load a third person on the plane. He said he was too far away to tell if the third person was a man or woman, but we're assuming it was your friend. Anyway, he said the pilot and the man got back in the car and drove to the parking lot, but only the pilot returned to the plane. The controller assumed the man in the car left after that.

"CHP walked the parking lot, looking for evidence. One of them spotted a white car beyond the lot, in a junkyard of old plane parts. They investigated and found blood on the ground by the trunk. They popped it open and found Goodwin. Plates were missing. We're trying to track the VIN number now."

"So, Muran definitely has Pebbles now," Jennifer said.

"It seems so. And we have no idea where they went. If they turn the transponder back on or try to land at an FAA-monitored airport, we've got a shot, but they probably flew south across the border into Mexico. It's less than a half-hour flight from Needles. If that's where they went, and I think they did, then we're screwed. We have no jurisdiction to go after them. At least, not until we can find out where they are. If they've gone somewhere with friendly ties to the US, we might be able to lobby the local PD or military to coordinate a rescue effort. But it means getting the State Department involved, probably the Defense Department, too. Red tape up the ying yang," Li said, punching her hand with a fist.

"Damn!" Jennifer said. "What about Interpol?"

"We can try once we find out where they went, but I'm not hopeful. They're better suited for investigation support, not rescue operations," Li said. She looked down at the terra-cotta-tiled floor and sighed. "Let's hope I'm wrong and they pop somewhere in-country."

Jennifer looked down as well, trying to gather her thoughts. If Muran expected to orchestrate an exchange, she would have to communicate a meeting place. When that happened, they would at least know then where Muran had gone.

"What did you come to see me about?" Li asked.

"Huh? Oh, nothing important. Just came to see if there was any update," Jennifer said.

"Well, that's all I got. Afraid it's not good news."

"Do you want me to tell Anlon, or should I stay out of it?"

"Actually, I'd appreciate it if you did. I could use the time to start calling folks in D.C. The earlier I can tee up DOD and State, the quicker they can get things rolling in case we need their help."

"Okay, no problem. You'll let us know when you get back anything on the car?"

"Yep. I'll have someone run over the composite sketch, too."

"All right. Thanks," Jennifer said, shaking Li's hand.

As Jennifer turned to leave the conference room, Li said, "Hey. Tell Anlon it doesn't change anything. As soon as he hears from Muran, I want to know about it, okay?"

"Got it," Jennifer said. Out in the hallway, she mumbled, "Better start working on a plan D."

Anlon sat in the corner of the conference room, looking down at the screen of his cell phone, willing Muran to call. He checked his email and texts, too, just in case. Frustrated, he slapped the phone down. "Come on, Muran, let's get this over with!"

He rose from the table and stood by the long bank of windows. Outside, a steady stream of white and red lights passed each other under the glow of orangish-pink streetlights. In the reflection of the window, he saw the remains of the pizza boxes the crew minting the bogus *Sinethal* had consumed earlier in the evening. He turned to grab a slice of the pepperoni and jalapeño pizza he'd requested in honor of Pebbles. As he munched on the cold, limp slice, he thought of how hard the crew had worked to fashion the forgery.

It had been fascinating to watch Mereau, Dylan and Antonio engineer the forgery together. Almost as fascinating as it had been to watch Mereau experience a car ride for the first time in his life. At first, the man had held onto Anlon's arm so tight, he cut off the circulation. Then, when Antonio had the driver lower the windows after Mereau announced he felt sick, Mereau had laughed like a child as the wind peppered his face.

Once they arrived, however, Mereau had been all business. Thankfully, Dylan had suppressed his childlike curiosity when introduced to the ten-thousand-year-old Mereau, and the three men had gone to work to create the gold, disc-shaped *Sinethal* mold. Mereau had accessed Malinyah's *Sinethal* to retrieve the disc dimensions, which he had then communicated to Dylan. When it had come time to design the notches on the back and Omereau's six-pointed star symbol for the *Sinethal's* front side, Dylan had trouble accurately incorporating the features. After several unsuccessful iterations, Mereau had handed Malinyah's *Sinethal* and a *Naetir* to Dylan so that he could meet with Malinyah and see the features with his mind's eye.

Dylan had been a trooper, Anlon thought. He had been badly shaken up by the experience of meeting Malinyah, but after a shot of *enjyia* supplied by Mereau, he had hopped on the computer and finished the mold design without asking a single question.

Meanwhile, Anlon and Antonio had discussed how to wire the booby trap inside the device. They agreed that if Muran somehow took possession of the gold disc, she would likely hold it as if she were using it, placing her fingers in the handhold notches. She would not suspect any electrical current given the absence of the *lyktyl*.

Antonio had huddled with some of his engineers on-site, and they came up with a design for high-voltage, pressure-sensitive shock nodes that could be placed beneath the surface of each handhold. While the engineers crafted the nodes, Antonio had described the concept to Anlon and Jennifer. "They're essentially high-tech joy buzzers, but they pack a bigger, more painful punch. If nothing else, it'll surprise Muran long enough to disarm her."

Once the nodes had been constructed, the mold casting had been modified to incorporate inner slots on each half of the mold to hold the nodes in place. Then had come the smelting process. Anlon, Jennifer and Katie had joined a dozen of Antonio's technicians as they peered into the lab from the hallway windows. Anlon had marveled at the ancient captain's nimble touch with the two Stones. First, Mereau had primed the *Tuliskaera* by grinding a *Naetir* against the base of the cone-shaped Stone. Once the snake design on the *Tuliskaera* glowed a reddish-orange, Mereau had turned the hockey-puck-shaped *Naetir* on its side and struck the base of the *Tuliskaera*. A laserlike beam had shot from the cone tip of the *Tuliskaera*, causing the technicians to ooh and aah. Within minutes, the gold bars had been liquefied and poured into the two mold halves.

Then, Mereau had used a *Breylofte* to generate sound waves that sped the cooling process, a technique used by the Munuorians when working with metals in building their ships, Mereau had explained afterward. Anlon had been further impressed by Mereau's craftsmanship when it came time to seal the two gold castings. Mereau had used *Dreylaeks* to reheat the inner faces of the castings enough for the two pieces to stick together. Once the two halves had been fused, Anlon could barely detect a seam around its edges.

Mereau had been quite pleased with the outcome, proclaiming to Anlon and Antonio that its appearance was authentic enough to fool Muran, which had prompted Dylan to respond, "Just pray she doesn't bring a metal detector."

"Why might that cause a problem?" Katie asked Dylan. She had been standing next to Anlon and Jennifer, watching the spectacle.

"Mereau told us the gold in the real-deal *Sinethal* is almost pure, which means it has a very low magnetic signature," Dylan had explained. "Our baby, on the other hand, has the shock devices inside, and with all the metal in them, they'll pop a much higher reading on a detector."

"I wouldn't worry about it. I doubt she'll have a metal detector," Anlon had said.

"I don't know, Anlon, I wouldn't be too sure about that. If she's figured out the medallion is a fake, she's likely to be super suspicious about both *Sinethals*. Wouldn't you think?" Antonio had replied.

With Antonio's words replaying in Anlon's mind, he sipped from a bottle of water to cool the jalapeños' bite and turned his thought to Pebbles. Based on what Jennifer had relayed from Li, she was now definitely in the presence of *The Betrayer*. As hard-nosed as he knew Pebbles was, Anlon worried about her health and state of mind. They would need her to be "in the moment," physically and mentally, when it came time for the exchange. If Muran attacked as Mereau expected, things would happen fast, and Pebbles would need to be ready to react.

There was a knock at the door and he looked up to see Jennifer standing in the doorway. She smiled and asked, "You okay? Mind if I come in?"

"Of course, come on over. Take a load off," Anlon said, pulling out a chair next to him and patting the seat cushion.

"Thanks," she said. She slid onto the seat and tucked a loose strand of hair behind her ear. Looking down at the table, she used her finger to trace along the wood-grain pattern. "I can't imagine what she's going through."

"Yeah, I know. I'm worried about her, too," Anlon said.

"I'm so angry at myself for not trusting my instincts. As soon as we heard about Anabel, I knew there would be trouble," Jennifer said.

"At least your danger radar was working. I never saw this coming. Not the way it rolled out," Anlon said.

"I talked with Griffin a few minutes ago," Jennifer said. "He feels awful, too. He had coffee with Pebbles the morning everything happened. He said she gave him shit for wearing shorts in the cold and wished him safe travels when he left."

"Where did he go?"

"Maui."

"Lucky duck."

"Yeah. He's back now. He came back as soon as he got my message from the hospital. I haven't had the chance to talk with him until now. He wanted you to know he'll take care of anything you need done at the house. He said all the cop cars are gone, but the police tape's still across the driveway and front door."

"God, I hadn't even thought about the house. We ran out so quickly, I'm not even sure I have my keys," Anlon said.

"I know how you feel. A bunch of my stuff's still in Burlington. I hope the hotel didn't trash it all," she said.

"I'm sure they didn't. I'll bet they had their security folks bag it all up and hold it. You should ask Katie to check on it. She'll probably get your gear here by sunrise," Anlon said, smiling.

"No kidding. She'd probably go get it herself!" Jennifer said.

They both laughed, and then Jennifer returned to her idle tracing of the table's surface. After a few minutes' silence, Anlon asked, "Something else on your mind?"

"Yeah, a few things, actually."

"Like what?"

"Mereau pulled me aside a little while ago to talk about a plan D."

"He did?"

"Yeah."

"And?"

Jennifer sighed. "You're probably not going to like his idea."

"Well, what is it?"

Without looking up from the table, Jennifer described Mereau's plan. When she finished, Anlon pounded the table and said, "No way. Out of the question."

Rising from the table, Anlon bolted from the room in search of Mereau.

Jennifer laid her head on the pillow and glanced at the glowing bedside clock. It was almost midnight. She was so exhausted she could barely hold her eyes open. With the little strength she had left, she pulled back the comforter and rolled her body between the sheets. She closed her eyes and said a prayer for Pebbles.

Rolling on her side, she clamped a pillow against her torso and nestled her head on another. She inhaled deeply through her nose and exhaled slowly through pursed lips. As she neared sleep, a jumble of the day's events and conversations went through her mind. The meeting with Malinyah stood out the most. Recalling the seaside encounter, Jennifer wiggled her toes. The feel of sand between her toes returned as she revisited the memory. She thought of meeting Mereau, his plan and the crafting of the "Trojan disc." She whispered a hope that the deception would work and shifted her thoughts to wonder what had happened to Omereau's *Sinethal*, mumbling, "What *did* you do with it, Anabel?"

The question was followed by a deep yawn. Jennifer curled into the fetal position and tried to clear her mind. Several deep breaths later, her eyes shot open and she gasped. She yanked away the covers and searched in the dark for her cell phone on the bedside table. She found it and pulled it from the charging cord. As she paced in the dark, she looked at the time. It was close to one in the morning, which meant it was approaching 4 a.m. in Vermont. Jennifer bit her fingernail as she continued to pace. Should I call him or text him? she wondered. If I call him and I'm wrong, he'll be pissed I dragged him out of bed and I'll look like an idiot. She opened the text app and typed out a quick message. "Call me as soon as you see this message!"

Jennifer had just pushed the send link when the doorbell to her room rang. The sound startled her and she dropped the phone. The doorbell sounded again, followed by pounding on the door. Jennifer reached for the switch to the bedside table lamp and called out, "Hold your horses, I'm coming."

Clad in T-shirt and undies, she padded to the door. "Who is it?"

"It's me," Anlon said from the other side of the door.

Jennifer cracked the door open. Anlon was fully dressed. He said, "Agent Li just called. They found Muran's plane. Grab what you need and let's go. We're headed to Mexico."

20

Hell's Angels

Laguna Milagros, Mexico
(The lagoon of miracles)
September 30

Pebbles closed her eyes and listened to the rhythmic patter of the palm fronds. In the distance, she could hear children splashing and a Jet Ski churning water. Closer by, a radio played a salsa tune, and a flock of gulls squawked at each other. Replace the rustling palms with whistling pines, and substitute hawks for the gulls, and the mix of sounds reminded her of the secluded cove on Lake Tahoe where she and Jennifer often sunbathed and practiced with their *Breyloftes*.

Opening her eyes, she looked around the windowless hut. Broad wood planks formed the walls and floor, while the pitched ceiling was made of thatch. Above the bed, a ceiling fan with blades of woven palm frond lazily circled. On the wall directly across from the bed, various masks were mounted. Painted with a variety of tropical colors, their eyeless faces stared down at her. Each mask depicted the head of a different animal, and depending on how Pebbles chose to look at them, their faces could appear menacing or cheerful. Whenever Kora came to check on her, the masks seemed to exhibit fear.

It must be all the *enjyia* she's feeding me, Pebbles thought. Kora's frequent visits began to make her think of the story of Hansel and Gretel. Pebbles doubted Muran intended to eat her, but there was definitely an unspoken purpose to the hourly feedings. She realized she shouldn't complain, however. Each cup of the Munuorian elixir gave her more strength and eased her various aches and pains. Plus, the feeding sessions provided respites from the muzzle covering the bottom half of her face and the shackles restraining her hands and feet to the bedposts.

She had tried on several occasions to pull free from the shackles without success and had learned that making any intelligible sounds through her clamped jaws was impossible. At least they hadn't beaten or zapped her again, thought Pebbles. Although, there had been a close call toward the end of the flight. Muran had exploded from the cockpit cussing and snarling, but Kora had corralled her before she reached Pebbles.

Since then, Kora had been the only one Pebbles had seen. Muran had not deplaned at the same time as they had, and she hadn't joined them for the drive to wherever they were now. As she had been blindfolded and stuffed in another trunk for the drive, Pebbles did not know much about her surroundings beyond the sounds she picked up and the visible contents of the small hut in which she was imprisoned. It was hot and humid, like Nicaragua, but absent of the jungle sounds or constant rain showers. She also knew they were near a body of water, but it wasn't an ocean, for she heard no crashing waves. It's either a lake or a river, Pebbles thought. She presumed they were somewhere in Mexico, given that the deejays on the radio station broadcasting the salsa music spoke entirely in Spanish and their station-break jingle ended with a bass-voiced "Meh-hee-ko." Pebbles had heard the jingle enough times by now to imagine various English translations. Her favorite was, "The best damn salsa music in all of Mexico!"

Wherever they were, they wouldn't be there much longer, Pebbles thought. Kora had interrogated her a few times since their arrival, and during their last "chat," Kora had brought Pebbles a fresh change of clothes. When Kora lifted the turquoise tunic for her to see, Pebbles had thought, "How Munuorian of you." In true Munuorian style, the sleeveless, mid-thigh-length tunic was all that Kora gave her. No shoes or sandals were provided for her feet, and no undergarments were offered. She had been allowed to bathe in private, and then was told to don the tunic.

"What's up? Are we going out for margaritas?" Pebbles had joked as she emerged from the hut's bathroom wearing the tunic, her first effort at levity since her ordeal began. Kora hadn't smiled. Instead, she'd shackled and muzzled Pebbles once again and left the hut, locking the door from the outside.

For the past hour, Pebbles had concentrated on Kora's wide-ranging questions. Instead of pummeling her endlessly about where Omereau's *Sinethal* was located, Kora had focused mostly on Foucault, Anabel and Devlin. She seemed most interested in "where, what, when" kinds of questions. When did you meet Foucault? Where? She asked about the location of Mereau's Maerlif again and wanted to know when Foucault had found it. She had asked if Pebbles had been to Anabel's house and if she'd seen her artifact collection. Kora wanted to know if Pebbles was aware of any recent travel Anabel might have taken. She asked Pebbles if she'd known Devlin and probed her about his collection.

In the last interrogation, she'd turned her attention to Malinyah. She wanted to know how much Malinyah had told Pebbles about Munirvo, Muran and Omereau. She asked Pebbles to describe her relationship with Malinyah, and about whether Malinyah was aware Muran was still alive. Kora asked about the *lyktyl*, wanting to know if Malinyah had worn it in the visions she shared with Pebbles. She'd also asked whether Malinyah had talked about the medallion or if she'd shown Pebbles its forging.

Pebbles had answered all the questions, but she had tempered the amount of detail she provided in several of her answers, and she had omitted some key pieces of information when answering others. She was most curious that Kora never asked about the Munirvo Maerlif map, nor did she spend much time on Omereau. At one point, Pebbles had asked Kora to tell her about Omereau, but Kora had ignored the question. The same occurred when Pebbles tried to learn more about how Muran and Anabel had known each other.

The only time Kora had shown any sign of anger had been near the end of the last interrogation. Pebbles, feeling like there was some sort of bond developing between them, had asked, "Why don't you let me call Anlon? I'll tell him you want Malinyah. I'll ask him about Omereau. Maybe he knows something I don't. He could ask Malinyah, too."

Kora had leaned over the bed and snapped at her to be quiet, but Pebbles kept going. "If she doesn't know, maybe Foucault does. I could ask Anlon to call him. Or I can ask Anlon to get Foucault's number so you can call him."

The suggestions had seemed to intrigue Kora. She had backed off and turned away. To Pebbles, it had looked like Kora was seriously considering her offer to help. Sensing a crack in the armor, Pebbles had said, "Look, I just want to go home. I don't care about the stupid Stones. I'll help you get what you want. I'll help you get Malinyah and see what I can find out about Omereau for you. In return, you let me go."

When Kora had turned back around, the expression on her face told Pebbles their conversation had come to an end. She'd roughly tugged the muzzle over Pebbles' mouth and then stormed from the hut, slamming the door on her way out.

So much for being a team player, Pebbles had thought.

Aja rocked back and forth, sipping *enjyia* and staring out at the lagoon's turquois-tinted water. The afternoon sun had passed behind the villa, casting a cooling shadow over the veranda. She smiled. Twelve centuries had passed since she had last been to the lagoon, and even though the landscape around it had changed somewhat over that time, the spot still evoked fond memories.

This is where it all began, she thought. The very best years of my life. Aja closed her eyes and recalled leading the young bride into a stand of trees by the water's edge. Wak Chanil Ajaw had been so afraid when the *Taellin* was pulled on her head. She had cried like a frightened child, begging to be set free. She had even tried to stand up and run, but the weight of the *Taellin* had made her stumble and fall. Once the girl had been returned to her knees, the teenager had turned wild, thrashing about just like Alynioria had. And just as Aja had done to Malinyah's precious daughter, she strangled Wak Chanil Ajaw until the bride slumped to the ground, unconscious.

The memory of squeezing the Mayan princess's throat aroused Aja. She could still feel the vibrations of the girl's screams in her fingertips. She remembered stroking the unconscious girl's shoulder while she whispered soothing reassurances to her. "It will be over quick. You'll feel no pain." Aja had even held the bride's hand while her *chac*, her assistant, erased the bride's memory, just as she had done with Alynioria, and the many other young girls sacrificed over the last ten thousand years.

Aja savored the idea of a fresh start. Her current body had housed her mind far longer than any she'd previously occupied, thanks to Evelyn's deceit. Aja was tired of looking at the same face in the mirror and was sickened by how much she'd aged. She longed to be young and vibrant again, and while she wasn't enamored with the idea of a new body marred by tattoos, it would suffice until she found a more suitable, long-term option.

Her thoughts were disturbed by the sound of a car pulling up to the villa. She turned her head toward the sound and listened closely, setting down the *enjyia* and reaching into her dress pockets for the *Dreylaeks*. A moment later, Kora came sprinting around the side of the villa. Her eyes were full of fear.

"We can't wait any longer!" Kora said. "They've impounded the plane."

"What?"

"The Mexican police. They've taken the plane from the hangar," Kora said.

"Calm yourself, child," Aja said. "They have no idea where we are."

"Damn it! Did you hear me? The Americans know we're in Mexico. We need to call Cully and get this over with," Kora said, bending over, out of breath.

Aja lifted the worthless medallion from her chest and squeezed it in her fist. Liars! Thieves! They would pay for their deception! Looking down at the glittering black stone surrounded by gold, Aja thought, I will kill every last one of them! "Very well. Is her body recovered enough to survive?"

"I think so," Kora said. She reached down and gently placed a hand on Aja's shoulder. "I'm sorry we didn't get Omereau."

"There is still hope. Once we are in new bodies, we can continue the search. At least we have a better sense of where to look," Aja said, patting Kora's hand. "Go get my phone."

"Yes, my Queen," Kora said. She bowed and entered the villa through the veranda door.

Aja finished the last of the *enjyia* and stared out at the lagoon. "Soon, sweet sister, we will meet again, and this time you will have no choice but to tell me what I want to know."

Chetumal, Mexico

The hotel staff hustled into the conference room with a fresh urn of coffee. As they set it up, Anlon yawned and stared blankly at the group of American and Mexican police officers gathered at the far end of the room. Jennifer and Antonio stood with them.

Katie walked up from behind and handed Anlon a fresh cup of coffee. "Here you go. Two creams, three sugars. Are you sure you don't want anything to eat? You didn't have breakfast or lunch."

"No, but thanks," Anlon said, looking down at his cell phone. "Have you seen Mereau?"

"Not since we arrived. Do you want me to call his room?"

"Nah, let him sleep," Anlon said in between sips of coffee. He understood Mereau had not responded well to his first airplane flight. Looking up at Antonio's energetic assistant, Anlon asked, "How are you holding up? You've been going nonstop for two days."

"Don't worry about me. I'm used to this kind of pace," she said. "You should see what it's like the last few days before Dr. Wallace buys or sells a company."

He smiled at Katie with admiration. Not a hair out of place, not a hint of bloodshot eyes. Not a wrinkle on her dress. How does she do it? Anlon wondered. He was just about to ask her for her secret when his phone began to buzz. His eyes darted down to the screen. Unknown caller.

His heart began to pound as he picked up the phone. Before answering, he said to Katie, "It's her. Go let them know."

Katie turned and scampered toward the police as Anlon took a deep breath and pressed the answer-call icon.

"Anlon Cully," he said, looking up at the rush of people heading toward him.

"I understand you are in Mexico," Aja said.

"I'm not sure how you know that, but, yes," Anlon said.

"You have Malinyah with you?"

"I do," Anlon said. "I also have Omereau."

"You what?"

"We found his *Sinethal*."

There was a long pause. Anlon's heart thudded so hard, he could feel it in his tongue. He reached for the coffee cup and took a quick sip. When Muran spoke again, her voice was tinged with skepticism. "Where did you find it?"

"You wouldn't believe me if I told you," Anlon replied.

"Tell me."

"Put Pebbles on the phone," Anlon said.

Another pause. Anlon heard a muffled conversation in the background. He put the phone on speaker and laid it on the table as the group of twenty around him leaned in to listen. The muffled conversation ended abruptly. At first, Anlon thought Muran had terminated the call, but the call timer on his phone screen showed the call was still active. A moment later, a voice said, "Hello? Anlon?"

Anlon had never heard a sweeter sound. The rush of emotion was so intense, he couldn't speak.

"Anlon? Are you there?" Pebbles asked.

"Thank God," he whispered under his breath. "Yes, it's me, Pebbles. Are you okay?"

The sound of sniffling came through the phone. Pebbles' voice cracked as she replied. "Hanging in there, I guess. You coming to rescue me?"

"I am. Count on it," he said, his own voice wavering. He looked up at Jennifer, who was wiping tears from her eyes.

"Good answer," Pebbles said.

Muran returned to the line. "Now, where did you find Omereau?"

"I'll tell you when I see you," Anlon said. "Name the place and time."

"The police are with you, no doubt?"

"Yeah. More than I can count. Say hello to *The Betrayer*, fellas," Anlon said, his anger rising.

None of the officers said anything. Agent Li's face wore a "what the f— are you doing?" expression. Anlon didn't care. He was exhausted and fed up with Muran's air of superiority.

"Careful, Dr. Cully," Muran warned.

Just then, Anlon looked up to see Katie push through the crowd of officers. With her was Mereau. Anlon leaned his elbows on the table and massaged his temples. "Where and when, Muran?"

"If I sense a solitary policeman, helicopter or anything hostile, I will kill her. Do you understand me? You are to come alone."

"Where? When?"

"Where are you now?"

"Chetumal. Downtown, near the airport," Anlon said.

"Good. Arrange for helicopter transport. I will call you later this evening with a time and place."

Laguna Milagros, Mexico

The candles flickered when Aja opened the villa door. Kora bowed and entered. Aja acknowledged her greeting and then motioned for Kora to follow her into the darkness. With the candleholder clutched in her hand, Aja walked slowly down a set of steps leading to the villa's sunken living room. When she reached the center of the room, Aja placed the candleholder on the table and turned back to face Kora.

The two women stood silently, bathed in the glow of candlelight. Aja reached out with both hands. Kora entwined her fingers around Aja's and smiled. Both wore white tunics trimmed in crimson and gold. The gold glittered with each flicker from the candles.

"We have waited so long for this moment," Aja said. "Are you ready, my child?"

Kora lightly squeezed Aja's hands. "Yes, my Queen. The *Tyls* are outside the hut."

"Good. I will enter first. You will wait outside until I call for you," Aja said, releasing Kora's hands.

"Yes, my Queen."

Aja gently stroked the black strands of Kora's hair, then caressed her cheek. Kora smiled and turned her face to kiss Aja's hand.

"It is time," Aja said. She lifted the candleholder and presented it to Kora. The two women slowly walked to the glass doors leading to the veranda, Aja following two steps behind Kora. They wound their way around the villa and headed for the small hut. The air was full of the buzz and chirps of nocturnal insects nesting around the lagoon and in the surrounding jungle.

The hut was completely dark. As they drew closer, Aja noticed the bulky shape of the *Taellin* resting on the concrete landing. When the candlelight reached the landing, she saw the cone-shaped *Tuliskaera* and the other *Tyls* laid out next to the *Taellin*. A flash of memories passed through Aja's mind. She saw the terrified faces of her previous victims, pleading with bulged eyes, as Aja approached the altar.

Her body began to tingle and her face flushed as she relived the erotic ritual. She licked her lips, recalling the salty taste of the tears running down their cheeks. Her hands trembled, remembering the feel of their quivering nubile bodies. Her loins prickled and she uttered a soft moan as she recalled slithering her hands around their necks.

When they reached the hut steps, Kora handed the candleholder to Aja and kissed her on the cheek. Aja was unaware of the gesture, her eyes glued to the hut door. The chatter of insects faded away as she mounted the steps, until only the sounds of her labored breathing and thumping heart penetrated her mind.

Kora sat on the steps and clutched the *Tuliskaera* in her hands. She closed her eyes and listened for the onset of the struggle through the hut's open door. She heard the creak of the bed and the tearing of fabric. Then came the muffled protests and Aja's coos.

As the creaking of the bed turned violent, Kora stroked the *Tuliskaera*, her fingers tracing the outline of the snake. Screams from beneath the muzzle barely rose above the din of insects. Then came the coughing and the scrape of the shaking bedposts. When the thrashing ceased, a throaty moan echoed from within the hut. Kora tensed her hands on the Stone and clamped her knees together.

For several minutes, no sounds emanated from the hut. Then Kora heard the bed creak once, followed shortly afterward by footsteps on the concrete landing. A burning hot hand touched her bare shoulder. A weak voice said, "Bring the *Tyls*."

Chetumal, Mexico

The hotel dining room officially closed at 10 p.m., but Katie had persuaded the hostess and chef to keep the kitchen open for a late dinner for Anlon, Jennifer, Mereau and Agent Li. Antonio, Katie and Henri had been invited, too, but they declined. Antonio had said he had business matters to attend, which necessitated Katie's assistance. Henri indicated a desire for a nap, saying he was weary from the day's events.

Though the meal had been enjoyable, the long wait for Muran's follow-up call had created a tense mood among the group, or at least it seemed that way to Jennifer.

She found it a stark contrast to the elation everyone had experienced upon hearing Pebbles' voice during the earlier call with Muran. For Jennifer, the brief conversation between Anlon and Pebbles had renewed her hope that they would find a way to get Pebbles back. But the shine had lasted only an hour or so. As the reality of the situation settled in again, so had the anxiety.

It reminded Jennifer of the antsy feeling she would get as a detective during a sting operation, waiting for the go-ahead to rush in and apprehend the criminals. In those situations, every second seemed to drag on as they waited for the bad guys to incriminate themselves, and the longer the limbo persisted, the more intense the desire to dash in and collar the suspects.

Mereau had seemed the most relaxed of the group, and Jennifer admired the several attempts he had made to lift everyone's spirits. The meal had been his first taste of food since assuming Foucault's body, and he'd savored samples from each person's plate. He had been most pleased to discover fish on the menu, and even more delighted when the Chilean sea bass had been placed in front of him. The Munuorians had called the fish by another name, he had told them, but its flavor and consistency were strikingly similar.

Anlon had barely looked up from his plate throughout the dinner, and even now he seemed distant. Jennifer didn't think he was depressed or deflated, just grim. She imagined it was the look of many a soldier about to charge an enemy line. Mereau had leaned over on several occasions to whisper to Anlon, a glint in his eye and confidence in his voice. It was the same confidence Mereau had exuded when he pulled Jennifer aside to describe his plan D.

Jennifer had seriously considered it. Mereau had asked for her permission to transfer her mind into his *Sinethal* so Malinyah could take on Jennifer's body. Mereau believed that, together with Malinyah, they could defeat any curve Muran threw at them. For Mereau had been clear: Muran would play for keeps. Jennifer hadn't interpreted his comments as defeatist. She viewed them as the observations of a realist. In this way, Jennifer considered Mereau a man who sought to achieve victory while minimizing their losses. And there would be losses, he'd been clear about that, too.

If the exchange went smoothly and they handed over Malinyah's *Sinethal*, he had said, it spelled the end for Malinyah. If Muran attacked before the exchange, Anlon, Pebbles or both might be caught in the crossfire between Mereau and *The Betrayer*, and Mereau himself might be cut down. If they managed to injure or incapacitate Muran, Mereau had said he fully expected the female confederate spotted at Needles to be waiting in the wings. With all their attention devoted to Muran, Mereau was convinced the confederate would take out at least one of them. If a full-scale melee ensued and the police descended on the scene, there would be even more carnage, he had cautioned.

Though Jennifer hadn't sought Anlon's permission to acquiesce to Mereau's request, she'd approached him for his opinion. Anlon's reaction had been more parochial than Jennifer had expected, but, afterward, during the flight to Chetumal, he had explained himself. "While I understand the value of a second, skilled Munuorian to face Muran, I worry whether Malinyah could confront Muran without her desire for revenge taking over. If she can't control her emotions, she might do something reckless and you'd risk an eternity inside a stone."

Anlon's view had been hard to argue against, and as Jennifer had thought about it more, she'd come to the realization that if she was going to die during the confrontation, she would rather do it on her feet than inside a stone. Mereau had taken the rejection in stride. He had smiled at Jennifer and said, "Then we will fight side by side. Muran will stand no chance!"

The sound of a phone buzzing cut short Jennifer's thoughts. She turned to see Anlon grab his phone and answer it. His face scrunched into a frown. "Who is this?"

The group watched Anlon intently. "I want to speak to Muran. Put her on the phone."

"God damn it! What do you mean she's not available?"

He bent over with the phone pressed to his ear, his free hand cupped across his forehead. "All right, all right. Just give me the location then."

Looking up, he clicked his fingers and mouthed a request for a pen. Agent Li had one out already and handed it to him. Anlon scribbled numbers on the tablecloth and requested the caller to repeat the numbers. He used the pen to touch each of the numbers and then asked, "What time?"

"Yes, yes, I know," he said. After a pause, he angrily spat, "I'll bring the f—ing things, don't you worry about that. You tell Muran to do her part, I'll do mine."

When the call ended, Anlon slammed his fist on the table, tipping over glasses and knocking silverware to the floor. Agent Li stood and examined the numbers. "Longitude and latitude?"

"Yes," Anlon said. "That's all she said."

While Li rapidly tapped on her cell phone screen, Jennifer asked, "It wasn't Muran?"

"No. Apparently, Muran was 'unavailable to speak with me.' Bullshit," Anlon groused.

"It's a place called Calakmul. Looks like it's in the middle of a rainforest," Li said. "What time is the exchange?"

"Calakmul?" Anlon asked. "That sounds familiar. I'm sure I've heard of it before."

"Great," Li said. "What time, Dr. Cully?"

"Midnight," Anlon said.

"Shit! App says it's over two hundred kilometers from here," Li said. "The only way to get there in time is by air. Damn, she's smart. If more than one copter comes in, she'll know it. If more than one person steps off, she'll know that, too."

Anlon slammed his fist on the table again. Mereau raised his hands and encouraged him to calm down. "Please, Anlon. You are playing into her hands. Muran's intent is to unsettle you. Don't fall for her ploy. Come, let us first learn more about this Calakmul and plan our strategy."

"But we need to move now, or we won't get there by midnight," Li said.

Mereau waved his hand dismissively. "She has waited ten thousand years for this moment, she will wait for us."

The conference room buzzed with conversation. Mereau stood at the map of the Yucatan Peninsula, focusing on the solitary road leading from Chetumal to the access road to reach the Calakmul ruins. Next to the map were pictures of the various structures at the site. Most were covered by vines or obscured by the canopy of the surrounding jungle. When he asked how long it would take to reach the ruins by automobile, he was told four hours. By helicopter, the distance could be covered in just under an hour, Henri informed Mereau.

Mereau asked if there were other forces in the area. The officer pointed to the modern town carrying the same name as the ancient Mayan site and another town near the entry to the access road. Both were a considerable distance from the jungle-bound ruins.

After a few more moments glancing between the map and the pictures of the ruins, Mereau said, "The site location is definitely to her advantage, except for one flaw in her thinking."

"What's that?" Anlon asked.

"Stone. There is a great deal of stone," Mereau said, as he broke into a smile. "Here is what we will do."

As the group prepared to leave for the airport, Mereau pulled Anlon aside. "I have a request. I would like to visit with Malinyah before we leave. She should know of our plan, and I would like to say good-bye…just in case."

"Of course," Anlon said. "I understand."

"Thank you. I will be quick," Mereau said.

They walked together to Anlon's room. When Mereau was ready to connect with Malinyah, he closed his eyes and exhaled deeply. Anlon stepped out of the room to afford him privacy and was met in the hallway by Antonio.

"Hey, I need to talk to you," Antonio said.

"Sure, what's up?"

Antonio looked up and down the empty hallway. "I don't like the whole setup, Anlon. It's too risky. Take these with you." He handed Anlon an oblong, black object with a red button in its center and four silver-colored bracelets. The black object was the weight and size of a small computer mouse and carried no markings. Antonio pointed at the device. "If shit goes south, you hide behind something and press the button."

"What is it?"

"Something I shouldn't be giving you," Antonio said.

"Come on, Skipper. What is it?"

Antonio wrapped his arm around Anlon and whispered in his ear, "I call it Hell's Angel. DOD calls it PLB R7X2."

"What does it do?" Anlon whispered back.

"It sends an angel into hell." Antonio smiled.

Anlon opened his mouth to respond, but Antonio cut him off. "Listen, it's classified. I mean, deep-deep-deep classified. Something the FBI can't know about. Something the Mexicans can't, either. No one can know about it. Not even Jennifer. You understand me?"

"No, I don't," Anlon said.

"All right, fine," Antonio whispered. "That, right there, is a military-grade personal locator beacon. It's linked with a nasty little experimental drone that's hovering ten thousand feet over the hotel right now. It's gonna follow you to Calakmul. When you get there, Dylan's gonna bring it down to treetop. Motherf—ing thing is silent. At night it will be invisible. The drone will spot you, Pebbles and anyone else registering a heat signal. It will track every movement of every person. Drone has AI. It can read a battlefield, discern hostiles from friendlies, but it won't fire unless you press the button or Dylan commands it at his end. Once the command is given, the drone will incinerate any and all hostiles. They'll never see it coming."

Anlon stared at him, mouth agape.

"It's some bad shit, Anlon. Just don't lose it in the jungle, all right?" Antonio said.

"I don't know what to say."

"Don't say anything. For the love of God and country, never, ever talk about it. If it comes into play, tell anyone left standing the lasers came from the Stones."

"What are the bracelets for?" Anlon asked.

Antonio wrapped his arm around Anlon again. "Consider it an insurance policy. The bracelets have a trace radioactive signature. Drone can detect them. Helps it identify friendlies. Give one to Mereau, Jennifer and the FBI lady. Wear one yourself."

"What about Pebbles?"

"Dylan's got that covered. He's not going to let anything happen to her. He's got a thing for her, you know."

"So I hear," Anlon said. He held up the bracelets. "What am I supposed to tell the others about these?"

"Tell them they're good-luck charms, but make sure they wear them."

"Why?"

"AI's still a little glitchy."

21

Firestorm

Inflight over Reserva de la Biósfera de Calakmul
Calakmul Jungle, Mexico
October 1

L ong before the helicopter crossed over the eastern border of the Calakmul jungle, Anlon had spied the vast dark void in the distance. It had instantly reminded him of the nighttime view of Lake Tahoe when flying from Reno toward San Francisco. Amid the outline of lights from the surrounding towns and cities, Tahoe looked just as desolate, nothing more than an inky thumbprint on the landscape.

Yet, as they drew closer to the jungle, Calakmul morphed in size. If Tahoe was a thumbprint, Anlon thought, the looming jungle was a handprint. The moment they passed over the last twinkle of civilization below, the helicopter was swallowed by an unending sea of black. Anlon squeezed the handle of the steel case on his lap and whispered, "Hang on, Pebbles. Almost there."

Turning to his right, Anlon observed Mereau. His eyes were alight as he gazed at the stars from ten thousand feet in the air. The large windows of the Mexican Federal Police copter afforded spectacular views of the entire horizon, and Mereau had been enchanted by the vistas above and below since leaving Chetumal. His demeanor had surprised Anlon. He had expected Mereau to lose his sea bass on the cargo-hold floor when they encountered the first roller-coaster-like turbulence. To distract Mereau, Anlon had leaned over to explain the source of the drops and yaws, telling him the bumpiness was caused by warm coastal air colliding with the cooler temperatures above the peninsula's mountainous interior. Mereau had smiled. "The feeling is familiar, like swells on the ocean."

Across the cargo hold sat Jennifer and Agent Li. Along with Mereau, the two women were decked out in black SWAT fatigues and body armor provided by the Mexican police. As Jennifer applied black greasepaint to her face, Anlon smiled at her. She nudged the headset microphone close to her lips and said, "You good?"

"Yeah. Was just thinking you'd make a mean-looking line-backer!" Anlon replied through his headset.

"Ha! Let's hope Muran thinks so, too!"

While Jennifer continued to camouflage her face, Anlon looked back out the window at the endless darkness. His thoughts drifted to the earlier discussion about Muran's choice of the ominous rendezvous point.

Before takeoff, Anlon, Mereau, Jennifer, Li, Antonio, Henri and several Mexican police officials — one of them the pilot who would fly the copter — had gathered around a map and various satellite images in the hotel's conference room.

The pilot had pointed to the satellite image of the area surrounding the coordinates communicated to Anlon. It showed dense jungle for miles in every direction. At the spot where Muran's latitude and longitude coordinates met, the image had revealed a clearing with light vegetation. According to the pilot, the clearing was roughly half a mile from the complex of Mayan ruins. Anlon recalled the image had shown the ruins as chunks of stone, poking out here and there from the canopy of the enveloping jungle.

"The clearing is the only realistic place for the helicopter to land," the pilot had said. "The next closest alternative is the parking area for the Calakmul museum and it is twenty miles north of the ruins."

Mereau had then reiterated his admiration for Muran's selection of the exchange site. "She is shrewd. She controls every aspect of the meeting, from timing to mode of transportation, right down to the landing site."

"But she left herself no means of escape," Li had objected. "She has to know that every exit will be covered, by air and road."

"You are wrong," Mereau had countered. "The officers have told us the jungle is nearly three thousand square miles. She will go to ground and exit at a time and place of her choosing. It will not be an easy task to track her. If she brings her *Tyls*, which I believe is a certainty, she may also attempt to waylay someone visiting the site and change bodies before trying to exit. In that case, it will be impossible to track her."

"And don't forget what she did to the police in Middlebury and Ticonderoga. Just because the exits are blocked doesn't mean she can't fight her way out," Jennifer had added.

The discussion had then shifted to the landing site. Specifically, how could Mereau, Jennifer and Li disembark to support Anlon without being noticed? The Mexican police had suggested using ropes to lower the three and an accompanying Mexican SWAT officer. The leader of the SWAT team, Major Martin Robles, had said, "The clearing sits next to the road from the museum to the ruins. The copter can drop down and hover over the road, a mile or so north of the clearing. We can rig four ropes and send down four people at once, two on each side of the cargo doors. I'll be your fourth."

"But won't Muran notice the sound of the copter hovering?" Anlon had asked.

Robles had shrugged. "She might, but if we're quick about it, I think we can make it work."

The pilot had agreed. "With all the structures and trees near the clearing, the sound of the copter will bounce all over the place at ground level. She won't know which direction we're approaching from. We can approach slowly, circle around the landing site, so it seems we're looking for a place to land."

"Right," Robles had said, "especially if we come in blacked out. If she can't see the copter and can't tell where the sound is coming from, and we don't hover for long, it should fool her."

Anlon had expressed reservations about the plan, but Robles assured him they had plenty of experience with black-out operations. "Drug cartels love to grow their crops in jungles."

"Won't it seem suspicious to land without lights?" Anlon had asked.

"After what she did to the chopper at Ticonderoga?" Li had replied.

"Good point," Anlon had said, before turning to query Jennifer. "So, how do you feel about jumping out of a copter?"

Jennifer's response had ended the debate. "How do you feel about going in alone?"

Anlon felt a tap on his arm. He turned to see Mereau standing next to him, gripping a handhold anchored to the cabin ceiling. Anlon was pleased to see Antonio's silver bracelet on his wrist. Mereau looked to each member of the landing party and said, "Let's run through it one more time."

Over the next several minutes, Anlon listened as Mereau reviewed their plan, supplemented by comments from Jennifer, Li and Robles, who would accompany them.

First, the helicopter would lower down everyone but Anlon. Since the drop zone would be a mile from where Anlon would disembark, Robles wanted to be on the ground ahead of Anlon so they had time to run down the road to the landing area.

Once the helicopter reached the clearing, the pilot would take his sweet time landing the copter, and Anlon was instructed to take his sweet time stepping out of the copter. The plan assumed Muran would light the clearing with flares or some other conveyance so as to clearly observe Anlon's solo departure. Whether Pebbles and the confederate who called Anlon with the coordinates would be there was an unknown. It was also unknown whether Muran would have other accomplices on-site. For these reasons, two SWAT snipers would remain in the copter and keep anyone in the clearing in their sights during the copter's slow ascent.

The combination of actions was designed to protect the exposed Anlon as long as possible, giving the other team members a chance to slim the gap between their drop zone and the clearing. Anlon's part in the plan was the simplest but most dangerous. He would wear no body armor nor carry any weapons. He would hop down from the copter wearing clothes that would make him easy to spot through the trees: a white T-shirt, tan cargo pants, and hiking boots with reflective piping along the seams. In his hand he would carry the steel case containing Malinyah's *Sinethal* and the freshly minted copy of Omereau's. In his pockets would be three items: his cell phone, a small flashlight and Antonio's beacon. Anlon considered the cell phone somewhat useless given the likelihood of poor cellular reception in the remote jungle, but he brought it anyway, holding out hope he would be able to get a bar or two in the event of an emergency.

The four members of the rope-jump party would dash for the clearing, expecting Anlon to delay or stall as long as possible before the exchange. Mereau reminded the group he would lag behind and encouraged them not to wait for him. Foucault's love of cigarettes and wine had taken a toll on his body, he told them. Jennifer said she thought she could cover the mile in under ten minutes. Even though the terrain was unknown to her, she indicated the night vision glasses provided by the police would help her navigate. Robles judged her ten-minute estimate as reasonable and indicated he would be with her every step of the way. Agent Li suggested she accompany Mereau, and the two would form a rearguard in case Jennifer and Robles ran into unexpected trouble.

They expected to take positions around the clearing perimeter and act, if necessary, to protect Anlon and rescue Pebbles. Once they were secure, Mereau and Li would pursue Muran to prevent her escape and recover Malinyah. While Jennifer escorted Anlon and Pebbles to safety, Robles would recall the helicopter for air support and then provide backup to Mereau and Li. Other police officers from the towns nearest the solitary road leading into the jungle would block the road. When SWAT armored vehicles, already en route, arrived at the jungle-road entrance, they would pass through the roadblock and drive to the ruins. As it was fifty miles from the highway to the ruins, Robles told them not to expect the armored vehicles to show up until everything was all over. As Anlon listened to the plan, he gripped the beacon in his pocket.

The four rope-jumpers would have Bluetooth earpieces allowing them to communicate with each other. Robles and Agent Li would also carry radios capable of calling back the helicopter. Anlon, however, would have no communication device other than his cell phone. He joked he would reach them the old-fashioned way: "I'll scream like hell."

When they finished running through the plan, Mereau said, "Above all else, remain calm. The exchange will not unfold as we expect. There will be things that go wrong, things Muran will do that surprise us. Keep your minds focused on the goals. Save Eleanor, protect Anlon, disable and apprehend Muran and retrieve the case with the *Sinethals.*"

"Landing zone coming up on our left. Looks like they've prepared a welcome." The pilot's voice sounded out in their headsets.

Anlon looked out the window. In the middle of the darkness, a fire could be seen.

"Looks like torches," Li said.

Robles crept across the cargo hold and raised binoculars. After focusing them on the fires, he said, "They are torches. They're set up around a landing on top of one of the pyramids. I see two people. One is laying down; the other is looking around to spot us."

"Laying down?" Anlon asked.

"Yes, it must be the hostage," answered Robles, adjusting the binoculars.

"There're no lights set up in the LZ," Jennifer said.

"Looks that way," Mereau said. "Anlon, I think Muran is expecting you to meet her at the top of the pyramid. It's a smart ploy. From that vantage point she will be able to see anyone trying to scale the pyramid."

"So you don't think she'll be at the clearing?" Anlon asked.

"I would say not," Mereau said.

"Should we alter our plan, then? Send in Anlon first?" Li asked. "She's above the treetops. She might spot us going down the ropes."

"She might spot us either way," Jennifer said.

"True, but if the copter heads to the clearing first, she'll likely be more focused on watching and waiting for Anlon to climb the pyramid than anything else," Li said.

Mereau and Robles agreed with Li. Jennifer turned to Anlon. "You cool with that?"

"Yeah, makes sense. I'll just walk real slow. Give you guys time to catch up."

Moments later, the pilot's voice was heard through their headsets: "LZ directly below us. Brace for landing."

Anlon crushed the handle of the case in his hands and exhaled several deep breaths.

The door slid open. Anlon waved to the others and said, "Don't be strangers."

The wash of the copter's rotors was intense. Anlon hopped to the ground and nearly toppled over. The case in his hand whipped about, testing the limit of his wrist's strength. Ducking down, he scurried away from the open door. When he looked back he saw the door close and heard the pitch of the engine rise as the pilot revved the engine.

He squinted through the turbulence, seeking to orient himself in the clearing. As far as he could tell, there was no one else in the darkened expanse. The copter began to rise as Anlon huddled in place. Soon it crested the treetops and disappeared. It took a bit of time before Anlon could hear properly, the decibels generated by the helicopter temporarily blocking out any other sounds.

He was aware of his own breathing, though. Rapid huffs echoed in his head as he scanned the tree line for any sign of movement.

As his ears began to clear and his eyes adjusted to the darkness, he could make out the faint glow of the torches in the distance. He stood and reached in his pocket to feel for the beacon. It was still there. Beside it was the flashlight. This he removed and clicked on. In a slow arc, he moved the flashlight toward the tree line closest to the torch glow. He saw no one. Turning in a circle, he observed the entire clearing. Behind him, the flashlight caught the outline of the road leading to the ruins. Anlon popped the flashlight into his mouth to move the case to his other hand, then pulled out the flashlight and started to walk slowly toward the road. In the distance, he could hear the engine of the helicopter fade away. He looked up and wondered if Antonio's killer drone was looking down on him.

Once he reached the road, Anlon's mind turned to the task at hand. He didn't care what Muran demanded, he would give it. He focused his thoughts on Pebbles, assuring himself that within minutes she would be in his arms and they would leave the rest to the professionals. He found it hard to walk slowly. The urge to be done with the whole affair caused his pace to quicken, though his conscience demanded otherwise.

The road curled to the right, and momentarily the glow from the torchlights atop the pyramid was blocked by another massive stone structure. As the road edged back to the left, however, he passed the structure and the torchlights came into full view for the first time.

Anlon had never seen as imposing a monument. Bathed in the orange-red glow from above, the shadows cast down the broad, stepped pyramid took on a threatening look. The reflection of the flames bouncing off the steps seemed like fingers, encouraging Anlon to ascend. There must be over two hundred steps, he thought, as he drew closer to the base of the pyramid.

He looked up and saw a figure staring down at him from the landing at the top of the pyramid. Arms crossed and legs anchored apart, the woman wore a white tunic. From Anlon's vantage point, he could not see the prone figure Robles had mentioned.

When Anlon reached the pyramid's base, he glanced at the steep incline of the narrow steps. It would be no problem to ascend slowly, he thought. *Just hope I don't pass out or fall off before I get there!* Reaching into his pocket, he felt for the beacon once more and then mounted the first step.

The rope decline had gone off smoothly. Jennifer had been surprised Mereau was the first to land safely on the road. He had smiled at her and whispered, "Must be the *enjyia!*"

She had given Mereau his first high five, then turned with Robles and took off down the road. As they ran, Robles whispered radio checks to each of the team members. Jennifer was pleased. So far, everything was going according to plan.

About halfway to the ruins, Robles whispered for her to stop. In between labored breaths, he suggested they check their weapons before proceeding. Jennifer nodded and reached into the front pockets of her pants. The *Dreylaeks* were ready for action. Reaching behind her, the small sack carrying a *Breylofte* bounced against her hip. Check. She slid her hand down the outside of each thigh. On her right side, her hand hit the butt of the holstered Glock. On the left side, her fingers found the hilt of the commando knife.

"All good," she whispered. Robles held up a thumb, and off they ran. Two minutes later, they slowed again as they reached the landing zone where Anlon had disembarked. The night vision glasses were excellent. Jennifer could see amazing detail all around, including the halo of the torchlights above the tree line.

"Follow me," whispered Robles. He crouched low and left the road, curling around the edge of the clearing. In his hands, he brandished a semiautomatic rifle with mounted sniper scope. With commandolike stealth, he stepped silently through the scrub brush. Jennifer followed close behind, the *Breylofte* now gripped by both hands above her chest. When Robles was satisfied the perimeter was clear, he relayed the information to Mereau and Li, trailing behind.

From the clearing onward, they kept to the tree line abutting the road. It slowed them down, but it provided cover. They serpentined around two bends in the road and then spotted the towering pyramid.

Jennifer, sweating profusely, wiped perspiration from her eyelids and looked up the near-vertical slope. There was Anlon, halfway up the pyramid steps. She whispered, "There he is. How close do you think we can get?"

Through her ear piece, Mereau asked, "Tell me, what do you see?"

"Anlon's a little more than halfway up. Someone's standing at the top. Can't see anyone else."

"Is there a way around the sides?"

"Yes. The main staircase is bordered by several tiers. They're decently hidden by trees."

"Good," the huffing Mereau replied. "Pick a side, left or right. We'll take the one you don't choose."

"We'll go right," Robles said.

"Go. We're not far behind," Li said.

Chetumal International Airport
General Aviation Hangar

Antonio stared at the black and green screen. Next to him sat Katie, chewing her fingernails. A speakerphone with a solid red light glowing provided the only other illumination in the plane's cabin.

"Is that Anlon on the steps?" Antonio asked.

Dylan Hollingsworth answered through the speakerphone. "Yes, it's him. He's got the case."

"All right. Give me some color, Dylan. Show me the good guys and bad guys."

Through the speakerphone, the sound of rapid typing could be heard. All of a sudden, the green figure ascending the pyramid turned blue, as did one of the two figures making their way around the pyramid's right side. The second one remained green.

"The green one on the right side has to be the SWAT guy. Turn him blue so we don't shoot at the wrong guy," Antonio instructed. He turned to Katie and mumbled, "Lord knows we don't want to take out a foreign national."

A few seconds later, the green figure turned blue. Another two green figures appeared on the screen, a few hundred yards behind. As they crossed the road and angled for the left side of the pyramid, Dylan turned them blue also. "That's all the good guys."

"What about the case?" Antonio asked.

"Hold on," Dylan said.

On the screen, an orange dot appeared beside the blue figure on the stairs. Antonio winked at Katie. "Mereau slipped a beacon in the case for me."

A dozen keyboard clicks later, Antonio saw one of the green figures on top of the pyramid turn red. The other figure, stationary and prone, changed color to pink. Dylan said, "I'm assuming the one on the ground is Pebbles. I've marked her appropriately."

"Yeah," Antonio said. "Can't imagine Muran would lie down at a moment like this. Anyone else?"

"Drone's not picking up any other heat signatures, but there's a lot of interference from the pyramid's stone blocks. I'll take it up a bit higher and circle the area."

"Okay, but don't go too high. Stay in firing range, and make sure you lock in the red bogey before you take it up," Antonio said. Turning to Katie, he smiled. "Muran's in for it now."

Structure II, Calakmul Mayan Complex

Anlon stopped a second time to catch his breath. He kept his eyes focused upward, as looking down induced vertigo. On the narrow steps, any wobble might send him and the case tumbling down.

He wondered if that was part of Muran's plan — get him to the top, then blast him over the precipice and down the stone staircase.

The figure at the top of the pyramid had moved back from view as Anlon drew closer to the summit. He was close enough now that he could hear the torches whip in the wind above the treetops.

Finally, he stepped foot on the landing. Panting heavily, he looked ahead. The landing had several rectangular blocks positioned in a square around a central courtyard. In this courtyard, an oblong stone block rested at the center. On it, Pebbles was laid out. She was blindfolded and wore a white tunic. Her hands were bound and rested atop her stomach. Her feet were bound as well. Torches lined both the inner and outer walls of the courtyard, casting wave-like projections of orange and red over Pebbles.

Behind Pebbles stood a woman. It was not Muran. And Anlon recognized her immediately.

Mereau turned to Li. "Will you trust me?"

The frightened FBI agent nodded and closed her eyes. Mereau hummed on the *Breylofte* and Li rose into the air. She cupped her hand over her mouth and bit down on her tongue to stifle the scream that begged to come out. Though she was terrified, she was amazed with Mereau's touch. It felt as if a giant had pinched her by the collar and lifted her silently and swiftly a hundred feet in the air, then placed her down as gently as she normally stepped out of bed.

When she landed, her eyes opened. The pyramid summit was still another fifty feet above, but in the shadows provided by the trees, Li was hidden from view. She turned to look down the slope for Mereau, only to find him standing beside her. He winked and raised a finger to his lips. Moving close to Li, Mereau whispered, "Stay here."

A moment later, she watched him take a running start and blow on the bowl-shaped Stone. He vaulted in the air and disappeared into the darkness on the side of the pyramid.

"Jonesey?"

"Ow ya goin, Dr. Cully," Jonesey said, her mouth twisted into a mocking smile.

Anlon stepped forward, his eyes locked on Pebbles. He was surprised she hadn't reacted to the sound of his voice. Her mouth was open but she hadn't turned her head toward him. In fact, she hadn't moved at all. Not even a twitch. Was she asleep? Had they drugged her?

"That's close enough," Jonesey said, her outstretched hand signaling Anlon to stop. In it, she clutched a *Dreylaek*. Anlon looked down and spied the companion Stone cupped in the palm of her other hand.

"Pebbles? It's me. Are you okay?" Anlon asked. Pebbles didn't reply. He looked at her more closely and saw red splotches around her neck. Looking up at Jonesey, Anlon asked, "What have you done to her?"

"You have the *Sinethals*?" Jonesey asked, her voice now devoid of the Australian accent.

Anlon felt dizzy. What was going on? What was wrong with Pebbles? What was Jonesey doing here? Where was Muran? His heart thudded violently. His eyes darted around. The case in his hand felt as heavy as an elephant. He took a step backward, teetering slightly as he neared the edge of the landing. Something was wrong. Very wrong.

"Talk to me, Pebbles. Say something," Anlon said.

Jonesey moved around Pebbles and stood between her and Anlon. "Open the case, show me the *Sinethals*."

He set the case down and anchored in position in front of it. "No. Not until I know she's all right. What did you do? Did you drug her?"

"Not exactly," Jonesey said. "Now, open the case."

Anger swelled inside Anlon, chasing away every scintilla of anxiety. As he glared at Jonesey, visions of the meeting to view Sinclair's tapestry filled his mind. Anlon recalled Jonesey questioning him about Malinyah's *Sinethal*, and her expertise in the mythology associated with Aramu Muru. Obviously, her interest in both went far beyond academic curiosity. It had been a setup. Had Sinclair known? Had he been in on it, or had he been duped too?

"Elton Sinclair part of your scheme?" Anlon asked.

Jonesey began to scrape the *Dreylaeks* together.

"Where's Muran?" Anlon asked.

From behind, Anlon heard the sound of shaking leaves and a thud. When he turned toward the sounds, his heel bumped into the case, knocking it over the edge of the landing. As the case began to tumble down the stairs, gunfire cut through the air.

Chetumal International Airport

"Holy shit!" Dylan called out through the speakerphone.

Antonio flinched as a leaping figure appeared from nowhere onto one of the lower tiers. The green blur immediately attacked the blue figure crouching on the tier's ledge. Katie gasped.

"Mark the bogey, damn it!" Antonio yelled at the phone.

The green blur turned red.

"Turn the AI on, now!" Antonio said.

Keyboard clicks. "On autofire?"

Antonio hesitated, watching the confrontation unfold. He saw the orange dot bounce down the stairs, passing the tier where the newly tagged red bogey stood over a fallen blue figure. Flashes of green obscured the red-blue tandem. Across the staircase, Antonio's eye caught two more blue figures. One leapt onto the staircase, rushing toward the scuffle on the far side. The other one chased after the orange dot. Darting his eyes up, Antonio saw Anlon's figure collide with the red bogey on the pyramid summit. Both fell onto the pink figure.

"Hold up," Antonio said. "They're too bunched up. Keep it on manual, but get ready to fire on my mark."

Structure II, Calakmul Mayan Complex

Jennifer was within twenty feet of the summit when she heard the "oof." She popped her head up and saw a blur of white disappear behind the far side of the staircase. Bright flashes lit up the trees, accompanied by the boom of gunfire. A second later, a shiny, spinning object crossed her field of vision. Before she could react, Robles was already on the staircase, rushing toward the gunfire. Jennifer shot a look up at the landing. There was no one there. Snapping her head back down the stairs, she caught a glimpse of the steel case as it twirled off the steps and into the darkness. She hopped from the tier's ledge onto the stairs and headed after the case.

She never saw Robles fly backward over the side of the pyramid, nor did she hear the scream as Muran fired a flaming bolt into Li. Jennifer was completely unaware Anlon had pried loose the *Dreylaeks* from Kora's grip, using one of the cookie-sized Stones to pound Muran's accomplice unconscious. With singular focus, Jennifer scampered down the steps, keeping her eyes trained on the spot where the case had disappeared.

As she neared the spot, the case came into view. It was perched on the ledge of a lower tier. When she was within three steps, she crouched down and jumped over the side. She landed awkwardly and rolled onto the ledge. A thud followed close behind. Jennifer scampered to her feet and found herself face to face with *The Painted Lady.*

Chetumal International Airport

"Fire!" Antonio said, pounding the desk.

The black-green screen, and the colored blotches moving upon it, disappeared behind a blinding flash. When the flash subsided, a smoky green haze hovered over the lower tier. As the haze began to clear, Antonio saw only a stationary blue figure on the ledge. The red bogey and orange dot were gone.

"Where'd they go? Did we get a hit?" Antonio asked Dylan.

"We hit something," Dylan said.

Structure II, Calakmul Mayan Complex

With the firefight raging below, Anlon dragged Pebbles behind the back wall of the courtyard. He whisked off the blindfold and saw her blank-faced stare. He shook her shoulders and called her name. Pebbles' head lolled to the side. He took hold of her chin and jostled her head. "Pebbles, God damn it! Wake up!"

No reaction.

Cursing, Anlon looked around for a means of escape. Behind the pyramid landing, he noticed another, taller structure. He squinted through the glow of courtyard torchlight to spy a way down from the landing and found himself staring at a sheer drop of at least twenty feet. Looking again at the other structure, Anlon realized it was part of the same pyramid — a second summit connected to the landing where he stood by a walkway below. In order to reach the walkway leading to the second peak, he would have to carry Pebbles down the pyramid's main staircase to the next closest tier. Cursing again, he picked up Pebbles and made for the staircase.

He reentered the courtyard from the backside and snaked around the slab where Pebbles had been laid out. He stepped over Jonesey's motionless body and exited between the blocks bordering the main staircase. A flaming bolt struck the steps a few feet away, exploding the stone block into shards that raked Anlon and Pebbles. He spun away from the debris and sought cover behind one of the blocks, hugging Pebbles against his chest.

A shrill voice called out, "Enough! Or your woman's mind is gone forever!"

Chetumal International Airport

"There she is!" Dylan said. "Should I fire again?"

"Damn! That bitch just won't die!" Antonio said. The "f" of "fire" hissed through his teeth as a blue blur soared from the darkness, landing on the steps between Anlon and the red bogey below. Antonio said, "Hold your fire."

To the left of the red bogey, a blue figure huddled on a ledge. Below, and to the right, Antonio saw another blue figure begin to move. The orange dot was still nowhere in sight. The fourth blue figure was missing as well.

"Move the drone behind our bogey," Antonio instructed. Once accomplished, Muran was surrounded on four sides. Antonio said, "Let's see you get out of this."

Structure II, Calakmul Mayan Complex

Hidden by the shadow of the main staircase, Li propped her back against the wall of the upper tier. One hand covered the bleeding hole through her body armor. The other trembling hand clutched her government-issued, Model 23 Glock. She heard a woman's voice call out. "Enough! Or your woman's mind is gone forever!"

She bit her lip as she raised up to peer over the wall. Before she could focus her gaze in the direction of the woman's voice, her eyes sensed movement above. It was just a flutter at first, just a speck in the black sky. Then a shadow crossed overhead, followed by a thump. A moment later, a male voice, Mereau's voice, said, *"Sae ut dote, Muran." It is over, Muran.*

Anlon slid down the block, his eyes blurred by dust from the exploding step. He lowered Pebbles to the stone floor on the landing and used the sleeve of his T-shirt to wipe away the debris. Woozy, he squinted through watery eyes at Pebbles. Her expression was unchanged.

He then heard Mereau speak. Where he'd come from, Anlon couldn't tell. Nor did he understand what the man had said to Muran. But he knew Mereau was close by, and his voice was firm. Anlon remembered the beacon in his pocket and pulled it out.

From below, he heard Muran reply to Mereau. "Ah, the hero-captain arrives. I'm afraid you're too late."

Rising up, Anlon cupped the beacon and shimmied along the block. Just as he prepared to peek around the corner, he froze. Jonesey was gone!

"Mereau," he shouted, "look out for the other one."

Anlon remembered he had stashed her *Dreylaeks* in his back pocket after braining her with one of them. He put away the beacon and retrieved the Stones. Ruing his inexperience with the weapon, Anlon started to grind them together. No time like the present, he thought.

Mereau looked down on the sneering Muran. Half her white tunic was covered in blood, and red rivulets trickled down her legs.

Around her neck was a lanyard, holding a swaying *Breylofte*. She warmed *Dreylaeks* in her palms.

The Munuorian captain stood his ground, *Breylofte* at the ready. To Muran, he said, "Surrender your weapons. You are no match for me."

"Don't be so sure, old man," she said. Raising her head, Muran shouted, "Kora? Kora come out. Join me. They won't do anything while we have the girl's mind."

"Kora?" Mereau exclaimed, looking around. A young woman emerged from the pyramid landing. Her head and tunic were bloodied as well. As she descended the steps, she spoke to Mereau in Munuorian: *"Halas, Fraendi."* Hello, Uncle.

Speechless, Mereau stared as Kora, his niece, Muran's daughter, passed by. Mereau had been told the girl had died in the Munirvo revolt, along with Muran's other daughter, Alaera. He asked, "How is this possible?"

"Bestill your wonder, Mereau. She is not the Kora you knew, the one who died at Malinyah's command," Muran said

"Malinyah's command? You used your children as shields, Muran. They died because you put them in your front lines, daring Malinyah to attack while you snuck off to take Omereau!" Mereau responded angrily.

"Lies!" Muran sneered, as Kora arrived by her side. "Now, where is my sister? And where is Omereau?"

"They are not here," Mereau said.

"As I expected. Another trick. Just like the *lyktyl*. I knew you were behind it, Mereau. These pathetic worms wouldn't dare try it on their own," Muran said. "Hello, worm."

Her greeting was directed at Anlon, who had emerged from the courtyard and now stood shoulder to shoulder with Mereau, *Dreylaeks* in his hands. She asked, "How is your drooling friend?"

"What have you done to her?" Anlon questioned.

"She has transferred her mind to a *Sinethal*. The one taken from the bank, I presume," Mereau said.

Muran smiled and nodded. As she spoke, she stared at Mereau. "And she will stay there forever. You will never find it on your own. I will tell you where it is, once you deliver Malinyah and Omereau… and the real *lyktyl*. Yes, now you see, don't you, Mereau? The trapper is trapped. Now, call off your minions and fetch me my *Sinethals*."

"I told you, they are not here," Mereau calmly said.

"Should I look for the case, my Queen? The one Cully was carrying?" Kora asked.

"There is no point. The *Tyls* in the case are forgeries," Mereau said.

Chetumal International Airport

"They're standing together, I have a clear shot," Dylan said.

"Steady, Dylan. Looks like they're talking," Antonio said. "Where's the damn case? It's not with either red bogey."

"I don't know. If neither of them have it, there are only two other possibilities. Either we destroyed it with the last shot, or it went over the side. There's too much stone in the way for me to tell if it fell into the jungle. If you want, I can take the drone over to the right and have a closer look along that side of the pyramid. Targets are locked, they're not going anywhere."

"Okay, do it. Careful, though. We don't want to attract any attention."

Structure II, Calakmul Mayan Complex

Anlon maintained a level glare at Muran and Kora, trying to suppress his anger. Muran had them beat, despite Mereau's bluff. The smile on Muran's face showed she knew it, too. She said, "I will be in touch, then. And, next time, sister-husband, you will crawl to me on your knees."

Below Muran and Kora, Anlon saw Jennifer perched on the staircase. She aimed a pistol at Muran. Anlon heard a click to his right. He looked over and saw Li's head and arm poking over the side of the staircase. She held a gun on Muran, too. Somewhere above, Anlon knew, was Hell's Angel. In the distance, Anlon heard the thumps of an approaching helicopter. Muran was absolutely trapped…and she would walk away free.

Muran slowly circled and laughed at the four of them. "Weaklings! Cowards! Idiots! You think me a fool? Come, Kora. They will not attack. They will not risk the girl's mind."

As they started down the steps, Mereau raised up the *Breylofte* and said, "Go no further, Muran."

"Or you'll what? Shoot me down? How do you feel about that, Cully? Your woman's mind inside a Stone for eternity," Muran said, continuing down the stairs. They were within ten feet of Jennifer.

"The *Sinethal* is not where you left it, Muran…and I have destroyed your *Taellin*," Mereau said.

Muran stopped in her tracks and wheeled to face Mereau. Anlon saw uncertainty cross her face, then fear. She looked to Kora, who shared the same terrified expression. And then Muran did the unthinkable. She grabbed hold of Kora and threw her down the stairs at Jennifer.

Rabbit quick, Muran leapt over the side of the staircase into the darkness. A mighty vibration shook the trees. Mereau pressed the *Breylofte* to his lips, took a running start and sharply hummed with the bowl pointed at the stone stairs. Up into the air he went, following Muran into the darkness.

The sound of a scuffle drew Anlon's attention back to the staircase. He turned to see Kora and Jennifer rolling down the steps. The gun Jennifer had gripped skittered down behind them. When they came to a stop, Kora was up first. As she resumed her descent, Anlon dropped the *Dreylaeks*, shoved his hand into his pocket and pressed the button on the drone beacon. Two white bolts crackled through the night air, one shooting over the pyramid courtyard, the other piercing Kora midchest. She tumbled down the rest of the pyramid, a smoke trail marking her path. Anlon released his hold on the button and side-stepped down the stairs to reach Jennifer.

Hidden by the shadows on the left side of the pyramid, Muran blew on her *Breylofte* to soften her landing onto one of the pyramid's lower tiers. Once there, she looked up and saw Mereau descending through the air toward her. Before he touched down, she blew again on the Stone to shoot her body up, past the falling Mereau, to reach the next tier. Mereau followed suit after landing on the lower tier. With the Munuorian captain trailing close behind, Muran hummed sharply on the Stone and the resulting sound waves vaulted her over the courtyard atop the pyramid's front peak. As she descended into the black chasm beyond, a white bolt clipped one of the courtyard's stone blocks near her head, peppering her face and torso with stone shards. Using the *Breylofte's* sound waves to again soften her landing, Muran tumbled onto the ledge separating the twin peaks of the pyramid. She jumped up, hummed on the Stone and propelled herself to the steps leading to the second peak.

Bloodied and enraged, she scampered up the steps. Mouthing obscenities, she snapped her head around to see Mereau again soaring through the air in pursuit. The torchlights of the courtyard behind him obscured all but his falling shape. As such, Muran did not notice he had cast away his *Breylofte*, and by the time she noticed the glowing Stones in his hands, it was too late.

She rolled on her back and raised her *Breylofte*, but before she could attack, Mereau sliced through her with a blast from the *Dreylaeks* pulsing in his hands. As the beam swept across her body, it shattered her *Breylofte*. The pieces of the Stone rattled harmlessly down the stairs as Mereau crashed against the jagged steps next to Muran. His leg bones snapped, and he screamed in pain. Muran howled and desperately tried to crawl away, her midsection on fire.

Mereau reached out and grabbed her leg, the sizzling *Dreylaek* in his hand boring into her calf. She wailed and tried to pull away. Mereau let go of her leg and propped his torso on the steps. Muran's eyes narrowed as Mereau started to scrape the Stones together again. *The Betrayer* spewed more obscenities, and with each Munuorian epithet, blood gushed from her mouth, spattering her face. When the Stones were red hot, Mereau pulled them apart and said, "For Alynioria."

When Anlon heard screams echo from behind the courtyard, he took off around the walkway he'd seen from the summit. Following close behind was Jennifer. As they came around the side of the ancient structure's front peak, they saw a fiery jolt cut through the darkness ahead. Another scream, a woman's scream, reverberated between the two peaks. When the bolt dissipated, they could see a small fire in the distance. They raced forward until they came upon Mereau and the burning, and quite dead, Muran.

Grimacing in pain, Mereau looked up and said, "Alynioria is avenged."

"Where is the *Sinethal*? Where is Pebbles?" Anlon frantically asked.

Mereau collapsed before he could answer.

22

Reunification

Structure II, Calakmul Mayan Complex
Reserva de la Biósfera de Calakmul, Mexico
October 1

Once the host of local and federal police arrived, the hunt for Pebbles' *Sinethal* commenced. With the unconscious Mereau on his way to Chetumal via helicopter, Anlon, Jennifer and the police were left with the daunting task of searching the one-hundred-eighty-foot, double-peaked pyramid with no clues as to where Mereau had stashed the Stone.

Major Robles, who had been discovered alive near the battered steel case in the jungle beside the pyramid, coordinated the search plan from a stretcher at the base of the ancient structure. He was assisted by Agent Li, who had been patched up and now sat in the open doorway of an ambulance beside Robles.

"Mereau was on one of the upper tiers with me, on the left," Li said, pointing up the steep edifice. "He jumped off the tier, heading toward the second peak."

"Did you see him come back to the main staircase?" Anlon asked. He sat on the pyramid's bottom step. Pebbles' body lay on a gurney next to him. "I was with Pebbles inside the courtyard. Did he come around the left or right side of the courtyard?"

"Honestly, I didn't notice him until he spoke up. I have no idea where he came from," Li said.

"Me, either," Jennifer said, while an EMT administered an ice pack to a new knot on her forehead. "I can't imagine him tossing it over the side, though. I'm sure it's up top somewhere."

"Well, we have plenty of men here, now. We'll find it," Robles said.

Aided by police officers toting flashlights, Anlon and Jennifer set off to comb the stone monument, starting with the temple atop the pyramid's rear peak. As they mounted the temple steps, Anlon realized it wasn't a temple after all. He'd been fooled by the light cast by torchlights set around the courtyard on the pyramid's forward peak. From the courtyard, the rear peak had looked to Anlon like a completely enclosed structure. Now that he was up close, he realized the tiered precipice he'd observed was really just a platform upon which a temple had one time been erected.

The contingent of police officers divided up and fanned out around the left and right sides of the platform's base tier. A call went up, and an officer waived his illuminated flashlight to Anlon and Jennifer. They followed the officer around the right side, stepping gingerly along the tier's narrow ledge with flashlights trained on the crumbling walkway. When they reached the back side, two officers pointed their flashlights down at a platform that jutted out from a vertical cut in the sloped pyramid wall. Ten feet below were two large, olive-colored backpacks sporting aluminum frames, propped against the platform wall. The light also revealed stone shards littering the platform. Anlon recognized a pile of greenish bits as the remains of a *Tuliskaera*, further evidenced by the sparkle of the *Tyl's* diamonds amid the debris. The pile was surrounded by larger, curved chunks. Mereau had been true to his word, Anlon thought. He had obliterated Muran's *Taellin*. Even if she had managed to escape, she would once again have been left without a *Sinethal*, *Tuliskaera* and *Taellin*. How Mereau had found Muran's gear, including her *Tyls*, was a story Anlon would have to wait to hear.

While there were stairs leading down the back side of the pyramid that the group could have used to reach the platform, they were severely decayed. In broad daylight, it would have been a daredevil feat. In the darkness, it was insanity. So, the group backtracked to the front of the temple steps and descended to a lower tier with a walkway that would allow them to reach the platform across a narrow strip of the decayed steps.

Once there, Jennifer and two police officers emptied the backpacks and discovered several more *Tyls*, including a *Naetir*, but found no *Sinethal*. Beyond the Stones, the packs were stuffed with clothes and wilderness survival gear. Holding up a GPS tracking device, she said to Anlon, "Looks like they definitely planned to hike their way out."

The search went on for another hour before the *Sinethal* was finally discovered. Anlon was examining crevices in the stone blocks surrounding the courtyard on the pyramid's front peak when he heard an excited voice call out. He quickly exited the courtyard and looked around. At first, he had a hard time picking out where the voice came from, but then he spotted a waving flashlight well below the pyramid summit, and the man called out again.

As much as Anlon desired to dash down the main staircase, the steep slope and precarious footing led to a slow, methodical descent. When he reached the officer, Jennifer was already there. Together, he led them again around the back side of the pyramid. To Anlon's surprise, the officer guided him to the entrance of a tunnel that penetrated beneath the pyramid's rear peak.

The tunnel had not been visible from above because it was cut directly beneath yet another platform well below the one where the backpacks had been stashed. The tunnel was guarded by a steel door, presumably placed there to discourage tourists and looters. The door was open, however, and Anlon noticed a singed hole where the lock had once been. The officer led Anlon and Jennifer down the tunnel's long corridor until it reached a T-branched hallway adorned with Mayan stone sculptures. The *Sinethal* rested against the base of one of the sculptures.

For many years to come, Anlon would recall sitting on the temple steps, Pebbles' *Sinethal* and a *Naetir* in his hands, as the sun broke over the horizon. The temple faced northeast and afforded an unobstructed view of the daily ritual from one hundred eighty feet above the jungle floor. With Jennifer seated beside him, they watched the gray sky turn pink, then orange, as the rising sun reflected off the broken clouds. Below the skyline, the jungle's green canopy extended to the limits of the horizon in every direction.

Anlon's hands trembled as he looked down at the Stones. Jennifer laced her arm through his and leaned against his shoulder. "What are you thinking?"

"I'm really nervous," he said.

"I know, it will be weird to be inside Pebbles' memories."

"Yeah, but in a good way," Anlon said. "I just hope Muran didn't lie. I'm worried the Stone will be empty."

"Positive thoughts, Anlon," Jennifer said, nudging him with her elbow.

"Right," he said, nodding. "Positive thoughts."

He inhaled deeply and closed his eyes, guiding the *Naetir* toward the *Sinethal*...

When the vision began, Anlon heard children loudly talking and laughing. As had been the case in visions with Malinyah, he could not see anything at first. But unlike his previous visits with the ancient Munuorian, the blank vista before him now was dark, instead of bright.

His ears detected the chirps of crickets and the croaks of frogs. From the banter going back and forth between the children, Anlon could tell they were playing a game of hide-and-seek. As his vision came into focus, he understood the reason for the dark vista. It was nighttime. The children ran about the edge of a forest, hiding behind trees while fireflies sparkled all around them.

Anlon found himself standing on a small rise of dewy grass, observing the children from across a field. Near the rise was a picnic table, where a group of adults chatted amiably, their faces illuminated by a campfire near the table. Pebbles was not among them.

He scanned the field and woods for a sign of Pebbles. For a moment, his heart fell. Were these someone else's memories? Then, a woman at the picnic table stood and cupped her hands around her mouth. "Eleanor Marie McCarver, you get down from that tree, right now!"

Lifting his head to follow the woman's gaze, Anlon saw a girl, no more than ten years old, balancing precariously on a thin branch. A boy emerged from the woods and pointed up at the branch. "Hey! No fair. You're it, now!"

"Mother!" the girl yelled back. "You gave me away!"

"I don't care. Tonight's not a good night for the emergency room," the woman replied.

As the girl climbed down from the tree, a man stood up and wrapped his arm around the woman. "All right, you wood elves, marshmallow time! Find a stick and get over here."

The four adults rose from the table as a half dozen children sprinted across the field, sticks in hand. A moment later, the children plopped down around the campfire as marshmallows were doled out. Anlon saw the girl from the tree adorn three marshmallows on separate twigs of her stick. The children laughed and teased one another as they hovered their branches over the fire.

A voice next to Anlon whispered, "What's going on? What did I miss?"

He turned to Jennifer and said, "It's a childhood memory of hers. She's the one on the far side of the campfire sticking her tongue out at the blond boy."

They watched the interplay between the two children. The boy levied a challenging taunt, leading the girl to respond by flexing her biceps. Anlon and Jennifer laughed. She said, "Oh, my God! That's definitely her!"

Motion from the woods caught Anlon's attention. He looked up and saw Pebbles approaching the campfire. She wore an oversized sweater and leggings. On her face, a soft smile could be seen in the glow of the fire. When she reached the girl jawing with the blond boy, Pebbles sat behind the girl and curled her knees up to her chest, wrapping her arms around her shins. Resting her chin on her knees, she watched the banter with twinkling eyes and the occasional giggle.

The woman from the table came around and sat down next to the girl. The girl climbed onto her lap. Once she had settled in, the woman kissed her on the cheek and wrapped her arms around the girl's waist. Anlon felt a warmth flow through his body. It was a familiar sensation — the kind of warmth one feels when all is right with the world.

"Come on," Anlon said, reaching for Jennifer's hand. "Let's see if they've got any extra marshmallows."

They were within fifteen feet of the fire when Pebbles spotted them. She uncoiled her arms and stood. A hand covered her mouth as Anlon and Jennifer smiled and waved. Chills raced through Anlon's body. The same happened to Jennifer, for he felt her shiver. Pebbles slowly walked toward them, her eyes blinking rapidly. Her voice cracked as she said, "Is this real? Are you really here?"

Anlon let go of Jennifer's hand and opened his arms. "We've come to rescue you."

Hospital General de Chetumal
Chetumal Mexico
October 2

"Is he awake? May I see him now?" Anlon asked. In his hand he clutched the handle of the dented steel case he had carried to Calakmul.

The nurse exiting Mereau's room nodded and gave Anlon permission to enter. The Munuorian captain sat against the raised back of the hospital bed. He smiled and waved his bandaged hands. Both legs were casted; one below the knee, the other extended all the way up his thigh.

"*Halas*, Anlon," Mereau said.

"Hello, Mereau. I see you are in good spirits," Anlon said.

"Yes, a great weight has been lifted from my spirit," Mereau said.

"I imagine so." Anlon took a seat on the guest chair next to the bed. "I'm sure Malinyah will feel the same way once she learns Muran is dead."

Mereau nodded and asked, "You recovered Eleanor's *Sinethal?*"

"Yes. It took a while, but I have it in here with Malinyah's *Sinethal,*" Anlon said.

"Excellent, I'm happy you found it."

"Me, too. Good hiding spot, by the way. Must have been really dark inside that tunnel," Anlon said.

"Not so. I used *Dreylaeks* to light my way, just as we do when our ships are submerged."

"I see. Interesting," Anlon said. Mereau's comment about the Munuorians' ships piqued Anlon's curiosity, but he had a more important topic to discuss. "Mereau, I need your help."

"I know. I've sent Henri to the plane to retrieve my *Taellin* and *Tyls*. He will be back soon. Then, we will go together to reunite Eleanor's mind with her body," Mereau said.

"It's going to be complicated, I'm afraid," Anlon said.

Anlon went on to explain the dilemma. He told Mereau that the EMTs at Calakmul had insisted on airlifting Pebbles to the hospital. Once there, the emergency room staff had treated her injuries and determined she was comatose.

She had then been moved to the hospital's small intensive care unit for further tests, after which the ICU doctor-on-duty had explained to Anlon that Pebbles had incurred severe brain damage. The doctor speculated that she had suffered catastrophic oxygen deprivation caused by strangulation. While Pebbles' autonomic brain functions appeared intact, the physician had explained, she was not aware of her surroundings. He had labeled her condition "unresponsive wakefulness syndrome." The physician had said only time would tell if the condition was temporary or permanent. "Some people wake from comas within weeks, some never do."

Anlon told Mereau he had listened to the doctor with a degree of concern. While Anlon knew the real reason for Pebbles' apparent coma, the doctor's description made Anlon wonder whether Pebbles' brain had indeed been damaged when Muran strangled her. After he explained the doctor's diagnosis to Mereau, he asked, "What do you make of it? Should we be concerned?"

"You have visited with her?" Mereau asked.

"Yes," Anlon said.

"And she seemed fine? You noticed nothing unusual about her manner?"

"I didn't notice anything unusual, but I'm more worried about damage to her brain than her memories on the Stone."

"Hmmm...I do not know the answer. There could be complications. For instance, she may be blind for a period of time after the transfer, just like I was. Beyond that, I cannot tell," Mereau said. "You must remember, Anlon, placing a person's memories into a new body was a banned practice among my people. While I have assisted fellow Andaers in moving their memories to *Sinethals*, I have never moved a mind back into a body. Yes, I showed Mathieu and Henri visions of how to do it before they transferred my mind into Mathieu's body, but I've never done it myself."

"Not the answer I was hoping for," Anlon said, rising from the chair. He paced to the room's window and gazed out at the parking lot. "If we do the transfer, and her brain is messed up, she might never recover."

"Unfortunately, that is true," Mereau said. "What does Eleanor have to say about it?"

Anlon stood and shoved his hands in the pockets of his jeans. With a frown, he said, "I haven't told her yet. I wanted to talk with you first."

"Ah," Mereau said.

After a moment's silence, Anlon returned to his seat and opened the case. He lifted out Pebbles' *Sinethal* and a *Naetir* and said, "Guess there's no time like the present. I've got another *Naetir* in the case. You want to visit with Malinyah while I talk with Pebbles?"

"I have already visited with Malinyah. Henri brought her to me earlier this morning. She is at peace," Mereau said.

"Excuse me?"

"Malinyah's *Sinethal* was not in the case. I replaced it with mine when I visited with her before we departed for Calakmul."

"What?"

"I am sorry for the deception, but I could not risk Malinyah falling into Muran's hands."

"Why didn't you tell us?" Anlon asked, stunned by the news.

"I thought it best to keep it to myself."

"But what if Muran had actually exchanged Pebbles for the case? You would have lost your *Sinethal*."

"I had no intention of allowing Muran to leave with the case under any circumstances. I came to end her curse or die trying. If she had prevailed, it would have meant she had killed me. But then Muran would have discovered she had been given an empty *Sinethal* and the Omereau forgery."

"So, that's what you meant when you told her both were forgeries. I thought you were bluffing," Anlon said.

"No, I told her the truth. I saw no reason not to. At that point, I'd already found and hidden Eleanor's *Sinethal* and destroyed the *Taellin*. I wasn't sure she would believe me, but it wouldn't have mattered if she hadn't. She was trapped and she knew it, despite her claim to the contrary."

When the mist cleared, Anlon found himself in a familiar place — his boat on a sunny afternoon on Lake Tahoe. Pebbles was sunbathing on the aft bench while the boat stereo played an Ice Zombies tune. From behind, Anlon heard the roar of Jet Skis. Turning, he spotted Jennifer and Griffin bouncing on the water's surface as they raced by. Their wakes jostled the boat, causing Anlon to wobble and grab the starboard railing. As the Jet Skiers disappeared into the distance, Anlon was distracted by another noise from the below-deck cabin. Directing his attention toward the cabin's open door, he received quite a shock. Anlon saw a clone of himself mixing up lemonade in the galley. So weird.

"Pebbles," Anlon said.

Without looking up from behind her sunglasses, Pebbles stretched and said, "Yum. Lemonade time."

"Uh…wrong Anlon," he said.

Pebbles' head slowly turned toward him. She lifted her sunglasses and stared at the Anlon standing before her, and then at the other one belowdecks. She said, "So weird."

She rose from the bench and the lemonade-concocting clone disappeared from the vision. She approached Anlon and wrapped her arms around him. "Is it time?"

"Kind of," he said, hugging her back. "Got a bit of a wrinkle to talk to you about."

Anlon felt her apprehension flow through his body. She asked, "What's wrong? I can tell something's wrong. You're nervous."

Proof positive the emotions of a *Sinethal* experience flow both ways, thought Anlon. "Uh, yeah. I am kind of nervous. Let's sit and talk."

Once they'd settled on the back bench, Anlon explained the situation to Pebbles and related his conversation with Mereau. He finished by saying, "What happens to the brain during a coma is a mystery. How, when and why brain cells reconnect and start firing again, nobody really knows. Point is, there's risk, but I can't tell you if it's a small risk or a big one."

Pebbles took the news better than Anlon expected, as evidenced by the sense of calm he felt pass from her mind into his. Without hesitation, she gripped his hands and said, "Let's do it."

"Are you sure you don't want to think it over?"

"I'm sure," she said. "Now, give me a kiss and let's get this show on the road!"

"How on Earth are we going to pull this off?" Anlon said.

"Don't worry. We'll get you all the time you need," Jennifer said.

"Yeah, don't sweat it, Anlon. Everything's going to be just fine," Antonio said.

As Anlon looked between his two friends, Jennifer took him by the arm and whispered in his ear, "Positive thoughts."

"I know, I know," Anlon said. He took a deep breath and started for the hospital elevator. When he reemerged from the elevator a few minutes later, Anlon was accompanied by Henri and the wheel-chair-bound Mereau. In Mereau's lap was a large gift box containing all the *Tyls* necessary for the transfer, including his *Taellin*.

As they approached Pebbles' room, Anlon looked up to see Jennifer and Antonio taking positions on each side of the door. Over Jennifer's chest swayed a lanyard connected to Agent Li's FBI badge. On her face, she wore a menacing "don't even think about entering the room" look. Antonio crossed his arms and widened his stance, adopting a similarly stern expression.

Although Pebbles was in a private ICU room, she was hooked up to all manner of diagnostic devices. The devices would go haywire and alert the nurse's station the moment Mereau began to zap the *Taellin* on Pebbles' head with a bolt of electricity fired from the *Tuliskaera*. A nurse or doctor or both would then likely head for Pebbles' room in haste, and that would present a problem.

Once the transfer started, Mereau had warned earlier, there could be no interruptions until the process was complete. So, it was imperative to either distract the nurses or disable the devices. With Jennifer and Antonio's assistance, Anlon crafted a plan to do both.

After Henri pushed Mereau and his wheelchair into Pebbles' room, Anlon joined them. He locked the door, sat down in a guest chair next to Pebbles and removed his shirt. While Henri helped Mereau prepare the *Tyls*, Anlon disconnected the first of the sensors adhered to Pebbles' head and reattached it to the corresponding spot on his own head. One by one, he repeated the process with the rest of the sensors dotting Pebbles' body. He did the same with the pulse oximeter and blood pressure cuff. Once complete, he asked Henri to switch off Pebbles' intravenous fluids. Lastly, Anlon leaned forward to kiss Pebbles on the cheek before Henri slid the *Taellin* on her head and placed the *Sinethal* in her hands.

Fifteen minutes later, Henri unlocked the door and invited Jennifer and Antonio in. They came through the doorway to see Anlon exchanging hugs with a conscious and smiling Pebbles. Cheers rang out and soon there wasn't a dry eye in the room.

As had been the case with Mereau's transfer into Foucault's body, Pebbles was blind, but that didn't dampen her euphoria. They kept asking her if she was okay, but she was too emotional to speak. She just nodded her head while reaching out to hug anyone and everyone who came within range of her outstretched arms.

The understaffed nurses working the ward had been too busy with other patients to notice the changes in Pebbles' diagnostic readings, or otherwise stop in to check on her during the transfer, but the commotion emanating from the room afterward attracted the attention of a nurse walking down the hall. When she reached Pebbles' room, the nurse was so excited to see Pebbles awake and interacting with others, she ran out immediately to find a doctor. The physician soon arrived and shooed everyone out so that he could examine Pebbles.

The doctor emerged a short while later, astounded by Pebbles' sudden recovery. "I don't know how to explain it. I've never seen anything like it. With the exception of her eyesight, she seems completely fine."

From inside the room, the group heard Pebbles call out, "Better than fine, doc! I feel awesome! Now, everybody come back in. I want to make sure I'm not dreaming all this."

Everyone, including the doctor, laughed. Anlon wiped tears from his eyes and turned to thank Jennifer, Antonio and Henri. Lastly, he bent over and hugged Mereau. "On behalf of Pebbles, on behalf of all of us, *kaeto!*"

23

Illumination

Hospital General de Chetumal
Chetumal Mexico
October 3

The following day, while Pebbles napped, Anlon stopped by Mereau's hospital room to check on his progress and to follow up on a few unanswered questions that had been rattling around in his mind since leaving Calakmul. Anlon brought along Cesar Perez, who had flown into Chetumal the previous night. Anlon found the Munuorian captain in good spirits once again.

"Mereau, this is a good friend of mine, Cesar Perez. He is an archaeologist and someone who's eager to speak with you."

"Very well, come in, come in. *Halas*, Cesar. I am Mereau."

"An honor indeed," Cesar said, bowing.

For the next half hour, the three men chatted casually about Munuorian culture and history. Although Anlon had gathered snippets of both through Pebbles' recounting of past visits with Malinyah, he learned many new things during the brief conversation. Cesar and Mereau seemed to bond during the discussion, and Mereau invited Cesar to visit him once he returned to Foucault's home in Pézenas.

"What do you plan to do, Mereau? Will you live there? Take over Foucault's life, as it were?" Anlon asked.

"No. I will help Henri settle Mathieu's affairs, but after that I am not sure what I will do. Mathieu's body, my body, is not well. Mathieu seemed to believe he only had a few years left to live, so I will have to ponder how best to use the time left to me," Mereau said.

"I'm sorry to hear that," Anlon said. "Maybe Mathieu was mistaken. You seemed pretty strong leaping around Calakmul."

"Believe me, it required every ounce of energy Mathieu's body could conjure, but I will see what I can do to reverse some of the disease. *Enjyia* is powerful, and there are other Munuorian medicines I can create. Mathieu's *gensae* is strong, so I might be able to extend his body's life," Mereau said.

"I hope you do. You let me know what we can do to help," Anlon said.

"A very kind offer, Anlon. Thank you."

"The very least I can do for all you've done," Anlon said. "So, before we go, I wanted to ask you a few questions about Calakmul. You up to it?"

"Yes, of course. What is on your mind?"

"How did you find Pebbles' *Sinethal* and the rest of Muran's *Tyls*?"

"I didn't sense Muran's presence when we arrived at the pyramid. I assumed she was lying in wait, so I went to look for her," Mereau said. "When I went around the side of the pyramid, I saw her come from behind the other structure in back."

"What do you mean you didn't sense her presence?" Cesar asked.

"Her *gensae*. I could not see it at first," Mereau said. "The stones of the pyramid provided her cover until she stepped into full view."

When Anlon probed how Mereau had been able to detect Muran's *gensae*, the Munuorian captain explained that Foucault had consumed *enjyia* for four hundred years, supplemented by a cryptochrome-rich diet. The combination had boosted the cryptochromes in Foucault's brain and eyes, ultimately allowing Mereau to "see" Muran's *gensae*, her magnetic aura, in the dark.

"But if you were able to see her *gensae*, how come she didn't see yours?" Anlon asked.

"Her *gensae* was weak. It may have been too weak," Mereau said.

Their conversation turned to Muran's purpose in storing her *Tyls* at Calakmul. Mereau reminded Anlon that he had predicted the possibility that Muran would bring her *Tyls*. "Whether the exchange went as planned or not, I believe she and Kora intended to switch bodies so they could escape the jungle unnoticed."

"Speaking of Kora, I meant to mention that Cesar and I met her less than two weeks ago. Can you believe that? She fooled us both pretty good," Anlon said.

"Oh?" Mereau asked.

"Yeah, you and Cesar will have a good old time chatting about a tapestry she was interested in. A tapestry featuring a mythical god named Aramu Muru," Anlon said. "Or, should I say, Omereau."

Cesar piped up. "Yes. I am most interested to learn more about Omereau. Perhaps a good starting point when I visit you in France?"

"Very well. Only, he was no god. He was a man. A tremendously gifted man, albeit unlike any other," Mereau said.

"Forgive my curiosity," Cesar said, "but was he one of your race? A Munuorian?"

A smile spread across Mereau's face. "What an intriguing question."

Down the hall from Mereau's room, Jennifer stopped by Elizabeth Li's hospital room to return her badge and to thank her for her help. When she entered her room, Jennifer found the FBI agent with a cell phone pressed to her ear while she maneuvered a finger on the touch screen of her laptop. Surrounding her on the bed were piles of paper and photographs. While Jennifer waited for Li to finish the call, she took note of the agent's ebullient demeanor. It was a far cry from the stressed-out, intense carriage Li had displayed in Ticonderoga.

When the call ended, Li smiled. "I love it when all the pieces fall into place."

"Me, too," Jennifer said. She handed over the badge. "Thanks for this. Turned out we didn't need it, but I appreciate your willingness to help. How are you feeling?"

"Good. Mereau's pilot stopped by this morning and gave me some of their elixir," Li said.

"Ah, no wonder you're in a good mood. *Enjyia* does kind of give a boost. From what I understand, it should help you heal faster, too," Jennifer said.

"That's what Henri said, too. I hope it's true. I need to get out of here and down to New Caledonia, ASAP."

"New Caledonia?"

"Yep. A few agents were dispatched to search Aja Jones' home there. They hit the jackpot."

"Really? What did they find?"

"Evidence linking her to the bank robbery in Middlebury, the rental house in Ticonderoga. Email exchanges between her and Kora, a.k.a. Diane Jones, and Charles Goodwin. Along with evidence at the various crime scenes, it'll be a clean sweep!" Li said.

Li also told her they found a manifesto penned by Muran. In it, the FBI agents discovered the ravings of a woman obsessed by the idea of restoring human civilization to its prehistoric glory with her as their queen. "There are parts of the manifesto we won't release publicly, but if you're interested, I can arrange for you and Anlon to view the volumes when the dust settles."

"Volumes? What's in them?"

"She recorded a history of her queendoms. The history goes back thousands of years. My supervisor in D.C. chalks it up to the overactive imagination of a lunatic. I'm not going to try and change her mind, but you and I know differently. Oh, and she apparently kept mementos from her conquests. The field agents can't tell if they are authentic ancient artifacts or modern reproductions, but we'll get them checked out by experts."

"Interesting. You mentioned Kora earlier. Did they find anything more about her?"

"Funny you should ask. According to the manifesto, what Muran said at Calakmul was true. There's a whole chapter devoted to her bitterness over the loss of her daughters, Kora and Alaera. She really did blame Malinyah for their deaths.

"Here's where it gets bizarre, though. In other chapters, Muran wrote of other children she bore in other lifetimes. Hundreds of them. Guess what? She named all her firstborn girls Kora, in honor of her first daughter. I guess she wanted to keep the memory of her fresh."

As Jennifer pondered Li's comment, another explanation came to mind. In order to transfer a mind from a *Sinethal* into a new body, Muran needed an assistant to operate the *Tuliskaera*. As Muran had painfully discovered at Fernando Pó, that person needed to be skilled with the *Tuliskaera*, so as to facilitate the electromagnetic transfer without blowing up the *Tyls*.

Her Kora replacements must have served as her assistants over the millennia. But, if that were true, Jennifer thought, something must have happened to the Kora living at the time when Muran was entombed on Fernando Pó. Someone had successfully transferred Muran's mind into her *Sinethal* before she died, and someone had constructed her Maerlif on Fernando Pó. Both required the skills of a person very experienced with the *Tyls*. If it had been one of the Koras, though, she hadn't stuck around long enough to find Muran a new body. She left Muran's *Sinethal* and other *Tyls* inside the Maerlif, and there they gathered dust for over a thousand years until Evelyn Warwick happened across it.

"Does the manifesto say anything about the last of the Koras? The one we dealt with at Calakmul."

"It does. She was born in 1944, during the years when Muran called herself Diane Caldwell. We checked with the Brits. There is indeed a birth record of a Kora Caldwell in 1944, with the mother identified as Diane Caldwell...and the father? Charles Goodwin."

"No way!"

"Yeah, I biffed that one. When we were in La Quinta, I told you and Anlon his social security number was issued in the 1940s. I assumed that meant he was born in the forties, but in those days, SSNs were issued when people entered the workforce, not when they were born. If I had looked closer at the records, I would have seen his 1922 birthdate."

"How would that have made a difference?" Jennifer asked.

"I guess it wouldn't have made any difference, really. Other than it would have further confirmed the SSN record was bogus," Li said.

"What about Anabel, or, Evelyn Warwick? I assume Muran's journal mentioned them?"

"There wasn't any mention of Anabel, but Muran had a lot to say about Evelyn. She did revive Muran, and she did botch it up. It's interesting, but Muran seemed to believe the mishap ultimately helped her."

"Really? How?"

"She believed the injuries made it easier to acclimate herself into the life of Clara Ambrose. People around her wrote off her new behaviors, and the loss of Clara's memories, as effects of the explosion. It sounds as if Evelyn helped foster the impression."

"Did Muran write about what happened between her and Evelyn? Does it pinpoint when Evelyn took her *Tyls*?" Jennifer asked.

"Uh-huh. She recorded the precise date. May 10, 1941. Happened during a Nazi bombing of London. They both went into the same air raid shelter. A bomb cratered the shelter. Diane Caldwell was trapped in the rubble; Evelyn was never found. Caldwell assumed Evelyn had been killed until she got home and discovered her artifacts had been taken," Li said. "Muran spent the last seventy-six years searching for Evelyn and the artifacts, with Goodwin's help, and at least one Kora in the mix, too."

"What about the reason? Why did Evelyn take them? What did Muran write about that?"

"Muran was just as baffled as we are. She called her ungrateful. She couldn't understand why Evelyn had betrayed her."

Later that afternoon, Jennifer and Anlon were visiting with Pebbles when Jennifer received a call from Tim Hall. She stepped outside the hospital room to take the call, then burst back into the room a few minutes later.

"I was right!" she said, startling Pebbles with her raised voice.

Pebbles, still blind from the transfer of her mind back into her body, flinched and cocked her head to follow the sound of Jennifer's voice.

"Oops. Sorry, Pebbles," Jennifer said.

"It's okay. What're you fired up about?" Pebbles asked, stretching her arms while suppressing a yawn.

"The Vermont State Police found Omereau's *Sinethal* yesterday! Right where I told them to look," Jennifer replied. "You can't see it, Pebbles, but I'm flexing my biceps!"

"Ha, ha," Pebbles replied. "Get your own move, copper!"

"Well? Go on. Tell us. Where was it?" Anlon asked Jennifer, rising to stand by Pebbles. He laced his fingers with hers as Jennifer began her explanation.

"Okay. So, you know when we were at Antonio's lab, making the fake disc?" Jennifer asked Anlon. "Well, when the disc was finished, Dylan said he hoped Muran didn't use a metal detector. And, later, I was thinking to myself, I wonder what Anabel did with the *Sinethal*? And then I remembered something Tim Hall said when we went through the crime scene," Jennifer said.

"And that was?" Pebbles asked.

"I'll get to that in a minute," Jennifer answered. Wrapped up in her triumph, she started to pace the room. "At first, I thought, I wonder if Muran did use a metal detector to search for the *Tyls*. I was thinking of all the stuff that'd been cleaned from the closets, the attic and such. Had they used a metal detector to hunt for signs of magnetized objects? Had they gotten pings that made them empty the chests in the attic, the pictures in the dining room, the drawers in the kitchen?"

"But, Jen, Dylan said Omereau's *Sinethal* would have had a minimal magnetic signature," Anlon reminded her.

"Right! Exactly!"

"Hold up," Pebbles said. "Why, exactly?"

"The *Sinethal* is almost pure gold. Gold's not particularly magnetic unless it's bonded to another mineral, like iron ore," Anlon explained. "A metal detector wouldn't have found it unless it was right on top of it."

"Or, unless Anabel had masked its magnetism," Jennifer said.

Pebbles squeezed Anlon's hand as soon as the words left Jennifer's mouth. "You mean, making the hiding place seem more magnetic? Like, putting something magnetic near it, or putting the *Sinethal* inside something else that was more magnetic."

"Yep." Jennifer smiled and flexed her biceps again.

"You know I can hear your shirt stretch when you do that, don't you?" Pebbles deadpanned.

"Haha," Jennifer said. "Anyway, if my gut instinct was right, there were two hiding places that stood out to me, right off the top."

"Ooh! I know one of them," Pebbles said, breaking away from Anlon's grip and raising her hand. "The refrigerator, or freezer."

"Correctamundo, señorita!" Jennifer said. "Most refrigerators have a magnetic surface, at least, most of the ones I've owned. So, I thought, Devlin had parked a *Naetir* inside his freezer, maybe he got the idea from Anabel, or vice versa?"

"A good deduction," Anlon said. "Cold temperatures actually boost magnetism, too. So, it was in the freezer?"

"Nope. I figured that was a little too out in the open," Jennifer said, a catty smile on her face. She paused, then said, "Okay...I did suggest the freezer to Tim, but it was my number two choice. Honest."

"You're killing the blind girl, here! Where'd they find the freakin' thing?"

"In the garden," Jennifer said.

"The garden?" Pebbles asked, her voice full of challenge.

"Yes, the garden! Remember, I told you six large objects had been removed from it. Magnetic objects. Stones. They had been arrayed in a circle, positioned equidistant from each other."

"The sign of Omereau," Anlon said.

"Exactly!" Jennifer gloated. "When I was at the crime scene, Tim said the entire garden gave off magnetic readings, but he also said the strongest readings were where the stones had been removed.

I thought, what if she buried it deep, and then put metal or magnetic stones on top of it, to mask the low-magnetic signature of the *Sinethal*? It would have created the same effect as putting it in the freezer, only it would have been harder to find. Turns out, it was buried six feet deep, under one of the holes where the magnetic stones had been removed. In case you're into symbolism, it was under the hole at the front left of the garden."

"If I'm not mistaken," Anlon said, "the bottom left icon on the *Sinethal* etching is the rhomboid, the one representing *Aromaeghs*."

"Right," Pebbles said. "And the *Sinethal* is a type of *Aromaegh*."

While Anlon chuckled at Anabel's trickery, Jennifer said, "You know what? When I went to visit her, she was gardening. I swear to God she was on her knees on the front-left side of the garden!"

Incline Village, Nevada
October 10

Anlon discovered the last missing piece to the mystery, the one that tied it all together, in the kitchen of his Tahoe home. After leaving Chetumal, Anlon had taken Pebbles to his winter home in Los Cabos. By then, her vision had been restored and her injuries mostly healed. He left her there with Jennifer and Griffin, who'd accepted Anlon's invitation to join them. Once Pebbles had settled in, Anlon had traveled to Tahoe to ensure every speck of the crime scene was wiped away or removed from the house before bringing Pebbles home.

For most of the day, Anlon stayed in his office while the crew he hired to do the heavy clean-up work sanitized what could be salvaged and removed that which couldn't. Late in the afternoon, one of the cleaning crew members popped up at the office door and asked Anlon to go through the packages and letters that had been strewn about the front hallway. "It's all on the kitchen counter. Just put what you don't want to one side and we'll take care of it."

When Anlon entered the kitchen and saw the blood-stained pile, he almost turned around and instructed the crew to trash the whole kit and caboodle, but he dutifully pulled up a barstool and evaluated each piece.

He pushed the dented book-package across the counter without even opening it. There was no way he would ever be able to look at the book inside without associating it with Muran and the kidnapping. Joining the dented package was the box with the howler-monkey stuffed animal. Given everything that had happened, the gag gift no longer seemed funny. Any other packages streaked with blood quickly found their way onto the growing stack across the counter, too.

Anlon approached letter mail in the same manner. Anything with blood on it was added to the trash heap…until he discovered a bloody envelope without a return address. It was postmarked Middlebury, Vermont. The postmark read September 9, six days before Anabel's murder had been reported. When Anlon opened the envelope, he discovered a long letter from Anabel inside.

> *Dear Anlon,*
>
> *I don't know where else to begin, but to say, I'm sorry. I'm sorry for the injuries you suffered on my account, I'm sorry for Devlin's murder, and Matthew's, too. I'm sorry I ever talked to Devlin about those horrid Stones, but most of all, I'm sorry for an awful decision I made long ago.*
>
> *You see, I'm responsible for it all, for everything that's happened. I wish I could tell you I had good cause for setting in motion all the wickedness that has transpired, but I would be lying if I did.*

From there, the letter went on to explain much of what Anlon now knew about her history. She confessed to her real identity and admitted to luring Clara Ambrose to Muran's tomb, and then helping Muran transfer her mind into Clara's body, essentially murdering Clara. She also described how Muran had coaxed her cooperation.

> *She seduced me. She made me feel special, loved and wanted. She begged me to help her come to life again, promising the physical and*

emotional closeness we shared when I visited her memories. She prom-
ised me long life, the end of servitude, greater beauty and her love,
and I fell for it. I fell for all of it. Every second in her presence was like
a dream come true, a fantasy that seemed so real, I could feel her body
against mine even after our visits.

I could have all I desired, she told me, if I would find her a body
into which she could pour her mind. Then, we could be together forever.
There is no excuse for what I did, what she suggested I do. She knew
how badly Clara treated me, I told her often enough. I was caught be-
tween a master who treated me like a slave, and a lover who treated
me like a princess. I chose to become a princess.

Later, Anabel described her relationship with Muran after *The
Betrayer* had taken Clara's body. The two had maintained the façade
of master and servant while their behind-the-scenes relationship
blossomed into a torrid love affair. An affair that eventually soured.

I discovered I'd traded one kind of slavery for another. She was
subtler in her cruelty than Clara, but she was cruel. Yes, she ful-
filled her promises, introducing me to enjyia and sharing her gold.
But we were never equals. She was always the master, I was al-
ways the servant. And the longer I served her, the more I came to
hate her. Soon, I found I was nothing more than her chambermaid,
and it made me angry. I confronted her, and she told me I would
have to live with it. When I threatened to leave, she threatened to
cut off my access to enjyia. When I told her I didn't care, she inti-
mated I would end up like Clara.

To prove her point, she dragged me outside and brought a Brey-
lofte. She blew on the Stone and lifted me high into the air and then
slammed me into the ground. It was hard to watch what Pacal did to
you, Anlon, in more ways than one.

Anabel barely touched on her theft of Muran's *Tyls*, but what she
did write explained her motivation for taking them and what she
did with them afterward.

I felt I had no way out. I stopped drinking enjyia, preferring to grow old and die to an eternity under her thumb. Then, a miracle happened, and I found a way to escape. But I did something petty. I took away some of her Stones, the ones she cared most about. I knew enough about them to understand why they were important to her, but I'd never actually used them. I don't know why I didn't destroy them, I guess I thought they might come in handy one day, so I kept them. I put them away, and I made a new life far away from her. My new life was more fulfilling than I could ever have imagined, and for a long time I forgot about Muran and the Stones.

She went on to describe highlights of her life after the theft — going to college, becoming an archaeologist, meeting Devlin and falling in love anew. At last, she detailed how and why she introduced Devlin to the Munuorians and their *Tyls.*

You may not believe me, but I never talked to Devlin about the Munuorians and their special Stones, until I got really sick. Yes, it's true, I stoked his interest in certain mythologies, and I did plant certain seeds that likely led him to the first Tyls he discovered, but he learned to use them on his own, and he realized their historical significance without any hints from me.

When I developed cancer, I thought I could overcome it by starting to take enjyia again. I'd never made it on my own, but I'd watched Muran make it enough times to know the process. It did slow the spreading of the cancer for a time, but not enough to stop it. I was desperate to keep my dream-life going. I had already lived three lifetimes, but I was greedy for more, and I knew it was possible to have more.

So, I compounded my earlier mistakes by confiding in Devlin. I gave him Malinyah's Sinethal, hoping he would talk to her and ask her for help. Yes, I knew what was on the black stone when I gave it to him, Anlon. Muran had talked of her sister often. I suppose I could have tried to talk with Malinyah myself, but I was afraid she would reject me. I thought she would sense my connection with Muran.

I asked Devlin to find out from Malinyah if there was a way to use the Tyls to kill the cancer, but Malinyah didn't understand Devlin, unfortunately. She thought he wanted to know where he could find more Tyls. She showed him a map where he might find more of the Stones, but not much beyond that.

Then, I learned my cancer was terminal, and I knew I was beyond any magic from Malinyah. When I shared the news with Devlin, he was heartbroken. He said he would try to talk with Malinyah again, but I told him it was too late for that.

But there was a way he could still help me. I told him I knew how to store my mind on a stone like Malinyah's, but I didn't have all the pieces needed to do it. I asked him to help me find a Tuliskaera and a Taellin. I gave him two statues I had taken from Muran that showed him what the Tyls looked like — the statues in the pictures Jennifer asked me about when she visited last month.

Don't you see, Anlon? I caused Devlin to stir up a hornet's nest to save myself, and he died because of it. Then, you got drawn into my mess and stirred it up some more. And now all the buzzing has attracted the attention of the queen hornet.

So, why am I writing to you? Why am I telling you all of this? Because she is coming for me, and for the Tyls I took from her, including Malinyah's Sinethal. Which means she will come for you, too.

The letter concluded with another apology from Anabel and a plea for forgiveness. When Anlon finished reading it, he walked outside and strolled to the end of his dock. Once there, he read the letter a second time, bowing his head when he was done.

For all the Munuorians' special gifts, for all the "fish-men" and their Stones did to save survivors of Munirvo, they'd created tools that, in the wrong hands, were still capable of wiping out all of humanity...ten thousand years after their creation. *Thank the stars that Muran never found the lyktyl!* Anlon thought. On his way back to the house, Anlon stopped by the patio firepit and torched the letter. Some things, he decided, are better left to the shadows of mythology.

Epilogue

Casa de Cully
Los Cabos, Mexico
October 24

Anlon looked out onto the patio and spied Pebbles staring out at the Sea of Cortez. He opened the door and poked his head out. "Hey, there. How was your nap?"

"Mmmm, delicious," Pebbles said, stretching out on the daybed. She patted the cushion. "Come join me for sunset."

"I was hoping you'd ask," he said, closing the door behind him.

Pebbles scooted to make room for Anlon and he slid in behind her, wrapping his arm around her waist. She nuzzled her body against him and covered his arm with hers. Anlon closed his eyes and listened to her breathe, his arm rising and falling with each respiration.

"How are you feeling?" he asked.

"Better, I guess. Still not all the way back, but getting close," she said.

Anlon was thrilled to hear the hint of optimism in her voice. Ever since the euphoria of her rescue had faded, the enormity of everything she'd endured had landed on top of her. For the past two weeks, she'd been a different person. Quiet and withdrawn, she spent her days staring out to sea, and sleeping. Her appetite had become nonexistent, but she wasn't glum or weepy, just quiet. Reflective.

Once Jennifer and Griffin had departed for Maui, Pebbles had opened up a few times, usually when they laid on the daybed

together and stargazed. In one of those conversations, she told Anlon she couldn't go back to Tahoe, not for a while. Anlon had said,
"Fine. We'll live here, or go somewhere else if you want."

In another conversation, she announced she didn't want to have
anything to do with the *Lifintyls*, Devlin's museum or Malinyah,
ever again. Anlon had said, "Done deal. I'll give all the Stones to
Mereau. They belong to him more than they do to us, anyway. I'll
get Cesar to deal with the museum."

At night, she had recurring nightmares. Visions of hands closing around her neck, or of guns pressed against her forehead. After one particularly frightening dream, she'd risen from bed in tears
and stomped out onto the patio. When Anlon came out to console
her, she'd turned to him and said, "I know people say that when
you get thrown off a horse you should get right back on, but when
the horse strangles you and tries to take your body, I think it's time
to look for a new ride, don't you think?"

But, she'd gone several nights now without a nightmare, and
earlier in the day she'd devoured fish tacos Anlon had prepared for
lunch. He had been so happy to see her eat, he had given her his
tacos too. Now, the optimism in her voice and the affection in her
touch seemed additional signs of improvement.

"Whatcha thinking?" she asked.

"Honestly?"

"Yes, of course."

"I was thinking about fish tacos," Anlon said.

"Mmmm…those were yummy," she said. She lifted his hand to
her lips and kissed it. "You were sweet to give me yours."

"Hey, if it'll get you to eat, I'll make 'em for every meal."

She laughed. It was the first laugh he'd heard from her since leaving the hospital. She rolled her body to face him. She kissed him
and tousled his hair. "What are we going to do, A.C.?"

He kissed her back. "I don't know. What do you want to do?"

"Honestly?"

"Yes, of course."

"How about we find some marshmallows and make a campfire?
We'll worry about the rest tomorrow."

The Anlon Cully Chronicles continues with *Priestess of Paracas*. And the adventure doesn't stop there! Look for more Anlon Cully mysteries in the years to come.

To receive updates about new additions to the series, <u>K. Patrick Donoghue - Novelist</u> on Facebook, or join the author's email subscriber list by visiting <u>kpatrickdonoghue.com</u> and click on the "Join Email List" link on the main menu.

On the author's website, you will also find more information about other books by K. Patrick Donoghue, including his science fiction thriller series, the Rorschach Explorer Missions, and *The GODD Chip*, book 1 of his new medical thriller series, the Unity of Four.

Illustration:
Sinethal Etching

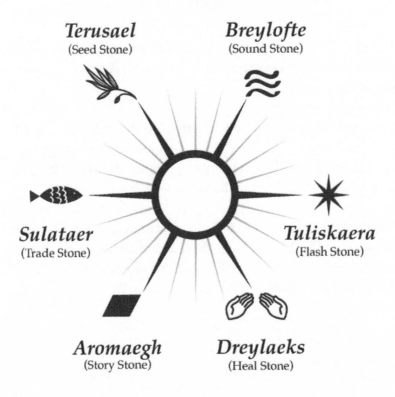

Terusael
(Seed Stone)

Breylofte
(Sound Stone)

Sulataer
(Trade Stone)

Tuliskaera
(Flash Stone)

Aromaegh
(Story Stone)

Dreylaeks
(Heal Stone)

Glossary of Munuorian Terms

ANDAERS – (and-airs) – the council of Munuorian elders/leaders. Malinyah and Muran were Andaers.

ENJYIA – (n-gee-yah) – a drink produced from flowers of plants whose seeds are altered by a *Terusael* (described below). *Enjyia's* taste is similar to sweetened herbal tea and it has a translucent, pinkish appearance. Munuorians who consistently imbibed *enjyia* were able to live for up to five hundred years.

GENSAE – (jen-say) – the Munuorians' magnetic sixth sense.

KAETO – (kay-toe) – thank you.

LIFINTYLS – (liff-in-tills) – Munuorian translation: survival tools. The set of six Munuorian tools/stones depicted on the etching carved into a *Sinethal*. The *Lifintyls* were magnetized devices forged by the Munuorian civilization. Except for *Sulataers* (described below), the composition of each *Tyl* (tool) was a combination of three magnetic stone types: olivine basalt, kimberlite and pure diamond. The *Tyls'* different powers were dictated by the relative concentration of the three magnetic stone types and their unique shaping. The six *Tyls* are described below:

AROMAEGH – (air-uh-may) – Munuorian translation: teacher, helper. A square or rectangular tile that houses virtual-reality-like recordings (sights, sounds, aromas, touch and taste). A *Sinethal* is one type of *Aromaegh*. *Aromaeghs* were created to store the collective memories, skills and accomplishments of the Munuorian civilization. They were used to transfer knowledge from one generation to the next, to teach specific skills and to retain important cultural events and memories.

BREYLOFTE – (bray-loft) – Munuorian translation: air mover. A bowl-shaped stone that amplifies soundwaves to levitate and move objects. Devised as a building tool, *Breyloftes* helped Munuorians place or remove large, heavy objects. They are also used as medium-range weapons to blast or throw opponents and objects.

DREYLAEK – (dray-lock) – Munuorian translation: healer, defender. A cookie-shaped and -sized stone. Two of them are needed to create their desired effects. When two *Dreylaeks* are rubbed together or slapped one against the other, different powers are generated. If slapped with no grinding, *Dreylaeks* can generate a close-quarters blast of air. If slapped together after grinding, *Dreylaeks* emit a thin laserlike beam that can be used to treat injuries (e.g., cauterize wounds, conduct surgery) or as deadly short-range weapons.

SULATAER – (soo-la-tare) – Munuorian translation: stone melter. A token/coin made of pure, 24-karat gold. *Sulataers* are embossed with a fish symbol on each side. The coins were used by the Munuorians to trade with foreign nations/tribes, and they also served as electricity conductors during *overtae*, the mind-transfer process, regulating the flow of electricity generated by a *Tuliskaera* into a *Taellin*.

TERUSAEL – (tare-uh-sail) – Munuorian translation: the refresher. An egg-shaped stone, used in conjunction with a *Breylofte*, to alter the chemistry of the seeds from poisonous flowers into seeds that produce life-extending flowers. The altered flowers are crushed into a tincture called *enjyia*. The enzymes in *enjyia* attack diseased cells in the body, which slows the aging process, thereby extending life.

TULISKAERA – (tool-uh-scare-uh) – Munuorian translation: fire cutter. A cone-shaped stone that produces a powerful laser when used in conjunction with a *Naetir* (described below). *Tuliskaeras* were used by the Munuorians to cut and shape objects (mostly stone objects). *Tuliskaeras* can also be used as long-range weapons against structures and people, and they provide the jolt of electricity needed to facilitate the transfer of a Munuorian's memories and consciousness into a *Sinethal*.

LYKTYL – (lick-till) –the device used to activate the unique *Sinethal* containing the memories and consciousness of Omereau.

MAERLIF – (mare-liff) – the vaults/chambers where the *Lifintyls* were stored prior to the Munirvo catastrophe. Maerlifs were also used as burial tombs of Andaers and prominent Munuorian citizens.

MUNIRVO – (moon-ear-voh) – the passing asteroid that nearly wiped out all life on Earth ten thousand years ago. The name means "star washer."

MUNUORIA – (moon-war-E-uh) –the Munuorian homeland.

MUNUORIANS – (moon-war-E-uns) –the lost civilization. The name means "star watchers."

NAETIR – (neigh-teer) – Munuorian translation: spark. A hockey-puck-shaped stone that served as a catalyst to operate *Tuliskaeras*, *Dreylaeks* and *Aromaeghs* (including the *Sinethal*).

OVERTAE – (over-tay) – the mind-transfer process that allowed the Munuorian civilization to store memories and partial consciousness into a *Sinethal*.

SEYBALROSA – (say-ball-rose-uh) – a Munuorian cliff-side shrine that features a massive ceiba tree surrounded by a garden of saguaro cacti.

SINETHAL – (sin-uh-thawl) – Munuorian translation: mind keeper. A specific type of *Aromaegh* that houses the memories and partial consciousness of select Munuorians, including Malinyah. Unlike other *Aromaeghs* (which contain static presentations or tutorials), *Sinethals* are interactive. A user can ask questions of, and receive answers from, the Munuorian whose memories and consciousness are stored on a *Sinethal*. Not only does a *Sinethal* interactively share sensory experiences (sights, sounds, aromas, touch and taste), but it also shares emotions associated with memories.

TAELLIN – (tay-lyn) – the helmet used by Munuorians to stimulate the brain's hippocampus to transfer memories and consciousness into a *Sinethal*. The helmet looks like an elaborate headdress that, when atop a user's head, gives the appearance of a fish head.

About the Author

Kevin Patrick Donoghue is the author of the Anlon Cully Chronicles archaeology mystery series, the Rorschach Exploer Missions science fiction series and the Unity of Four medical thriller series. His books include:

THE ANLON CULLY CHRONICLES:
Book 1: *Shadows of the Stone Benders*
Book 2: *Race for the Flash Stone*
Book 3: *Curse of the Painted Lady*
Book 4: *Priestess of Paracas*

THE RORSCHACH EXPLORER MISSIONS:
Prequel: *UMO* (novella)
Book 1: *Skywave*
Book 2: *Magwave*

THE UNITY OF FOUR:
Book 1: *The GODD Chip*

WAYS TO STAY IN TOUCH WITH THE AUTHOR:
Follow <u>K. Patrick Donoghue - Novelist</u> on Facebook, join the author's email subscriber list by visiting <u>kpatrickdonoghue.com</u> and clicking on the "Join Email List" on the main menu.